This Golden Land

Barbara Wood

iUniverse, Inc.
Bloomington

This Golden Land

iUniverse books may be ordered through booksellers or by contacting:

iUniverse
1663 Liberty Drive
Bloomington, IN 47403
www.iuniverse.com
1-800-Authors (1-800-288-4677)

ISBN: 978-1-4502-6816-5 (pbk)
ISBN: 978-1-4502-6818-9 (cloth)
ISBN: 978-1-4502-6817-2 (ebk)

Printed in the United States of America

iUniverse rev. date: 12/14/10

ENGLAND
April 1846

Lady Margaret awoke in sudden pain.

Lying in the darkness, trying to determine the hour of the day, she heard the rain pelting the mullioned windows and remembered that she had decided to lie down before dinner.

She must have fallen asleep—

Another sharp pain. *No! It's too soon!*

With great effort—the baroness was eight months pregnant—she managed to sit up and swing her legs over the side of the bed. It had been daylight when she had come into the bedroom; now it was dark and no lamps were lit. She groped frantically for the bell rope and as she gave it a pull, she felt warm dampness spread beneath her.

"No," she whispered. "Please God, no...." Another sharp pain made her cry out.

By the time the housekeeper arrived, the pains had become stronger and closer together. Mrs. Keen rushed to the bedside, where the glow from her oil lamp fell upon bed sheets soaked in blood. And Her Ladyship— "Dear God," whispered the housekeeper as she eased the shockingly white baroness back down onto the pillows.

"The baby," gasped Lady Margaret. "It's coming...."

Mrs. Keen stared at her. Lady Margaret's long red hair, streaming down her back and over her shoulders, made her seem younger than her twenty-three years. She looked frail and vulnerable. And now the premature pains.

Earlier, when Lady Margaret had said she was feeling out of sorts, Lord Falconbridge had gone himself to fetch the doctor at Willoughby Hall. But that had been hours ago. Had the storm washed the road out? "Don't you worry, Your Ladyship," Mrs. Keen crooned. "Your husband and Dr. Willoughby will be here shortly."

Leaving a maid to sit with the baroness, the housekeeper flew down the stairs, calling for Luke, her husband, who was the estate manager.

Falconbridge Manor exploded with life as word of Lady Margaret's premature labor brought maids, footmen, the butler, the cook, and assistant cooks from their rooms and various tasks, some of whom had been in the process of getting ready for bed, with others still dressed in work uniforms. Lord Falconbridge was extremely rich, and the manor, dating back to William the Conqueror, required a large staff.

Luke Keen, having just come in from seeing to the hunting dogs, the cold and damp of the evening on his tweeds, said, "What's all this then?"

The housekeeper took her husband to one side. "Her Ladyship has begun labor. She is three weeks early. Something is wrong. You must send someone to find His Lordship and Dr. Willoughby. They should have been here by now."

He nodded gravely. "I'll send Jeremy. He's our fastest rider."

A scream from the second floor made them look up and then at each other. Luke twisted his cap in his hands. His sister, God rest her, had died in childbirth. "Should I go for Doc Conroy?"

Mrs. Keen bit her lip. Although John Conroy lived just on the other side of the village, and he *was* a doctor, he did not belong to the same social class as the baron and his wife. Conroy took care of the villagers and the local farm folk. And there was that *other* matter about Dr. Conroy, which Mrs. Keen knew displeased Lord Falconbridge. His Lordship would certainly not approve of such a man, doctor or no, laying hands on his wife.

But then, recalling Lady Margaret's miscarriage the year before that had very nearly taken her life, the housekeeper said, "Very well, Mr. Keen, ride into Bayfield yourself. And pray that Dr. Conroy is home!"

As Keen saddled his horse, he wondered if he was doing the right thing. Lord Falconbridge had a terrible temper and took it out on everyone when something was not to his liking. He was also a man to lay blame. Poor Mrs. Delaney, the cook who had been at Falconbridge Manor for thirty years— out on her ear because His Lordship insisted that it was her onion soup that had caused his wife's miscarriage. If something happened to Lady Margaret or the baby tonight, who would the baron blame? Keen and his wife could not risk losing their positions. Times were hard and jobs were scarce.

On the other hand, Keen told himself as he mounted the horse, His Lordship could be generous with rewards. If the Keens, by their quick action, saved Lady Margaret's life, and the baby's, there was no telling what favors His Lordship could bestow on them. Perhaps a retirement cottage of their own, and a small pension....

As Luke Keen rode off into the rainy night, he prayed that he wasn't about to make the worst mistake of his life.

It was good to be home, Hannah Conroy thought as she set the table for supper. Good to be back in Bayfield, back in her own home where a fire burned cozily against the miserable night, while her father worked in his small laboratory off the parlor. This past year in London, the intensive training in midwifery at the Lying-In Hospital—with the lectures and demonstrations and exams, the long hours on the wards, taking care of patients, emptying bedpans, mopping floors, and living in cramped quarters in a dormitory with one afternoon off each week for church and personal laundry—it had all been worth it. Perched on the fireplace mantel and ready to be hung out on the lane was the freshly painted new shingle: *Conroy & Conroy ~ Physician & Midwife.*

For as long as she could remember, Hannah had wanted to follow in her father's footsteps as a healer, but since the medical profession was closed to women, she saw midwifery as a back door into that world. When she turned seventeen, her father had sent letters of recommendation to the Lying-In Hospital in London. Hannah had then gone to the city for entrance exams and, having passed, was enrolled. She started the course on the morning of her eighteenth birthday and received her certificate of completion one year later, when she turned nineteen, one month ago. Hannah dreamed of someday having a modest practice of her own and had already been informed that Mrs. Endicott, wife of a local egg farmer, was willing to have Hannah attend to the delivery of her ninth child, due in a week. Mrs. Endicott, Hannah had no doubt, would then refer Miss Conroy to friends and neighbors.

Hannah was also happy to be home for another reason—in the year that she had been away, her father's health had declined, so much so that she was going to suggest that he scale back his medical practice and take care of himself for a change.

At forty-five, John Conroy was a tall, attractive man with dark hair touched with silver, his shoulders square, his back straight. In his way of dressing "plain" whenever he went out—long straight black coat over black trousers, black waistcoat and white shirt; no cravat, shirt buttoned to a simple collar; and a low-crowned black hat with a wide, flat brim—John Conroy cut a striking figure. When he walked through the village, ladies' heads turned.

With tenderness, Hannah recalled how, after her mother died, the women of Bayfield and surrounding areas had come around—the widows and spinsters and mothers of marriageable daughters—bringing quilts and food to the handsome Quaker widower. But none could penetrate the wall of grief nor break through the barrier of dedication to a new cause that was born the night of Louisa's death: to find a cure for what had killed her.

Hannah paused in slicing the bread and listened to the wind and rain. Had she heard the sound of horses' hooves in the distance? She prayed it was not someone coming to fetch her father for an emergency. He would go, of course, as there was no other doctor around.

The village of Bayfield, in the county of Kent, was located halfway between London and Canterbury on a brisk stream that branched off the River Len. Although it was speculated that people had lived in the area since the Stone Age, and that possibly Caesar's legions had marched through here, the settlement could be specifically traced back to the year 1387, when a group of pilgrims returning from Canterbury had rested "by a hay field" and decided to stay.

Hannah listened to the horses' hooves draw nearer until they arrived in the courtyard. Opening the front door to see a lone rider jump down from his mount, Hannah recognized Luke Keen from Falconbridge Manor. "Mr. Keen! Please come inside."

As Hannah closed the door behind him, he removed his soaked cap and dashed it against his leg. "Is your father home, Miss Conroy? He's needed at once."

John Conroy's voice came from the parlor. "Hannah, did I hear—Oh, good evening to thee, Luke Keen."

"Sorry to bother you, Doc, but there's an emergency at the Manor."

"I'll be right along. What is the problem?"

"It's her Ladyship, Doc."

Conroy turned. "What did thee say?"

"She's in a family way and something's wrong."

Conroy exchanged a look with his daughter. Although they had been to Falconbridge Manor, it was to tend to the household staff. They had never been summoned by the Falconbridges. "Where is their own doctor?"

"His Lordship went to fetch Dr. Willoughby hours ago and they ain't returned. My wife says it's bad. She thinks Her Ladyship might die!"

Luke Keen helped them hitch their horse to their buggy and then he left, to ride ahead and let Her Ladyship know that help was on the way.

As the Conroys set off into the night, the rain pelting the leather roof of the small carriage, John snapped the reins and the chestnut mare broke into a fast trot while Hannah clasped her bonnet to her head. She searched her father's face for signs of fatigue. Although Hannah was not herself a doctor—nor could she ever be—years of assisting him had given her a sharp diagnostic eye, especially when it came to detecting the onset of a condition he had developed during the course of his research. Because of experimenting on himself with infections and test cures, her father now suffered from a chronic heart ailment for which he had concocted a medicine—an extract of the foxglove plant that was called *digitalis* because of foxglove's resemblance to a human finger, or "digit."

But there was no fatigue on his face tonight, no telltale perspiration or pallor. He looked rugged and healthy. And then Hannah was wondering how Lord Falconbridge was going to react to their presence at the manor. The few times she had seen the baron, he had not looked pleased. It was because, when he rode through Bayfield, the citizens removed their hats out of respect. But Hannah's father did not. Like all Quakers, he refused to pay "hat honor" to any man, believing that all people were created equal in the eyes of God. She recalled the look in His Lordship's eyes on those occasions when he had looked back at the impudent Quaker—a look that now chilled her to the bone.

"Here we are," John Conroy said when the lights of Falconbridge Manor appeared ahead through the light rain. As stable boys ran up to take their rig, Conroy and his daughter were met by an agitated Luke Keen, who led them to the tradesmen's entrance, which opened into the kitchen. Instead of being taken to the back stairs which led to the servants quarters, where John Conroy had seen to many an injury or illness, they were led through a corridor into the grand baronial hall that was the heart of Falconbridge Manor. It was the first time Conroy and his daughter had been in the residential part of the mansion, and Hannah tried not to stare at the suits of armor, fabulous paintings in ornate frames, and collections of exquisite porcelain and military memorabilia in glass display cases.

After relinquishing damp capes and hats to a maid, the Conroys were led up the vast, curving stairway by the housekeeper, a somber woman in black bombazine who was pale-faced and shaken.

The Conroys found Lady Margaret in a vast and luxurious bed chamber with magnificent tapestries, handsome furnishings, and flames roaring in the fireplace. The baroness was lying on a massive four-poster bed, her rounded body covered by a satin counterpane.

John Conroy said to Mrs. Keen, "I shall need a basin of water."

"Yes, doctor," she said stiffly, and disappeared into an adjoining room, where Hannah glimpsed beautiful gowns, hats, and shoes.

Conroy went to Lady Margaret and, laying a hand on her clammy forehead, said in a soothing tone, "Margaret Falconbridge, I am John Conroy. I am a doctor. Can thee speak?"

She nodded.

"Is thee in pain?"

"No ... pains stopped ...."

Conroy shot his daughter a look. The cessation of birth pains could be a serious sign. "Margaret," he said quietly. "I am going to examine thee. Do not be afraid."

Conroy opened his black medical bag that contained tongue depressors, silk sutures, gauze and bandages, as well as arsenic tablets, powdered cocaine, and vials of strychnine and opium. He brought out his stethoscope. It was the latest design, made of rubber tubing and equipped with a listening bell and two ear pieces. With this he was able to hear the desperate faint galloping of the baroness's heart.

"Hannah, if thee will please," he said, drawing back the white satin cover and gesturing for his daughter to lift Lady Margaret's blood-stained nightgown. Out of deference to his patient's modesty, John Conroy would have Hannah conduct the visual examination.

Hannah did so and then said in low voice, "Lady Margaret is not in labor, Father. But she continues to bleed. I suspect placentia previa." It meant that the placenta had broken free from the uterine wall and was blocking the birth canal. If intervention was not initiated soon, the lady would bleed to death and the baby would perish.

Mrs. Keen returned with a porcelain basin filled with water. Setting it on a small writing desk, she watched in curiosity as Dr. Conroy retrieved a bottle from his bag. As he decanted a dark purple liquid into the water, the housekeeper wrinkled her nose at the pungent smell that rose up. When Conroy removed his coat and rolled up his sleeves to plunge his hands into the horrible stuff, her eyebrows shot up. What on earth was he doing?

She was suddenly alarmed. Quakers weren't like normal Christians. Was John Conroy going to do something unorthodox to Her Ladyship?

Mrs. Keen opened her mouth to protest when loud noises exploded in the hallway beyond—booming shouts and stamping feet. The door to the bedchamber flew open, and Lord Falconbridge rushed in. Still wearing a wet cloak and top hat, he fell upon the bed and drew his wife into his arms. "Maggie, my love. I am here! The main road was washed out. We had to go around. Maggie, are you all right?"

A second man entered the chamber at a more sedate pace—portly and white-whiskered, calmly handing his top hat, cape and walking stick to Mrs.

Keen. He barely glanced at the Conroys as he went to the bed, standing opposite His Lordship, and lifted one of Lady Margaret's wrists between his thumb and finger. Hannah and her father recognized him as Dr. Miles Willoughby, doctor to Bayfield's wealthy and privileged.

"If Your Lordship will permit me," he said in an authoritative voice.

Falconbridge eased his wife back onto the pillows. Margaret was unconscious now, her face as white as the sheets.

Pulling out a gold pocket watch, Willoughby counted Her Ladyship's pulse, then laid her arm down. He pursed his lips as he looked at the rounded abdomen beneath the white nightgown. He then looked at Margaret's face. "Mrs. Keen," he said to the housekeeper without taking his eyes from his patient, "when did the labor cease?"

"About half an hour ago, sir."

"Very good," he said. "Now if Your Lordship won't mind giving us some privacy?"

"Save her, doctor," Falconbridge pleaded as he rose from the bed. "I could not bear to lose her." The baron's face was the color of cobwebs.

"Do not worry, Your Lordship. A little blood-letting is what Her Ladyship needs."

John Conroy stepped forward and said, "Friend, blood-letting is not wise. Margaret Falconbridge has suffered a separation of the placenta and is hemorrhaging. What must be done is to deliver the child and stop the bleeding."

Willoughby barely looked at him. "Mrs. Keen, I suggest you assist His Lordship to his private chambers."

"Yes, Doctor," she said and waited anxiously while Falconbridge tore himself away from the unconscious Margaret. The baron was a thin, severe looking man in his forties, known for being humorless and a crack shot at pheasant shooting, and not very popular among his tenants and the villagers. Margaret was his second wife, and he was as yet without an heir.

Falconbridge turned to John Conroy, noticing him for the first time. "What are you doing here?"

"I was summoned," Conroy said.

The baron nodded vaguely, cast a final woeful glance at his wife, and then strode out of the room with the housekeeper close on his heels. When the door closed behind them, Willoughby set his medical bag on the bed and undid the buckle. "You can go, too," he muttered without looking at the Conroys. "I'll take over now."

Dr. Willoughby pulled a stethoscope from his bag and applied it to

Her Ladyship's chest. It was the old fashioned kind—a long wooden tube, one end of which was applied to the patient's chest, the other end for the doctor's ear. The length was designed to keep a doctor's face from coming too close to a female bosom, and the instrument was not nearly as accurate as the modern stethoscope Hannah's father used.

"My daughter can help," John Conroy said. "She is a trained midwife."

Willoughby ignored the suggestion as it was beneath consideration. That a country girl of little breeding should attend to the wife of a baron.

Hannah took no offense. She had never imagined she would attend to ladies of title and high birth.

Willoughby reconsidered his choices for treatment. All disorders of the body, from a simple headache to cancer, were universally treated with one of four prescribed methods: bleeding, purging, vomiting, and blistering. In this case, purging of the bowel to relieve pressure on the womb was out of the question as the patient was unconscious and would not be able to swallow the mercury preparation. Likewise, Willoughby could not administer an emetic to cause vomiting. He decided that blistering, created by the application of a caustic chemical on the skin, would not be sufficient in this case. That left his initial choice of blood-letting.

"Friend, I suggest thee hurry," Conroy said. "The baby has but minutes."

"Sir, the baby is fine," Willoughby replied as he set aside the stethoscope and placed his hands on Lady Margaret's large, round abdomen. "The labor was false. And the hemorrhaging you are so overly concerned about is simply a matter of Her Ladyship having too much blood. It is putting pressure on the womb. After I have treated her, the pressure will be relieved and her pregnancy will resume its normal course."

He paused and lifted his nose, sniffing. "What is that?" pointing to the bowl of purple liquid on the writing desk.

"Tincture of iodine."

"Tincture of what?"

"Iodine. An element extracted from seaweed."

"Never heard of it." Willoughby wrinkled his big nose. "Why is it there?"

"I wash my hands in it."

"And why would you do that?"

"It is a solution of antisepsis and it—"

"Oh not that humbug!"

"The solution will protect—"

"It is a *French* idea, sir, and totally unfounded."

"Protect the patient," Conroy finished quietly.

"Protect her from what?"

"From anything the doctor might infect her with."

"And that, sir, is another absurd notion, French, too, I believe, or possibly German. Protecting a patient from her doctor indeed. Doctors are gentlemen, sir, and gentlemen have clean hands."

"I implore thee to please wash thy hands before touching Margaret."

Ignoring him, Willoughby removed sharp lancets from his bag and set them on the counterpane. John Conroy said in alarm, "Then thee truly does intend to bleed her?"

"Precisely so," Willoughby replied as he tied a tourniquet around the baroness's upper arm. "Twenty-four ounces should do it," he murmured, looking around for a receptacle to catch the blood.

Conroy said softly, "Friend, this is not the time for blood-letting."

Willoughby gave him a look. He did not like the Quakers' refusal to address anyone with honorific titles such as Sir, Madam, Your Honor, or even Your Majesty. "I will ask you again, sir—" Willoughby began before he suddenly stopped, drew a long intake of breath and sneezed heartily into his bare hand. Running his finger under his nose and then down his coat, he said, "I am asking you to leave now, or shall I call for someone to escort you out?"

Conroy watched as Willoughby reached with the same hand for a lancet. "Friend, I mean no disrespect, but I ask that, for the sake of our patient, thee washes thy hands first."

Willoughby scowled. He wanted to tell Conroy to stop calling him "friend." And then he thought: Conroy. Irish. "Lady Margaret is not *our* patient, sir, she is mine. Now get out."

"Brother Willoughby," Conroy began.

"I am not your brother, sir, nor your friend!" Willoughby bellowed. "I am a licensed physician with a medical degree from Oxford University and I will thank you to address me respectfully."

Conroy blinked. What could be more respectful than "friend" and "brother"? He turned to his daughter, nodded, and collected his coat and medical bag. As they left the bedroom, they saw Dr. Willoughby retrieve the chamber pot from beneath the bed and place it under Lady Margaret's arm. "We will pray for her," Conroy murmured to Hannah.

When he heard the door click shut behind the Conroys, Willoughby shivered and wondered if he should call for more coal in the fireplace. The long cold ride through the rain had left his clothes damp, and his flesh was chilled. When he sneezed again, cupping the explosion with the hand that held the lancet, he looked around for the cause of the sudden sneezing.

When his eye fell on the bowl of purple solution—what had the Quaker called it? Iodine?—Willoughby decided that *that* was the source of his sudden sinus problem. As soon as he bled Her Ladyship, he would open a window and pour the blasted poison to the ground below.

Tapping the pale arm until a blue vein rose, he made a cut with the lancet and watched the blood trickle into the chamber pot, sure in the knowledge that he was practicing medicine as Hippocrates had practiced it two thousand years ago.

Miles Willoughby was sixty-five years old, having been born in 1781 to an English peer, and because he was the youngest of four sons and therefore destined to inherit neither title nor estates, he had decided to make his way in the world as a gentleman physician. He had attended Oxford University where he had learned Greek, Latin, science and mathematics, human anatomy, botany, and skills in blood-letting and applying leeches, the foremost treatments of the day.

As Willoughby watched the rich blood drain from Her Ladyship's arm, he thought of the impudence of that Quaker to insinuate that the oldest tried and true method of treatment should be avoided in this case! Miles Willoughby had been practicing medicine longer than that upstart had been alive. And who was *he*—a country doctor who never even went to medical school, who in fact had served an *apprenticeship*, like a common tradesman—to tell a *gentleman* physician what was to be done?

And that foul smelling concoction now filling the air! Miles Willoughby was convinced that the notion of antisepsis was a European conspiracy to set medicine back thousands of years. He had already heard of the crackpot notion that doctors should wash their hands—it was a theory coming out of Vienna. They even had the audacity to claim that doctors were the *cause* of infections!

"There now, Your Ladyship," he said when the chamber pot was a quarter full. "Let's see how we are doing." Although Lady Margaret was unconscious, Willoughby spoke to her in the reassuring way he had for years, especially with female patients whom he believed needed the fatherly touch because they really were like children.

He would have liked to lift her nightgown to see if the hemorrhaging from the womb had abated. But while such intimate visualization was permitted in lower-class women, for a lady of Margaret Falconbridge's rank it was unthinkable, even for a gentleman physician. So he decided that a little more blood-letting from the arm was called for.

Mrs. Keen escorted the Conroys from the upper floor, but when they reached the bottom of the stairs, John Conroy paused and, looking back up the massive staircase, said, "I think perhaps we should not leave so quickly, Hannah. We will wait."

Instead of being taken to a parlor or drawing room, as a doctor of Willoughby's social standing would have been, John Conroy and his daughter were taken to the kitchen. Hannah noticed that her father looked weary. "We should go home, Father."

He shook his head. "Not just yet, daughter. I am worried about that poor woman upstairs." John Conroy lifted his face to the ceiling, as if to peer through the stone and wood and mortar and observe what was happening above. He was fearful for Margaret Falconbridge's life, yet he knew he could not interfere. Closing his eyes, he offered a silent prayer to God, asking for guidance.

As a young man, John Conroy had known that he wanted to pursue a career in service to others, such as law or business that would lead, perhaps, to a position in the managing of a humanitarian institution. But Quakers were forbidden to enter Cambridge or Oxford Universities where such professions were taught. And so when young Conroy had voiced his frustration to the local Bayfield physician, the doctor had confessed that he had been hoping to retire in a few years and had been entertaining the idea of training a successor. He had offered John the apprenticeship, which would be eight years, at the end of which John Conroy would receive his *medicinae doctor* certificate.

While serving the apprenticeship—visiting patients with his mentor, reading Greek and Latin, learning how to diagnose and treat—John had found that he enjoyed helping people in this way, and wondered if perhaps there was something more he could do. When he suggested he might consider becoming a surgeon, his mentor did not discourage him. But the older doctor secretly suspected that the young Quaker was too kind-hearted and compassionate to handle the terrible screams he would hear in the surgical theater (not to mention the hemorrhaging the surgeon caused, the gangrene and pus that inevitably followed, and the high death rate among such patients). He advised John to avail himself of the public operating theaters in London. And so John Conroy had gone to the city and had bought a ticket for a seat in the public gallery of St. Bart's Hospital to watch a surgical procedure—a woman undergoing the amputation of a cancerous breast.

While John did not pass out as some in the audience had—at the sound of the patient's agonizing shrieks and the sight of the rivers of blood—one thing did convince him that he could never be a surgeon. For the sake of the patient, a surgeon must be fast. In fact, surgeons were timed with stopwatches. A cancerous testicle or breast must be amputated in less than a minute or the patient would die of shock. John Conroy was too slow and methodical to be a surgeon.

Physicians, on the other hand, dispensed medicines that eased pain and discomfort. The quiet Quaker had decided that bedside medicine was best suited to his temperament, and as it turned out, Dr. Conroy did more than dispense pills and ointments, wrap sprains, and set bones. He listened to his patients' woes, even if it was about failed crops or a cow's milk drying up, knowing that a friendly ear was sometimes the best medicine.

Now he was troubled. News should have reached them of the birth of the child. He feared that Miles Willoughby was not focusing on the baby but on the number of ounces of blood he could squeeze from Margaret.

Miles Willoughby could look back proudly on a distinguished career, the first thirty years of which had been as a practitioner in London, catering to the elite and blue-blooded of Belgravia, where he had also had a fine home. When he turned fifty, however, Willoughby discovered that the dampness and fog no longer agreed with his joints, and so he had left London for life in the milder climate of Kent, where he had taken over the practice of a retiring physician who was not only himself a man of upper class breeding but who boasted a clientele that included two Members of Parliament, a High Court judge, and an Earl.

In the fifteen years since, Willoughby had carved a pleasant life for himself in the Bayfield countryside. He enjoyed the prestige, weekends at estates, invitations to balls and hunts, and he especially liked the way people deferred to him. All he had to do was take care of "vaporous" ladies (blood-letting in every case), colicky children (leeches on the abdomen), and the occasional gentleman's back pain (opium mixed with brandy). Anything less pleasant, such as boils to be lanced, or the more noxious illnesses, he referred to colleagues in London, whom he called specialists (although they were simply men who were not as fastidious as Willoughby), and sometimes to surgeons, who were a step down the social ladder from physicians.

Willoughby was pleased now to see the blood from the baroness's arm slow to a trickle, which meant the excess had been successfully drained from her body so that the congestion of the womb had been relieved. "Well done, Your Ladyship," he said as he removed the tourniquet and set aside the chamber pot swimming with dark blood. "I'll just take your pulse and then I shall call in your ladies to have you bathed and changed, and then you can visit with your husband." He would also give her some arsenic tablets as a tonic.

He shifted his thumb and finger on her limp wrist. He frowned. He looked at her face, which was the normal pale color after a blood-letting. But then he noticed that her chest was not rising and falling.

Dropping her arm, he pressed a fingertip to her neck, feeling on the right side and then the left for a throb in the carotid artery.

There was none.

"Lady Margaret?" he said. He patted her cheeks. Then he bent and pressed his ear to her chest. No heart sounds.

He straightened and frowned down at her. "Lady Margaret?" And then he placed his hands on her abdomen and felt no movement within. "Good Lord," he whispered. The baroness and her child were dead.

How was that possible? He looked at the lancet and tourniquet and then at the dark blood in the chamber pot. He had performed this procedure hundreds of times. What could have gone wrong? And then his eye fell upon the bowl of foul, purple solution sitting on the writing desk. Willoughby's heart jumped in shock. The Quaker had poisoned the air! Collecting himself, he went to the door and, knowing that Falconbridge was pacing in the hall beyond, said, "Your Lordship may come in now."

When the baron stepped into the bedchamber, Miles Willoughby closed the door behind him and said, "I am sorry, Your Lordship. I did all that I could."

Falconbridge stared at him. "What are you talking about?"

"If only I could have been here sooner."

Falconbridge ran to the bed and took his wife by the shoulders. "Maggie? Wake up, my darling!"

Then he looked at the rounded abdomen where his child once slumbered but was now entombed. He lifted a tear-stained face to Willoughby. "How did it happen?"

"Everything was going as I expected, the blood-letting was easing her distress when suddenly she expired."

"But she was fine this afternoon when I rode to fetch you. Just a little queasiness."

"I blame myself, Your Lordship. When I saw the bowl of toxic fluid, I should have thrown it out at once. But, of course, my main concern was with seeing to Her Ladyship—"

Falconbridge blinked. "Toxic fluid?"

Willoughby pointed to the bowl on the writing desk, and Falconbridge immediately realized he had been detecting a strong odor in the air. It was coming from the bowl. "What is it?" he asked, rising from the bed.

"The good Lord only knows," Willoughby said, throwing up his hands. "The Quaker had set it out for reasons that are beyond me. It is not normal medical practice, I assure you. But I do chastise myself for not throwing it out. I fear the air has been poisoned, and, in fact, you and I would do well to leave this room at once, Your Lordship."

Falconbridge stared into the pungent-smelling fluid, feeling its fumes assault his nostrils and swim up into his head to engulf his brain. Margaret was dead. The baby dead. He felt the room tilt and sway, heard the wind howling beyond the windows. "What am I going to do?" he sobbed, and covered his face with his hands.

Willoughby laid a fatherly hand on the baron's shoulder and said, "I will take care of things for you, Your Lordship. I suggest, however, that we detain the Quaker and his daughter, and send for the constable. A crime has been committed here tonight."

Luke Keen came into the kitchen. "Sorry, sir, but His Lordship has asked that you be detained. Come this way, please." The estate manager led the Conroys to a small library off the main hall, where no fire burned in the grate, and only one candle had been lit so that the room was cold and gloomy. "If you'll wait here," he said, not meeting them in the eye, and then he left, closing the door behind himself.

"What do you suppose—" Hannah began, when Willoughby came striding in, looking somber and officious.

"How is Margaret Falconbridge?" John Conroy asked. He had removed his wide-brimmed Quaker's hat and stood taller than the older doctor.

"*Lady* Margaret," Willoughby said archly, "has died."

"Oh no," Hannah whispered, standing at her father's side. "And the child?"

"It perished as well."

"Thee could not save them?" Conroy said.

Willoughby drew himself up as tall as he could and jutted out his whiskered chin. "And how was I to do that when you poisoned them both?"

Conroy's eyebrows arched. "What does thee mean?"

"You poisoned her with that concoction in the bowl."

"Dr. Willoughby," Hannah interjected. "Iodine cannot cause illness. It *prevents* illness."

Willoughby skewered her with a look. A lifelong bachelor, the Oxford-trained English gentleman was contemptuous of women, as he was of Irishmen, foreigners, and Quakers. "I did not say you made Her Ladyship ill," he said archly. "I said you *poisoned* her. You filled the air with toxins."

John Conroy said quietly, "I did not."

"Will you swear to that?" Willoughby asked, knowing that the Quaker would do no such thing.

"Friend, my way of speaking is plain speech, which is truthful speech. Therefore I have no reason for making a sworn statement. Instead, I offer an affirmation that my witness is true."

"The high court in London will want more than that, sir. You must place your hand on the Holy Bible."

"That I cannot do. But I affirm before God that I did not poison Margaret Falconbridge."

"We'll see about that. His Lordship has sent for the constable. In the morning, your case will be presented to the magistrate. There will be a formal inquest, and I shall recommend charges of medical malpractice, professional malfeasance, and criminal negligence be brought against you."

Willoughby turned to leave when his eye fell upon Conroy's black medical bag. Without asking, he undid the clasp, looked inside, and lifted out a bottle containing purple liquid. He read the label: *Experimental Formula #23.* "You experimented on the baroness! You might have at least saved it for one of your farm wives, sir!"

"I was not experimenting," Conroy said. "I merely call it my experimental formula. There is a difference. I have used it in my treatment of other patients. I assure thee, Friend, no harm came to Margaret Falconbridge through my use of the iodine."

"And I will thank you, sir, to stop calling Her Ladyship by her Christian name!"

"I know of no other to call her," Conroy said quietly.

"She is *Her Ladyship* to you, sir. You will show some respect to your betters."

"Can he do that, Father?" Hannah asked after Willoughby had left. "Can he accuse us of those things?"

"A man can be accused of anything, Hannah," John Conroy said as he sank into an upholstered chair and turned melancholy eyes to the rain washing the windows. Shadows crept along the cold carpet, shifting, changing shape—ghostly phantoms, he thought, mustering for an attack. His eyes swept the shelves of books that had a look of neglect, and he thought of the forgotten knowledge they contained, the undisturbed passions, suspended lives and ecstasies lost to memory.

"Don't worry, Father," Hannah said as she looked around for a blanket. "You have friends, and there are your patients. They will speak up on your behalf." But even as she said it, Hannah thought of how rich and powerful Lord Falconbridge was. A High Court judge would sooner heed him and wealthy men than farmers and village shopkeepers.

"I shall ask Mrs. Keen to bring some tea." Hannah went to the bell pull by the dark fireplace, gave it three firm tugs. When she came back to her father's side, she searched for anything that might keep him warm but found nothing. Musty furniture stood in ancient shadow, giving the room an eerie, abandoned feel. Hannah took the one burning candle and lit a candelabra of six, bringing it closer to her father. The additional light did little to add warmth to the sepulchral atmosphere.

As Hannah moved about this room that was not hers, taking over as if she were the lady of the manor, drawing heavy drapes against the rain, tugging the bell pull once more, examining the coal bucket and seeing if there were tinder for a fire, John Conroy marveled at his daughter's new self-assurance. Thirteen months ago she had left Bayfield a shy, quiet girl of eighteen, but she had returned a confident nineteen-year-old woman eager to tell stories of patients, fellow students, and professors. "It's a waste of time to educate a girl," friends and villagers had warned Dr. Conroy. "It makes them uppity with notions of reaching beyond their station. No man will want to marry her." John Conroy had turned a deaf ear. And look how he had been rewarded! A year's course in midwifery had gifted his daughter with a lifetime of wisdom and skills, or so it felt to a very proud father who had looked forward to sharing his medical practice with his daughter.

Until now ....

"Medical malpractice, professional malfeasance, and criminal negligence."

Words sharper than knives and deadlier than bullets. John Conroy felt his heart quiver beneath the assault. A body can take any punishment, he thought, but the soul is a vulnerable thing. He whispered, "Hannah, bring me my bag."

She was suddenly at his side, searching his face, gently touching his wrist to feel his pulse. When she had left for London, her father had still been in good health. But when she had returned, Hannah had been shocked by the change. That was when she had learned the extremes to which he had gone in his obsession to find a prevention for childbed fever. On the evening of her return from London, with her luggage still crowding the parlor, her father had called from his small laboratory: "Hannah! Hannah, come quickly!" Lifting the hems of her skirts, she had hurried through the house to find her father bent over his microscope. "Take a look, Hannah. Tell me what thee sees."

Because the room was small and crammed with a workbench, stools, a desk and boxes of records and supplies, Hannah had had to move carefully so that her wide crinoline skirt did not knock anything over. She bent to the eyepiece. "I see microbiotes, Father."

"Are they moving?"

"Yes."

He had removed the slide and replaced it with another. "Now look."

She peered again through the eyepiece. "These are not moving."

"The first is from a patient, Frank Miller at Bott's farm. He has a gangrenous wound. I collected pus from it and smeared some on my hands. I then washed my hands in the latest formulation."

"Father! You have been experimenting on *yourself?*"

"Watch, Hannah. Verify it for me."

Using the remaining supply of matter harvested from Miller's wound, Dr. Conroy had smeared it on his hands and then scraped off a sample and placed it on a slide under the microscope. Hannah peered in and saw the sub-visible creatures squirming there. Conroy then washed his hands in a bowl filled with a strong-smelling solution, rinsed his hands in a bowl of clear water, filled a tiny pipette with the rinse water, dropped it on a slide, and positioned it under the lens. "Now what does thee see?"

Hannah looked. "They are not moving, Father."

John Conroy murmured, "Praise His name." Then, with more animation: "Hannah, I believe I have found the formula at last. The cure that I have been searching for. I will go to London and present my findings to the learned men there."

"But, Father, last time …" That day, two years ago, was burned painfully into Hannah's memory. She and her father had gone to London where he was to speak before the College of Physicians. Prior to his speech, they had taken a tour of Guy's Hospital, where Hannah had seen doctors in frock coats smeared with blood and pus. These, she learned, were badges of a doctor's popularity. The filthier his coat meant the more patients he attended to. Hannah's father was of the radical and unpopular belief that such fluids, even when dry, possessed contagions that could be spread from patient to patient. Which was why Conroy advocated that a physician wash his hands before touching a patient and even change into clean clothes on a daily basis.

"No one knows what causes fevers," the gentle-spoken Quaker had said that day as he addressed the respected gathering of Britain's elite physicians. "No one knows why the human body burns where infection is present. But I believe …"

He had gone on to describe to his learned audience his belief that sickness was the result of unseen beings invading the bloodstream. John Conroy had even invented a word for them: "microbiotes," from the Greek *mikro*, meaning very small, and *bios*, meaning life. Conroy believed that microbiotes secreted a poison that made a person sick.

But his audience was not won over. One gentleman had shouted from the back of the auditorium, "It has been demonstrated time and again, sir, that fevers are the result of too much blood in the body, and that only by blood-letting can a fever be reduced."

Conroy had countered with: "I have personally examined, under microscope, blood drops from healthy people and from those with fever. In the blood of the sick person I have seen white cells in greater preponderance than in the blood of a well person."

"You mean greater *preposterousness*, do you not?" called a man from the front row, and everyone laughed. "White cells! Microbiotes! Are you sure you are not a novelist, sir, dishing up a fiction?"

Hannah had been in the visitors' gallery watching as her father became the target of insults, mocking laughter, and stamping feet until he was finally forced to step down, albeit it with solemn dignity.

"Daughter, my bag," he said now. "I am not feeling well."

Hannah brought his medical bag to him, and then she went to the door and opened it upon a deserted corridor. Closed doors beneath Tudor arches and two silent suits of armor were all she saw. Why had no one answered her ring? "Hello? May we please have a fire in here? It is terribly cold." She listened. Muffled voices—male, upset, authoritative—came from upstairs. Had the constable already arrived? Hannah could not believe how she and her father were being treated. He had come out in the rain for Lady Margaret.

She returned to his side and brought the candelabra closer. Judging by his sudden pallor and the way he grimaced, she knew it was the pericarditis. Exposing himself to infection had caused a chronic inflammation of the membrane around the heart. She opened his bag and searched for the familiar vial. "Father, I cannot see your medicine."

His head dropped back against the back of the chair. "I must have left it at home...." Closing his eyes, he listened to the rain beyond the windows and felt the chill of the small library penetrate his coat and shirt to meet the pain that was building behind his breast bone. He felt as if he were in a vise, and he knew that, without the medicine, he would most likely not survive this attack. So he sent his thoughts to God, praying for guidance, for forgiveness and for peace.

"Father," Hannah said decisively, rising to her feet. "I shall send for a carriage. Can you tolerate the ride home?" She looked around the room and saw no bottles of brandy or wine. It was a dark, saturnine chamber illuminated by the occasional flash of lightning. "Are you able to walk?"

Conroy labored for air. "Hannah ... I must tell thee the truth about thy mother's death ... it has been on my conscience ..."

"Do not speak, Father."

"The letter, Hannah, read the letter ..."

She blinked. "Letter?"

The walls of the tomb-like parlor were hung with ancestral portraits, men in padded doublets and women in farthingales. As Hannah knelt at her father's side, she felt their eyes on her, the greedy eyes of the jealous dead hungry for her father's life force. You can't have him, she wanted to cry.

John Conroy didn't breathe for a moment, and then he looked at her, at the face that was so like Louisa's, the high forehead and delicate cheekbones, eyes the sparkling gray of mother-of-pearl framed by black lashes. Hannah wore her hair the same as Louisa had: the black tresses parted in the middle and swept over her ears like raven's wings, to lie at her neck gathered in a silk net. He lifted a weak hand and placed it on her cheek. "How like thy mother thee is."

John Conroy's life had begun, he always said, the day Louisa Reed came into his life "like a fabulous butterfly." Hannah thought it a love story for the ages. Louisa Reed had been touring southeast England with her theatrical company when she had sprained her ankle in Bayfield. Since she was an actress, Miles Willoughby's distinguished predecessor would not see her. And so she was taken to the local practitioner, a shy young Quaker with a brand new shingle.

What had it been like on that fateful day, Hannah often wondered, when Louisa had brought her gaiety and outgoing personality into that quiet, modest cottage? What had the beautiful young woman with the midnight hair and lemon yellow gown seen in the softly-spoken man in black? John and Louisa must have been like night and day—and yet, like night and day, they had complemented each other and had fit together into a perfect unit. Hannah's mother had fallen so deeply in love that she had given up the stage to be with John, and he had been so in love with her that he had allowed himself to be expelled from the fellowship of the Society of Friends in order to marry her.

Reaching into his medical bag, he brought out the bottle of experimental formula. "If I had had this miracle six years ago, I could have saved thy mother." Taking Hannah's hand, he pressed the small bottle into it, saying, "I pass it to thee, Hannah, as my legacy. Use it in thy midwifery. Save lives."

"We will use it together," she said in a tight voice.

He rolled his head from side to side. "My time in this mortal life is at an end, daughter. God calls to me. But I must tell thee the truth about thy mother's death ... I should have spoken long ag ...." He swallowed painfully. "The letter explains.... but it is hidden ... find it....."

"Father, I do not know what you are talking about." Hannah squeezed his shockingly cold hands. "I will fetch Dr. Willoughby—"

"No!" A harsh whisper spoken with the last of his strength. "It is my time, Hannah. We must accept." He opened his eyes, tried to focus on her face, and then let his gaze roam the room. He paused, frowned, and said, "Who is that?"

Hannah looked over her shoulder. "Who is what, Father? There is no one there."

"Why ...." John Conroy whispered. "I know thee, sir...." His face cleared, the shadows retreated, and Hannah was startled to see her father suddenly smile. "Yes," he said, nodding toward the specter that only he could see. "I understand ..."

And then: "Oh, Hannah! The light!" He brought his eyes back to hers, and she was stunned to see focus and clarity in them, and an intensity she had not seen in years. He reached for her hand that still held the bottle of formula and said, "I see so much now. Hannah, this is the *key*!"

Tears rose in her eyes. "Father, I do not know what you are talking about. Let me take you home."

A strange glow seemed to suffuse his features; his smile now was one of ecstasy. "I was blind, Hannah. I did not understand." His cold fingers grasped her hand tightly so that the small bottle dug painfully into her palm. "This is it, the key to everything. Oh, Hannah, my dearest daughter, thee stands at the threshold of a glorious new world! A wondrous adventure—"

John Conroy died then, smiling, while generations of arrogant Falconbridges looked down gloatingly from their ancient canvases, and Hannah, suddenly left alone in the world, wept against his chest and clutched the tiny bottle that had, ultimately, killed him.

THE CAPRICA
August 1846

-2-

"If the boy dies, Captain, we take over this ship and sail for the nearest land. Because it's a death ship for sure, and we ain't gonna let our families perish in the middle of the ocean." The angry Irishman curled his huge hands into fists to punctuate his threat.

"I assure you," said Captain Llewellyn, Master of the *Caprica*, "Dr. Applewhite is doing is utmost best to stop the contagion."

"Yeah?" shouted a Scotsman who clutched a heavy belaying pin. "Then how come we're dropping like flies down here and that lot up there ain't even touched?" He flung his arm toward the quarterdeck, where the ship's four paying passengers enjoyed privacy and better accommodations than the *Caprica*'s two-hundred-plus immigrants who were crowded into steerage.

Captain Llewellyn drew in a steadying breath to curtail his temper. As the three-masted square-rigger rolled and swayed along its nautical course, alone on a vast sea that sparkled to the far horizons, Captain Llewellyn, a gruff, thickset man with bushy white whiskers and a brusque manner, took the measure of the enraged Irishman. He might not be armed, Llewellyn thought, but the crew and officers wouldn't stand a chance should mutiny erupt. The Irishman was not alone. Nearly a hundred angry Scotsmen, Welshmen, and Englishmen were lined up with him on the deck, for once forgetting their political and religious differences, united in one cause: to take over the ship if the Ritchie boy died.

As more immigrants appeared on the deck, faces twisted in fury, Captain Llewellyn glanced up at the quarterdeck where he saw a lone man watching. Neal Scott, the young American, one of the *Caprica*'s four paying passengers—a scientist bound for Perth to work on a survey vessel for the colonial government. A pleasant fellow, Llewellyn thought, if a bit mysterious, traveling with those strange crates right in his cabin instead of stowing them in the hold. The captain did not care for Mr. Scott's current keen attention on the brewing trouble. Scott would tell the others, and then the captain would have a panic on his hands.

Llewellyn brought his attention back to the Irishman and fixed him with a stern gaze. The Master of the *Caprica* had small bluebell-colored eyes, like two pin pricks set deep in the creases of his weathered face, and they did not miss a thing. Behind the angry men, womenfolk were starting to line up, widows who had buried husbands and children at sea and who now brandished broomsticks and rolling pins. It will be a bloody slaughter, Llewellyn thought. And neither side will win.

He was a good and fair captain who treated his crew better than most, but a seaman's life was hard. If the immigrants did take control of the ship, would his sailors be only too happy to sail her to the nearest rock? Turning to his First Officer, he said quietly, "Send for Dr. Applewhite."

Mister James hesitated. "Will it do any good, sir? The doctor's been down there numerous times already."

During his long career at sea, with each voyage carrying a ship's doctor, Captain Llewellyn had learned that medical men were unpredictable. They were not regulated the same way sailing men were. Llewellyn had had to serve many years as an ordinary seaman, and then had had to study long and hard at navigation, the stars, weather, how to read maps, how to handle a sextant, and to read the wind before he got his master's ticket. But any man could call himself a doctor. There was no general standard, no regulations, nothing by which to measure a medical man for competency. Private medical schools dotted the map like mushrooms, with courses as short as six months and then the diploma was awarded. And so when one hired a ship's doctor, one never knew if he was of the barest education and experience, who didn't know a boil from a scab, or an Oxford scholar who could name every nerve in the body and who spoke in words that cost a shilling apiece. Llewellyn himself had sailed with his share of charlatans and snobs, and in the grand scale of things, he counted Applewhite among the more capable. If the contagion could be stopped, Applewhite was the man to do it.

"Fetch him," he said quietly, "if only to make these ruffians stand down."

"It's awfully quiet out there," said Mrs. Merriwether, looking toward the open doorway that led from the salon to the companionway. "I'm used to hearing the pipes and fiddles of the immigrants on the main deck. I don't like that silence."

"There there," said her husband, Reverend Merriwether, in a tone of comfort that he himself did not feel.

Seeing the distressed look on both their faces, Hannah Conroy said, "I am sure Captain Llewellyn is handling things."

The Merriwethers were a missionary couple on their way to Australia, and Hannah liked the reverend's wife, a plump lady in her fifties, tightly corseted into a blue and white striped gown. Like Hannah, she wore her hair in the fashion of the day—parted in the middle and swept back into a chignon (although the reverend's wife sported old-fashioned and slightly girlish ringlets that quivered over each ear when she spoke.)

The Reverend himself was portly, with a pleasant disposition, and a scalp so bald that it was shiny (a deficit, Hannah suspected, that was compensated for by prodigious bushy gray side whiskers).

The Merriwethers had literally rescued Hannah back in London.

Although a formal inquest ruled Lady Margaret's death as due to natural causes, and although Hannah's father's name was cleared, things were not the same after that. As much as the local people loved John Conroy, they feared Lord Falconbridge more. And as the baron and Dr. Willoughby continued to rail against the Quaker for the untimely death of the baroness, the name of Conroy was destroyed forever. Mrs. Endicott, the egg farmer's wife who had asked Hannah to attend her ninth birth, said, "Sorry, but I've my customers to think of." As if someone named Conroy could spoil all their eggs. Hannah knew that no one would hire her, that Bayfield was no longer her home.

England is no longer my home. Wherever she went, she would encounter the same class prejudice, the same narrow-minded thinking that had killed her father. With his final breath he said, "Thee stands at the threshold of a glorious new world!" And so to a new world she would go. And perhaps, while she was building a new life for herself, she would solve the mystery of John Conroy's other final words, for which Hannah had no explanation: the "truth" about her mother's death, and a mysterious letter she was supposed to read but which she had not been able to find among his belongings.

After burying her father and selling their cottage, Hannah went to London to buy passage to Australia, where she had heard the sun shone like gold and opportunities were as vast as the continent itself. But she discovered that no ship's captain would take on a young, unmarried lady who was not escorted or chaperoned. "You would be a severe distraction for the officers and crew," one captain declared. "I dare not risk a breakdown in moral order." As Hannah could not afford to hire a lady's companion, she was beginning to despair of leaving Britain when the booking agent found a husband and wife missionary couple traveling to Perth. He sent a note to the inn where they were staying, inquiring if they wouldn't mind chaperoning a young woman on the voyage. Hannah then met with the Merriwethers, and they decided she was a young lady of good character, albeit in reduced circumstances, and graciously offered to watch out for her welfare aboard ship.

But now, weeks out of Southampton, in the tastefully appointed salon of the *Caprica*, as three of the four private-cabin passengers tried to pay attention to their midday meal of boiled beef and potatoes, Abigail Merriwether was more concerned about her own welfare than Miss Conroy's. She had not confessed her rising fears to her husband as he would take it as a lack of faith in God, but she could not help it. Each day that brought them closer to Australia brought more dread. What were they doing? Surely they were too old for such an arduous undertaking. Caleb was past his prime but deluded himself into thinking he was a younger, stronger man. We shall perish in that wilderness, Abigail thought, as she smiled at her table companions. And now there was this dreadful contagion to worry about.

The claret sparkled like rubies in crystal glasses. The china and silver on the table caught glints of light as overhead brass lanterns swayed with the roll of the *Caprica*. The small salon was also used for recreation between meals, with a little round table for cards and backgammon, its oak surface bored with holes to secure drinking glasses. The bulkheads were hung with lithographs of sailing ships and watercolors of pleasant landscapes. The floor was covered with a fine Turkish carpet. Luxury sailing for those who could afford it.

But the three passengers were too nervous to enjoy the meal. They sat in silence, listening to the creak and groan of the ship

After a brief call at the island of Madeira, the *Caprica* had found fair skies and a forgiving ocean. She was "running before the wind," according to Captain Llewellyn, and therefore was making good time, which meant they should arrive at their destination within the promised four months. It had been pleasant sailing, with the days blending into one another as the lone ship scudded over the sea, sails snapping and billowing, sailors in the yards and rigging, or making repairs, swabbing decks, and playing concertinas in the evening. The four cabin passengers spent their days reading, playing cards or chess, or writing in diaries to chronicle the progress of their remarkable journey.

And then Dr. Applewhite had reported an unexpected death among the immigrants. The next day, more had fallen ill to a sudden contagion, so that now the entire ship's company was in the grip of fear. It had been days since those in the salon had heard the pipe and the fiddle on the main deck, where the immigrants spent their days. Although illness and injury were part of any long voyage, nonetheless, one person's illness was a major concern as it could spread. Entire ships were known to succumb to devastating illness, to limp into port with only a fraction of their crews and passengers.

"Dr. Applewhite," Reverend Merriwether said, "is there a chance the dysentery will reach *us?*"

The ship's doctor, a bulky man with ruddy jowls, shared the passengers' table and was the only one eating. He shook his head. "Not a chance, sir. We've all the fresh air up here." Although the salon was situated below the quarterdeck, it had portholes that admitted ocean breezes. Applewhite speared a potato and popped it whole into his mouth, the ship's doctor being a man of appetite, with the paunch and chins to prove it.

Hannah leaned forward in concern, her food cold and neglected. "Mr. Simms told me the latest victim is a child." She did not know the boy's name or who he belonged to in the mass of immigrants traveling in steerage, but the tawny-haired child had become a source of joy every morning as Hannah had watched the families line up on deck before breakfast for roll call by Mister James. She had first noticed the boy at the beginning of the voyage, about six years old in a tattered pullover sweater and short pants, standing at attention for the First Officer's inspection. Someone had fashioned a paper sailor hat for the child, and he wore it proudly as he snapped and held a proper salute, keeping his hand to his forehead during the entire roll call.

Hannah's heart had gone out to the sweet little boy who seemed to her to embody the hope and optimism of the people traveling to the far ends of the earth, and so she had come to seek him out each morning.

But he had not made an appearance in days.

The fourth passenger came into the salon then, filling the doorway with his breadth and height. Hannah looked up to see the broad-shouldered American, Neal Scott, standing there.

Mrs. Merriwether turned a hopeful expression to him. "Is everything all right out there, Mr. Scott? It's so frightfully quiet."

"The captain's just having a talk with some passengers," Scott replied as he took his seat at the table. Although his tone was casual, Hannah saw concern in his eyes.

Hannah thought Mr. Scott an attractive man. In his mid-twenties, with dark brown hair and long sideburns that framed his square face, he was a robust man who struck Hannah as more suited to outdoor labors than the cerebral studies of a scientist. His attire was casual: country tweed trousers and jacket with leather shoulder and elbow patches, a checkered waistcoat and loosely tied cravat. The bowler hat was always cocked at an angle, giving him the appearance of a man on Derby Day.

Although Hannah had made the acquaintance of many young men in the Bayfield area, and then among the male staff at the London Lying-In Hospital, none had affected her the way this man did. She wondered if it was due to his exotic appeal—she had never heard an American accent before, and found his speech intriguing—or perhaps it had more to do with the curious intimacy of ocean travel, being forced into a stranger's close company for months at a time.

The paying passengers occupied four small private compartments below the quarterdeck, and although Hannah had known that Mr. Scott occupied the one next to hers, she had received a shock when she had wakened one night from a nightmare—it was a recurring dream: Hannah locked in the cold library with her father—to hear a muffled voice from the cabin next door, saying, "Are you all right, Miss Conroy?" Hannah had called through the thin wall that it was a nightmare, nothing more, realizing that they must be sleeping next to each other with just a bulkhead separating their berths. Hannah had had difficulty falling asleep after that, knowing that, immediately on the other side of the wall, the handsome American also slept.

Besides being attractive, Mr. Scott possessed an energy and enthusiasm that Hannah found infectious. She had heard that Americans were less reserved than Englishmen, and more inclined to speak their minds, which Mr. Scott most definitely did. A scientist by training and education, with emphasis on geology and the natural sciences, Neal Scott had been hired by the colonial government in Perth to sail on a science vessel that would be surveying the western coast and offshore islands. "That is why I am going to Australia," he had told his fellow travelers the first day at sea, "to uncover mysteries and explore the unknown and to answer such questions as why Australia has animals found nowhere else on Earth, and why other animals in the rest of the world are not found here. There are no bears in Australia, no large predatory cats. The entire rest of the world has its lions, tigers, panthers. No such thing exists in Australia. Why? Even the very name Australia comes from the Latin *Terra Australis Incognito*, which means Unknown Southern Land."

Neal now turned to Dr. Applewhite, who was tucking into his boiled beef with gusto, and said, "I believe, Doctor, that the captain will be sending for you shortly. Just to take a look below. Nothing urgent," he added, with a quick glance at the others.

"Oh dear," Mrs. Merriwether said, not at all mollified by Mr. Scott's calm demeanor. "What are the symptoms, Doctor?" She felt her own pulse and then laid a hand on her own forehead.

"You have nothing to worry about, my good woman," Applewhite replied as he refilled his wine glass.

When Hannah saw that Mrs. Merriwether was still worried, she laid a hand on the woman's arm and said, "You exhibit none of the signs and symptoms of the flux, Mrs. Merriwether. Your pulse and temperature are quite normal. I believe we are safe here."

Neal Scott was amazed at the affect Hannah Conroy's conciliatory words, her comforting tone, had upon Mrs. Merriwether, who immediately calmed down and decided she should at least taste the claret. The young lady seemed to have an inborn talent for calming the distressed. Miss Conroy also did not seem to recoil from unpleasantness as she had offered Dr. Applewhite assistance down in steerage if he needed it. Not the offer one would expect from a young lady of gentle breeding.

Miss Hannah Conroy, Neal had discovered, was full of surprises. When they first boarded the *Caprica*, he had thought she was the Merriwethers' daughter. He had been surprised to learn that she was traveling alone. She had further impressed him when she had declared, "It's a ship of dreams, Mr. Scott," when the *Caprica* set sail and everyone—officers and crew, the four cabin passengers, and the two-hundred-plus immigrants—watched England become a memory. "Every soul on board is sailing to a cherished dream and new beginnings. It is very exciting, Mr. Scott."

"Why did you become a midwife?" Neal had later asked, when they were far out to sea and he had heard the story of her father's passing, how Miss Conroy had sold their cottage and sought passage to the colonies on the other side of the world.

He had heard passion in her voice as she had replied, "When I was eight years old, an injured farmer was brought to our cottage, bleeding and in tremendous pain. Within minutes, my father took away the pain, cleaned up the blood, and mended the wound. I was mesmerized. And I thought: I want to do this. But I was told that girls could not become doctors. And then when I was fourteen, a visiting midwife came to Bayfield. A very professional woman who carried a medical bag and did more than just deliver babies, she helped women with their private ailments. Since I could not go to medical school, I realized that I could enter the healing profession through midwifery."

"And why did you choose to go to Australia"

She had looked at him with a steady gaze and said, "I could not stay in England, for it was archaic class divisions that killed my father. I will start my life anew in a land where there are no Lords, no men born into a title and privilege they did not earn." Neal decided she must be a strong-minded, independent young lady to travel to the other side of the world on her own. Yet her appearance was deceiving. Her slender figure, poise and grace, her quiet way of speaking, those lovely pale hands, and the high forehead over wide, expressive eyes gave Miss Conroy the appearance of a high-born lady with nothing more taxing on her mind that what to tell the cook to serve for dinner.

Such speculation about a young lady was not a habit with Neal Scott. Ever since Annabelle—*"You should have told me the truth sooner, Neal. I can never hold my head up in this town again. You have made me a laughingstock."*— he had trained himself not to get too interested in a young lady. But because, at the end of this voyage, he was disembarking at Perth while Miss Conroy was continuing on to Adelaide, placing more than a thousand miles between them, Neal felt safe lowering his barriers just enough to permit himself to wonder about her.

Why, for example, was she not married? She did not even seem to have a fiancé or a beau. He found that hard to believe. And what of the nightmare that had made her cry out in her sleep one night, waking him, causing him to lie sleepless afterward, troubled that such an engaging young lady should be plagued by bad dreams. Perhaps it had to do with her recently deceased father. Her gray gown, edged at the cuffs, collar, and buttons with black piping, and the black lace cap covering her dark hair indicated that she was in mourning (although Neal thought the color suited her, and in fact brought out the lovely gray of her eyes).

A crewman appeared in salon then, informing Dr. Applewhite that one of the immigrants was in serious need of his help.

"Which one is it?" the doctor asked, his mouth full.

"It's the little boy, sir."

Giving his plate a rueful look, the doctor hoisted his bulk out of the groaning chair, pardoned himself, and followed the crewman out.

Deep within the ship's belly, where more than two hundred people slept with the stench of vomit and feces, Agnes Ritchie sat in the darkness as she stroked her little Donny's head. He had been so robust and healthy just a few days ago. The doctors back in London had said so.

Because the voyage to Australia was long and hazardous, the weak and undernourished were weeded out during a screening process before the ships even set sail. Small families were preferred, especially those with older children who could get to work once they had landed. Everyone in the colonies was meant to work, from convicts to settlers to soldiers to the bureaucrats. And no one worked harder than Agnes Ritchie, a Scots Presbyterian trained as a seamstress and dressmaker.

A job in Sydney had been arranged for her—at triple the wage she could expect in Glasgow. *And* her passage was being paid for. She had worried, back in the immigrant depot at the docks where they had all been quarantined until it was time to board the *Caprica*, that the sudden disappearance of her husband would void her ticket. But the immigration officials had been very understanding—the lure of jobs and land overseas was strong, they said, until it came time to actually board the ship, and then many folks experienced a change of heart and ran back home. That was what Agnes's Andrew had done, asking her to come with him, and then just leaving when she had said no. He hadn't even tried to take Donny, their son, with him, allowing that the boy would have a better life in Australia than back on their farm that hadn't produced in three years.

The officials had looked into Agnes's case—the pros and cons of a woman on her own traveling with a small child had to be weighed. But when they examined her papers they agreed to let her continue to Sydney because she was a skilled artisan, and such workers were in great demand in the colonies. That, and the fact that she had a healthy child. So Agnes Ritchie had placed herself and her son in God's care and, with their small bundle of possessions, had climbed the gangway of the *Caprica*.

The first four weeks had been a harrowing time of terrible sea sickness, scalds, burns, broken limbs, and bruising during rough seas. Agnes had stoically accepted it all as God's will, praying day and night that he keep her and her son well. And then contagion had broken out, what everyone was calling "the bloody flux" because of the severe diarrhea. It had started shortly after they stopped at some islands for fresh food. A few fell ill but managed to recover. But then came the first death and burial at sea. After that, the contagion spread so quickly that panic set in. The immigrants grew afraid to go belowdecks, insisting that the open air of the main deck was safer. But even up there, as the men and women had bunked down on the boards, despite the captain's orders that they go below, the contagion continued to spread.

Four more deaths. Four more burials at sea. And then Agnes's Donny fell ill and stopped eating.

The ship's doctor called it dysentery. It dehydrated the body, he said, and so Mrs. Ritchie was to see that her boy drank as much water as he could. But it didn't seem to matter how much she managed to get him to drink, the dehydration was accelerating. His skin was hot and dry, his lips cracked and bleeding. He moaned with pain.

Agnes had not left his side in days, even though she herself was weak from the illness and felt on the verge of collapse. "You'll be missing your lessons," she murmured as she stroked his hair. "Just think how you've loved being up on deck everyday, my boy. And wasn't it kind of the captain to arrange for you and the children to have lessons all through the passage?" She forced a chuckle. "I could hear you, sweet boy. The wind carried your voice below every time you recited for the teacher. Now have some water, Donny lad."

He had been in and out of torpor for three days, and always she coaxed him to open his eyes and drink.

But this time, Donny Ritchie did not wake up.

"It's about bloody time!" boomed a voice at the other end of the vast, crowded belly of the ship. Agnes looked up to see Redmond Brown, a potato farmer escaping the famine in Ireland, raising a fist to Dr. Applewhite, who had just arrived. "How come that high and mighty lot up there ain't falling sick like us?" Brown shouted.

"Allow me to pass, sir," Applewhite said, and made the mistake of laying a hand on the man.

Brown shoved back, and the crewman who was escorting the doctor seized Brown's arm and pulled him away with such force that the Irishman staggered backward into a large barrel, knocking it over so that contents rushed out like a broken dam.

"Now look what you've done!" Brown cried, scrambling to his feet. "That's our drinking water."

As few lamps were burning in steerage, due to the high risk of fire, Dr. Applewhite had to make his way through darkness, pushing his bulk between beds and crates, bundles of clothing stowed on the floor or swinging from the rafters. He went to the wooden shelf that was Donny's bed and examined the unconscious child in the light of the swaying lantern. As he searched for a pulse, the doctor made a secret vow: never again to sail on an immigrant ship. In fact, he amended, once they were docked in Adelaide, he was going to set foot on solid ground and never set foot off.

The steward was clearing away the barely touched lunch when Mister James came into the salon. The Merriwethers had retired to their cabin, leaving Neal Scott and Hannah Conroy to wait for news from Dr. Applewhite. At the sight of the First Officer in his marine-blue tunic, brass buttons, and gold braided cap, Neal and Hannah rose anxiously.

"Mr. Scott," said James in a grave tone, "are you able to handle a gun?"

"What's going on?"

"The boy has gotten worse and the immigrants are threatening an uprising if he dies. We will need every able man to defend this ship."

Hannah draped her shawl around her shoulders and started for the door. "I will see if Dr. Applewhite needs assistance."

As Mister James handed Neal a pistol, he said, "You do *not* want to go down there, Miss. It's not a fit place for a lady like yourself."

But Hannah walked past the officer, with Neal following.

From the quarterdeck, beneath a blue sky, with a stiff wind filling the sails, they saw the crowd down on the main deck, looking angry and dangerous. The silence was ominous. Captain Llewellyn, in his long dark coat over white trousers, with his dark blue visored cap bearing the gold braids of his rank as commander of the *Caprica*, stood squared-off with the rag-tag crowd that figured they had nothing to lose. Standing with Llewellyn were merchant marine sailors who wore blue bellbottom trousers and white shirts with square collars. Since their long hair was braided into ponytails and smeared with tar to prevent them getting caught in the ship's equipment, the men were nicknamed Jack Tars. Tough-looking sailors, Hannah thought, but no match for the enraged mob.

Tucking the pistol into his belt, Neal took Hannah by the arm, protectively, and led her down the companionway. Hundreds of wary, suspicious eyes watched them as they went. As they descended into the foul-smelling belly of the ship, a crewman said, "Watch your step here, Miss. A barrel of drinking water got knocked over. The floor's slippery."

"Ah, Miss Conroy," Dr. Applewhite said when she and Neal reached Donny's bedside. "I'm glad of your help. I've three new cases to look at.

Revive the boy and give him as much water as he will tolerate. We'll need to keep this up 'round the clock if we're to save him."

But when Hannah saw the deep torpor, the sunken eyes, and felt the barely detected pulse, she recalled an epidemic of dysentery that had swept through Bayfield, and she knew that the boy could not be revived and the subsequent lack of hydration would lead to his death. But when she voiced this to Applewhite, the physician said, "Oh, the boy will revive. At least once anyway. Use this." And he produced from his medical bag a small vial stoppered with a cork.

Removing the cork, Applewhite slipped his arm beneath Donny and, lifting him up, moved the vial from side to side beneath the boy's nose. To Hannah's astonishment, Donny's eyes snapped open, and he drew in a sharp breath. Quickly stoppering the vial, Applewhite brought a tin cup of water to Donny's mouth and held it there while the boy took in a few sips. When Donny closed his eyes, Applewhite lowered him to the soiled bedding and said to Hannah, "It is called spirits of ammonia. It is made from ammonium carbonate, a compound that stimulates the lungs, thereby triggering the inhalation reflex, causing a patient to come 'round. A little trick I learned in India."

Hannah was astounded. Her father's own recipe for smelling salts was ordinary table salt dampened by a dozen drops of lavender, and it would not have been strong enough to revive Donny Ritchie.

When Hannah suggested that bringing him out of the hold might help, Applewhite agreed. "Take him to my cabin. The sickbay has a bunk with a porthole above for fresh air." He handed her the vial of smelling salts and said, "Slap the boy until he comes 'round and then force him to drink water. As much as he can tolerate without throwing up. Keep at it, Miss Conroy. Keep him conscious and keep giving him water. I shall stay here with the new cases."

At that moment, Agnes collapsed. Neal picked her up and laid her gently on a bunk, but as he started to turn away, she seized his hand in a surprisingly strong grip, and whispered, "Take care of my boy. He's all I have. He's why I came on this voyage. Without him I have no reason to live." In the dim light of the odorous hold, while the ship groaned and creaked, and a mutiny brewed topside, Neal was captured by Agnes's wide, pleading eyes. And as he stood momentarily frozen, he felt something react deep inside himself, a nameless quake that jolted him.

Dr. Applewhite intervened. "Now, now, madam, your boy is in good hands. You must look after yourself." Then he gestured to a crewman near the companionway. "You there! Break open another barrel of drinking water!"

As Neal gathered the child into his arms, he heard Mrs. Ritchie say in a weak voice, "Please God, I beg of you, take me instead."

-3-

The tiny compartment adjacent to the doctor's cabin was cramped, with a narrow bunk along one wall, and cabinets and shelves containing medical supplies on the other. There was barely enough room for Neal as he bent to place Donny on the bed. He then returned to the door to allow Hannah to go to the boy's side, where she knelt and tapped his face the way Dr. Applewhite had. "I don't know how long I can keep this up," she said as she waved the smelling salts under Donny's nose. He awoke abruptly, sucking in breath, and she immediately brought the cup of water to his lips. Although his eyes were closed, Donny took in a few sips before he sagged in her arm. "It seems so barbaric. But there is no other way to get water into his body. And if he doesn't get adequate water, he will die."

She looked up at Neal, who kept glancing over his shoulder. "What is it, Mr. Scott?"

When he did not reply, but kept his eye on the corridor as if danger lurked there, Hannah said, "What is the matter, Mr. Scott?"

"I'm sorry," he said, bringing himself back to Hannah who knelt by the bed. "I was just thinking … Agnes Ritchie … something she said."

"And what was that?"

He frowned, unable to put his feelings into words. For reasons Neal could not fathom, the Scotswoman had reached a place deep inside him, had touched his soul in a way it had never been touched. He could not shake her wide eyes, her whispered plea, her prayer to God from his mind.

Take me instead …

"Miss Conroy," Neal said suddenly, startled by the idea that had just jumped into his mind. "There is something I would like to try, with your help." Even as he spoke, Neal was amazed at what he was saying, the audacious experiment he was suddenly gripped to try. It had to do with Donny and his mother, but there was something more, an emotion so powerful within himself, nameless and foreign, that Neal knew he was acting upon pure impulse. For now, he must do this. He would analyze it later.

"I would like to take the boy's photographic portrait."

"Portrait!"

He spoke quickly, the words tumbling out as the idea expanded in his mind. "Two years ago, a neighbor's child was killed in the street by a runaway wagon. The mother was inconsolable. She tried to commit suicide on the day of the child's funeral. But a photographer was there—you have heard of photography, Miss Conroy?"

She nodded.

"The photographer made a portrait of the deceased child lying in her coffin and—it was like a miracle, Miss Conroy. The distraught mother was so greatly calmed that she never thought of suicide after that."

"But Donny hasn't died!"

"He might, and I am afraid, Miss Conroy, that if he does, Agnes Ritchie's grief might be enough to spark a rebellion on board this ship. A photographic portrait might bring his poor mother some comfort and help quell the uprising. And I would rather capture his likeness while he is alive, Miss Conroy, than when he is a corpse. Mrs. Ritchie would know the difference."

She looked at him uncertainly. "You really think that a portrait—"

"I have the equipment," he said quickly, wondering how on earth he was going to accomplish such an impossible feat on a moving ship. "A camera is part of my scientific equipment."

"How long will it take? I must keep reviving him and administer the water."

"We need keep him immobile only for fifteen minutes."

"But how?" she said, looking down at the unconscious child. Donny's head rolled from side to side with the rocking of the ship. "The mayor of Bayfield had a photographic portrait taken, and the whole village turned out to watch. He had to sit with his head fixed into a clamp. The photographer said there must be absolutely no motion for the entire sitting."

"I know," Neal said, rubbing his hands together, "but I'm wondering if we can immobilize Donny's head somehow, and then stabilize my camera so that when the ship rolls, the boy and the camera would roll synchronously. In essence, it would be as though there was no motion at all."

But more importantly, Neal had to make sure of adequate sunlight. "Can the window in your cabin be secured open, Miss Conroy? Mine does not. The thing keeps crashing closed, and we will need ten minutes of sunlight to make a positive image from the negative."

"Yes," she said, having no idea what he was talking about.

"We shall have to move quickly."

"Tell me what to do," she said.

He knew they hadn't much time. The immigrants on the main deck were growing angrier by the moment. Shouts could be heard, threats. "I will fetch my equipment," Neal said.

While Mr. Scott was gone, Hannah moistened her handkerchief and pressed it to Donny's lips. She looked at his pale face, the sweet features peaceful in repose. She knew that if he died, it would spark a bloody conflict on the *Caprica*.

Neal returned with his camera box and tripod, and he slipped into the small sickbay, leaving the door open. As he began to set up his equipment, he said, "Geologists have been sketching rock layers and formations for years, but *I* believe the new technology for capturing photographic images will revolutionize science. Geologists will be able to record precise details without possibility of error. That is why I was hired by the colonial office to help survey the western coast of Australia."

With the ship dipping and creaking, Neal used ropes to immobilize the wooden box-camera on its tripod, tilting the lens downward at the child. To stop Donny's head rolling from side to side, Hannah removed a ribbon from her chignon and laid it on his forehead, firmly tying each end to the bed. She brushed Donny's bangs over the ribbon, and disguised the ends by bunching the sheet on either side. Hannah and Neal shared an unspoken worry as they worked quickly: What if this backfired? What if a photographic image of her child sent Mrs. Ritchie into such hysterics that the main deck became a bloody battlefield?

As Neal secured the camera at the foot of the bed, he watched Hannah's slender body bend over the child, tenderly counting his pulse, studying his face, listening to his soft respirations. Hannah's hair had come loose at one side and streamed over her shoulder, giving her a disheveled look that was strangely erotic.

Stepping past Hannah, Neal lifted the horizontal glass pane in the port hole, flipping it up so that daylight streamed into the cabin. He looked at Hannah. She nodded. They were as ready as they were going to be.

From Neal's supply of photographic paper, prepared by himself back in London and stored under his bunk in his cabin, he had retrieved one sheet and painted it with gallic acid and nitrate, and fixed it in a wooden frame which he now slid into place at the back of the large box camera. Shifting the back of the camera to and fro until he saw Donny's image come into focus in the view finder, Neal removed the brass lens cap and looked at his pocket watch. The exposure would need fifteen minutes.

While Neal studied the watch, Hannah kept her eyes on Donny. She prayed she was not making a mistake. Was fifteen minutes too long to let him go without water? She realized she was frightened. And the silence in the narrow cabin only served to heighten her fear. She looked up at Neal Scott, who studied his timepiece. "You must be very close to your own mother," she said.

He snapped his head up. "I beg your pardon?"

"To go to such trouble to comfort Mrs. Ritchie. You said it was something she had said.... I thought perhaps she had reminded you of your own mother."

He stared at her. He felt the ship creak and groan around him, rock gently from side to side as minute by minute Donny's features were captured inside the box. Neal wondered if he dared tell Miss Conroy the truth. *If I had told Annabelle sooner, would things have gone differently?*

Had Annabelle known the truth ahead of time, before Neal asked for her hand, she would not have flung his engagement ring at him, her father would not have brought a lawsuit against him for breech of promise and defamation of his daughter's character, and the whole ugly mess that had brought shame and embarrassment to Neal's protector, Josiah Scott, would never have happened.

He looked at Hannah, sitting on the floor next to Donny's bed, looking up at him with an open expression, those nacreous eyes framed by dark lashes and finely shaped eyebrows—

Suddenly it was very important to Neal that Miss Conroy knew the truth. "I am not close to my mother, Miss Conroy," he replied. " I don't even know who my mother was. You see, I was a foundling."

He allowed a moment for it to sink in, a moment in which Miss Conroy could adjust to the fact that he had just told her in polite terms that he was a bastard.

"I see," she said softly.

Neal returned his attention to the face of his pocket watch. "Twenty-five years ago, a young lawyer named Josiah Scott came home from his Boston law office to find a cradle on his doorstep. It was made of oak, very nicely crafted, with a hood. I was a few days old, wrapped in a white satin christening gown edged in pearl-beaded lace. There was a note, asking Josiah Scott to place me with a good family. But Josiah Scott kept me, thinking that whoever had left me might have a change of heart and come back. But weeks and then months went by and no one came for me, and in that time Josiah Scott grew fond of me. He kept me and raised me, and then he adopted me, giving me his name."

Neal lifted his eyes from the watch face and said, "I was lucky. Josiah Scott is a kind and decent man. He never married. It was just he and I. We have had a good life together." As Neal studied the sweeping hand tick away the seconds, he thought of the chemically treated paper coming to life within the camera, and of a young unmarried lawyer with an infant suddenly on his hands.

"Did you ever find out," Hannah began and then stopped, realizing she was prying.

Neal did not mind talking about it. "I thought of searching for my real parents. But they left no clues, and I took this to mean that they did not wish for me to find them. Besides, I had no idea how I would even begin such a search, and now it's been twenty-five years."

"So you do not know if you have brothers and sisters?"

"No idea." He cleared his throat and looked at her. "What about you, Miss Conroy? Do you have siblings?"

"My older brother and two younger sisters died in a diphtheria epidemic. Now both my parents are gone and I am alone in the world."

There eyes met in the dim confines of the cabin. "As am I," Neal said softly.

And then, remembering himself, he returned to marking the time.

The sweep hand ticked off the seconds as the *Caprica* rolled and groaned along its course. Sounds from the rigging—clanking, snapping—drifted through the open window. Heavy footfall thudded on the deck above. Neal kept his eyes on the watch. Two minutes to go. He thought of the angry immigrants lined up against the *Caprica*'s crew, while Hannah watched Donny's face, his chapped lips, wondering if this had been a mistake. The little boy desperately needed water.

"You know, Miss Conroy," Neal said, wondering why he felt the need to explain such things to her, "in a way I am a very fortunate man."

"How so, Mr. Scott?"

"Most men are born into a predetermined station in life. There are expectations of them at the moment of their birth, and few can break from that mold. But I was born free of those societal and familial fetters. Josiah Scott raised me to be anything I wished. When the day came in which I declared my desire to go away to university and study science, he did not forbid it on the usual grounds—that I had to follow in the family business, or join him in his law practice. And when I told him I wished to come to Australia and explore this new continent, he did not say to me whatever young men are told to discourage them from answering the call of wanderlust. In fact, he gave me his blessing. There! That will do it!" Neal said as he snapped his watch closed and replaced the brass lens cap on the camera. "Now we must hurry."

Quickly dismantling the apparatus, Neal silently exited the sick bay and returned to his cabin.

Hannah retrieved her ribbon, tied her hair back, and then revived Donny with the smelling salts. He took a few more sips of water this time and seemed to remain conscious a little longer. Making sure Donny was secure in the bunk, comfortable and dry, she went to her cabin to clear space and fix her porthole window open, as Mr. Scott had requested.

Working in the semi-darkness of his own cabin, Neal donned protective attire, and then he removed the fine, semi-transparent paper that had captured the image of Donny Ritchie and dipped it into a solution of potassium bromide to stabilize it. Next he pressed the sheet into a glass frame that contained a stronger, light-sensitive paper and brought it into Hannah's cabin where he exposed the framed papers to the sunlight streaming through the porthole. This would require ten minutes.

Hannah stared at Neal as he situated the glass frame on top of her trunk, where the light was the strongest. He wore goggles, rubber gloves, and a rubber apron. When he saw how she looked at him, he said, "The chemicals used in the developing process can be quite harmful, dangerous in fact."

When the exposure was done, Neal picked up the frame and hurried back to his cabin. Hannah said she must return to Donny and that she would await the results.

With his cabin door shut against the outer light, Neal rinsed the positive print in water, applied a coat of gallic acid and silver nitrate, and then dipped it into a bath of sodium hyposulfite. When he was finished, he removed his goggles and gloves, gently dried the new photograph, and lifted the stained glass pane of his porthole, holding it open to admit light. He stared at the astonishing image in his hand.

It was perfect.

Neal studied the details from an objective point of view, satisfied with the balance of shadow and light, pleased that there was no clouding and very little grainy effect. And then he took it down the corridor to the sickbay, where he found Miss Conroy once again giving Donny small sips of water. When she was done, she rose to her feet and gave him an expectant look.

He handed her the photograph. "What do you think, Miss Conroy?"

She stared at the picture, her eyes wide. "Mr. Scott," she said in a whisper. "This is a miracle."

He smiled. "It *is* rather a good image."

"A good image," she said, her gray eyes filled with wonder. "Mr. Scott, this is the most beautiful thing I have ever seen. I had no idea … the boy looks so peaceful. One would not guess that he was so dreadfully ill. Oh Mr. Scott, you have worked a miracle!"

Neal had thought of it as a basic scientific experiment with nothing miraculous about it. But when he looked at the image of Donny Ritchie again, he saw what Miss Conroy saw: an angelic little face, eyes closed in peaceful slumber, boyish hair combed down on his forehead. Because the calotype photographic process didn't produce the sharp focus that Daguerre's process did, Donny Ritchie lay in a soft glow, the edges blurred so that it almost appeared as if he floated on a cloud. The ragged sweater did not look torn and threadbare, but soft and woolly like a lamb's coat.

"It's wonderful, Mr. Scott!" Hannah said, and he was taken aback by her sudden smile, the glow on her features. His heart rose to his throat. Her pleasure washed over him like a sweet rain, and he realized he was experiencing genuine happiness for the first time in ages.

Suddenly, they heard a commotion on the deck. Mr. Simms, the cabin steward, materialized in the outer corridor to inform Neal and Hannah that Mrs. Ritchie had become so hysterical that some of the immigrants had brought her topside and made a bed for her on the deck. But her wails were agitating the immigrants all the more. "Captain's distributed weapons to all the men, myself included, sir, and I've never fired a pistol in my life!"

"Our timing couldn't be better," Neal said to Hannah. "Shall we show this photograph to Mrs. Ritchie?"

"Oh yes! But you go. It's your miracle, Mr. Scott. I will stay with Donny."

Two sailors on the quarterdeck tried to block Neal's way, for his own protection they said. But down the stairs to the main deck he went, through the crowd to where Captain Llewellyn faced a knot of angry men.

"Stand down, you lot, or I'll lock you all in irons."

"Can't lock up more than two hundred of us," came the growled reply, and the immigrants curled their hands into fists. "We want to know what you're going to do about the contagion."

"Captain," Neal said.

"This is no place for you, Mr. Scott."

Neal found where Mrs. Ritchie had been laid, and he knelt next to her, holding the photograph up for her to see. Everyone fell silent as they wondered what the gentleman was up to.

They saw Agnes wipe her eyes and frown at the piece of paper that looked like it had a picture of some sort on it. They saw her squint at it, and then look more closely, her expression turning to one of puzzlement. They saw her blink. Her mouth opened. Her eyes widened. And then they saw all the lines and shadows vanish from her face. "Why …" she said in a whisper, reaching for the photograph and bringing it closer. "It's my Donny." She looked at Neal in wonder. "How did you do this, sir?"

"It's called photography, Mrs. Ritchie."

Agnes looked at the picture again. "Look how peaceful he seems. Like he isn't sick at all."

Agnes's friends helped her to sit up and then crowded around to gawk at the picture. Soon it was being passed from hand to hand, as everyone stared and remarked and marveled over the likeness of Donny Ritchie. Many who had never seen a photograph turned it over to look at the back, to see where the image was coming from.

Neal found himself smiling. Watching the picture go from man to woman to child, passed around and back again to Agnes Ritchie, who filled her eyes with Donny's face and then passed the picture around once more—to feel their excitement and joy made Neal Scott's heart warm in a way it had not in a very long time.

Agnes Ritchie looked up at him then and said, "God bless you, sir," in her thick Scottish brogue. "I know now that my Donny will get better. Just look how healthy he is here. There is a place in heaven for you, sir, and that's the truth."

Neal modestly accepted everyone's praise, including that of Captain Llewellyn, who said that, for now, the mutiny had been averted, adding cautiously that it still depended on whether the boy lived or not. Then Neal returned to the sick bay to give Hannah the good news. He found Dr. Applewhite there, examining Donny. When the doctor told Hannah she could leave, Hannah insisted upon staying. And as there was little room for the doctor and his girth, Applewhite retreated to his own cabin for a much needed rest.

Neal brought in a small wooden chair for Hannah, but she said, "It won't fit. There's no room."

"But you can't sit on the floor all night, Miss Conroy."

"I shall be fine, Mr. Scott."

He left again, to return with the two pillows from his own bunk. "Then at least sit on these." And Hannah gratefully made a cushioned seat for herself, her pearl-gray skirts billowing out around her, making Neal think of a cloud.

Situating the chair in the doorway, he took a seat and watched as Hannah placed her ear to Donny's chest. She could hear his heart fluttering like a tiny sparrow struggling to get out.

"What are his chances?" Neal asked quietly, listening to the hammering of his own heart. His emotions were heightened and he did not know why. It had to do with the strange, nameless feelings Mrs. Ritchie had aroused in him—well, Mrs. Ritchie at first, but now Hannah Conroy as she sat so devotedly at Donny's side. Neal Scott, scientist and explorer, a man who believed that everything in the universe could be measured, quantified, and categorized, was at a complete loss to identify the alien emotions that had invaded him today.

"Dr. Applewhite said the next few hours are crucial," Hannah said. "If I can wake Donny enough times to get water into him, he will be fine by morning. But the smelling salts are having less effect on him. I think his lungs are becoming used to the shock from the chemical."

Daylight waned, and Simms the steward brought Neal and Hannah a dinner of sausages, potatoes, and peas, with wine and bread and butter, but their trays went untouched. He asked about the boy, reported on the other dysentery cases in steerage, not as bad it seemed, likely to pull through, and then left after saying ominously, "It's this boy we're all worried about."

When darkness fell, Neal offered to give Hannah a break. "Go topside, get some air."

But she would not leave. So Neal went to stretch his legs and see what the situation was with the immigrants, while Hannah roused Donny, gave him sips of water, and sponged his hot skin. When Neal returned, Hannah had him lift the boy from the bunk so she could change the soiled sheets. There was less discharge this time, she noted, and it had been hours since Donny had vomited.

"How is Mrs. Ritchie?" she asked.

"She is much better. Able to keep water down. She keeps looking at the photograph. I think it is helping. And I think you should get some rest, Miss Conroy. You'll be no good to Donny if you drop from exhaustion."

"Yes," Hannah whispered as they stood close together in the dimly lit cabin, rocked together in the embrace of the *Caprica* on the undulating ocean. Neal brushed a stray lock of hair from her cheek. She looked up at him, his face so near that she detected the fragrance of shaving soap. She wanted to lean into him, let him take her weight and her fatigue, hold her for a while. Neal wanted to put his arms around her and draw her against him. But that was not why they were here. There was sickness on the *Caprica*, and possible mutiny brewing. This moment, this night, was not a luxury for them to enjoy.

While Neal took a turn at the beside, Hannah went no further than the wooden chair. She was soon asleep, her head resting against the doorframe. As Neal watched her, he thought of the nightmare that had wakened him one night, with Hannah crying out in her sleep. What was it that haunted her? Her father's death, perhaps? And what had truly caused her father's death? When Hannah spoke of his passing, it seemed to Neal to be in symbolism and ideals—"It was class prejudice that killed him."—but the details, Neal did not know. Exactly how did class prejudice kill a man? He wanted to ask her, and suspected Miss Conroy would freely tell him, but he was afraid of her secrets, because once he possessed them, then he was in danger of growing too close to her, of allowing himself to fall in love, and that he could not permit. He knew there was no future for himself and Miss Conroy—she a Quaker, he an atheist, she gentle born, he a bastard, she looking to settle down and build a midwifery practice, he under a spell of wanderlust so strong that he could never stay in any town for long.

Insurmountable odds.

And so he would not ask her about her nightmare, would not inquire about her father, but would leave their relationship as the shipboard friendship that it was, doomed to end once they were on land and thirteen-hundred miles apart.

Just before dawn, Donny opened his eyes and asked Hannah if she was an angel. He then asked for his mother and said he was hungry. Giving the boy some warm broth that Mr. Simms had brought, Hannah then cleaned him up and, with Neal carrying the boy, they walked up into the morning sunlight.

As soon as Hannah and Neal appeared on the quarterdeck, the crowd that had spent the night under the stars rose to their feet and cheered in a blazing sunrise that was turning the ocean to gold.

-4-

"I do not like the look of that scud, Mister James," Captain Llewellyn said as he studied the black clouds on the horizon. Through the brass spyglass, he inspected every mile of the approaching squall and arrived at the grim conclusion that before him lay a storm for which there was no way around, nor was there any nearby port where they might find safe anchorage until the storm had passed.

"It's a big one, sir," the First Mate said quietly. "And it is approaching fast."

"That it is, Mister James," the master of the *Caprica* said solemnly.

"What are your orders, sir?"

Llewellyn thought for a moment as he studied the height and breadth of the approaching squall, its speed, and the look of the seas in its path, and then said, "We will not fight it, Mister James. We will lie ahull, and may God have mercy on us."

The First Mate swallowed in fear. Lying ahull meant bringing the sails down and locking the tiller to leeward, allowing the boat to drift freely and at the mercy of the storm. He was suddenly thinking of his young wife, Betsy, and their baby back home in Bristol.

"Batten all hatches and portholes," Captain Llewellyn said. "Secure all cargo and make fast the livestock. Check the scuppers. Extinguish all fires and flames. And try not to alarm the passengers."

"Aye, aye, sir," the younger man said, knowing that he and Llewellyn were thinking of the same thing: the *Neptune*, in these waters at this time last year, going down in a storm with more than three hundred souls on board.

Llewellyn looked at his passengers who were out on deck, enjoying the mild weather. After passing over the equator without incident, he had informed them that once they had made it through the Doldrums, they would navigate away from Africa and toward Rio de Janero where they would pick up a south-westerly to carry them to Australia. The Doldrums lay far behind them now, but there was no longer a possibility of picking up the favorable south-westerly. A storm bigger than any Llewellyn had ever seen lay in their path, and they had no choice but to put themselves at its mercy.

The captain prayed that the loss of life would be minimal.

Up on the quarterdeck, unaware of the approaching storm, three of the cabin passengers were enjoying the warm sun and cloudless sky.

Reverend Merriwether, seated in a wood and canvas deck chair, was engrossed in one of the many books he was transporting to the colony, while his wife knitted at his side. Abigail wished she could loosen her corset and divest herself of the cumbersome crinoline and petticoats. Women's fashions were not designed for the semi-tropical climate of the Southern Atlantic Ocean. But she was used by now to the inconveniences of long-distance travel. She had grown accustomed to the constant sway and yaw of the *Caprica*, and the ship's every creak and groan, to hearing the sound of the ship's bell marking time and regulating the crew's watches, and to hearing the bosun's whistle issuing high-pitched commands.

She wished they could keep sailing forever. The aboriginal mission had been described as "in the back of beyond, and the savages go about naked."

Swallowing back her secret fears, Abigail focused her attention on her fellow cabin passengers. They seemed not to mind the inconveniences of ocean travel. In fact, since the day the little immigrant boy had recovered from the dysentery—and the others also recuperated with no new outbreaks—Mr. Scott and Miss Conroy seemed to be possessed by a curious zeal. They had also grown friendlier with each other, Abigail thought as her knitting needles flew. She noticed how Miss Conroy occasionally raised her head from the book she was currently reading to look out over the main deck, her gaze always going straight to Mr. Scott who was toiling away at a perplexing labor, with the assistance of a few brawny immigrants. Mrs. Merriwether suspected that a special bond was forming between the two young people. She had even confessed to her husband that it would be a great delight if Miss Conroy and the American were to marry on board the ship, with either the captain or her husband presiding.

As if sensing Mrs. Merriwether's scrutiny, Hannah paused in her reading to look up and smile at the older woman. Then she saw the captain on the bridge, where he stood at the wheel in his white trousers and long dark blue coat with the brass buttons, his little blue eyes squinting out to sea. Earlier, Captain Llewellyn had been peering through his spyglass and having what appeared to be a serious dialogue with Mister James. The First Officer had then left the bridge, on an urgent errand it had seemed to

Hannah. What could the problem possibly be? The sky was clear, the ocean calm, and things appeared to be normal aboard the ship.

Hannah's gaze went to Neal Scott, who was down the main deck working at his new invention—a camera stabilizer that would allow photographs to be taken from a ship. Mr. Scott had made friends among the immigrant men, some of whom now helped him with the sawing and hammering of his wooden contraption. He had removed his jacket and worked with his shirt sleeves rolled up, suspenders criss-crossing his broad back. Neal Scott was a husky man, like the wrestlers Hannah had seen at country fairs taking on challengers for prize money, and she thought again how much more suited to physical labor he seemed than the gentlemanly pursuits of scientific study.

Forcing her eyes away from him, Hannah returned to the book in her lap.

Since the dysentery, Hannah had been helping Dr. Applewhite see to the medical needs of passengers and crew. She had learned more from him—the use of powdered ginger, for example, as a medicine for sea sickness—and had even assisted him in setting the compound fracture of a sailor who fell from the rigging. From these experiences, a new curiosity had germinated in Hannah's mind. After Donny, there were no new cases of dysentery. No more deaths. The contagion disappeared as quickly and mysteriously as it had first appeared. Why? Where had the contagion suddenly come from, and why did it end so quickly and mysteriously?

When Hannah had sold her cottage in Bayfield, she had packed her father's medical instruments and microscope to take with her, as well as a thick portfolio of laboratory notes chronicling his research in the cause and cure for childbed fever. Hannah had not looked at these things, as they brought back painful memories. But her curiosity about the contagion on board the *Caprica* prompted her to open her father's portfolio—a collection of loose papers held between two stiff covers and secured with a ribbon— hoping to learn more of his techniques for treating illness. She had expected to find remedies, pointers on how to diagnose, and medical answers. Instead, his personal portfolio was filled with baffling notes, equations, recipes, and even more questions. And they were all out of order. John Conroy, as conscientious a Quaker as ever lived, abiding by rules, ethics, careful thought and rigid ways, had been surprisingly haphazard in his laboratory practices.

But what baffled Hannah most of all was a question stated on the first page of the notes, written six years ago: "What killed my beloved Louisa?"

Hannah thought it a strange question since he had known Louisa's death was caused by childbed fever. In fact, it was that very fever that had driven him to six years of obsessive research. Or did the question have something to do with his final, cryptic words to Hannah as he was dying: "The truth about thy mother's death"?

Since her father's notes were undecipherable, Hannah had put the portfolio away and looked elsewhere for a way to quench the thirst that now budded within her. Dr. Applewhite had generously invited her to avail herself of his small collection of medical books, which she did so with enthusiasm. The tome in her lap was *Pathology & Medicine* by Sir William Upton, and already Hannah had learned things her father had never taught her.

She looked up from her reading again. Hannah had never felt so distracted. As much as she desired to concentrate on satisfying her new curiosity about medicine and disease, she could not stop thinking about Neal Scott. Especially at night as she lay in her bunk, achingly aware that the handsome American lay just on the other side of the thin wall. She would toss and turn as she pictured his muscular body—wearing what?—the breath would catch in her throat, she would perspire, and when she finally drifted off to sleep, it would be to find Mr. Scott in her dreams.

Sir William Upton lay neglected in her lap as, once again, Hannah allowed her gaze to travel down to the activity on the main deck where she saw, in the sunlight, Neal's sweat-soaked shirt clinging to his muscular back.

Neal was demonstrating to his new friends how he wanted the camera box to be mounted. He paused to mop his neck and looked up at Hannah sitting demurely in a deck chair, her lovely round head embraced in a dainty silk bonnet. She had been watching him, and now quickly looked away.

He had not been able to stop thinking about her since the night they spent with Donny Ritchie. To sit with her in the salon, to stroll on the deck with her—each moment now took on a unique quality. He knew he could fall in love with her if he allowed himself to, but at the end of this voyage they would be going their separate ways.

"Pardon me, sir, a word if you please?"

Neal looked up to see the First Officer with a grave expression on his face. "What is it, Mister James?"

"I will have to ask you to go below now, sir. There's a bit of rough weather headed this way."

"Rough weather? How bad?"

"Captain's expecting it will be as bad as it can get, sir. I suggest you secure those crates of yours. And if you can help the others in any way, I would appreciate it. Especially the young lady," Mister James added, nodding toward Hannah, who was holding onto her bonnet as the wind tried to snatch it away.

As Neal headed for the quarterdeck, sailors and deck hands were suddenly everywhere, running, shouting, climbing the rigging. Officers were ordering the immigrants to go below and, as Neal reached Hannah, he saw crewmen sealing the hatches to the steerage hold.

The day grew dark, the wind brisk. Sailors had donned broad-rimmed hats and rubber Macintoshes as they wrestled with shrouds, lanyards, and buntlines. The Merriwethers had already gone to their cabin to secure their possessions and themselves. Neal helped Hannah down the companionway, as the sea was growing choppy and walking was a challenge. Hannah went to her cabin, while Neal addressed the task of making sure his crates were properly stowed.

As the Merriwethers secured their trunk, the Reverend said, "My spare glasses! They must have fallen from my pocket up on deck. I'll be right back."

"Caleb, no!" Abigail hurried after him, trying to grab his arm. "It's too dangerous."

"If I break my glasses and don't have a spare set, I'll be of no use in Australia," he called back, gesturing for her to return to their cabin. But Abigail followed as her husband struggled up the steps of the companionway and, pushing up the hatch, emerged into a violent day.

Deciding it would be reckless to search for his glasses, Caleb Merriwether started to close the hatch when he saw, sprawled on the deck, what looked like an unconscious sailor. Caleb could not be sure as the man was lying against a coil of ropes, and seemed, in fact, to be just another coil. "My goodness," he said to Abigail, who was behind him, "is that a man?"

"Caleb, please, come down!"

The middle-aged missionary, whose hardest labor in recent years had been to weed his marigolds, took a quick measure of the scene—the low black clouds, the squall line driving toward the ship, the spray shooting up over the side—and made an instant decision.

As he pulled himself topside, Abigail climbed after him, calling for him to come back. But the sailor would for certain be washed overboard, and no one else seemed to have noticed the fallen man. As Reverend Merriwether fought his way across the slippery deck, with the *Caprica* pitching and rolling, he prayed that the man was still alive. Had he fallen from a yardarm?

At the companionway, with her hair flying in the wind, Abigail watched in horror as her husband stumbled to the stricken man, slip twice on the wet boards, and reach him as the ship gave a great lurch. She frantically searched for help, but the few sailors on deck were struggling with sheets and lines, and the roar of the wind drowned out her cries for help.

Caleb fell two more times, but he managed to seize the unconscious man—whose forehead was bleeding—by the collar of his rain slicker and struggle back, pulling him along the sodden deck as the rain grew torrential and higher spray came over the sides.

Abigail's eyes were wide with terror as she was certain that, at any moment, the two men would be washed over the side. And then, to her astonishment, Caleb was at the companionway, drenched and pale, but holding on to the unconscious sailor. Together, the missionaries lowered the man down and carried him back to their cabin, where they tied him to a bunk and then held onto each other as the storm hit.

Working quickly in his own cabin, Neal tied the last of his boxes and equipment to the lower bunk, securing them with ropes given to him by Mr. Simms. Hannah appeared in the doorway. "Do you need help, Mr. Scott? I have but a trunk, and it is well secured."

"You should not be here, Miss Conroy. These chemicals are very dangerous." He noticed that Hannah had removed her cumbersome crinoline so that her skirt hung straight down, giving her an alluring, more feminine shape.

"You said they were flammable. If you extinguish the lantern…?"

"They are more than flammable, I'm afraid. The ether that is used in preparing the collodion can be explosive." Back in Boston, not far from Josiah Scott's law office, a photographer had been killed in his darkroom when a bottle of ether burst and the fumes were ignited by a candle. Stored properly and in a cool and stable place, such volatile photographer's solutions as potassium cyanide, ammonia, and silver nitrate were not a hazard. But Neal had no idea how these liquids were going to react when tossed about in a storm.

"Then all the more need for an extra pair of hands," Hannah said, and she picked up a length of rope to help him fasten it around a box labeled FRAGILE SCIENTIFIC INSTRUMENTS. When all was secure, Neal tossed his jacket onto the upper bunk, and then a leather satchel. At that moment, the ship lurched and the satchel fell to the floor, snapping open, the contents spilling out. Hannah helped him retrieve the shaving brush, soap mug, handkerchiefs, combs. She picked up a small glass bottle and looked at it in the light from the lantern that swayed overhead. It was made of a lustrous emerald-green glass, shaped like a teardrop with a long neck and sealed at the mouth with red wax. The bottle was flattened, like a hip flask, but miniature—only two inches long—and it was suspended at the end of a beautiful gold chain, as if it were meant to be worn like a necklace.

Snapping the satchel shut, Neal tossed it onto the upper bunk and said, "That's everything! Now Mr. Simms said we should be tied to our bunks. Let's go to your cabin and I will secure you with a—" He stopped when he saw what Hannah held in her palm.

"This fell out of the bag," she said. "It's lovely."

His face darkened. "Josiah Scott found it among the blankets that swaddled me in my cradle."

"How extraordinary."

"I believe it belonged to my mother, that she placed it in my blankets as a memento. I don't know what it is exactly. It probably contains the most expensive Parisian perfume money could buy."

"Why would you say that?" Hannah said in surprise.

"Over the years I have speculated about the owner of that bottle, what she must have been like, what her motives were to leave it with me while depositing me on a stranger's doorstep. I believe," Neal said as the ship gave another lurch and he reached out to steady himself, "my mother left that expensive little bottle with me as a symbol of her bloodline, to let me know that I did not come from humble folk but from what passes for aristocracy in America."

"Mr. Scott," Hannah said. "This is not a perfume bottle."

"It isn't? How do you know?"

"Because I recognize it. This is a tear catcher."

He frowned. "A what?"

The ship rolled. Hannah put her hand on the wall. "A small bottle for holding tears that have been shed on special occasions. They can be tears of sadness or of joy."

"I've never heard of such a thing."

"They're mentioned in Psalms. When David prays to God, he says, 'Put Thou my tears in a bottle.' It's an ancient custom that goes back centuries.

Mourners collect their tears in bottles and give them to the person who has lost someone. Or you can give tears of joy as a gift."

Hannah handed it to him. "They are very popular in England. Those mourning the loss of loved ones collect their tears in bottles with special stoppers that allowed the tears to evaporate. When the tears have evaporated, the mourning period has ended. But this particular bottle, you will notice, was stoppered so that the tears would not evaporate. Your mother meant for you to carry her tears with you throughout your life." He gave her a startled look. "Are you saying my mother's *tears* are in here?" He looked down at the emerald-glass, casting off shimmering green lights as the overhead lantern swayed.

"Mr. Scott, she wanted you to know that she cried when she left you on Josiah Scott's doorstep."

Neal stared at Hannah, and then at the tiny emerald bottle in his hand. He suddenly felt as if the breath had been knocked out of him. "Do you really think that's so?"

She smiled. "I'm sure of it."

"I … I had no idea. My God," he whispered. And suddenly there it was: the nameless emotion that had had him in a grip since the day he took Donny Ritchie's photograph. Mrs. Ritchie had pleaded with God to take *her* instead, and something had shot straight down to Neal's depths, to stir feelings so powerful and alien in him that they had frightened him. Now he knew. His own mother had abandoned him. She had not asked God to take her instead. She was a selfish woman who, unlike Agnes Ritchie, did not want her child, but discarded him without a worry. That was what had driven him to take the photographic portrait of a sick child. Not to calm a hysterical woman or quell a mutiny, but to satisfy something within himself, to reassure himself that not all mothers were as selfish as his own.

But now … the perfume bottle was no longer the expensive bauble of a vain and selfish woman but a receptacle for her tears.

The ship heaved at that moment, and Hannah fell against Neal. "We have to get you tied down," he said, pocketing the little glass and gold tear catcher. "And this lantern must be extinguished." He reached up and drew the lamp down, blowing out the flame, plunging them into darkness.

The ship grew momentarily calm, but they imagined the forces of nature gathering and building above them. "We have to get you to your cabin," Neal said huskily, holding tightly to Hannah, not wanting to let go, unable to move. What on earth had happened just now, in these past minutes, in the confines of this small compartment? How had this young woman with gray eyes and a compassionate smile pulled scales from his eyes that he had not even known were there?

His mother had left her tears with him.

Strong emotions surged through him, rocking him as surely as the *Caprica* rocked him. His embrace tightened around Hannah. In the utter darkness of the cabin, his pressed his mouth against her hair.

Hannah thought of the violent storm that was about to hit, but she could not stop holding onto Neal. She held tightly to him. She could feel his warmth through the fabric of his shirt, the hard muscles. Without her crinoline, she could feel his legs against hers, a startlingly erotic sensation. She trembled. He drew her tightly to him.

In the darkness, Neal brought his hand to her chin, lifted her face to his. When he bent to kiss her, the first line of rain was upon them, and then the first monster wave struck.

Neal and Hannah were thrown off their feet. She cried out. He grappled for her in the dark, found her, pulled her to him.

In the other cabins and steerage, where lanterns and candles had also been extinguished, the passengers rode out the storm in terror, as blind as moles as they heard the sickening groans and creaks of the ship's beleaguered timbers. Mrs. Merriwether held onto her husband, who prayed in a loud voice as the ship rocked violently. Dr. Applewhite plied himself with so much medicinal brandy that he was barely aware of the storm. And Captain Llewellyn, alone in his cabin where he had lashed himself into his bunk, decided that, all in all, he had had a good life at sea.

When Neal heard a terrifying crash next door, he ran out and, fighting his way into the corridor that was so dark it was as if he were blind, he felt his way along the wall until his came to Hannah's door. He lost his footing, and he realized in horror that the floor was wet. Water was coming from Hannah's cabin. Neal flung the door open and saw gray daylight.

Sea water was pouring through the smashed porthole.

Hannah rushed in behind him and frantically gathered up a blanket to stuff into the opening, but she slipped when the ship lurched. Neal fell forward, landing on the sodden bunk, and more water poured in. As he struggled to get upright, Hannah cried, "We shall drown if we do not block this window!"

The ship rolled again, and the two fell backward. Enough light came through the porthole to show Neal that there were already about six inches of water in the cabin.

Knowing that there was no way he could go for help, he pulled sheets off a bunk, and then the mattress, and pushed toward the window, straining against the steep list of the vessel. Suddenly the *Caprica* was flung the other way, and Neal was dashed forward, helplessly, to crash against the bulkhead.

The ship careened so far over, and so much water poured in that Neal thought surely this was going to be the sinking of the *Caprica*.

And then Hannah was there, dragging the mattress from his arms and struggling to lift it to the window. Gaining his footing, Neal lifted the rest of the bulky mass of feathers and ticking, and together they jammed the mattress into the opening, filling in the edges with sheets so that the cabin was once again plunged into utter darkness.

The groaning and creaking of the boards sounded as if the ship were about to be torn apart while the storm roared and bellowed and kicked up the seas. "Mr. Scott!" Hannah called out in the darkness. "Are you all right?"

"I'm here!" he shouted, holding out his arms, blindly searching for her. Their hands met, and he pulled her to him. The *Caprica* lurched and then dropped suddenly, and Hannah threw her arms around Neal to hold tightly to him. She was soaked. Her gown clung to her body, and her wet hair streamed down her back and over her breasts. Neal could feel her trembling flesh beneath his hands.

In the darkness they held onto each other, falling this way and that until Neal caught hold of the doorframe and wedged himself against it so that with the next tossing and falling of the ship, he stayed rooted, holding Hannah tightly in his arms as she shivered and buried her face in his neck.

Neal thought of their lives ending in this unknown and unmarked spot, and he pictured the watery grave that awaited them below. He thought of the young woman quivering in his arms. He pressed his lips to her cold wet hair and drew her more tightly to him. The *Caprica* was thrown into a sickening yaw that seemed to spin her in a complete circle. Neal held on and kept himself and Hannah upright. The seas grew high, lifting the ship like a twig on a raging river, to drop it again in such a steep plunge that Hannah screamed. With freezing water swirling about her ankles, she dug her fingers into Neal's back and held onto him as if he were a life preserver.

A giant wave slammed the *Caprica* abeam, and she careened so far over that Neal and Hannah knew this was the moment of capsize. Hannah pressed her hand against Neal's neck. He lowered his head. Hannah lifted her face and their lips met in the terrifying darkness, in a deep kiss driven by passion, fear, and a last desperate grasp for precious life.

"Land has been sighted, Captain. Fremantle dead ahead."

"Thank you, Mister James. Full and by, Mr. Olson," Captain Llewellyn said to the helmsman at the wheel.

"Aye, aye, Captain."

The passengers gathered on deck along with officers and such crew as were not working the lines. It was a somber moment. They and the *Caprica* had survived the storm, but the memory of that terrible night weeks ago would stay with them for the rest of their lives.

By dawn the next day, the enormous squall had passed and the sun had broken through clouds to illuminate a drenched and broken *Caprica*—but still seaworthy, Captain Llewellyn had found, and so he had given orders for a new course to Cape Town, where they would shelter and make repairs. The immigrants had then been brought on deck, first to kneel on the soaked boards to pray, and then for a head count. Six had perished in the storm, two of them infants. Among the crew, eight had been washed overboard, while the officers had come through, albeit with injuries.

But the sailor whom Caleb Merriwether had risked his life to save had come through the ordeal with but a scratch on his head.

And now the west coast of Australia lay before them, bright and vibrant like a beacon of hope.

As Hannah stood on the deck in the golden sunshine, she thought of Neal Scott and their desperate hours together in her cabin as he had held her so tightly, and she had felt his warmth and strength when she was certain each breath was their last. And their kiss, which had lasted an eternity before a scream from Hannah had broken them apart.

They had not kissed again, during the storm, or afterward when they realized they were alive. Nor had they spoken of that moment. Each needed to think about that night, to examine startling new feelings, and find a way to understand the new life they had emerged into that next morning—because both Neal and Hannah had been changed.

At Hannah's side, Neal Scott watched the shoreline of Western Australia as it grew more distinct on the sunlit horizon. He thought of the remarkable young woman standing next to him. He had held her in his arms, thinking they were about to die, they had kissed in a way that had been both erotic and desperate, they had clung together and kissed as they thought they were about to die, and everything had changed. Neal was no longer thankful that they were going their separate ways. He did not want to leave Hannah. But he had no choice. He was to disembark here, and she was to continue on.

There was so much he wanted to say to her, but there had been no opportunity for private conversation after the storm. Hannah's cabin had been so severely damaged that she had moved in with Mrs. Merriwether, while the Reverend had bunked with Neal. The ship had been a beehive of activity, with seaman hammering, sawing, boiling tar, Neal joining them, along with able-bodied immigrant men, repairing the *Caprica* as she limped toward Cape Town. Hannah had had her hands full assisting Dr. Applewhite with injuries, infections, and hysteria. The only times Neal and Hannah spent a few minutes together were at meals, and that was in the company of others. They would look across the table, eyes meeting, and the hungers born the night of the storm flared between them.

They stood close together now at the rail, watching the approaching mainland. The other passengers also stood in awestruck silence beneath a vast, blue sky and sparkling sunlight. As the *Caprica* neared the coast, everyone saw deep-blue ocean turn shades lighter until finally they glimpsed lime-green water embracing white-sand beaches. Beyond lay a tree-covered plain stretching away to mountains.

But it was the tropical lime-green waters that stopped the breath in every throat. People from damp, misty isles had never seen such a blessed sight, and they prayed that their own destinations of Adelaide, Melbourne, and Sydney were as heavenly.

Standing with the four cabin passengers, Mr. Simms, the steward, said, "Perth was founded seventeen years ago, and right from the beginning hostile encounters erupted between the British settlers and the local aborigines. Those blackfellahs put up a mighty big fight to hold onto their land, considering they weren't doing anything with it. The English settlers were planting crops and running livestock, doing *something* with the land, you see. But the blacks didn't understand. There were some terrible battles, but that's all over with now. Three years ago a local chief died, and his tribe fell apart. They've retreated to the swamps and lakes north of the settlement, and they don't bother anyone."

When no one commented, Simms added, "You see before you one of the most isolated settlements on Earth. Did you know that Perth is closer to Singapore than it is to Sydney? And the summers here are hot and dry, with February being the hottest month of the year."

"Imagine," Mrs. Merriwether declared. "February being the middle of summer!"

"Imagine," Neal Scott said quietly, "three million square miles of land and nearly all of it never before seen by human eyes. Some speculate that there is a great inland sea and that what we think is the coastline of a continent is really a great reef surrounding that sea. Some speculate that the ruins of ancient cities lie in Australia's heart. Atlantis, perhaps. Or unknown races of humankind. Maybe the lost tribes of Israel live there, and they have built a second Jerusalem."

Hannah trembled with anticipation at the thought of this new world! A land that had been occupied a mere eighty years, with no centuries-old castles and antiquated lords and ladies. A place of new beginnings and fresh starts.

A tender had been deployed from the mainland, rowed by eight sailors, and as it came up alongside the *Caprica*, the Merriwethers said their good-byes. To Hannah, Reverend Merriwether said that, should she ever find herself in Western Australia, she would be welcome at their mission. "We are not there just for the redemption of aboriginal souls, Miss Conroy. All who seek the truth are welcome."

As Abigail watched her husband say good-bye to Miss Conroy, she marveled at the change that had come over him in the weeks since the storm. Caleb had lost weight and gained muscle as he had helped with the ship's repairs. His skin was tanned. He was the picture of health and vigor. Her fear of living at the aboriginal mission had vanished when she had witnessed her husband's act of bravery. She had not known Caleb possessed such courage and fortitude.

The Merriwethers were second cousins, and when they were children it had been understood that they would one day marry. Abigail had dutifully complied and had given Caleb five children. A respectful affection had existed between them, but no passion. How strange and unexpected, Abigail thought now in excitement as she looked forward to her new life in this sunny land, to fall in love with one's husband after thirty years.

As their luggage was being lowered into the tender, Mrs. Merriwether took the opportunity to offer Hannah some advice: "You are very bright and highly educated, Miss Conroy. But let me tell you, no man likes a woman who is smarter or more educated than himself. You must learn to hide your light under a bushel, my dear, at least until you are married."

"But I have not come to Australia to seek a husband."

"You need one, whether you want one or not," Mrs. Merriwether said, gray ringlets quivering beneath the brim of her bonnet. "A midwife is expected to be married and have children of her own, otherwise it is improper that a young unmarried lady be exposed to bedroom matters. And women will not care a fig for your formal training if you have never experienced childbirth yourself. If you expect to survive here, my dear, you must first marry."

And then it was time for Neal and Hannah to say good-bye, as his crates and trunk had been lowered to the tender. In a voice tight with emotion, he said, "I'm not used to putting my feelings into words. I can talk endlessly about the earth and all that is upon it, but when it comes to matters of the heart, I am tongue-tied. But before I leave you, Hannah, you must know of the profound impact you have had upon me. Ever since the day Josiah Scott told me the truth of my birth, I have held such a resentment in my heart against my mother. It is unreasonable, I know, but I have never been able to forgive her for giving me up. But you cracked that stubborn wall, my dear Hannah, when you told me about the tear catcher. It has shown me another side to the woman who is my mother and has planted within me the urgency to learn the truth of my birth and my parentage. I will write letters home, to everyone I can think of, government offices, local town councils and even to church registries. I am eager now to know my mother's name."

He did not voice the rest, the real reason he was going to search for his origins. It was too soon. Some things needed to be spoken at the proper time. The truth was, he had fallen in love with Hannah Conroy. He wanted to marry her. But while he suspected that Hannah herself did not mind that he was a bastard, he knew that others would. Society did not forgive birth out of wedlock. His past would come back and haunt their present, even to the point of harming their children. And so before he could ask her to marry him, he needed to know who he was, he had to know who he was offering to her.

Neal knew that if went home right now, bought passage on one of the ships anchored in the harbor, returned to England and from there, to Boston, that he could conduct a more thorough search for his mother, and would have a greater chance of success in finding her. But he didn't want to leave Australia, because Hannah was here. "This is a most difficult farewell," he said to her.

"Indeed it is," Hannah said softly as she filled her eyes with the sight of tall and handsome Neal Scott. It was exactly six months since they had set sail from England, and she hated to part ways with him. She was tempted to disembark here, but she was also eager to find her place in the new world and begin her midwifery practice. That was the change the storm had worked on her. Hannah had emerged from the tempest filled with new urgency and the thought that not a day must be wasted.

She looked toward the mainland and saw a young colony—a few warehouses near the pier, military barracks, wooden buildings, scattered homesteads, shacks near the beach. Not the thriving community where she could build a practice and at the same time explore her new interest in healing and disease. And anyway, Neal was embarking on the science vessel and would not be back for a year.

"I pray you find the answers you seek," she said. Hannah suspected that, although Neal claimed that because he was unfettered and without roots he was free to roam the world and explore mysteries, she did not believe he was free at all, but rather a prisoner of deeply buried hurts. He was not roaming the world to explore mysteries but rather to solve the mystery of himself, to find his place on earth. Until he uncovered the truths about his mother, Hannah suspected, and the circumstances of his birth, Neal Scott would never truly be free.

She wanted to give him a token of remembrance, something personal from herself that he could carry as a memento of their time together on board the *Caprica* and perhaps, she hoped, as a reminder of her affection for him. But she was unsure of the rules. Society dictated decorum and the proper etiquette regarding behavior between unmarried ladies and gentlemen. But weren't shipboard friendships different?

Caught in a moment of not wanting to leave and unable to speak, Neal memorized every detail of Hannah as she stood there in the golden sunlight, to carry with him like a mental photograph: the reed-straight posture, the pearl-gray gown that made her eyes luminesce, the proud tilt of her head, the dark hair swept up into a chignon, the little hat with the dainty black veil that covered her high forehead.

And as he held her with his eyes, oblivious of the activity on the ship around them, it struck Neal that he and Hannah shared a special bond, other than their life and death experience at sea, and that one desperate kiss. They both didn't quite fit into society. For Neal, it was his illegitimacy, a fact that he must keep secret because otherwise polite society would have nothing to do with him. For Hannah, she did not fit into society's model of a normal young lady, because she read medical books, asked probing questions, and voluntarily placed herself in situations that a proper lady would not.

A very unconventional young lady indeed. And one with whom, despite a promise to himself that he would never again fall in love, he was in fact falling in love.

"Miss Conroy," he said at last. "I would like to give you a token of remembrance, if you do not think it too forward of me." He reached inside his tweed jacket and brought out a handkerchief, freshly laundered and folded into a square. As she accepted it, Hannah saw the initials N.S. embroidered on one corner.

"Thank you, Mr. Scott," she said, tucking the linen into her bag. Then, removing one of her gloves made of soft kid and dyed gray, she offered it to him, saying, "And I hope you will accept this in return."

When he took the glove, it was as if she had slipped her hand into his, and Neal knew he was never going to let go.

He wanted to take Hannah into his arms then and press his mouth to hers, right there in front of God, the ship's crew, the *Caprica's* immigrants, and the seagulls overhead. "Although we say good-bye for now, my dear Hannah," he said quietly, "it will not be for long. In a year, when my contract is up, I shall travel on to Adelaide, and there we shall meet again."

They looked at each other beneath the bright October sunlight, while Perth's harbor bustled about them and the salty scent of the sea filled their nostrils.

"In a year then," Hannah said quietly, in love, excited and thinking of her father's last words, that she—with Neal Scott—stood on the threshold of a glorious new world.

ADELAIDE
February, 1847

-6-

"You're very young, Miss Conroy," Dr. Davenport said as he examined Hannah's certificate and references from the Lying-In Hospital in London.

"I have recently turned twenty," she said, wishing she could fan herself. It was warm in the doctor's office, and the open window did little to help. Instead of a breeze, all that came in from the street was more heat, dust, flies, and the smell of horse droppings. But Hannah, like the rest of Adelaide's predominantly British female citizenry, would not dream of doing without a tight corset and a heavy crinoline under her skirt. Mr. Simms, the cabin steward on the *Caprica*, had been right when he said February was a hot month in Australia.

It made her think of Neal Scott and wonder how he was doing in Western Australia, where she had heard it was even hotter than South Australia. Four months had passed since they had said farewell at Perth, and in that time Hannah had thought of him every single day. She prayed he was well and that he would be coming to Adelaide, as he had promised, in eight months' time.

"And you said you are *not* married?" Dr. Davenport said, peering at her over his spectacles.

Unfortunately, Mrs. Merriwether's prophecy had come true: no one would hire a young, inexperienced, and, most especially, unmarried midwife. "You should lie and say you're a widow," had been the advice of Molly Baker, one of the young ladies with whom Hannah shared Mrs. Throckmorton's boarding house. "No one can disprove it, and it will admit you into the sisterhood of wives. Unmarried girls aren't supposed to know what goes on behind bedroom doors. So how can you deliver babies if you don't know how they got there in the first place?"

Molly had a point, but Hannah could not begin her new life with a lie. "I am unmarried," she said to Dr. Davenport.

Hannah's marital status wasn't the only obstacle to getting a midwifery practice started. She had discovered that the established midwives in town jealously guarded their territories, making it impossible for a newcomer to attract patients. She had advertised in local newspapers, posted notices on public bulletin boards, and had introduced herself to the town chemists— she had even chatted up nannies who congregated in the city park, asking them to pass her name along. But the few calls she had received, coming by messenger to the boarding house, had resulted in disaster. *"You're* the new midwife? You're barely out of girlhood. And unmarried, with no children of your own?"

With her money running low and the rent due, Hannah had gotten down on her knees and prayed as she never had before, this time speaking to her father, asking him to guide her. That night she dreamed again of the cold, gloomy library at Falconbridge Manor, as she had many times, in which he pressed the iodine bottle into her hand, saying, "This is the key," or "Thee must know the truth about thy mother's death." Mysteries that plagued Hannah's sleep and puzzled her in waking hours. But in this last dream her father had said something new: "Thee helped *me*, Hannah, thee can help other doctors."

Collecting newspapers and visiting the post office and other public places where notices were posted, Hannah searched for employment advertisements and answered those placed by physicians. But that, too, had proven fruitless as they either wanted a male assistant or a domestic maid. Hannah fell into a category that did not seem to exist.

Finally, she had decided she must take matters into her own hands. With a list of physicians in Adelaide, she had set out to present herself before them, offer her services, and somehow persuade them that they needed her help. Three had already turned her down. "Stop this folderol, young lady, and get married." "I already have a maid." "You should be ashamed."

Now she sat demurely in Dr. Gonville Davenport's stifling office opposite Light Square, praying that he was more open minded than the others. She had even used some of her precious dwindling money to invest in a new wardrobe. On this hot February morning she wore the latest fashion: a drop-shouldered, narrow-waisted gown of lavender silk with purple velvet piping and buttons, the sleeves wide and split to reveal white ruffles. Matching gloves and a dainty bonnet finished the ensemble.

But she did not purchase one of the new handbags, which she thought rather frivolous as they were too small to carry anything larger than a handkerchief. Hannah cradled in her lap a carpetbag of luxuriant blue velvet shot through with shimmering silk and gold threads woven into an exotic design. Her mother had purchased it in Morocco and had used it for her stage cosmetics. Now it contained Hannah's most precious possessions: the instruments and medicines from her father's medical bag; the bottle of Experimental Formula #23, three-quarters filled with the iodine preparation; her mother's prized book of poetry, given to her by John on their wedding day with an inscription that read: "To my Beloved, who is Pure Poetry herself." And finally, from her father's small laboratory, the leather portfolio that held his research notes, the sum of his life's work.

As Hannah politely waited while Dr. Davenport read her reference letters, she thought of Mrs. Merriwether's warning: "Hide your light under a bushel." The last three doctors had not only been uninterested in Hannah's education, they had seemed, for some reason, to find it offensive and not at all proper. Hannah wondered if this time she should stay quiet.

Tucked inside her bodice was Neal's monogrammed handkerchief. She felt it there now, a gentle pressure on her bosom, as if Neal himself were touching her, urging her to spread her wings in this land where not even the sky was the limit. But how to do both—reach for her dream and yet hide her light?

She tried not to let her desperation show, but she was growing anxious about her living situation. Hannah wasn't used to a noisy, bustling town, or sharing a house with six women. She had had trouble sleeping during her first days at Mrs. Throckmorton's: the traffic outside seemed never to cease, especially in November and December when great mobs of sheep were driven straight through town to the harbor six miles away. There was the constant clip-clop of horses' hooves beyond her window, the crack of a whip, the driver of a dray shouting at his bullocks. Hannah had been born on the outskirts of sleepy Bayfield in a small whitewashed cottage with four rooms and a patch out front for growing flowers. She had grown up there. It was the life she was used to, the one she aspired to recreating here in South Australia. Hannah hoped that when her practice built up, she could move to a small place of her own further out of the center of town.

She tried to take the measure of the physician behind the desk. Dr. Davenport was an attractive man in his late thirties with a head of thick black hair that fell over his forehead in a boyish curl. His large nose and arched brows gave him a severe look, yet his tone was kind and his manner polite.

"I'm afraid I don't need a midwife," he finally said in a genuinely apologetic voice, "as I prefer to attend to childbirth myself."

"I can help in other ways. I assisted my father in his office, and I accompanied him to see patients in the countryside." Would it sound too pretentious if she added that they had even been called to the bedside of a baroness?

Davenport set the letters down and made a frank study of the young lady. She certainly presented herself well. Attractively dressed, well spoken. A spark of intelligence in her lively eyes. She had said her father was a Quaker, which meant she had been taught honesty. And the letters of recommendation from her teachers at the Lying-In Hospital spoke highly of her (although one professor of obstetrics noted that Miss Conroy was prone to asking too many questions). She was demure without being shy, ladylike but with enough assertiveness to present herself at his office asking for employment.

His practice *was* growing, and he had in fact been considering taking on an assistant. But not a young woman who was not even married!

Uncomfortable beneath the doctor's scrutiny, and worried that she was going to blurt something that would ruin her chances with him, Hannah looked around the tidy office lined with books, anatomical charts, ferns in brass pots, a human skeleton hanging from a stand, the doctor's desk cluttered with papers, books and journals, and a glass-doored cabinet stocked with medicines, bandages, instruments, sutures, basins and towels. Dr. Davenport's impressive library would be a bonus if he hired her.

Her eye came to a small ivory statue on the doctor's desk. "How lovely," she said.

Dr. Davenport glanced at the statue that stood eight inches tall and glowed ivory-white in the sunshine. He reached for it and smiled in fond memory. "Antiquities is a passion of mine, Miss Conroy. I purchased this statue in a small shop in Athens. The proprietor assured me it is at least two thousand years old."

"May I?"

"Please." He handed it to her.

"She's exquisite. Who is she supposed to be?"

"The goddess Hygeia."

"Oh yes, the daughter of Aesculapius," Hannah said. "An apt addition to a doctor's office."

Davenport's arched brows rose. "You are familiar with Aesculapius?"

Hannah hesitated then said, "He was the ancient Greek god of medicine, and Hygeia was the goddess of health, cleanliness, and sanitation."

Davenport nodded. "She is called upon at the beginning of the Hippocratic oath, when a new physician recites, 'I swear by Apollo, Asclepius, Hygeia, and Panacea, to keep according to my ability and my judgment, the following Oath.' But I'm afraid, Miss Conroy, that despite her standing in the oath, Hygeia wasn't an important goddess in the Greek pantheon. It was her father who worked the cures. But Hygeia prevented disease, which in my mind is more important."

Hannah was amazed at the intricate details of the carving—the goddess's robes, the flowers in her hands, the tiny sandals on her feet. She would have been carried by a woman, Hannah decided. Perhaps a physician herself, because Hannah had read that there were women doctors in ancient Greece. She tried to picture that ancient woman now, with her flowing robes and soft speech as she administered gentle medicines.

Hannah paused. No, this is not a goddess of healing. Hygeia was the goddess of *preventing* disease. The woman who carried this would have been a teacher.

As she handed the statuette back, saying, "She's beautiful," Davenport thought: She resembles *you*. The sudden notion startled him, but it was true. Not the Grecian gown, but the goddess's round head, the thick hair parted in the middle and swept up to an intricate knot at the back, the long graceful neck, even the delicate facial features.

This gave him pause. A widower who had lost his wife on the voyage from England, he had not realized how much he missed female company until now. His own dear Edith had been intelligent and lively, educated and well read, a woman with whom he could discuss all manners of issues, a woman delighting in lively debates and passionate nights.

He had decided not to hire Miss Conroy, but now he found himself saying, "Your duties will involve sweeping and mopping the floor each night. Light dusting. Washing my medical instruments. Rolling bandages as needed. And seeing that my medicinal stores are kept stocked—for that you will need to visit Krüger's Chemist shop once a week. If the patients come to accept you, then I will be glad of your help with frightened children and hysterical woman. And when the need for a midwife arises, you can assist me, and we shall see from there."

It was agreed that Hannah would work three mornings a week to begin, for a probationary period of six months with provisions for more hours after that. Hannah was so giddy with joy when she left his office, she could swear her feet did not touch the ground. When I have proven my skills and competence, she thought in excitement, I shall ask Dr. Davenport to add my name to the shingle outside, then I shall place adverts in the newspapers, informing the city of my association with the fine doctor.

As she stood on the wooden sidewalk in front of Dr. Davenport's two-story brick building, with horses trotting by, and carriages kicking up dust, Hannah pressed her hand to her bosom and thought, I shall write to Neal tonight, telling him the good news.

When they had said good-bye at Perth, they had arranged to write to each other in care of General Post. "If the *Borealis* makes any port, I shall strive to send you a letter," Neal had promised.

He had done more than that. To Hannah's delight, just two weeks after her arrival in Adelaide, she had found a letter awaiting her at the Post Office. Neal had written it the very day after he arrived in Perth.

It started in a formal tone and consisted of dry facts: "The HMS *Borealis* is a Cherokee class, 10-gun brig-sloop of the Royal Navy, a veteran of the Napoleonic Wars, and refitted for scientific survey. I shall be part of a fifteen-man team and the captain is keen to adopt my invention in which the camera will be stabilized for photography from the ship."

But then he must have warmed to his task, for the letter grew more personal. "I had dinner yesterday evening at the home of Perth's Lieutenant Governor—not as grand an affair as you might think—and the Merriwethers were also guests. As there were other scientists at the table—members of my expedition—a lively debate on current scientific progress ensued, and I fear I shocked the Reverend and his wife with my confession that I am an atheist and that I believe that someday science is going to explain all mysteries, perhaps even including the mystery of God himself. Dear Hannah, I do believe the well-meaning Merriwethers would have kidnapped me and whisked me off to their aboriginal mission had they been able to!"

He had then written, "I am enclosing a photograph of myself. I wanted to give it to you on the *Caprica*, but it struck me as too forward and perhaps rather vain. But I do not want you to forget me, so I have overcome my reservations and am including it in this letter."

Hannah had been thrilled to find, tucked into the envelope, a small piece of stiff paper, roughly the size and shape of a slice of bread. A black and white image was imprinted on it, Mr. Scott gazing out of the picture with dark soulful eyes. He wore a dark loose jacket over a white shirt, and he sat with one leg crossed over the other. His head was bare, exposing his closely cropped dark hair, and behind him hung a backdrop painted with trees and hills.

But the amused eyes and smiling mouth that she had come to know on the *Caprica*, were not evident in this photograph, which actually gave Mr. Scott a melancholy look.

As if anticipating her observation, Neal had written in the letter,

"Forgive the seriousness of my aspect. It is hard to hold a smile for fifteen minutes. In fact, my head is fixed in a brace that you cannot see. I'm afraid that, until the process is somehow quickened, photographic portraits will always look serious."

But Hannah liked the serious look, thinking it made him even more handsome, and added a distinguished air, as suited a man of learning and science. What a marvelous invention! A photograph was not at all like a painting that hung on a wall. Neal's small picture went with her everywhere, she could look at him any time she wanted, and at night, before she turned her lamp down, she would gaze at Neal's face and marvel at the strange intimacy, the staggering connection to him that it created.

And each time she looked at his face, she remembered the kiss during the storm—her first kiss, and one so desperate and passionate that reliving it overwhelmed her with desire and the terrible ache to be kissed by him again.

Neal had closed his letter with well wishes and a cryptic, "There is so much more I wish to say," and the promise to meet her in Adelaide in a year's time. Hannah had written back, telling him of her new life at Mrs. Throckmorton's boarding house, her eagerness to get her practice started, and had ended with the hope to see him next October.

Now it was only eight months away, and Hannah felt so good that she decided to try for an additional employment position, something to fill in her alternate days so that she would work a full week. Next on her list was Dr. Young on Waymouth Street.

When she neared the address of the small, white bungalow set between two empty lots, with a yellowing lawn in the front, Hannah saw a beautiful carriage with two horses waiting in the street. Coming down the path from the front door was a distraught young woman. She wore the black dress, white apron and white mob cap of a house maid, and when she reached the carriage, she came to a standstill, wringing her hands.

"Are you all right?" Hannah asked, noticing now that the girl was on the verge of tears. Hannah noticed also that there was something wrong with her face.

"I don't know what to do, miss. Dr. Young's housekeeper said he's gone to Sydney and might not come back and there's something awful wrong with Miss Magenta, they can't wake her up!"

Hannah glanced toward the small house, and saw that someone had hung a cloth over the doctor's brass plaque. She looked at the carriage—

clearly the possession of a wealthy family. Finally she looked at the maid, whose face was pinched and pink, her blue eyes wide with fear.

"I work for Dr. Davenport," Hannah began.

But the girl said, "He won't come! Dr. Young was the only one who would come! What shall I do? I can't go back alone."

"Perhaps I can be of help," Hannah offered, wondering why the girl was so certain Dr. Davenport would not take the call. "My name is Hannah Conroy, and I do have some experience taking care of people."

The blue eyes widened. "*You*, miss?" The maid looked up and down the street, wringing her hands savagely as if she were trying to dislocate her fingers.

"What's your name?" Hannah asked in a soothing tone.

"I'm Alice. And Miss Magenta needs a doctor bad!"

"What happened?"

"We don't know. She said she wasn't feeling well and now she won't wake up."

"Are you sure you don't want to see Dr. Davenport? His office is just—"

"None of the doctors will come," Alice cried, adding, "It's Lulu Forchette's house," as if that explained everything.

Glancing up at the coachman, who was smoking a cigarette in complete disinterest, Hannah said, "I'll go with you, Alice. I might be of help."

The drive took them beyond the city limits and out into the countryside, which Hannah had not yet visited. As the coach raced along the rutted road, and Hannah held onto her bonnet and her carpetbag, with dust and grit flying through the open window, she looked out and saw green rolling hills patched with farmland and sheep paddocks, barns, and shearing sheds. Cottages and houses lay far apart, and once, in the light of the setting sun, she thought she spotted a church steeple through the gum trees. As they passed under a canopy of tall eucalyptus, Hannah saw a flock of white cockatoos fly up, turning pink and orange as they flew off into the sunset. And as the carriage slowed to cross a narrow bridge over a creek, Hannah was startled to see a large, dark-orange animal, impossibly tall with tiny forelegs, jump gracefully out of the way. Hannah's eyes widened. It was her first kangaroo.

Alice didn't speak during the thirty-minute journey but sat rocking with the carriage, chewing her lip, and twisting her hands. Hannah thought the girl, who she guessed was around twenty, was on the verge of terror, as if she were more worried about her own safety than that of the mysterious Miss

Magenta. Hannah tried not to stare at Alice's face, but she was curious. Her left cheek was puckered with scarring. She had no left eyebrow, and from what Hannah could discern beneath the mob cap and yellow curls, Alice seemed to be missing some scalp and her left ear. It was a tragedy because, when Alice turned her head to look out the window, Hannah saw that in her right profile, Alice was actually quite pretty. She wondered what had caused such an unfortunate disfigurement.

"Here we are, miss!" Alice said as the coach slowed and an elegant house came into view.

Three stories tall, with verandahs and balconies, intricate lattice work and eye-pleasing columns, the home of Alice's obviously rich employer was set amid lawns and gardens, at the end of a long drive that turned off the main road. The ornamental ironwork was a trifle gaudy, the verandahs and balconies crowded with too many plants, and there was an array of imported weather vanes on the roof, giving the effect of the occupant showing off new wealth. The only neighbors were a sheep station a mile back, and what appeared to be a dairy farm up ahead, so that the elegant mansion stood alone amid gum and pepper trees, and country wilderness that fanned out to low hills and dappled brooks.

It seemed a strange place for so posh a residence, especially as there seemed to be no significant outbuildings, and no crops or livestock. Just a house, big and beautiful, in the middle of nowhere.

As the coachman gave her a hand down to the dusty path, Hannah heard music and laughter pour from the open windows, and now that the sun had dipped behind the trees, she saw that lamps had been lit in all the rooms. When she saw, around the side of the house, the saddled horses tied up, and the various carriages and conveyances, she realized there must be a grand party going on.

Alice quickly led Hannah around to the rear and into a brightly lit, very noisy kitchen where pots boiled and ovens gave off tremendous heat. "This way," Alice said, as cooks and maids looked at Hannah in curiosity. Alice led her to a back staircase where she found, at the top, several ladies anxiously milling about. They were young, two of them attired in nightgowns and peignoirs, the third in knee-length drawers and a camisole of white eyelet cotton. All three had their hair undone and streaming over their shoulders, as if they had just wakened from afternoon naps. As Alice explained to the nervous young ladies that Dr. Young wasn't coming, and Hannah heard murmured words about Miss Forchette being terribly angry, she followed the young ladies into a bedroom cluttered with gowns and shoes, a dressing table laden with jewelry and cosmetics, and a rumpled bed with a scarlet counterpane upon which a young lady in a lacy nightgown lay sprawled, shockingly white and deathly still.

As Hannah rushed to the bedside and lifted the young woman's wrist, and as she heard the piano music down below, accompanied by men's deep laughter, Hannah realized that this was no ordinary residence. Although she had never visited such an establishment, had never accompanied her father to a certain cottage on the road out of Bayfield, where a family of women were known for their hospitality, Hannah had no doubt what sort of house this was.

"What happened?" she asked as she searched for a pulse at the girl's neck and found it dangerously weak and irregular.

"She complained of a headache," said one of the girls. "She also said she was nauseated."

Hannah lifted Magenta's eyelids and saw dilated pupils.

"And she was terribly thirsty but couldn't drink any water," added another.

So Magenta had a dry mouth, Hannah thought, and difficulty swallowing. Hannah had seen this before. But it wasn't one of her father's Bayfield patients. The unfortunate victim had been one of Hannah's fellow students at the Lying-In Hospital. She had, in fact, occupied the dormitory cot next to Hannah's, and one night had dosed herself with tincture of belladonna to alleviate severe menstrual cramps. Like Miss Magenta, the poor girl had ingested too much, and although the students had sent for a doctor, it was too late.

"We have to wake her up," Hannah said. "We have to make her vomit."

"We've tried to wake her up, miss. Smelling salts don't do it."

But Hannah still had Dr. Applewhite's supply. She retrieved the tiny vial from her carpetbag, removed the stopper, and moved the vial back and forth under the girl's nose.

Magenta gasped, her eyes flying open. Working quickly, Hannah said, "Help me turn her onto her side." As the others rolled Magenta over, Hannah pried open the girl's mouth and thrust her fingers in, causing Magenta to gag. "Get me a basin, quickly!" Hannah said, and the bowl was produced just in time. Everything Magenta had consumed in the past two hours came up. The girls watched with held breath as their friend retched into the basin until her stomach was empty. Then Hannah said, "Help me get her to her feet. We have to walk her as much as she will tolerate. Fill that glass with water, please. We need to dilute her blood."

Half an hour of to and fro in the cluttered bedroom, with Hannah under one arm, one of the girls under the other, forcing the groggy Magenta to stagger back and forth, stopping only to force water between her lips, finally brought her pulse, pupils and skin temperature back to normal. Easing the girl into a chair, with orders to the others to keep her awake and talking, Hannah collected her bag and asked to be taken to the owner of the house.

As it was, Alice was out in the hall, having been instructed to bring Miss Conroy to a private parlor when she was finished with Magenta. When they reached the foot of the stairs, Hannah was taken past an archway that opened upon a large, sumptuously furnished parlor where she saw men in frock coats or evening tails, well-dressed and prosperous looking, socializing with an extraordinary collection of women. She tried not to stare. Although most were young attractive ladies in gowns (albeit with immodestly low décolletages and hems so high as to expose stockings), Hannah saw one very small woman, a midget of perfect proportions, dressed as a little drummer boy sitting on a gentleman's lap, while in a corner among potted palms, a seated gentleman sipped champagne in the company of a pair of Polynesian twins dressed only in grass skirts and flower garlands over their bare bosoms.

The men smoked cigars, pipes, and cigarettes, and the air was filled with the pungent scent of cannabis, familiar to Hannah because her father frequently prescribed hemp tobacco for nervous disorders. A long table was set with platters of appetizing food, and a barefoot girl dressed in a Japanese kimono moved about with a tray of champagne-filled glasses.

But the biggest surprise came when she was taken into a smaller parlor, with Alice quickly retreating, closing the door behind herself.

"G'day," said Hannah's hostess. "I'm Lulu Forchette."

The owner of the house was the largest woman Hannah had ever seen. Robed in dazzling blue silk, her wrists, fingers, and fat neck adorned with jewelry that blinded, and egret feathers rising from her flaming red hair, Miss Lulu Forchette reclined on a red velvet chaise with a glass of champagne in one hand, a cigarette in a long holder in the other.

"Alice reported that you revived Magenta. You brought her around and saved her life. Have a seat, dearie, I want to know all about you and this miracle you performed!" Lulu Forchette's voice, like the rest of her, was larger than life.

Hannah took a seat on a brocaded chair. In contrast to the main parlor that was like something out of a fantasy, this was a prosaic scene—the walls covered in flocked wallpaper, with watercolors of landscapes hung for display. Plants in pots, polished lamps, shiny knick knacks, books, antimacassars on the sofa and upholstered chairs. There was even an ottoman with silver elephants stamped into blue leather. Actually a lovely parlor, with some expensive, tasteful appointments—a red and gold Chinese vase on the mantelpiece between a pair of wide-eyed Staffordshire dogs.

"Pardon me if I don't get up," Lulu said. "I've got a bad ankle."

"Would you like me to look at it?"

Lulu waved a chubby hand. "Alice told me you revived Magenta with strong smelling salts. How is it you did that? Nothing we tried worked."

Hannah brought the vial out of her bag and handed it to Lulu, who took one whiff and jerked her head back "Crikey! It's powerful. We could use this. My girls sometimes faint. It's the tight corseting. Men can't resist tiny waists."

She reached out to a plate of sugared almonds, popped one into her mouth, and munched thoughtfully. "So how is it that I sent Alice for a doctor and she came back with you? And who are you exactly?"

Hannah explained the circumstances outside Dr. Young's office and then gave Miss Forchette a bit of her own background.

Lulu chuckled. "So you're a midwife and fresh off the boat. I expect you were surprised when you got to my place. Alice wouldn't have told you the kind of house this is. At least you didn't demand that my coachman take you right back to town. I'll hand you that. But you disapprove, I'm sure." She held up a hand, even though Hannah had said nothing. "It's the way of life in the colonies. You find a need and you fill it. Like you," Lulu Forchette said, narrowing her eyes as she looked Hannah up and down. "Saying you're a midwife but dispensing medicine, too. We do what we can to survive. Me, I was transported for stealing an apron. I completed my seven years and got my pardon. Trouble was, I couldn't sew, I didn't know how to cook, and laundresses were a penny a dozen. I had no skills, no occupation, like so many girls. Before I knew it, I was on the street, begging. The first man to offer me money for a quick service was a banker, of all things. We went into an alley, and I came out with sixpence. He liked me, and I stayed with him for a while. He introduced me to his rich friends, and making a long story short, here I am. Thanks for what you did for Magenta. I've told that girl time and again to stay away from the belladonna, but she won't listen."

"Perhaps," Hannah ventured to say, "she is unhappy here."

"Unhappy?" Lulu released a short laugh that sounded like a cough. "Why would she be unhappy? Magenta's my daughter, this is her home."

"Your daughter—"

"The good Lord blessed me with four girls, all of them good looking. And I'm proud to say they're more in demand by my customers than any of the other girls." Lulu laughed again, her great bosom heaving, with lights shooting off her necklaces and earrings. "Don't look so shocked, dearie. We're a happy family here. We like what we do, we wear pretty clothes, and we've got no husbands to get drunk and beat us up. Most of all, we don't go hungry in this house. That's the worst of it," Lulu said, her face going dark, her look going inward. "The hunger. A starvation so bad that you fight dogs for scraps in the street. And then a man comes along and offers you a sixpence for a few minutes of your time, and all you can think of is the meat pies the sixpence will buy. After a while, you'll do anything. Don't matter what a bloke asks for, as long as you've got a meal and a roof over your head at the end of it."

She brought herself back. "And ain't that what marriage is all about, anyway?"

"I've never thought about it," Hannah said truthfully.

"And as for being happy, well, all my girls are happy here. They are free to leave any time they want, but they don't." Lulu reached for another sugared almond and then paused and pressed her hand to her jaw. "Can you do something for a toothache?"

"Oil of cloves will help."

"What about a red, itchy rash?"

"I've found that a salve made of lamb fat and camphor will clear up most rashes. You can obtain both at the chemist in town."

Lulu's small, keen eyes studied Hannah, from her lavender bonnet to her dusty shoes. "So you know a lot about medicine and healing, things like that? You can stitch up cuts and such?"

"Yes."

Lulu rubbed her jaw again in thought. "Doc Young was the only physician who would come out and see my girls. The rest are too snobbish to cross my doorstep. Alice tells me he's gone to Sydney to retire. What would you say to entering into an agreement with me, Miss Conroy? Like, when a need arises, can I send for you? I'll pay you well for your trouble. We get the occasional illness, but mostly it's accidents. You'd be surprised."

Hannah thought for a moment. If her father didn't object to visiting a house of hospitality on the road out of Bayfield, then his daughter shouldn't either. "If I can be of help. I am staying at Mrs. Throckmorton's boarding house on Gray Street."

Lulu held up Dr. Applewhite's little vial. "And where can I get these smelling salts?"

"Please keep that. I can make up more."

"You're *giving* this to me? Free of charge? Let me tell you something, dearie." Lulu shifted her bulk and farted delicately. "Don't give away what you can sell. It's the rule in this house, and it's what's made me rich. These smelling salts are strong medicine. I doubt there's anything like this in the colony. I know Mr. Krüger doesn't carry anything this powerful. My advice: bottle it and sell it, and you'll soon be rich too."

Lulu gestured toward the closed door and the music beyond. "Those men out there in the expensive clothes, drinking fancy champagne and paying top price for my girls, they come to this shore with dirt behind their ears. Nobodies back home, they buy five hundred acres and run sheep or cattle and grow so rich their pants don't fit. It's what everyone comes to Australia for. You'd be a fool not to join the parade."

Hannah asked about Alice's facial disfigurement. "The poor child," Lulu said. "When she was twelve, a brush fire went through her farm. It was night. Her entire family perished, but Alice was saved by a ranch hand. She was caught under a fallen beam and her rescuer tugged hard, not knowing her hair was pinned down. It pulled away some of her scalp and ear. The bloke rushed her to a neighbor who took care of her and nursed her back to health. They even offered to let her stay with them in exchange for work. But they discovered that Alice had gotten a sudden fear of fire. She couldn't light a lamp or go near a stove or a fireplace without screaming. As they were barely subsisting themselves, they couldn't keep a girl who couldn't earn her food. She was taken into town where a charity for orphans tried to place her in domestic work, but Alice's fear of fire kept getting her sacked. Finally, she was old enough for the authorities to stop worrying about her and she found herself on the street. That's where I found her, poor raggedy thing, down by the docks begging."

"That's what I do, share my good fortune with those in need. Every now and then I go into town in my carriage and search the streets for girls in desperate situations. I rescue them, bring them home, fatten them up, and they join my family." The great, pale bosom, laden with necklaces, rose and fell in a dramatic sigh. "That's me, softy at heart. Most of the girls appreciate what I do, but some can be ingrates. It isn't always easy being charitable, you know. Will you stay for supper? My cooks put out the tastiest roast beef and Yorkshire pud."

"No thank you, I should get back to town."

Reaching for the bellpull near the chaise, Lulu gave it two impatient yanks, and a young, red-haired woman appeared, bearing a striking resemblance to Miss Forchette. "Rita, escort Miss Conroy back to the carriage. And give her a pound note for coming out tonight." To Hannah, Lulu said, "I'd get up and see you out myself, but the ankle is bad."

Hannah noticed the cane by the chaise: a handsome piece carved from mahogany with a curiously shaped gold handle. Not the sort of cane one purchased for temporary injuries. Hannah wondered if Lulu's weight prevented her from walking.

Rita led her through the house to the large kitchen, where the staff were busy at the stoves and ovens. As they neared the rear door of the house, with Rita going ahead out into the evening, they passed a deep linen cupboard, and Hannah heard singing within. It was the familiar "Ballad of Barbara Allen," and the voice was so beautiful, it sent chills down Hannah's spine.

She looked in and saw Alice at the shelves, collecting folded pillow cases and sheets. Sensing that she was not alone, Alice turned abruptly, the song stopping in her throat.

"I have never heard such a beautiful voice," Hannah said.

"Thank you, miss," Alice said shyly, blushing so fiercely and covering the left side of her face with her hand that Hannah suspected Alice only sang when she thought there was no one around.

Hannah found Rita waiting for her outside in the sultry summer evening, with stars now winking in the black sky. "Just follow this path," Rita said with a charming smile. "The coach is waiting."

The air was perfumed with flowers and filled with the noisy songs of crickets and frogs. February, Hannah thought as she followed the path. Easter was around the corner, and it would be celebrated in autumn.

But even more remarkable than upside-down months was her visit to this incredible house. She thought of Lulu and Rita and Magenta, and the other girls within, the gentleman callers, and the lights in all the windows. Hannah could not even imagine what went on in those rooms. And what had Lulu meant by "accidents"?

Hannah's thoughts turned to Dr. Davenport and her first day at work tomorrow, and she was suddenly so excited and full of speculation that she did not see a strange, dark shape materialize on the garden path ahead. It was the growling that caught her attention.

Hannah stopped and stared. The dog emerged from the shadows, and Hannah saw by the moonlight that it was orange coated with a long snout and sharp upright ears that gave it a fox-like appearance. Its fur was filthy and ribs were clearly delineated. The creature was starving.

Hannah froze as the snarling beast bared its fangs, hackles rising.

Her mouth ran dry as she forced her feet to move back one small step. As she did so, the dog took a wary step toward her. Hannah went back another, and the dog advanced another. Hannah continued to retreat, hoping she would reach the light and noise of the kitchen, which might send the dog away, but with her last step she felt a tree at her back. She could go no farther, and the dog continued to advance.

Hannah was wondering if calling for help would drive the dog off, or make it attack, when she suddenly heard a low voice nearby. "Don't move. Stay perfectly still."

Hannah held her breath as a man stepped out of the darkness and moved in front of her, his back to her. He spoke to the dog in a calm voice. "It's all right, mate. We're not here to harm you. We're just passing through."

The night's cacophony seemed to grow louder as the stranger stared down the snarling dog, speaking calmly to it. Hannah had no idea who the stranger was. He had come from the direction of the road, and he wasn't dressed like the gentlemen in Lulu's house. He seemed, in fact, to be wearing work clothes. His head was covered in a wide-brimmed slouch hat, and he smelled of tobacco.

"I'm sorry we've taken your territory," he said calmly to the dog, "but that's just the way of things now. Let's part friends, all right?"

The moment stretched and became surreal as floral fragrance filled Hannah's head, and she could hear music and laughter from the house, while a strange man stood between herself and a savage dog.

And then the growling stopped, the hackles lowered, and after a moment the dog turned and slunk away into the night.

The stranger stepped back and turned to face Hannah. "Are you all right?"

She placed her hand on her chest as she released a shaky sigh. "My heart is racing! Whatever it was you did, thank you."

He glanced back through the darkness and said, "They don't understand that this isn't their territory anymore. They come for what they can find in the rubbish, now that their hunting ground is gone."

"What kind of a dog was that?"

"That's what the aborigines call a dingo. You can't tame them and they're often dangerous. Where are my manners? Jamie O'Brien, at your service," the stranger said with a smile as he lifted his hat.

Hannah saw dark blond hair, and in the shadow of the wide brim of the hat as he reseated it, eyes that squinted over craggy cheeks and rugged jaw. Mr. O'Brien's skin was weathered like a sailor's—his squint reminded her of Captain Llewellyn's—and she wondered if the hair was naturally blond or sun-bleached. He stood a head taller than herself, but he was neither husky nor broad-shouldered; rather he was lean, and as he wasn't wearing a jacket—over his white shirt he wore a black leather waistcoat with silver buttons—she saw a tight, compact figure. His sleeves were rolled up, and Hannah saw well-muscled forearms. She noticed something attached to his belt: a leather sheath with a knife handle sticking out. A man used to fending for himself.

Hannah sensed strength in him, despite his slender build, and guessed that he was not a town man but one of those rugged types who come in occasionally from the farms and ranches and even the Outback. A drover, perhaps. His hands, she thought, would be calloused.

She realized he was staring at her in an odd way. He had told her his name, and now he was studying her as if he was expecting a reaction. Was she supposed to know who he was? Was he famous in some way?

And then she realized he was waiting for the courtesy to be returned. "Hannah Conroy," she said, aware that he stood close, giving her no room to move away from the tree. His eyes, the pale blue of a man who spends all his time outdoors, held hers, and she saw creases of amusement at the corners. Yet she did not feel he was mocking her. When she detected the scent of fresh clean soap and shaving cream, and because he was on the path leading to Lulu's house, she guessed why he was here.

"What's a fine lady like yourself doing at a place like this?" he asked, glancing past her toward the house.

She explained that she was a midwife, called to help one of the girls.

He glanced down at the carpetbag in her hand. "A midwife is it?" he said softly, the corners of his eyes crinkling in amusement. "For someone in *Lulu's* house?"

"One of the ladies fainted."

"Ah." He fell silent then, and Hannah saw changes in his pale-blue eyes, like ocean tides. "Ah," he said again as if suddenly understanding something new, and trying to find a way to understand and accept it. He couldn't seem to stop staring at her.

"Thank you again for sending the dog away," she said, and looked right and left, to see how she could gracefully sidestep him. His frank stare, that had begun in amusement and curiosity, had turned grave, and Hannah wondered for an instant if he was dangerous.

The colony of Adelaide was the gateway to the country's vast interior, with opportunists flocking from all over the world to come in search of opals, gold, diamonds, even the lost treasure of King Solomon. There had been no strikes of gold or opals as yet, but rumors were a powerful draw. Already copper and silver had been discovered, promising that more riches lay just on the other side of Adelaide. And so this frontier town of eight thousand souls that was the staging platform for explorers, visionaries and gold seekers, was also teeming with men and women looking for get-rich-quick schemes—confidence artists, swindlers, grifters, gamblers, and flimflam men, along with the usual petty thieves, pickpockets, and purse snatchers.

Perhaps this stranger was one of the latter. But he surprised her by plucking a rose from a nearby bush and handing it to her. "The aborigines say that flowers were created by the ancestors back in the Dreamtime, which was a long, long time ago. The ancestors were magical people, and everything they did or thought was transformed into something solid. It's said that every time an ancestor laughed, a flower was created. And because people laugh more in the springtime, that's why there are more flowers in springtime. That's what the blackfellah says anyway."

Jamie O'Brien's accent intrigued her. In this colony of immigrants from all over the British Empire, one heard a range of accents from the Queen's English to cockney, Irish, and Scottish brogues, and the sometimes incomprehensible speech of the Welsh. But there was another accent, a newer one, which Hannah suspected was a hybrid of all the rest, and it was spoken by those few who were native to the continent. Hannah realized that her rescuer might not be a fortune hunter after all, newly arrived at these shores, but was in fact native born to Australia, a rarity in the colony.

The evening was suddenly suffused with a strange enchantment. The air was too warm. Summer nights in England were never this warm. Hannah's corset felt tight and uncomfortable, her legs encumbered by the petticoats and crinoline. She thought of the nubile South Seas twins entertaining men in Miss Forchette's parlor, swaying in their grass skirts.

Her heart quickened beneath the stranger's nearness and bold scrutiny. He was no gentleman. Yet he seemed to fit in with the night; the ambience suited him. There was a wildness in the air, and in him.

"I must go," she whispered, finding her throat tight, the breath trapped in her chest. It was fear, she told herself. What else could it be?

He stared at her for a moment longer, and then the grin came back, carving creases in his craggy cheeks and jaw. Stepping away, he tipped his hat and said, "It was a pleasure meeting you, Miss Midwife. I sincerely hope we meet again."

Jamie O'Brien struck off on the path toward the house, and Hannah heard the coachman call, "Miss? Are you all right?"

And the enchantment was broken.

"There she is," Ida Gilhooley said to her husband sitting next to her in the wagon. "There's Miss Conroy, going into the post office, just like her landlady said."

Walt Gilhooley spat a stream of tobacco juice onto the street, which was muddy from a recent autumn rain. "I don't like this, Ida. I say we should leave well enough alone. If Miss Forchette were to find out—"

"I'm not afraid of that cow," Ida said, thrusting out her chin. In truth, the plump middle-aged Ida was terrified of Lulu Forchette, but Ida Gilhooley, chief cook at Lulu's house, was more afraid of what would happen if they didn't secretly fetch Hannah Conroy. If that poor girl were left to die, it would be on Ida's conscience, and she firmly believed in a God who punished sinners. Coming like this to get Hannah Conroy without Miss Forchette knowing might result in an unpleasant confrontation and even more unpleasant consequences, but it was preferable to eternal damnation. "I've got to go in and get her."

"All right," said Walt, who was Lulu Forchette's coachman and man-of-all-work, and who wished at that moment he was any place on Earth than in front of Adelaide's Post Office, about to drag a lovely young lady into an ugly, and potentially dangerous, situation.

The central post office was a large brick building with Grecian columns at the main entrance, flanked by post boxes labeled: ADELAIDE, MELBOURNE, SYDNEY, and THE WORLD. The main hall was noisy as people came to send letters and collect mail, or stood writing at counters where inkwells were provided. A long counter staffed by postal workers saw lines of people, and beyond lay the great sorting center for letters, newspapers, and parcels.

Hannah waited patiently in line, but she wasn't really expecting a letter from Neal Scott. After the HMS *Borealis* set sail on her year-long survey mission, she wasn't expected to make port where there was postal service. Still, Hannah held out hope that one of these days there would be another letter to add to the one she had received back in November, seven months ago. She had written to Neal about Dr. Davenport and how much she enjoyed working for him. Hannah had wanted to write more; in fact, she wanted to write every day as it made her feel closer to Neal, and connected to him, but she didn't want him to return to Perth to find an embarrassing mountain of letters awaiting him.

But if she were to write another letter on this overcast autumn day in May, Hannah would tell Neal about her busy mornings with Dr. Davenport, how he was allowing her to do more and more, such as applying dressings and dispensing salves, how much she was learning from him, and how fond of him she had become. Dr. Davenport reminded her of her father. He was gentle with patients, respectful, didn't rush them. And his treatments were conservative. He wore clean clothes everyday and he even washed his hands. Hannah had assisted him at three childbirths and he had promised her that the next one, should it be without complications, would be hers entirely.

She might also tell Neal in her imaginary letter that, two weeks ago, she had marked the anniversary of her father's passing, and her decision to leave England, by spending a day alone in the park. Sitting on a bench beneath a pepper tree, Hannah had opened her father's laboratory notes for the first time since the *Caprica*, and once again thought of his last words to her. He had spoken of a letter. But there was no letter among his notes, and she still could make no sense of the collection of scraps of paper, notes, receipts, equations, formulas, and entries in Greek and Latin. Perhaps when she was more educated she could unravel the mystery of her father's portfolio. And so, to that end, Hannah was borrowing from Dr. Davenport's impressive medical library. Although much of it was difficult reading, Hannah was determined to learn.

She would *not* tell Neal, however, in her imaginary letter to him, that she had been hired by a certain madam who lived outside of town. It was an unusual occupation to be sure, tending to the health issues of a bordello. Hannah had been summoned to Lulu's on a variety of problems: a fight between two girls resulting in one sticking the other in the eye with a hat pin; a brief spell of diarrhea for the whole household for which Hannah had prescribed ginger and rock salt; a sprained ankle; a kitchen scalding; a gentleman breaking his nose during vigorous sport with Ready Rita; and another crisis involving Miss Magenta and the belladonna.

Hannah didn't know how she was going to tell Neal about her association with the house of ill-repute. She wasn't even sure how she herself felt about it. Lulu Forchette's domain was a world unto itself. Although Hannah never visited the private rooms when they were in use, as she passed by closed doors she nonetheless heard the range of human emotion in the cries and sighs, yells and moans, weeping and laughter coming from the other side. Lulu's house troubled her, but the girls insisted, when asked, that they were happy there because otherwise they would be on the street.

"Sorry, miss," the postal clerk said. "No letters today."

Thanking him, Hannah stepped aside and worked her way back through the throng toward the main entrance. As was her habit, she paused at the wall of bills and notices.

The central post office was the nexus of the city's important news, with one wall devoted to government announcements and front page news. Here one could read about the latest ordinances, recent elections, new laws, rules and edicts. There were also police broadsheets—posters advertising rewards for wanted outlaws.

Hannah perused the police broadsheets in idle curiosity.

A fugitive named Jeremy Palmer of Warrington, Lancashire,

"Did on the 18th Day of March in 1842, stab and kill his employer, Mr. McMasters of Billiluna Station. Palmer is aged twenty-three, average height, brown hair, is crippled with a clubfoot."

Another broadsheet advertised a reward of fifty pounds for the capture of a prisoner who had absconded from the Female House of Corrections in Hobart Town on the 19th of January: "Mary Jones alias Middleton. Sentenced to three years Penal Servitude. Age thirty-eight years, height 5ft 2in, complexion swarthy, stout build, hair dark auburn, a scar on first finger on left hand."

When Hannah came to the next poster, one recently added, she stopped short and stared.

£50

REWARD

For the capture of one

JAMIE O'BRIEN

Wanted for crimes committed in the Colonies and Territories, which include theft through fraud, tricks, and confidence games. He is also wanted in New South Wales for impersonating persons of authority, forging government documents, and evasion of the Law.

Description: O'Brien is five feet ten inches, slim build, aged thirty with dark blond hair and pale blue eyes. O'Brien has scars on his wrists and ankles from iron shackles. O'Brien is a cunning racketeer known locally as a "sharp" and a "gyp artist."

Hannah blinked. Jamie O'Brien. Wasn't that the name of the stranger who had saved her from the dingo in Lulu's garden? She remembered the scars on his wrists, as his shirt sleeves had been rolled up. And now she understood the reason for the expectant look on his face when he had told her his name.

Hannah had wondered if she would see the mysterious stranger again. Every time she was called to Lulu Forchette's house, she had thought of the enchanted encounter in the rose garden. She had difficulty analyzing her curious attraction to O'Brien. It wasn't the same as her feelings for Neal. Jamie O'Brien was more like one of the strange wonders of Australia, like the kangaroos and kookaburras, the vast skies and breathtaking vistas. Hannah was becoming captivated by this land, and perhaps that was what it had been with O'Brien. He was born here. He was simply another unique aspect of this fascinating continent.

As she started to move away, Hannah recognized Ida Gilhooley, pushing through the crowd. "Miss Conroy! There you are! Your landlady said we'd find you here, miss. Can you come to the house? Alice is hurt bad."

"Alice! How?" Hannah followed Mrs. Gilhooley out the main entrance and down the steps toward the waiting wagon.

"She fell and hit her head. Miss Forchette didn't want to send for you, she said it was nothing and that we shouldn't bother you about such a small thing. But, miss, Alice is groaning and says she feels sick. So I told Her Nibs we got weevils in the flour. It was the only way me and Walt could come into town. *She* don't know we're fetching you for Alice. She'll raise hell when she finds out, but Alice is in a bad way and we just couldn't stand by any longer."

As Hannah climbed into the wagon, she looked at Ida and said, "What do you mean 'any longer'?"

Ida climbed in next to her, so that the three sat snugly on the bench while Walt snapped the reins. "It's terrible what that woman does to those girls," Ida said. "Keeps them as slaves, and mistreats them something awful."

Hannah looked at her in surprise. "I thought the girls were happy there."

"They're not," Ida said as her husband maneuvered the wagon into the busy traffic on King William Street. "Lulu goes out in her carriage and goes up and down the streets, looking for girls begging. She gets them as young as she can so she's sure they're virgins and don't have the French disease. Lulu seems kind at first, offering them a room and meals. And after a few days asks them to entertain a 'friend.' You know the rest."

Hannah felt her stomach tighten. Surely what Ida said wasn't true. "But the girls can leave any time they want."

"Lulu charges the girls for room and board. She keeps a ledger. They have to pay off their debt, and Lulu sees to it that they can never save enough money to pay it off. Walt and I owe her too. D'you think we'd work there willingly? Lulu tricked us like she tricks everybody. Our little farm suffered a drought and the bank was threatening to take it from us. Lulu offered us a loan, which we jumped at. A few months later, she called in the note. We couldn't pay, so she took our farm and then made us work for her to pay it back. That's how she does it. She preys on people in trouble, pretends to be their rescuer, and ends up getting free labor."

"And Alice?"

Walt suddenly said, "I'm not sure about this, Ida, going behind Lulu's back. There's no telling what that woman will do when she lets her temper loose."

"Keep going, Walt," Ida said firmly. "I've got a fond spot for Alice. She sings like an angel, and I draw the line at—"

When Ida didn't finish her sentence, Hannah looked at her. "Draw the line at what, Mrs. Gilhooley?"

But Ida pressed her lips together and kept her eyes on the traffic ahead.

Feeling apprehensive, Hannah tried to settle into her place between Walt and Ida, as it would be at least a thirty-minute ride out of town. She held firmly to her blue carpetbag, cradled in her lap. Molly Baker, a fellow resident at Mrs. Throckmorton's, had suggested Hannah trade the bag in for something more stylish, but Hannah would not part with it, even after she had treated herself to a new outfit. As it was May and winter was around the corner, Hannah had purchased the newest style of dress, one that came with a jacket bodice worn over a high-necked blouse and unbuttoned to reveal a waistcoat (which was false, because it was unthinkable for a lady to wear a real waistcoat). The sleeves were very wide with white lacy undersleeves, and the hem swept the wooden sidewalk in a festoon of scalloped ruffles. From her bonnet to her boots, Hannah's outfit was an array of autumn colors—russet, pecan, and bronze.

King William Street was wide but not macadamized, so that mud was kicked up by dense traffic that consisted of wagons and carts, drays and buggies, open carriages and closed carriages, men on horseback, and even a sixteen-passenger omnibus drawn by four horses. But the wooden sidewalks made it possible for pedestrians to stroll comfortably past businesses and look in the windows of fish and chip shops, bakeries, banks, haberdashers, dry goods shops, tea houses, pubs, chemists, and dressmakers' salons. Up and down Adelaide's main north-south thoroughfare ranged a hodgepodge of architecture and design, with four-story red brick commercial buildings interspersed with small weatherboard cottages and even shacks.

When Hannah first arrived, she had been fascinated by the fact that Adelaide had been a *planned* city. She had assumed that all cities were like London, having sprouted long ago and then grown willy-nilly in every direction. But men had come to these plains with an actual plan, and had set about to creating a grid of wide, straight streets, with the city blocks marked off into lots, and a large square in the center, named for Queen Victoria, and four smaller planned parks planted with grass and trees. The nearby plains and foothills had since become a patchwork of wheat farms, vineyards and sheep runs. Nearer to the town were two flour mills, factories processing raw materials, a brewery, several distilleries, a candle manufacturer, and slaughterhouses that emptied their refuse into the river.

The newness of Adelaide also amazed her. In Bayfield, the tavern was four centuries old. Here, the oldest pub had been built only twelve years ago. People had occupied Bayfield's region continuously back to prehistoric times. But Hannah had learned that when the first white settlers arrived in South Australia, the only inhabitants were handful of Aborigines who had since been re-settled elsewhere.

Finally, Hannah and the Gilhooleys were out of the congestion and following a pleasant country lane, but the mood of the three in the wagon was far from joyful. Hannah noticed that Walt's face was set grimly, and Ida now clasped her gloved hands tightly. Neither had spoken a word in the half hour ride. And Hannah herself was anxious. In the past three months, she had become very fond of Lulu's chambermaid.

Whenever Hannah visited the house, she made a point of seeking Alice out, to exchange a few words with her and then ask her to sing a song—just in the kitchen for the cooking staff, because she knew how cripplingly shy Alice was, and knew that she never sang for anyone else, or in any other part of the house. Hannah saw how beautifully Alice blossomed when she sang for her small audience, how she closed her eyes that were the color of cornflowers, lifted her chin, and sent golden tones over the heads of her silent admirers. Hannah herself was moved each time by bittersweet emotion, as Alice's ballads reminded her of Bayfield and her father, their little cottage, and even her mother, who had died when Hannah was thirteen.

When Hannah had commented once to Alice how her voice moved

others, Alice had shyly said, "I did not know before the fire that I had a voice. It was afterward, when a neighbor was nursing me back to health. I was in such emotional and physical pain, that I would go for long walks in the countryside, away from people. One day I was listening to a songbird, and the sound so lifted my spirits that I opened my mouth and sent my own song up to the sky. I sang out my soul, and at once I felt the healing begin. Since then, I cannot stop singing. I think that if I were to be silenced, I would die."

Hannah thought it a shame that Alice could never sing professionally, that her amazing voice would never be shared with the rest of the world. But there was no venue for her. Her facial scars saw to that.

"Here we are," said Walt at last, as the familiar house came into view.

Ida Gilhooley took Hannah to a small room off the kitchen where Alice lay moaning on a pallet.

The girl was dressed only in undergarments—a white cotton shift over cotton drawers—and lay curled on her side, whimpering and shaking. Hannah saw a nasty gash in the scalp, the blood already blackening in Alice's yellow-blond hair. But there were also red welts all over her body, and small cuts. And one eye was purpling, an angry swelling of the lids.

Hannah knelt at her side, and when she gently laid her hand on Alice's shoulder, the girl started. "Shh, it is only me, Miss Conroy. Can you tell me what happened?"

When Alice didn't reply, Hannah looked up at the others gathered around, but none would meet her eyes. "What happened here?"

One of the kitchen girls coughed and said, "She fell."

Noting the wound on her scalp, Hannah examined Alice's eyes and then asked if she still felt nauseated. But it appeared that the danger of concussion had passed. She made a closer examination of Alice's other injuries, confirming for herself that they had not been caused by a fall. Alice had been beaten. And among the bright red welts, Hannah saw yellow and green bruises, indicating they were days old.

Strangely shaped bruises, she noticed.

Hannah realized that they were are all the same oval shape, and there was even a scar that had once been closed with stitches—it, too, was the same shape. Hannah realized in shock where she had seen that oval before—it matched the unusual gold handle of Lulu Forchette's walking cane.

Hannah looked up at those around her. "Alice didn't fall, did she?"

"Lulu wants her to sing for the men," Ida Gilhooley said.

The light from the kitchen doorway was suddenly blocked. Hannah turned to see the mountainous Lulu standing there robed in a bright red ruffled dressing gown. She stood supported on her cane, with a stormy expression on her face. "What's going on here? Get away from that girl."

Hannah rose to her feet. "You have been beating her."

"The silly cow needs it."

Hannah noticed that, despite her girth, Lulu had no trouble walking. The cane, Hannah suspected, was put to other uses. As the kitchen workers looked on in silence, Lulu and Hannah locked gazes. When Lulu took a step forward, Hannah stood her ground. But her heart pounded, and she was reminded of the wild dingo in the rose garden. There would be no Jamie O'Brien to rescue her now.

As calmly as she could, Hannah turned her back on the three-hundred-pound madam and knelt next to Alice. "Would you like to come home with me, dear?"

Alice's eyes widened in fear. She glanced past Hannah at Lulu and swallowed painfully. Hannah moved so that she blocked Alice's view of Lulu, and said again, "Would you like to come home with me? You will be safe, I promise. No one will harm you."

When the girl hesitated, Hannah said, "You have the right to be treated with respect and dignity like anybody else."

Alice finally said in a tiny voice, "Then yes, miss, I should very much like to go with you."

"The girl owes me," Lulu barked.

But Hannah ignored her, helping Alice to her feet and wrapping the blanket around her. There would be no time to fetch what few possessions Alice had. With her arm protectively around the girl, Hannah faced her opponent. "You have received your fair payment, Miss Forchette. Alice will not be coming back here. Nor shall I."

Lulu said nothing, and the air became charged with tension. Some of the "upstairs" girls had come to see what was happening, dressed in night clothes or undergarments, looking sleepy and tousled. Their work day would not begin until afternoon.

Hannah moved her gaze among them, meeting each one in the eye, girls she had helped, had chatted and even laughed with—Ready Rita and Easy Sal, Gertie the midget, Acrobatic Abby, and the Polynesian twins. "If any of you wish to leave, you can come with me right now."

They looked down at the floor and nervously cleared their throats.

"I am at Mrs. Throckmorton's boarding house on Gray Street," Hannah said. "You can come to me any time and I will help you find proper jobs and a decent place to stay."

To Lulu, Hannah said, "I think the authorities will be interested in hearing about this house."

Lulu laughed. "Who do you think are my best customers?"

When Hannah started toward the rear door that led to the rose garden, helping Alice along, Lulu said, "And how do you expect to get back to town? Walk? It's ten miles."

"I'll take them," Walt Gilhooley boomed from the back steps. "Ain't nothing you can do to me and Ida that you ain't already done." And he gestured for Hannah to come along.

As the two stepped through the door, Lulu called out, "You'll be sorry you did this, Miss High and Mighty. Dead sorry!"

-8-

Gonville Davenport, MD, hummed a lively tune as he combed scented pomade through his thick black hair and inspected himself in the looking glass over his wash basin. He frowned at the first sprouts of gray at his temples and wondered if he should try some boot black on them. The pomade was new. He had purchased it the day before from Butterworth's, telling himself it was to look more presentable to his patients.

In truth, this recent extra attention to grooming had to do with Miss Hannah Conroy.

Davenport held two cherished beliefs: the basic goodness of humankind, and that it behooved a man, once in a while, to step outside convention and his own personal boundaries and take a leap of faith. Miss Conroy had put those two beliefs to the test when she had sat in his office, three months prior, offering the most outrageous proposition: that she work for him as an assistant in his medical practice! Having at first been suspicious of her intentions, and then having been convinced of her honesty, Davenport had decided to give her proposal a try. And the result had been a success.

Not only had Miss Conroy proved to be a boon for his practice, she had wakened old interests in him, so that Davenport found himself looking forward to going to work once more. He had become jaded since arriving in Adelaide, a childless widower. Patients' woes had long since ceased to interest him or make him care. But with Hannah Conroy asking questions, he felt like a medical student again, curious about everything, wanting answers just as she did, and hunting for solutions.

Miss Conroy had even presented him with a curious personal conundrum of her own. "My mother died of childbed fever," she had said one afternoon when his office hours were over and he was writing in medical charts while Hannah was sweeping the floor. "My father said so, the coroner said so, her symptoms were even what is called textbook, and my father launched a career in searching for a prevention and cure for childbed fever. And yet, after my father's death, I found his laboratory notes and in them he had written a question: 'What killed my beloved Louisa?'

"Is it possible, Dr. Davenport," Miss Conroy had said as she set her broom aside and looked at him with those remarkable gray eyes, "that my father realized my mother had died of something else?"

Davenport had asked Miss Conroy to describe the course and nature of her mother's final illness, and after she had done so, he could only agree that Louisa Conroy had indeed died of childbed fever. Why her father had subsequently questioned it, he did not know.

Davenport had said he was sorry that he couldn't help her, but that night he had opened books not touched in years and found himself getting lost in medical texts. For the first time since Edith's passing, Gonville Davenport was interested in things once more, even if, ultimately, he had not found the answer to Hannah's personal conundrum.

Dr. Davenport had also discovered that he enjoyed being a teacher, and Miss Conroy was proving to be an eager and enthusiastic pupil. He smiled now to think of one particular medical mystery they had solved together.

Mr. Paterson, a married shoemaker in his sixties, had come in complaining of headaches. He had also exhibited a strange skin color that he said was driving his friends and his customers away, as they feared he was contagious, and his wife wouldn't let him touch her. Davenport knew at once that such pronounced evidence of jaundice meant advanced liver disease, but Davenport never liked to snatch hope from his patients, and so he had given Mr. Paterson a "tonic" and sent him home. The tonic was harmless sugar-water dyed pink, and he instructed Mr. Paterson to have three spoonfuls a day, not to miss a dose. Most doctors kept such a placebo in their medicinal stores, since it was a kindness to send a patient home with at least something. And as false hope was better than no hope, sometimes the harmless placebo even effected a cure.

After Mr. Paterson had left, however, Miss Conroy had expressed concern about him because the cobbler was a nice old man whose business was failing, and she felt sorry for him. She had then made the observation that the shoemaker's jaundice wasn't the same color as the cases of jaundice her father had seen in Bayfield, and so she wondered if the problem could be something else. "He is more orange than yellow," she had said. "Could it be his gall bladder?"

Davenport had been taken aback, unused to having his diagnoses and treatments questioned, especially by a woman. But he had learned by now that Miss Conroy's questions were not due to any lack of confidence in him, or arrogance on her part, but merely an expression of genuine curiosity. When he had explained that the absence of epigastric pain ruled out gall bladder disease, Miss Conroy had brought up Mr. Paterson's headaches, which Dr. Davenport could not explain.

After Miss Conroy had left for the day, Gonville Davenport found that he had a medical mystery on his hands. Miss Conroy had observed correctly: the extreme orange tint of the skin, plus the headaches, were not fully explained away by either liver or gall bladder problems.

What, then, was ailing Mr. Paterson?

It had sent Davenport to his medical references, and as he searched, he began to recall an article he had read not too long ago in a foreign medical journal. He spent nearly a night searching his stacks of magazines and periodicals, but had finally found it and, reading the article, had discovered what he suspected was the true cause of Mr. Paterson's strange color. The next morning he had presented himself at Mr. Paterson's Wright Street shop and had asked a few questions he had not asked back in the office—namely, the cobbler's diet.

"I had read recently," Dr. Davenport reported to Hannah upon returning to the office, "that a substance found in vegetables had been isolated and identified by chemists at the Sorbonne. They named it *carotene*, after the carrots in which it is found. This got me to thinking. When I asked Mr. Paterson if he ate carrots, he took me out back and proudly showed me his carrot garden. It seems he so loves the root that it's all he eats—boiled, steamed, baked, or raw! Miss Conroy, it was the carrots that had turned him orange."

"And the headaches?" she had asked.

"I also learned that he wears his hat too tight."

Mr. Paterson switched to potatoes, bought a larger hat size, and was cured. They had laughed about the case, Gonville Davenport and Hannah Conroy, and now it was their secretly shared joke. Davenport had not felt such satisfaction with the practice of medicine in a long time. Nor such pleasure in the company of a young lady.

Hannah was also a boon to the women patients. Whereas a physician had access to a male patient's body, and could even ask a gentleman to disrobe, it was unthinkable that a physician should glimpse what lay beneath a lady's clothes. A doctor had to rely on what the patient told him, and very often, women were too shy or embarrassed to be explicit, with ailments couched in delicate terms, leaving the doctor to guess. When a lady blushingly confessed that her "regularity" was off, he didn't know if she was referring to her menstrual cycle or her bowels. Miss Conroy, however, allowed women to speak freely, and she in turn, having had vast experience of this sort of thing with her father, was then able to convey to Dr. Davenport precisely what ailed the patient, thus making his treatments more effective.

It was no wonder more and more women were flocking to his office! Davenport had decided to expand his hours from three to five mornings a week, increasing Miss Conroy's hours as well.

As he left his upstairs apartment and descended the rear stairway that led to a kitchen, his private office and the outer waiting room where patients were beginning to congregate, Davenport arrived at a decision. Before Miss Conroy had presented her remarkable offer, three months ago, Davenport had been seriously considering going back to England to marry a distant cousin of whom he was rather fond. But all that was changed now. He had new plans in mind. Although they had only been acquainted for three months, he decided it would not be too forward of him to invite Miss Conroy to a horse race on Sunday, at Chester Downs, a mile outside of town, where there would be a musical band, a buffet of German sausage, bread and beer, and two Frenchman reportedly demonstrating something called a "hot air balloon flight."

Entering his office and drawing back the curtains to reveal morning sunshine, he went to his desk where he saw that his housekeeper had placed the morning mail. Davenport sifted through the envelopes—bills, adverts, a letter from the cousin back home in England. One envelope caught his attention. He opened it and frowned. As the contents of the letter began to sink in, he stared in disbelief.

Dr. Davenport went over the letter a third time until his knees buckled, and he dropped like a dead weight into his office chair.

"I know you will like him. His name is Robert," Molly Baker said with enthusiasm, "and he's a clerk for a solicitor!" Moon-faced Molly was an apprentice to a posh seamstress on Peel Street, a position that gave her such confidence that she was boldly outspoken on all manner of topics, a trait her friends suffered patiently.

The residents of Mrs. Throckmorton's boarding house were in the downstairs drawing room, preparing to leave for the day. "He wears a white collar and has clean fingernails," Molly added as she pinned her bonnet to her head, using the hallway looking glass.

This was the fourth young man Molly had tried to introduce to Hannah, and no matter how many times Hannah insisted that she was waiting for a young man to join her in Adelaide, an American scientist currently working on a survey vessel out of Perth, Molly wouldn't listen. Plenty of girls boasted of having young men coming out to join them, and few of those swains rarely materialized.

"Really, Hannah, you are such an innocent. Yet you are twenty years old!"

Molly was twenty-one and liked to brag that she had been kissed not just by one young man but by an impressive three. None of the kissing relationships had led to anything serious, but she remained hopeful. Marriage was Molly's main goal in life. And marriage not to just any man. He had to work in an office and wear a clean shirt everyday. "I would wager," she said, "that a man has never even held your hand."

Not just my hand, Hannah thought as she tied her bonnet ribbons under her chin. Neal held my whole body, as we thought our ship was sinking. And then he kissed me ....

But Hannah could never tell anyone these things because it was too private and special, and also because no one who had never been through such an experience could possibly understand. She also could not tell Molly and the others about Lulu Forchette's house, and that, in many ways, because of her visits there, she was far more knowledgeable about intimate matters than a girl who had been kissed three times.

"I am sure Robert is a very nice young man," Hannah said, "and I do appreciate your efforts at introductions, but I am not looking right now."

When Hannah saw Molly's cheeky smile, she knew what her friend was thinking: that Hannah had her eye on Dr. Davenport. "He owns his own house," Molly had said only last week over a dinner of Mrs. Throckmorton's steak and kidney pie. "With the entire upstairs for living, and downstairs for his practice. A *doctor*, Hannah, with a good income. And not bad looking, if a bit old."

Hannah allowed Molly to believe what she wanted, knowing that Molly could not fathom Hannah's true reason for working at Dr. Davenport's office. That she wanted to make a career of healing people.

Bidding Molly a good day, Hannah left Mrs. Throckmorton's house and struck off into the crisp autumn morning. When she reached the muddy street, she turned and looked up at a third floor window, where Alice was looking down, waving. Hannah waved back and continued on her way.

Alice was recuperating from the severe beating Lulu had given her a week ago, and she could not go outside until the facial bruising was entirely gone. But Alice, Hannah had discovered, despite her frail looks and shyness, possessed a strong inner fortitude. She was not a girl to languish in self-pity. Alice had promised that when she was better, she was going to look for a job in town. Her time at Lulu's house had forced her to face and overcome her fear of fire, so that now she could work at any domestic occupation, and be glad of it.

Thinking that it would aid Alice's recovery, Hannah had persuaded her to come downstairs one evening and sing for the other boarders. They were enraptured. One girl had said, "Alice's voice is like an unexpected break in the clouds sending down a ray of sunshine on a dismally rainy day." Another enthused, "She makes me feel sad and joyous at the same time." And Molly Baker had declared, "She could catch a rich husband with that voice!"

But out of Alice's hearing, they all agreed that it was such a shame about her facial disfigurement.

It had been a difficult seven days. First, Hannah had had to lie to Mrs. Throckmorton about Alice's "accident," persuading the landlady to allow the injured girl to share Hannah's room. At the same time, Hannah's conscience had become greatly troubled by the house of ill-repute. Now that she knew the women were held there against their will, and physically abused, she knew must do something about it. But she had no idea what. Alice had begged her to forget it. "The authorities won't do anything. They are Lulu's best customers. I could name judges, bankers, men high up in the colonial government who go to her house on a regular basis. They won't want you making this public. It could backfire on you."

For a week, Hannah had struggled with the moral dilemma, torn between her conscience and the truth of Alice's warning, and now she had come to a decision. She would seek Dr. Davenport's advice. He was a smart man, educated, and wise to the ways of the world. She would take him into her confidence and explain about the house beyond the edge of town—he would undoubtedly be shocked to hear of the existence of such an establishment, and that men in high positions were patronizing it, but Hannah needed counsel on what to do.

She reached Dr. Davenport's a few minutes later, as Light Square was not far from her boarding house. Going up the front steps of the two-storey brick residence sandwiched between a dress shop and a bookstore, Hannah smiled at the shiny brass plaque with Dr. Davenport's name on it. Someday, she knew, her name would be there, too.

The street door opened onto a tiny foyer that offered two doors. One was labeled *Private* and it led to the kitchen and servants' area in the rear.

The other door said *Waiting Room*, and Hannah entered it to find a small crowd already waiting to see the doctor.

A bench ran along two walls. When a patient came out of the doctor's office, the next person in line got up and went in, and everybody slid along. As she passed through, Hannah smiled at everyone. A few of the men stood, others touched their caps, murmuring, "Good morning, miss." There was Mr. Billingsly, the haberdasher, with an infected toe, and the baker's wife, Mrs. Hudson, with a cough that wouldn't go away. A man with his right arm in a sling was Sammy Usher, a drover who fell off a bullock dray and dislocated his shoulder. Hannah noticed that Mrs. Rembert was back with her arthritis, and Mr. Sanderson had no doubt returned to collect another bottle of the doctor's tonic, which he declared had given him the vitality of a twenty-year-old. There were a few whom Hannah did not recognize. She knew that some came out of curiosity as word had spread of a woman working in a doctor's office, and people came to see for themselves.

As she opened the inner door, she prepared herself for another day of learning, and her excitement rose because one never knew what the day was going to hold. Like the case last Monday, when a woman had come running into the office to declare that a neighbor family were dire ill and dying.

Davenport had gone at once, walking at a fast clip through a light drizzle, as the house was not far. He and Hannah let themselves in and found the father and mother lying ill in one bedroom, five children in the other, all down with severe abdominal pain, vomiting, and weakness. As Dr. Davenport examined the children, Mr. Dykstra had managed to drag himself out of bed and into the children's room. He was dizzy, staggering and giggling, and, in fact, appeared to be drunk.

Helping the man back to bed, Dr. Davenport asked for a report on when and how the illness had started. It appeared to have been shortly after breakfast, with the youngest falling ill first. By noon they were all nauseated and stricken with diarrhea and pain.

"What did you eat for breakfast?" Dr. Davenport asked, and was told of sausage, eggs, and tomatoes. Leaving the Dykstras as they lay groaning under Hannah's watchful eye, Dr. Davenport went through the modest little wooden house and out to the back where he found the typical garden of most Adelaide citizens. Neat rows had been planted with lettuce, carrots, and tomatoes. Dr. Davenport looked around, and when he found the empty kerosene tins, came back to the bedside and asked, "Mr. Dykstra, did you use lamp oil on your garden?"

"Had to, Doc. Aphids and spider mites got into my tomatoes again. The plants were young, and I knew I'd lose them. So I doused the whole crop with kerosene. It worked."

"Mr. Smith, kerosene is a poison to humans as well as to insects. Your breakfast tomatoes were poisonous."

"But my wife washed the tomatoes real good before we ate them."

"Mr. Dykstra, the kerosene seeped into the soil and was then drawn up by the roots of the young plants. By the time the tomatoes matured, they were full of kerosene. Find another way to kill aphids, Mr. Dykstra."

Dr. Davenport prescribed large doses of water hourly, to dilute the blood, and peppermint to control the vomiting. That night, Hannah recorded two notes on the case, writing on a small piece of paper: "Unexplained euphoria or giddiness is a symptom of kerosene poisoning," and, "If one poisons pests when plants are young, the poison will be present in the mature plant and make those who eat the plant sick." She slipped the note into her father's portfolio, hoping that it was only the first of many she would add to his already impressive body of observations and knowledge.

As she entered Dr. Davenport's office on this morning filled with promise, Hannah saw the distraught look on his face, and she was instantly alarmed. "Oh dear, has someone passed away?" Hannah took a seat in the patient chair. "Was it Mrs. Gardener? Her heart was so weak."

Street sounds drifted through the window as Davenport found his voice. "Miss Conroy, have you been paying visits to a house on the outskirts of town, owned by a Miss Forchette?"

"Yes, doctor. As a matter of fact, I had planned to bring up this very subject with you. You see—"

"Miss Conroy, what on *earth* possessed you to visit such an establishment?"

Taken aback by his sudden, uncharacteristic impatience, Hannah described her encounter with Alice, three months prior, outside Dr. Young's office. "As no other doctor would go out there, I offered to help."

Davenport released a heavy sigh. "You do realize that this has cast serious doubt upon your integrity? That your reputation has been damaged?" He held up a sheet of stationery. "Someone is upset and is threatening to tell Adelaide society of your connection to that house."

"Who?"

He showed her the letter. It was signed, *A Concerned Citizen*. "They didn't sign their real name."

"No doubt not wishing to admit that they even know of such an establishment.

"Dr. Davenport, I assure you, I went there for no immoral reasons. I went only to help the girls. Certainly they are as entitled to health care as anyone else."

"No one denies that. But, Miss Conroy, that is a house of ill-repute. Anyone associating with it is going to come up suspect. Surely you see that?"

Hannah frowned. "Dr. Young went there regularly. Why didn't this 'concerned citizen' spread the word out about *him* going to Lulu's house?"

"Because he went there as a doctor, to see to health issues."

"As did I. Dr. Davenport, I was called to wrap sprained ankles, to suture wounds, to treat rashes. Why is that different from what Dr. Young did?"

"That is because a doctor takes care of myriad ailments, from sprains to fractures to fevers. A midwife, on the other hand, is concerned with but one function of the human body. No one could possibly know that you went to that house for other reasons. You are not, after all, a doctor. You are a *midwife*, and midwives visit such houses for only one purpose."

"And what is that? Surely the author of that letter doesn't think I delivered babies there."

His eyes widened. Did she truly not know? "Miss Conroy," he said, choosing his words carefully, "what other reason might a midwife be called to an establishment like Miss Forchette's?"

"I have no idea."

Dr. Davenport saw the genuine innocence in her eyes, the lack of guile on her face. He looked at the delicate throb of pulse at her pale neck, her gloved hands clasped patiently in her lap, and he was rocked with a nameless emotion. "Miss Conroy, there is a certain secret and illegal treatment which midwives are known to practice on occasion." He said no more, hoping she would finally grasp his meaning.

It was Hannah's turn to stare, and as she looked at handsome Dr. Davenport with the boyish curls dropping over his forehead, despite the gleam of pomade that was intended to tame such curls, and as she saw the embarrassment on his face, his obvious discomfort with the subject, the full meaning of his words sank in.

Hannah gasped. "I assure you, Dr. Davenport, I performed no—" She could not say the word.

"I know that, Miss Conroy," he said, "but the rest of the world does not. If you were not a midwife, the allegations would not be so severe. In fact, there might be no allegations at all, but a simple questioning of your character. Unfortunately, if word gets out, this will have serious ramifications for me and my medical practice. The fact that I hired an abortionist...." He let his words trail off.

Hannah closed her eyes. "I had no idea."

"I know that, but the damage is done and cannot be undone." He lifted eyes so bereft that it took her aback. "I'm afraid I must discharge you."

She stared at him. "Discharge me—" The breath caught in her throat. "But I have broken off my association with that house."

"It doesn't matter. The harm has been done. If I do not terminate your employment here, I risk losing every patient I have. And if my practice closes, people who have come to depend on me might end up going to doctors of dubious credentials."

"I am so sorry," she whispered.

When he saw the tears sparkle in her gray eyes, Gonville Davenport had to fight the impulse to dash around the desk and gather her into his arms. She looked so *vulnerable*. He wanted to hold her and tell her that everything was going to be all right, that he didn't care what the citizens of Adelaide thought, that he would protect her and help her through this.

But he knew he could do no such thing. He had to think of his patients.

Davenport blamed himself for this mess. Hannah was only twenty years old, fresh from England, and without family. Her maturity and capabilities had blinded him to the innocent girl underneath. He knew now that he should have taken better charge of her, inquired into her off-hours activities, asked about friends and associates. But it was too late now. Her naiveté had done irreparable damage. The horse race at Chester Downs, the German sausage and beer, and the Frenchmen with their hot air balloon flight would carry on without him.

As Hannah started for the door, Davenport said, "Just a moment, Miss Conroy." Reaching for the ivory statuette of Hygeia that had stood on his desk since his honeymoon in Athens, he held it out and said, "I want you to have this."

Hannah barely saw the traffic and pedestrians of Adelaide as she made her way back home. How could she have been so blind? Of *course* people would think of only one reason why a midwife would visit a house of ill-repute. How could she not have realized it herself? Tears blinded her as she dodged carts and horses to cross the street. This was not Bayfield. She was not assisting her father, protected by his wisdom and experience. She was a green girl who had possibly made the worst blunder in her life!

Hannah was met in the downstairs parlor by a grim-faced Mrs.

Throckmorton. Alice was also there, looking whey-faced and frightened. And then Hannah noticed that her trunk was there as well. "I am sorry, my dear," the elderly landlady said in genuine sadness. "You have been a good tenant and I hate to see you go. But I received this letter...."

"I understand," Hannah said.

"But Alice doesn't have to leave," Mrs. Throckmorton said. "I've told her she can stay, and when she's all better, I'll give her a job and a room."

But Alice went to stand at Hannah's side. "I'm going with Miss Conroy," she said, trying to look as dignified as she could with her poor black eye and bandaged head. She turned to Hannah. "It's my fault, miss. I was the one who took you to Lulu's. And then you rescued me. I will make it up to you, I promise. I shall work two jobs and pay you back."

Hannah turned to the landlady. "Mrs. Throckmorton, may I have a look at the letter?"

Hannah perused the page, reading the inflammatory words, threats, ending with the signature, *A Concerned Citizen*. But this time she saw something she had not noticed in Dr. Davenport's office. The handwriting was unmistakably Lulu's.

"Yes, you can come with me, Alice," Hannah said as she lifted one end of her trunk and Alice picked up the other. "We'll be all right, you'll see."

They managed to get to the street corner, where carriage and wagon traffic made it impossible to cross, when two men on horseback shouted, "Hoy there, ladies!" To Hannah's surprise, they jumped down—men in dusty work trousers and shirts, with bush hats and sunburned skin—and each took an end of Hannah's trunk. They gave Alice an odd look, but grinned and touched their hat brims at Hannah and said, "Where to, miss?"

She and Alice followed the helpful strangers for several blocks until they came to a modest hotel with a sign in the window that said, "Lady Guests Must Be Accompanied."

Hannah tried to pay the two men, but they only winked and said it was their pleasure, and as they made their way back down the busy street to where they had tethered their horses, Hannah saw a boy in ragged clothes and bare feet sloppily pasting posters to the brick wall of the hotel.

They were all the same: the latest front page of the *Adelaide Clarion*.

And the headline story was about troubling news from Western Australia, something about an aboriginal uprising near Perth, colonists slaughtered, missionaries massacred.

And a government coastal survey party, their vessel docked in a deserted cove, had been attacked—with loss of life.

-9-

Alice dreamed of the fire again last night.

It was the fourth time since leaving Lulu's. Before that, Alice had not dreamed even once of the fire that had claimed the lives of her parents and her siblings, sparing only herself. Why? she wondered as she finished her morning tea and decided to go for a walk, today being Sunday. Why had she not dreamed, or even really thought about the fire, for the past eight years, only to have it haunt her now in such detail that she woke up soaked in perspiration?

"I'm sorry, miss, but I won't wear cosmetics," she said quietly but firmly, responding to a suggestion Hannah had made for concealing her disfigurement. "Lulu paints her face. She forces her girls to paint their faces. I won't be like them."

Hannah gave Alice, who might otherwise have been very pretty, a thoughtful look. It was a cool autumn morning in May, and they were finishing their breakfast in the room they shared at the Torrens Hotel on King William Street. Hannah had asked Alice to call her by her first name, but Alice was too unused to such familiarity with anyone to stop addressing Hannah as "miss." Besides, in order to secure a room at the hotel, the two had to pass themselves off as a lady traveling with her maid, as hotel policy did not allow unaccompanied women to register.

A week had passed since their eviction from Mrs. Throckmorton's. Alice's injuries were fading, and now she was anxious to search for employment. But Hannah suspected that Alice was going to run into the same problems she had before she went to work for Lulu: no one wanted a disfigured servant. Hannah had an idea of how Alice could solve the problem with cosmetics, but Alice would have none of it.

"You're really quite pretty," Hannah said. "With your lovely blond hair and its natural curls, your blue eyes. From the right side, you have a perfect profile and flawless skin. Now if we could just cover …" When she saw the closed look on Alice's face, Hannah said, "Let me show you something."

She was determined to help somehow. Alice's disfigurement was crippling. Strangers, when they saw her face, could be insensitive and even cruel. Everywhere Alice went, she met looks of curiosity, pity, and revulsion. It resulted in her developing a defensive gesture: she would bring her hand up to the scarred side of her face and let her fingers flutter at the edge of her maid's cap, as if she were trying to hide behind her hand. The unfortunate result was that she just brought all the more attention to the disfigurement.

"My mother was a Shakespearean actress," Hannah said as she opened her blue carpetbag and brought out her mother's book of poetry. Folded inside was a playbill that Hannah had kept as a memento. Unfolding it now, she held it up for Alice to read.

A Winter's Tale
by William Shakespeare
On which occasion,
Miss Louisa Reed
Will perform
Being The Last Night of Their Performance This Season
Theatre Royal, Shakespeare Square, Edinburgh 29 July 1824

"This was my mother's last performance," Hannah said. "She had met my father months prior, during a tour of southern England. She had twisted her ankle, and he had treated it. They had fallen in love. After this performance, my mother returned to Bayfield and to John Conroy, giving up the stage forever."

As Hannah spoke, a memory from her childhood returned in vivid detail. She was no more than six or seven at the time, and her mother was showing her a most remarkable bag. She called it her "kit," and it was full of boxes and bottles and little cases. Stage make-up from her days as an actress. Hannah was dazzled by the sticks of greasepaint, the gums and pencils and powders designed to give the actor a different face than his own. "With these I can be a Chinese Princess," Louisa had said merrily. "Or an African Negress or a maiden aunt in Lincolnshire. I can make myself ugly or beautiful, young or old. Anything I wish to be!"

Recalling that distant afternoon, Hannah thought, *Stage cosmetics can create artificial flaws.*

Or cover them up.

"You see? My mother wore cosmetics, and she was very respectable. Alice, have ever seen a stage play? Then I shall take you to one as soon as we can afford it."

"Thank you, miss," Alice said, thinking, *When we can afford it.* They were already in arrears with the hotel rent, and soon they would have no money for food. The problem was, how were they to earn an income? So far, no one would hire Alice, and Hannah had gone through the employment adverts in the newspapers, only to decide in the end against applying for positions. She had not explained why to Alice, but Alice knew the reason: that Hannah might put a future employer in the same jeopardy as she had Dr. Davenport. Both Alice and Hannah knew that whoever she worked for would be a likely target of Lulu Forchette's poisonous pen. Unfortunately, leaving Adelaide, and thereby Lulu's reach, was not an option. Alice knew that here was where Hannah was to meet the American, Neal Scott, in October—or so she prayed.

After reading a frightening newspaper account of aboriginal uprisings in Western Australia, Hannah had written letters to authorities in Perth, asking after the welfare of a ship called the HMS *Borealis*. She had also written to an aboriginal mission, inquiring about a missionary couple she had met on the voyage from England.

Alice had heard all about the miraculous journey of the *Caprica*. And she had seen Neal Scott's photograph. He was a very good looking man, and from the way Hannah had talked about him, he was smart and educated, adventurous and courageous, and quite the gentleman. Alice was envious, as she herself could never hope for such romance in her life. Long ago, before fire had robbed her of family and home, Alice had dreamed of being a wife and mother. But that dream had died.

After removing the maid's apron that she insisted upon always wearing, Alice straightened the cuffs and buttons of her maroon dress that was slightly out of date in that the sleeves were tight and there was no crinoline under the petticoats. She then affixed her simple straw bonnet to her hair and took a long look at her face in the mirror—one side supposedly pretty, the other side puckered with scars. She looked at Hannah in the reflection, seated at a desk, her head bent over quill and stationery. Through the open window came the melodic peeling of bells from Adelaide's numerous steeples. "How come you don't go to church, miss?"

Hannah looked up. "I beg your pardon?"

"You said your father was a Quaker. Don't they go to church?"

Hannah studied Alice's eyes that were a remarkable shade of blue, and she saw only innocent curiosity there. "When my father married a stage actress, he was banned from the fellowship of Friends. But he kept the Sabbath in his own way."

Alice paused and then said, "Do you pray, miss?"

Hannah thought about this. She did not mind the question but did not know how to respond. Prayer was something that had never come easy to Hannah. She thought of how her father would stand in the parlor of their small cottage, beginning his day in silence, his Irish Quaker feet planted firmly on the braided rug as he gathered his soul and his thoughts together before the first pink of the morning sun—before he knew what surprises or disappointments the day was going to hold. Hannah had always sensed about him, in that silence, as he stood tall and thoughtful, a brink of excitement, as though he were living in just that moment, as if no other moment was ever going to exist. Was that when he prayed? Was that when he walked in the Light? He never talked about it. The sun would crest through the trees, yellow rays would sneak into the parlor, and John Conroy would shake himself loose from the invisible hold of the supernatural and begin his day.

Hannah had tried to emulate him. But all she could do, she had found, was just stand and be silent. It never went farther or higher or deeper than that. As always, standing in her bedroom before the bed was even made, still in her nightdress with her bare feet on the cold floor, she would try to travel where her father had traveled, send her eyes and ears on a spiritual journey as he did, but her thoughts inevitably would tug her in the direction of the kitchen and flood her mind with prosaic details: a curtain that needed mending, a lamp that needed a new glass chimney, a bill to be paid to the butcher, and would a letter arrive at last from the Lying-In Hospital?

"I do my best," Hannah said with a smile. "But I think God listens to us no matter how we phrase our words."

"I remember, before our farm burned down, on Sundays my father would open our big Bible to any page and read from it." Alice looked inward for a moment and then said, "I don't remember the voyage over. I was four when we left England. My parents had such high hopes here." Her voice caught.

"Alice," Hannah said gently. "Would you like to go to church?"

She shook her head. "I will just go for a walk."

"Why not go to the horse races at Chester Downs? I understand that city omnibuses will be departing hourly from Victoria Square."

"Perhaps," Alice said, and she left.

But horse races were not on her mind as she followed one of the main thoroughfares out of the city, joining many pedestrians who were out for a stroll, and open carriages going up and down the streets for the Sunday outings the citizens of Adelaide so loved.

Alice had a long walk ahead of her, but her injuries from Lulu's beating were nearly cleared up now, the pain was but a memory, and she felt strong as she followed the country lane past houses and gardens and sheep paddocks until the city was far behind and farms became so vast that houses were miles apart. Passing through dappled sunlight, waving to the occasional passersby in carriage or on horseback, Alice fought down her fears. When doubt crept in and she wondered if she was making a mistake, wondered if Lulu would trap her and keep her prisoner once again, Alice reminded herself of newly learned words: fairness, equality, justice. And they kept her resolve strong.

These were concepts Alice had never really known. Memories of her early life on the farm were vague. She had lost much of her recollection after the fire that left her family dead and herself disfigured. It was probably an ordinary life, possibly even a happy one. After that, all she had known were impatient Juvenile Care authorities who tried to place her in homes only to have her returned, followed by snappish employers who could not understand her fear of fire, and then finally the harsh streets where she slept in alleys and doorways and stayed alive by begging at back doors. After that, it was Lulu's house.

And then Hannah Conroy had entered Alice's life and things had changed. For the first time, Alice knew kindness and sympathy, and even a little hope. And so it was these that propelled her along the Kapunda Road where traffic had become almost nonexistent as most folk were at Chester Downs for the horse races and outdoor fête.

As she neared the house, Alice saw how quiet it was in the morning sunlight, with no carriages or horses outside. As powerful as some of Lulu's customers were, she knew better than to keep her house open on Sundays. There were limits even to corruption. And so it was a day for the girls to rest, do mending, even pay visits into town under the watchful eye of Walt Gilhooley. On this particular Sunday, the girls and the house staff could not resist staying away from the horse races (although they would dress modestly and keep a low profile) and so the house would be silent. Lulu would not go, Alice knew, but would be in her parlor either snoring away in a nap, or eating sweets while counting her money.

Alice paused at the back door to take in a breath and square her shoulders. She had come because she knew that the letters to Dr. Davenport and Mrs. Throckmorton would not be the end of it. Lulu would not rest until Hannah

Conroy was destroyed utterly. Hannah had wanted to confront Lulu about the letters, but Alice had talked her out of it. Lulu would not stop in her vendetta against Hannah, and Hannah trying to appeal to Lulu might only make things worse. Alice had said, "Lulu will drop it in time, miss, just forget about it," and Hannah had taken her advice.

No one knew Lulu's background, where she came from, who her folks were. It was doubtful even that Lulu Forchette was her real name. Alice had heard that the deadliest snakes in the world were found in Australia, but she would vow that none held a candle to the cold and ruthless Lulu. It was impossible to believe that a genuine human heart beat beneath that fleshy bosom. Lulu's girls weren't allowed to have babies. If Lulu's pennyroyal tea didn't do the trick, then Dr. Young was summoned with his sharp instruments. Girls died. Lulu didn't care. There were plenty more in the streets, with more arriving from England each day.

Alice didn't bother to knock. She found Lulu sprawled on her chaise, her henna-red hair loose about her plump shoulders, the hem of her expensive silk and lace dressing gown trailing on the rich Turkey carpet. Her head was back, her rouged mouth opened in a soft snore. On a small table beside the chaise lay the remnants of Lulu's usual breakfast: fried eggs and potatoes, beefsteak and sausage, buttered toast and hot chocolate.

Alice cleared her throat and Lulu's eyes were instantly open. They narrowed when they saw who stood there. "Come crawling back have you?"

"I've come to ask you to leave Miss Conroy alone."

Lulu snorted. "Not bloody likely. She put you up to this?"

"She has done you no harm—"

"No harm! That self-righteous cow has stirred discontent among my girls. Three asked to be let go, another tried to run off. Miss High and Mighty needs to be taught a lesson. Five more letters go out tonight, to some very influential people."

Alice glanced at Lulu's cluttered desk where, lying on top of ledgers and bills, five sealed envelopes lay. "I will stay with you if you do not post those letters."

Lulu laughed. "What do I want you for, ugly thing?"

"I will sing for your customers."

The fat madam gave this some thought and then said, "It won't change my mind. Miss High and Mighty needs to be taught a lesson."

"I feel sorry for you," Alice said quietly.

Lulu's nostrils flared. "Don't know what *you're* feeling so superior about.

How far do you think you'll get in life with that face of yours that scares children? You had a good thing here. You were hidden. Ungrateful cow. I took you in."

"Yes you did. And you forced me to work eighteen hours a day. You made me sleep on the floor. You starved me. You treated me worse than someone treats a dog. I made a mistake coming here. I thought I could appeal to your sense of mercy. But I was wrong." Alice reached the desk in three strides, grabbed the five envelopes and toward the door.

"No you don't," Lulu grunted as she hauled herself to her feet, steadying her great bulk with the cane, and tried to block the way. But Alice was quick. She darted around Lulu and was out the door.

Lulu lumbered after her, shouting at her to stop. But Alice kept going, down the main hallway and into the kitchen.

"Go ahead, take the bloody letters," Lulu said as she came into the kitchen, "I'll just write more."

Alice stopped. Lulu was right. Stealing the letters was a futile act. Alice turned and looked up at the large woman who towered over her with malevolence in her eye, the deadly walking stick in her hand. Slender, small-boned Alice realized she had to find some way to stand up to her. As she looked around the deserted kitchen, cluttered with pots and pans, meat cleavers and milk jugs, her eye fell upon the kitchen table where she saw a red and white cardboard box with writing on it: *Stowe's Noiseless Matches. Positively Will Light A Flame Anywhere.*

The box was decorated with bright red flames.

And suddenly Alice's ears were filled with the roar of a raging fire. She looked at the fireplace, and although it was cold and dark, Alice saw flames leaping before her eyes. She was confused. Was she remembering the recent nightmare, or the real fire of long ago? When she heard a woman's high pitched scream, she couldn't tell if it was herself in the nightmare, or her mother on that fateful night.

As memories began to flash rapid-fire behind her eyes—yellow and gold flames, heat, sheer terror, her nails torn from scraping at the door to get out, Alice heard herself say in a quiet voice, "But the worst thing you did was lock me in the cellar in total darkness with nothing but matches and a lamp."

"Had to be done," Lulu snapped. "What good is a chambermaid who can't light lamps and candles, who screams at the sight of a fireplace? I did it for your own good. And it worked, didn't it?"

The days and nights locked in the cellar, starved, terrified of the dark, while she screamed and begged to be let out. With Lulu on the other side saying, "Light the lamp, and I'll let you out."

"Yes," Alice said. "It worked. I am no longer afraid of fire." She picked up the cardboard box, pulled out a match, and struck the phosphorus head on the side of the box.

"What are you doing?" Lulu said.

Alice held the flame before her eyes. "Showing you how well you got me rid of my fears. I came to ask you to stop writing poisonous letters about Miss Conroy. I reckon the best way is to burn them."

"What—"

Before Lulu could react, Alice set fire to the envelopes, and then tossed the burning paper down so that it landed on the hem of Lulu's expensive silk gown. As Lulu quickly bent to snuff the flames, crying, "Look what you did, idiot!" Alice struck another match and tossed it onto the voluminous silk that floated around Lulu's fat legs.

"Stop it, you little bitch!" Another match and more silk took flame. Lulu started screaming, as she smacked her thighs and stamped her feet. "Throw some water on me!"

But Alice just stood there as the flames rose and engulfed Lulu's body, and the air filled with the stench of burning silk and the sound of crackling and snapping.

"Help me!" the madam shrieked, her red hair standing out as she turned into a column of fire, her arms held out, flapping like the wings of Satan's angels. Lulu stumbled toward Alice, who fell back a step, unable to tear her eyes away from the look of horror on a face that started to blacken and char, with a strange, keening sound coming from the gaping mouth. As bits of lace and flesh floated down to the flagstone floor, Lulu dropped to her knees. She was no longer recognizable.

Alice spun about and was out the door, slamming it behind herself and locking it from the outside. As she heard Lulu Forchette screaming for help, Alice whispered, "You had to be stopped. I could not let you hurt Miss Conroy or anyone else any more. And you are wrong. I *will* get on in the world. I will cover my ugliness with cosmetics because now I know that actresses wear cosmetics and actresses are respectable. And if I can, I will learn to sing for other people because the girls at Mrs. Throckmorton's boarding house showed me that I can." As she watched smoke roll out from under the door while the unearthly screaming continued, Alice murmured, "I pray that God forgives you," and then she left.

By the time Alice was heading back down the tree-lined road toward

Adelaide, with kookaburras laughing in overhead branches, and sheep bleating in nearby paddocks, and the blue winter sky filling with puffy white clouds and the choreographed flights of cockatoos, as Alice tread the red earth of South Australia and felt new strength invade her limbs and spine, she lifted her chin and drew in the wind, to fill her lungs with fresh hope and courage for a new future, while far behind her on the road, behind the gum trees, a high pitched wail of agony rose to the sky and then, gradually, died.

-10-

It was August, the dead of winter, and a cold rain lashed the streets of Adelaide. As Hannah and Alice made their way through the downpour, struggling with wet capes and umbrellas, they began to question the wisdom of venturing out on such a day. But they had no choice. They were desperate.

Hannah and Alice hadn't twopence between them, they were behind in their hotel rent, and neither had even the remotest prospects of employment. It was this desperation that had driven them out into the winter rain that turned Adelaide's streets into rivers of mud. A new store had just opened, and from what Hannah and Alice had heard, it might offer opportunities.

Alice was going there in the hope that Kirkland's Emporium sold cosmetics, while Hannah planned to introduce herself to the proprietor, giving him her calling card, and telling him what she had said to the various town chemists: "If you will let your customers know about my midwifery service, I shall tell my patients about your wonderful shop." So far, she had gotten only one referral through a chemist—an emergency delivery at one of the hotels—and although mother and baby had done just fine, the family had only been in town for a few days before continuing on to Melbourne. Hardly the start of a practice.

Hannah was driven by another need as well. She wanted to move out of the hotel, which was public and noisy, and so terribly impermanent. She had never known such rootlessness. Her dream of owning a little cottage of her own grew each day, and if Kirkland's selection of commercially made medicines, and home health books, was as impressive as Hannah had heard, then this could be the start she needed.

"Here we are!" she said breathlessly when they reached the emporium. They closed their umbrellas and hurried through the front doors to join the few other citizens whose curiosity about the new store was greater than their aversion to rain.

"My goodness," Alice whispered, her blue eyes going wide at the immense size of the store, the rows of aisles, the endless counters, and the stacks of shelves along all the walls. "A person could get lost in here, miss!"

"Let's divide up, Alice. You look for cosmetics, and I shall search for the public board." Kirkland's boasted a large notice board, like the one in the Post Office, where people were free to post advertisements and messages. Hannah had come to look at employment notices, and to leave her calling card, as she had on other public boards around town. Now that Lulu Forchette was no longer a threat, Hannah was actively seeking ways to earn a living.

Following the news of Lulu Forchette's bizarre death—she had been found burned to death in her kitchen—Adelaide had been abuzz with rumors about what sort of house Miss Forchette had run. Colonial officials from the Lieutenant Governor to the Post Master had expressed shock and outrage that such an establishment had been plying illicit trade so close to the fair city of Adelaide, and had called Lulu's death a judgment from God.

What became of the girls, Hannah did not know. Ready Rita and Easy Sal found her at the Torrens Hotel one day in June. They had shown up in capes and bonnets, and carrying valises. They had not come to ask for her help, but to thank her for her kindness when she visited the house. They were on their way to Sydney, they said, in the hopes of finding better employment. They told Hannah and Alice that when they all returned to the house after a day at the races, no one had shed a tear over the grisly discovery. Miss Magenta had fainted at her mother's funeral and died a short time later of a belladonna overdose. Lulu's other daughters had had to forfeit the house due to back taxes, and all the girls had packed up their belongings and scattered. The Gilhooleys, they said, had found positions on a large sheep station and were happy. Hannah said good-bye and wished them well, saying she would miss them, and meaning it.

Dr. Davenport was gone, too.

When Hannah had discovered that the Concerned Citizen letters were forgeries, back in May when Mrs. Throckmorton had evicted her, she had sent a note to him, explaining that he no longer had anything to fear. She had received a letter in return, in which Dr. Davenport explained that he was closing his practice and sailing back to England to marry a cousin who was recently widowed and left with five children. He wished Hannah well, and said he would always remember their three months' association with fondness. She kept his statuette of Hygeia beside her bed.

Also on her bedside table was Neal's photograph in a pewter frame. She still had not heard news of the *Borealis* or the fate of the Merriwethers at the aboriginal mission, even though she had sent follow-up letters. And now she was worried about Neal, wondering if there was some way she could go back to Perth and look for him herself.

For the moment, however, earning a living took priority, and as Hannah searched for the public notice board, she surveyed Kirkland's in awe. She had never been inside such a large establishment and was amazed at the variety of merchandise crammed onto shelves, covering display counters and hanging from the walls. A sign on the main counter said, "We have everything. And if we don't have it, we can get it." Neatly piled next to it were imported newspapers: the London *Times*, *Punch*, the *Illustrated London News*, and the *Quarterly Review*.

There were displays of ladies' handkerchiefs and gloves, handbags and muffs, bolts of calico, cotton and silk in a surprising variety of colors, and a stack of men's work trousers proudly identified as "Kentucky Jeans From America." A glass confectioner's case was stocked with marzipan, peanut brittle, cubes of thickened treacle, called "toffee," and Yorkshire pennies—little shiny black licorice buttons. Shelves were stocked with Charles Dickens's *Oliver Twist*, *Pickwick Papers* and *A Christmas Carol*, the books of Jane Austen, William Makepeace Thackeray, and Sir Walter Scott. Tennyson, Keats, and Byron, the Collected Works of Shakespeare, and a sign saying "All the way from America" pointed to Melville and Richard Henry Dana.

And then Hannah turned the corner from one aisle into the next and what she suddenly saw made her come to a standstill, her eyes wide in surprise.

As Alice wound her way through the warren of aisles and shelves, she prayed she would find what she needed. Miss Conroy's suggestion that she cover her scars with makeup had proven more difficult to achieve than she had expected. Ladies did not wear cosmetics. There were encouraged to bite their lips and pinch their cheeks before entering a room, but use of pencils and rouge were scandalous for they were the mark of "loose" women. Although some commercial makeup was available, mostly manufactured in France—powders, bases, and waxes containing light, "natural" color—they were prohibitively expensive. Hannah and Alice had gone to the Victoria Theater on North Terrace to inquire among the acting company if they had any cosmetics to sell, but all jealously guarded their secret formulas and recipes. And so Alice continued to go out into the world with her scarred cheek and missing brow, with the bald patch on her scalp and the mutilated ear kept disguised with her own hair and maid's mob cap pulled low.

When they had heard of a new store in town, announcing "many departments"—a new concept fresh from London—that sold everything from thread to gum boots, Alice wondered if they might carry makeup. As she perused enticing displays of needles and thread, buttons and yarn, tape measures and pins—as she walked down aisles stocked with candles and lamp oil, doilies and soap; garden seeds from England; coffee from Arabia, cocoa from Mexico, tea from India; blankets and basins; hand mirrors and hair brushes; galoshes and sun hats, Alice came upon a large cork bulletin board, "For the convenience of our customers." Calling cards, adverts, announcements, and notices were tacked up, many placed by people looking for employment or offering jobs.

Alice had once declared she would take any kind of work, but now she was not so sure. She had gone to one interview at a rich man's house near North Terrace where she had been admitted through the rear door, and the lady of the house had conducted the interview in the kitchen, asking personal questions for the cooking staff to overhear. The woman's attitude had been haughty and snobbish, worse even than Lulu's, and she had begun to recite a list of prohibitions, should Alice be lucky enough to get the job, when it had occurred to Alice that she would just be entering into another kind of slavery. She had thanked the surprised lady and left.

Alice did not know what to do. Since breaking away from Lulu Forchette's grasp, she had felt adrift. For all of her twenty-one years, Alice Starky had been told what to do, what to eat, where to sleep. Not for a single hour in all her life had she been her own mistress. But now she was and she had no idea how to live. "You can be anything you want to be," Hannah had said. But what did that mean?

Alice paused when a poster caught her eye. It was large and busy, and framed in a fancy decorative border. Large letters shouted: "Coming Soon To Adelaide, One of the New Music Halls So Recently Seen In London!"

Alice read the words again. Her education was rudimentary, and as she had never heard of a music hall, she made sure she read it correctly. She was able to pick out a few words—magic acts, piano player, musicians, acrobats, jugglers, trapeze artist. One in particular jumped out at her: *Soloist singer.* "Requirements are fine voice and good looks. Female preferred."

Alice struggled over the big word at the top of the poster. AUDITIONS. She didn't know what it meant, but she gathered from the rest of the information that it had something to do with entertainers trying out for acts to be performed on a stage. "Salary paid on scale according to talent and popularity. See Sam Glass, proprietor."

Alice's heart began to race. Was it possible? Her hand went protectively to her scarred cheek, and her fingers fluttered at the ruffled edge of her white mob cap as she pictured the stares of the imaginary audience, deaf to her voice because they were so shocked by her looks. People had told her that when she sang no one noticed her disfigurement. But was it true, or had they only been speaking kindly out of pity?

As her heart continued to race, and she felt excitement steal through her bones, Alice made a note of the date when the try-outs were to be held. October 10. Six weeks away. Would she be able to fix her face in time?

Hannah could hardly believe her eyes as she approached the impressive display of commercial and manufactured medicines. Like most people, she visited a chemist when she needed something for a headache, a rash, or an upset stomach. But it required a prescription from a doctor, and then a visit to a chemist shop, and then there was the waiting time while the ointment or syrup and elixir was made up, and sometimes it could be a long wait if the chemist was busy. *These* medicines, however, appeared to be already prepared and ready to buy.

One display of bottles was topped by a sign that boldly declared, "Absolutely Safe and Healthy Childbirth With No Danger To Mother or Baby!" Hannah looked at the bottles of red liquid, which were labeled, "Dr. Vickers' Antisepsis Compound," and her eyes widened. Had someone found a formula before her father had? The label said nothing other than "use of this miracle compound will guarantee safe and healthy childbirth with none of the dangers and sicknesses that attend such a blessed event."

She picked up one of the bottles and held it to the light. What *was* it?

Uncorking the bottle, Hannah lifted it to her nose. There was no scent. She removed her glove and dipped her finger in, bringing it to the tip of her tongue. No taste.

She frowned. It was just colored water. How, then, could the label and this big sign make such a preposterous promise?

Recorking the bottle and replacing it, she scanned the other medicinal offerings that covered the countertop: boxes, packets, tins, and bottles of medicines of all kinds—elixirs, nostrums, tonics, and remedies—in liquids, powders, syrups, or creams. Crowning one pyramid was a hand-lettered sign that said, "Safer than leeches! No need for unpleasant purging! Avoid doctors' fees! Cheaper than the chemist!"

Hannah looked at *Dr. Brogan's Cure-All*. The label promised to eradicate everything from pimples to gout and also worked as a hair restorer, stomach settler, and menstrual regulator. "A generous dose of cocaine in every teaspoonful, guaranteed!"

She noticed that some labels did not list ingredients, while others boldly promised generous amounts of cocaine, opium, and alcohol. And if a product bore a person's name, it was always preceded by "Doctor" or "Professor."

Dr. Doyle's Infallible Worm Destroying Lozenges: "They cure where others fail." *Prof. Barnard's Health Tonic*: "Contains over sixty ingredients including rare snake oil!" *Dr. Palmer's Female Pills*: "Guaranteed to calm a distressed womb." *Swami Gupta's Elixir of Life*: "Proven in India! Will definitely eradicate all forms of cancer." *Dr. Harrow's Fertility Tonic*: "A baby in every bottle!"

Hannah had had very little exposure to commercial medicines. Bayfield's chemist made up prescriptions from doctors, selling only a few manufactured medicines. Occasionally, a traveling salesman would come through the village, selling miracle cures from the back of his wagon, but Hannah's father cautioned his patients against buying such "humbugs."

A gentleman came up the aisle just then, a thick-set man in a neat black suit and shiny bald head, with a bushy black and gray beard framing rosy lips. He introduced himself as Mr. Kirkland, owner and proprietor of this fine establishment. "For whatever ails a body," he boasted as he waved a hand over the medicinal offerings, "I have the cure."

"This is most impressive," Hannah said, a bottle of *Cocaine Tooth Drops For Children* in her hand.

"Indeed it is! As you can see, these come with guarantees. A chemist can't guarantee that his medicine will work. And these cost a lot less than what a chemist mixes up for you. Save time, too, no going to the doctor first."

But how, Hannah wondered, could all these medicines promise cures when not even a doctor could? And then she realized: they couldn't. Now she knew why her father had called such products "humbug." They were nothing but fakery. But there was no law against it, and the public, desperate to cure their aches and pains and ills, believed the printed word.

Mr. Kirkland pointed out that he carried health books too. Hannah picked up a manual on "Care of the sick In Home." She turned to the chapter titled, *Giving the Patient A Bed Bath*. "When patient is too sick to be removed from the bed for a bath, bring basin of soapy water to bedside and, using a cloth, wash the patient starting with the neck, washing as far down as possible. When that is done, start with the feet and wash up as far as possible. When that is done, wash possible."

She picked up another, *Safe Child Delivery*, and scanned its contents. "Step One: when the mother goes into labor, send all gentlemen out of the house. Step Two: place the mother behind a privacy screen." Hannah could not believe her eyes as page after page of useless information went by. There were no specific details on how to assist with a delivery, no advice for cases of emergency, and certainly no mention of using clean linens and washing one's hands. The manual was mostly about keeping the mother cheerful and optimistic. "Ply her with plenty of spirits, whether gin or rum, although wine will do."

"These books and medicines are my biggest sellers," Mr. Kirkland said proudly, clasping his lapels as if he were a politician looking for votes. "Folks come in from the country and buy up all they can. Some farms are so remote that people there never see a doctor. They have to make do for themselves."

A stranger came up the aisle just then, tipping his rain-soaked bowler hat and saying, "Greetings, friends. Farley Gladstone, at your service." He handed them each a damp calling card, inscribed: *Dr. Gladstone, Painless Dentist.*

Gladstone had putty-colored hair, a narrow face, and small, feminine hands that Hannah thought would be an asset in his profession. In a thick Liverpool accent, he explained that he had transported barrels of Waterloo teeth to Australia.

"*What* teeth?" Mr. Kirkland said.

"Most dentures are made with the teeth of animals," Gladstone said, speaking rapidly in the manner of salesmen with a pitch, "although human teeth are preferable. But where can one obtain a sufficient supply, with so many people requiring dentures? Other than, of course, those extracted from executed criminals and the destitute who willingly have their incisors and molars extracted in exchange for a few pence. But the Battle of Waterloo proved a boon to dentistry! Fifty thousand young and healthy soldiers perished on that battlefield, but their teeth live on! After being harvested, those teeth have found their way into the mouths of many Britons. And now, because of me, Australians will benefit as well."

Mr. Kirkland studied the calling card and wrinkled his red nose. "A dentist is it? Then why are you calling yourself Doctor? You're a barber, aren't you?"

"I am a doctor of dentistry, my good fellow. There is a city in America, a place called Baltimore, that recently opened an actual *college* of dentistry, the first dental school in the world. We dentists, like surgeons, are breaking away from our barber affiliations and becoming respectable, like physicians. So great is my vision of the future in which dentists are addressed as 'doctor' that I embrace the designation myself in anticipation of that future."

The proprietor sighed and gave Hannah a look as the ebullient "Dr." Gladstone moved on to introduce himself to others in the aisles. "Fancy a dentist calling himself Doctor," Mr. Kirkland said with a shake of his head. "That's what Australia does to people. Gives them ideas."

As Kirkland walked away, Hannah returned her attention to the display of medicines and books, and she thought of the far-flung homesteads Kirkland had spoken of, the scattered settlers, the isolated families so far from the services of a doctor. And she found herself thinking of Bayfield, and the days her father went out in the buggy, to follow the country lanes and byways as he visited his patients. And an idea so new and perfect sprang into her mind that she found herself suddenly smiling.

When she saw Alice coming up the aisle toward her, Hannah noticed that, by coincidence, her friend was also smiling. And she realized that venturing out into the storm had been worthwhile after all.

-11-

As Hannah guided her one-horse buggy along the tree-lined lane, she was so enchanted by the shimmering countryside, she thought it was as if, overnight, the world had been turned into gold by the unseen hand of a magical alchemist.

She could not stop marveling over the miracle that had taken place. The golden wattle, a native Australian acacia, was in full springtime bloom, producing large fluffy yellow flower heads that were in fact clusters of many tinier flowers, casting green trees and brown bark in gold that shimmered blindingly in the sunlight.

The whole world in fact seemed bursting with new life and fresh color as the rust-red earth of South Australia gave forth an abundance of emerald-greens, deep sky-blues, and flowers ranging from blood-red to canary yellow. Fields of clover, acres of wheat and corn, and vineyards mantled in lush grape vines all swept away to rolling hills where sheep and cattle grazed, and the occasional red-roofed farmhouse stood beneath the sun.

Riding along the road to the clip-clop of her mare's hooves, Hannah heard the wind in the gum trees, many of which she was now able to identify—the spotted gum, the blue gum, the thin-leaved stringy bark, the red flowering gum, and the mountain ash—and they seemed to be whispering, "Come live with us."

There was that strange enchantment again, redolent of her encounter with the outlaw Jamie O'Brien eight months ago. She had not heard news of him since, but his Wanted posters were still up around the city, so she assumed he was still at large. This drive through the country, far from noisy Adelaide, reminded her of that enchanted night. In retrospect it seemed that when she had been in imminent danger of being attacked by a starving wild dog, out of the night a stranger had materialized to rescue her, a man with an exotic accent, weathered skin, tilted smile. Hannah had the oddest notion that it was almost as if Australia itself had come to her rescue in the form of a person, for just those few minutes. Where did Jamie O'Brien disappear to afterward?

He went back into the red earth and the ghost gums and the never-ending sky.

Such a romantic notion no longer startled her. Hannah knew she was falling in love with her adopted land. Its uniqueness delighted her. The flocks of white cockatoos flying up from the tops of gum trees. The sudden appearance of an emu, tall and fat, trotting across the track. Kangaroos grazing alongside sheep brought over from England. And signs over gateways identified holdings as Wattle Run, Billabong Station, Fairview Farm.

They were new signs, Hannah noticed, erected in just the past few years. In Bayfield, the roads themselves were hundreds of years old. One could not pass a farm that hadn't been in a family for generations. The very oaks and glens were steeped in tradition and customs. But here! Cottages with their original coat of paint, not yet re-painted. Fields that had just been planted for the first time. Newcomers arriving to stamp their identity on the land, to make something of this country and of themselves.

The very newness of Australia captivated Hannah. There would be no gloomy libraries where snobbish physicians could pass unfair judgments on a man who had no title, no lineage. She thought of Neal, who did not know who he was or where he came from—this would be the place for him. A place of new beginnings and fresh starts, where it did not matter what came before, what prior generations had done in this place, where all that mattered was what a man did today.

She wished she could share this discovery with Neal. And perhaps she soon would. Hannah had finally received a letter from the colonial government in Perth. Neal's science vessel had not been affected by the recent native uprisings, had not in fact yet returned to port from its year-long voyage of survey and exploration, but was due in soon. Perhaps he was already there now, looking for a ship to bring him to Adelaide.

She saw a turn-off up ahead, a dirt track disappearing among gum trees. A sign by the road said Seven Oaks Station, with an arrow pointing right.

Once she had heard that Neal was all right, Hannah had given up the notion of going to Perth to search for him and had come out to the countryside where she hoped to start a midwifery practice. The idea had come to her at Kirkland's Emporium, when the proprietor had said the settlers were so far from medical help. Hannah had decided that getting away from the city and its established midwives who so jealously guarded their territories would be just the start she needed.

She and Alice were staying at the Australia Hotel, a bustling establishment farther along the Kapunda road than where Lulu had lived.

It was owned and run by a cheerful widow named Mrs. Guinness who had no qualms about unmarried ladies renting a room. The hotel had been built a couple of years prior, after copper was found in Kapunda and the great ore drays came and went along the country road, filled with men in need of food and rest. A few other buildings had sprung up around the hotel—a dry goods store, feed and farm supplies, a blacksmith. Mrs. Guinness handled the mail that came up from Adelaide for the region, and so farmers and cattlemen frequently tramped up the steps of her hotel for their letters from home.

Hannah had been out here in the open spaces for five weeks now, trying to get herself known. Each morning she would set out in the borrowed buggy and, equipped with her blue carpetbag, a map of the district, and a lunch of cold chicken or beef, bread and cheese, and a bottle of sweetened tea, she would cover as much of the countryside as she could, visiting farms and homesteads, introducing herself, leaving her calling card: *Hannah Conroy, Licensed Midwife, Trained in London.*

Alice did not go with her. Because Mrs. Guinness had by good fortune needed help in the kitchen, Alice had a job at the Australia Hotel. But in the evenings she rehearsed in Mrs. Guinness's drawing room, to the piano accompaniment of Mrs. Guinness's daughter, because she had her heart set on the auditions at the new music hall. Alice tried out various selections on whoever occupied the room at the time, gauging their reactions to see which song she should choose for her audition. The drawing room audience changed every night, as drovers, cattlemen, and shearers came and went. But all sat spellbound while Alice sang, and all agreed that her voice sounded like spun gold (although one tactless fellow had said within Alice's hearing, "She's beautiful if you don't look at her").

As Hannah guided the buggy off the main road, through a wide gate and beneath a sign that said, "Seven Oaks Station," she looked for oak trees. Adelaide's wide avenues had been planted with the oaks and elms of England. Even Lulu Forchette's house had been landscaped with flora imported from Europe. Other homesteads in the gently rolling countryside had been cleared of much of its original brush to make room for the willows and poplars of home. But apparently, Seven Oaks had kept its native gums and acacias, as Hannah could not spot a single oak.

It was lambing season, and she rode past a paddock occupied by hundreds of ewes with little ones at their sides. Beyond, Hannah saw another fenced area where Angus cows grazed as they suckled new calves. She saw farm dogs at work among the stock, racing this way and that, while men on horseback oversaw order in a noisy cattle yard. It was a busy, prosperous station, with stables, shearing sheds, woodchip yards, milking sheds, and even a chicken house. And the morning air was filled with the cacophony of bleating sheep, mooing cows, barking dogs, shouting men, and even great flocks of crows screeching overhead.

When the main house itself came into view, Hannah slowed the buggy to a halt and stared in wonder.

The house at Seven Oaks was large and rectangular, comprised of a single storey with a gabled roof. A deep verandah went all the way around and was enclosed in an intricate railing, its roof supported by decorative iron posts. Although the wood siding of the house was the natural color of the timber, the window trim, door jambs, railing and posts had been painted white. It was a simple house, yet stately and elegant. Around the homestead a beautiful landscaped garden sloped down to a pond where black swans mingled with ducks and other bird life.

Hannah remained perfectly still in the buggy, the reins forgotten in her hands. There was something about the house at Seven Oaks that struck a chord deep within her. She could not say why. How to explain why some places called to a person, and others did not? She looked at the way Australian gums sheltered the house, shedding silver bark and dollops of golden sunlight onto its roof. She heard the buzz of insects in the air, felt the warmth of the sun penetrate the top of the carriage and enfold her in timeless suspension.

For here it was, nestled in green rolling hills covered in flocks of white sheep, beneath a blue sky that went on forever, amid the silence and the noise of the Australian countryside—the house of her dreams.

She resumed her drive and brought the buggy to a halt next to a hitching post. As she mounted the steps of the front verandah, toward a solid front door with a glass pane set at eye-level, Hannah knew exactly what she would find inside: a tidy entry with a polished floor, the hallway stretching to the back of the house where kitchen and laundry would be, doorways leading off either side into rooms that would be perfectly furnished with sofas and chairs, tables covered in lace cloths, braided rugs in bright hues. She would smell lemon polish, her eye would catch the gleam of brass and glass. There would be one of the fashionable new lamps that had little crystals dangling from the glass chimney, and they would make a charming tinkling sound.

She knocked.

A harried maid answered with a frown, barely listened to what Hannah had to say, bade her come inside, and then rushed off down the hall to disappear at the rear. Hannah looked around. The interior of Seven Oaks was exactly as she had imagined. To the right, an open doorway revealed a tastefully appointed parlor. To the left, a dining room with a polished table and six chairs, an armoire displaying china. Hannah surmised that the bedrooms were at the back of the house.

From the far end of the hall a woman appeared, coming toward Hannah with long, purposeful strides. Stripping off a work glove, she extended her hand and introduced herself as Mary McKeeghan, mistress of the station.

Hannah handed her a calling card, and explained that she was going around the district to let people know of her services.

Mary McKeeghan released a gruff laugh. "We don't need a midwife here!" she said, but she was smiling and Hannah took an instant liking to her.

Mary McKeeghan was a handsome, broad-shouldered woman with a sunburnt face. She wore a dusty white bodice over a skirt that appeared to be made of soft kid leather. And on her orange, fly-away hair she wore a man's bush hat. Hannah guessed that she was in her thirties, and she wore a wedding ring.

And then Hannah noticed with a start a black cloth band around each of her upper arms.

Seeing Hannah's look, Mrs. McKeeghan said, "We're a house of mourning. But I've a mob of men to feed," and she gestured to the end of the hall where Hannah pictured the kitchen and a hungry crowd, "and haven't had time to go into town and buy a black dress. No crepe to hang on the front door either. It's our busiest time of the year."

Hannah had already been told this at every cattle and sheep station she had visited, and if it wasn't stock, it was planting time at the crop farms. But as busy as folks were, babies were still being born and midwives were needed.

"I am sorry for your loss," she said.

"It was my sister," Mary said, grief flooding her green eyes. "Fell off a horse and broke her neck. It was bad enough, but she left behind a newborn as well." Mary McKeeghan glanced over her shoulder and shifted on her feet, as if she was going to dash off at any moment. A woman with little time on her hands.

"A newborn!" Hannah said.

"Well, five months old, and him not doing well either."

"What's wrong?"

Mary's green eyes seemed to size Hannah up, taking in the dark orange dress with the little black cape that went just to the middle of Hannah's back, the black gloves and small black bonnet tied under Hannah's chin. Hannah knew she gave an impression of maturity and professionalism, hoping it would make folks overlook her age. "Would you know something about babies, beyond delivering them, I mean?"

"I have some experience, yes."

"It's this way," Mary McKeeghan said and she walked with such a long, quick stride that Hannah had to hurry to keep up.

The bedrooms were indeed in the rear, and the one Hannah now entered was spacious and sunny, with a four-poster covered in a patchwork quilt, a colorful braided rug on the scrubbed floor, and handsome dressers of dark wood. Near the window a cradle stood on a rocking stand. No sounds came from it.

"He's five months old, and he was fine until two weeks ago. We came back from the funeral and it was as if he knew his Mum had gone. Sylvie nursed him for three months and then switched him to sugared milk, which he took to with true appetite. She could leave him with the pap boat and he would feed himself. Now look." Mrs. McKeeghan bent over the cradle, picked up the ceramic pap boat, and brought the nipple to the baby's lips. He turned his head away. "Won't feed," Mary said.

The pap boat was made of Staffordshire ceramic and resembled a bottle, slightly curved, and lying on its side. Cow teats preserved in spirits were usually tied onto the end as a nipple, but in this case, cheesecloth covered the spout for the infant to suck on.

Hannah drew the baby's blanket back and was shocked to see how skinny and undernourished he was. She snapped her fingers on one side of the infant's head. He did not turn in the direction of the sound. "Is he deaf?"

"Oh no. He used to respond. It's as though he doesn't care."

"Does he roll over?"

"He started to and then stopped."

Hannah also noticed that no matter what sounds she made, how she tickled him, or grinned at him, she could not get the baby to smile. Retrieving her stethoscope, she listened to the tiny chest and heard the miniature heart within, struggling to survive. As she folded the instrument back into her bag, it was on Hannah's lips to tell Mary McKeeghan that a baby needed more than to have a pap boat placed in his crib. He needed to be held. He needed to feel human warmth and touch, without which he would wither and die. But when she looked into Mary's tired face, saw the lines of grief and worry and stress around her eyes and mouth, Hannah realized that this woman's life was filled with demands that were pulling her every which way.

As if she could read Hannah's mind, Mary said, "Between the baby and my own Mum, I'm at my wits end. It's our busiest time. I've even got my two children working the tar sticks in the shearing shed."

"What's wrong with your mother?"

Mary took Hannah into the next bedroom where a woman in her fifties, with graying hair and blank eyes, lay on her side, facing the wall. "Been like that since the funeral. I've begged her to get up, to eat, but she won't. I don't think she can even hear us."

Hannah lifted the woman's wrist, getting no response, and felt her pulse. She touched the woman's neck, felt her forehead, tried getting her attention. But Mary McKeeghan's mother lay as still as death, staring lifelessly at the wall.

Hannah thought, *One failing to thrive, the other giving up.*

Going back into the nursery, Hannah lifted the baby from the cradle and, picking up the pap boat, went back into the other room. "What are you doing?" Mary McKeeghan asked.

"Something I saw my father do once." Hannah placed the pap boat on the table by the bed, then she bent over Mary McKeeghan's mother and, nestling the baby next to her in the covers, warm against the woman's bosom, took one of the spare pillows that sat on top of a wooden chest and tucked it behind the baby, so that he was snug between pillow and grandmother. Neither made a sound.

Hannah straightened and said, "What is your mother's name?"

"Naomi."

Hannah laid a hand on the woman's unresponsive shoulder and said, "Naomi, if you want to feed your grandson, the pap boat is right here by the bed."

Out in the parlor, Mary McKeeghan said, "What will that do?"

"I'm not sure," Hannah said truthfully. "It might not work. But it's a chance, as I can think of nothing else to save either."

"Thank you stopping by," Mary said, escorting Hannah to the front door. "And for trying to help. It's not easy," she said, and Hannah saw guilt steal into the green eyes, "helping at lambing and shearing time, all those mobs of men to feed and see to. I had hoped my Mum would take care of little Robbie, and now they're both sickly and me with no time to spare."

Hannah guided the buggy back toward the main road but stopped and pulled over to look back at the house. She carried paper with her, and a pen and inkwell, for recording her experiences and jotting down observations. She retrieved a sheet of paper now, spread it on her lap and, dipping her pen into the ink, proceeded to sketch Mary McKeeghan's house on it.

When Alice saw the beautiful girls lined up outside to audition at the new music hall, she wondered if she had made a terrible mistake. Did she have even the slightest chance of being hired?

Since Hannah had been called away to deliver a baby, Alice had come into town on her own. Hannah had wanted to accompany her, but Alice had insisted that, with Hannah trying to build up a practice, it was more important she went on the call.

Since they had not been able to find makeup, Hannah and Mrs. Guinness had helped Alice choose a bonnet that sufficiently covered her head so that most of the scarring was hidden, and then they had used a writing pencil to fill in the blank eyebrow. "The idea is to emphasize your positive attributes," Hannah had said as she coaxed a few of Alice's natural blond curls out from the other side of the bonnet, and over her forehead, to show off her beautiful tresses and to frame her lovely blue eyes. They had also spent precious money on a new gown that, although not showy and expensive, was tasteful and the latest fashion.

Her hopes had run high as she had walked toward the music hall, and then she saw the line of beautiful women waiting to audition. Not all were singers, but those who were possessed stunning faces and figures. Alice felt like a stick next to them, and an ugly one at that.

The doors opened and everyone crowded in. Alice found herself in one of the new style of saloon-bars where patrons sat in chairs at small tables, allowing them to eat, drink alcohol and smoke tobacco whilst watching the show.

The proprietor moved through the crowd, sending various applicants to different parts of his establishment, where men went to apply for jobs as waiters, bartenders, janitors, and women hoped to work in the kitchen or back stage. The artistic applicants, Sam Glass saw to himself, calling them onto the stage one by one and either watching patiently as they juggled, tumbled, and pulled doves out of their coats, or dismissing them with an impatient wave of his hand.

Glass wore a brown suit with a checkered waistcoat and a tweed cap on his head. He spoke in a deep, gravely voice that made one think of sandpaper, and chewed constantly on a soggy cigar. He sported a strange moustache—a straight black line along his upper lip that looked as if it had been drawn there with a lump of charcoal.

The auditions moved swiftly as most acts were too amateurish for the new Elysium Music Hall, and when it came Alice's turn, as she mounted the steps to the stage, Glass looked her up and down. Pretty eyes. Was the hair natural blond? That would be a plus. "Take off the bonnet," he said.

"My bonnet?"

"You aren't going to wear it on stage. Folks'll want to see your hair. Take it off."

Alice looked at the crowd, most of whom were so involved in preparing their own songs, recitations, and musical instruments that they weren't watching. She came back to Glass, who sat at a table with a large schooner of beer by his hand. "Hurry up!" he barked. "I haven't got all day. Take off the bonnet or clear the stage."

She did so, and when her face and scalp were exposed in the stage lights, Sam's eyebrows shot up. "Jesus Christ! Are you having a joke on me?" He narrowed his eyes and leaned forward. "Did Jacko King put you up to this?"

When he saw that she was serious, Glass said in a kinder tone, "Listen, love, I imagine you have the nicest voice in the world. But my customers will have eyes as well as ears. Know what I mean? There's pubs by the harbor that can use singers and don't care what they look like." He gestured for her to leave the stage, and shouted, "Next!"

Alice didn't move. As Glass turned to say something to the man who shared his table, Alice thought of Hannah Conroy's kindness, and Mrs. Guinness's encouragement. She recalled evenings in the hotel parlor practicing and rehearsing, with Hannah and Mrs. Guinness telling her what a beautiful voice she had. She thought of Lulu Forchette who kept telling her she was ugly. And she thought of all the faces that had come to the music hall, unblemished faces with perfect cheeks and intact eyebrows.

Alice squared her shoulders and drew in a deep breath. The drovers and shearers at the Australia Hotel had said, "Sing something merry to cheer everyone up." "Sing something risqué, like they sing in pubs." "Sing something funny and make everyone laugh." But when Alice opened her mouth and began to sing, there was nothing merry, risqué, or funny about the hymn that came from her throat.

"Amazing Grace, how sweet the sound,
That saved a wretch like me.
I once was lost but now am found,
Was blind, but now, I see."

Those standing near her turned and stared. Hearing the pure, high voice, they stopped talking and listened.

"T'was Grace that taught
my heart to fear.
And Grace, my fears relieved.
How precious did that Grace appear
the hour I first believed."

People backstage, and those beyond the footlights also fell silent, giving Alice's voice more room to reach walls and rafters and glittery chandeliers, until performers in the sidelines, tuning their instruments or practicing their moves, ceased their tasks and turned in the direction of the hymn.

"Through many dangers, toils and snares
we have already come.
T'was Grace that brought us safe thus far
and Grace will lead us home."

Sam Glass looked up with a frown, and the silence spread through the tables and chairs and back to the liquor bar at the rear. Carpenters stopped hammering. Painters lowered their brushes. Men on ladders steadied themselves as they swiveled about to see where the hypnotic sound was coming from.

"The Lord has promised good to me
His word my hope secures.
He will my shield and portion be
as long as life endures."

People out in the foyer now came into the hall, silent, listening. Not a sound was heard except for the golden tones that floated like silken ribbons over the heads of the awestruck crowd.

"When I've been here ten thousand years,
bright shining as the sun.
I've no less days to sing God's praise
then when I've first begun."

Sam Glass stared at Alice as men produced handkerchiefs and blew their noses and women wiped their eyes. He looked around and saw the faces of colonists far from Mother England and knew they were remembering loved ones left behind. He returned his eyes to the lone girl on the stage, petite, slender, fragile. What was it about her? It wasn't just that she had a nice voice and could carry a tune—so far all auditioning singers possessed those qualities—there was something more in this pale, ethereal creature. She didn't just sing the song. It was the way she breathed, the way she emphasized some notes, softened others, threw in pauses where no one ever did, and held those high notes for longer than he thought her small lungs capable. Feeling his own throat tighten, Glass realized there was something almost spiritual about the way she sang, that filled one with sentiments of hearth and home, angels and the Virgin Mary.

"Amazing Grace, how sweet the sound,
That saved a wretch like me....
I once was lost but now am found,
Was blind, but now, I see."

When the last note from Alice's throat had rung in the rafters, the silence remained, no one moved. They continued to stare at the girl with the disfigured face. Then they tore their eyes away, trying to understand how deformity and beauty could go together, and they looked at the sawdusted floor and then at each other, and conversations took up again, slowly somberly, with everyone wondering if it was all right to applaud a hymn.

Sam Glass shot to his feet. "Christ Almighty! Where did all that voice come from? You're just a little slip of thing. Don't look capable of blowing out a candle, never mind belting out God's most blessed hymn."

He gestured for her to come down from the stage, and when Alice reached his table, Glass spoke quickly. "We open in four weeks. I'll put you in the middle, so we're sure to get everyone's attention. I'll have some of the girls fix your face with cosmetics, and we can do something with your hair, too. I want you to dress to dazzle. A short skirt, mind, that gives the gents a glimpse of stocking. Bare arms. And the neckline cut low to reveal as much bosom as you can without getting us raided. What's your name?"

"Alice Starky."

He thought a moment, then said, "From now on, you are Alice Star. And you are going to be a sensation."

-13-

As Hannah guided the buggy along the shady drive of Seven Oaks Station, she experienced two joyous emotions. The first was her feeling, as she approached the main house, of coming home. The second was thoughts of Neal. He should arrive in Adelaide any day now, and Hannah could barely eat or sleep with excitement. And now Alice was going to sing at the new music hall. The world, golden with blooming acacia, was glowing with promise.

Hannah was not surprised to see Mary McKeeghan and her mother sitting in rocking chairs on the wide verandah, with the chubby, smiling Robbie in Naomi's lap. Mary had sent a message to Hannah at the Australia Hotel, informing her that both baby and grandmother were recovering from their spell of malaise. Mary invited Hannah to tea, and Hannah greatly appreciated the opportunity to make a friend in the district.

As Hannah took a seat, Mary McKeeghan said, "I've already spread the word about you, Miss Conroy. We don't have a doctor out here, and God knows we need one. But I reckon you're as good as any doctor, and I know that folks around here will be comforted to know that there's someone who can help in times of need. Perhaps you can look in on Edna Basset on your way back? She's down poorly with croup, at Fairview Farm."

-14-

The sign on the marquee said: "Grand Opening! Entertainment for the sophisticated upper classes only: music, singing, plays and other outstanding acts. Rowdies and drunks will not be admitted."

Carriages were lined up along the wooden sidewalk as ladies in evening gowns and gentlemen in formal attire stepped down. A crowd had gathered to watch the parade as many of Adelaide's prominent citizens came to attend the opening of Sam Glass's extraordinary supper-theater. Overhead, the southern sky's million stars winked down at them.

Inside, a colorful and noisy throng milled beneath glittering chandeliers, to sip champagne and socialize in the lobby before finding tables in the main hall, where musicians tuned their instruments. A grand red velvet curtain hid the stage from view. Unlike traditional theaters, Glass's music hall, called The Elysium, had a liquor bar along the back wall, carved of dark mahogany, outfitted with mirrors, shiny brass beer taps, and pyramids of crystal glasses and schooners. The kitchen was adjacent to the theater, and when the audience was settled at precisely seven o'clock, supper would be served by young waiters in white shirts, black trousers, and white aprons. Tonight's offering was spring lamb, roast potatoes, and baby carrots, followed by French cheese and English custard. At eight o'clock exactly, the dishes would be cleared away, after-dinner drinks served, and the curtain raised.

"I am so nervous, miss!" Alice said as Hannah waited with her backstage with other performers. Sam Glass had provided Alice with makeup so that her scars were hidden. It was not perfect, but with her blond hair combed a certain way and held in place with a rhinestone tiara and an egret feather, Alice's deformity would not be seen in the stage lights. Besides, with every gentleman in the audience smoking a pipe, cigar, or cigarette, there was enough smoke in the air to make details indistinct.

"You will be fine," Hannah said, trying not to be in the way of the men in tights, or clown costumes, or dressed like gentlemen in evening wear. They were singers, acrobats, magicians and actors. The women were garbed in glittering costumes that exposed a lot of skin. Alice, on the other hand, despite Sam Glass's instructions, had chosen to wear a simple white gown,

Empire style, with a high waist and neck, long sleeves, and absolutely no skin showing.

The stage manager came through, ordering all non-performers to leave as the show was about to begin.

Hannah gave Alice a hug, wished her well, and hurried back to the table she was sharing with Mrs. Guinness. The curtain rose and the small band in front of the stage played "God Save the Queen." The audience cheered and applauded the various acts that came out one after another, laughing at the clown, singing along with a balladeer and his banjo, jeering at a magician who kept dropping his wand.

At the rear of the packed house, Sam Glass chewed his cigar and watched and worried. A few mishaps had occurred, but nothing the patrons could have guessed. The kitchen ran out of spring lamb and the bar ran out of claret, but everyone seemed happy. Glass had a lot invested in this venture. He was counting on this mob to go home tonight satisfied, and tomorrow tell all their friends about The Elysium.

It was three-quarters through the evening when the curtain came down, the audience grew restless with anticipation, but when the curtain rose again and Sam Glass saw Alice Star—wearing an Empress Josephine gown, looking like a choir angel—he felt a fierce throb at his temples. He had given her explicit instructions on the sort of costume she was to wear. So far the audience had been treated to bare ankles and low-cut necklines. They had been awe-struck by the lady trapezist in tights. Alice Star was supposed to follow suit.

He chomped his cigar and spat juice into a brass spittoon. For the successful running of a supper-theater, it was necessary for everyone to obey the boss. What sort of chaos would ensue if everyone did what they chose? He would let her sing this once, and after the performance she was getting the sack.

Alice waited on the stage. The audience grew restless, conditioned now to performances with brassy, explosive openings. The girl in the virginal gown and yellow hair did nothing to grab their attention. She just stood there. Hannah's heart pounded. Her mother had told her, long ago, of something called stage fright. Was that what gripped Alice now?

And then she saw Alice nod her head ever so slightly, and the violinist in the band stood up and began to play. Alice drew in a breath and began to sing.

"All in the merry month of May

When the green buds were swellin',
Young Jimmy Grove on his deathbed lay
For love of Barbara Allen."

The audience released a collective sigh. It was a familiar song, a sweet song, and a sad one. People reached for their glasses filled with ruby-red liquids, or their tea cups, while they remembered the first time they had heard the song of Barbara Allen.

"He sent his man to find her then,
to the town where she was dwellin'.
"You must come to my master dear,
if your name be Barbara Allen."

The audience grew hushed as they watched the girl dressed in white, standing alone in a column of light, her voice seeming to come from no human throat but perhaps from the whiteness of her dress. An angelic voice, many thought.

"For death is printed on his face
And o'er his heart is stealin'.
Then haste away to comfort him,
O lovely Barbara Allen."

Some began to remember bittersweet moments in their own lives, loved ones lost, nights of comforting, days without comfort. Tears sprang to a few eyes. Sam Glass's ire grew. His audience was sinking into sadness! He was ruined!

"And very slowly, she came up
and slowly she came nigh him,
and all she said when there she came,
'Young man, I think you're dyin'.'"

Sniffs were heard throughout the hall. Hannah herself needed to retrieve a handkerchief and dab the corners of her eyes. It was made of fine linen and was embroidered with the initial NS. Neal's handkerchief, which she carried with her everywhere, a memento made all the more precious as Alice's pure, clear voice reminded Hannah of her desire for Neal, and how she missed him. Mrs. Guinness swallowed painfully as she recalled a young man from long ago, whom she had not called to mind in years, but who now materialized behind her eyes, handsome, smiling, going off to fight Napoleon. She, too, needed a handkerchief.

> *"When he was dead and laid in grave*
> *Her heart was struck with sorrow.*
> *'O mother, mother, make my bed*
> *For I shall die tomorrow."'*

The voice of gold, accompanied by the sweet-sad tones of the violin, held the audience captive, keeping them silent, frozen. Not a hand moved, not an eye blinked. Sam Glass wondered if they were breathing even. A fine thing. Promising them an evening of merry entertainment and giving them instead a dirge.

> *"She on her deathbed, as she lay,*
> *Begged to be buried by him*
> *And sore repented of the day*
> *That she did e'er deny him."*

The song was over; the hypnotic voice grew silent. No one moved and Sam Glass imagined a stampede for the box office and demands for money back.

And then the applause began, gaining momentum as Alice stood on the stage, with people getting to their feet and shouting, "Bravo!"

"You were wonderful!" Hannah enthused when she found Alice in the chaos backstage. Sam Glass was there, congratulating her, telling her that he was going to put her on last from now on. The acts that had followed Alice had not done as well as the ones before—either the performers' hearts were not in it, or the audience's mood had changed, or both. But everyone agreed that Alice had been the high point of the evening, and that was how Sam wanted his patrons to go home.

"I owe you so much, Hannah," Alice said, as others crowded around to congratulate her. Alice couldn't put it into words, not yet, not until she was alone and could look back on this moment—but as she had sung out her soul and felt the emotions of the onlookers, had seen their faces, even their tears, Alice had been struck but a shuddering emotion that had overwhelmed her and even now left her at a loss for words. All she knew was that, while she had sung for these people, she had suddenly realized that this was what she was meant to do. Alice had found her calling in life.

"Not at all," Hannah said, noticing that Alice no longer addressed her as "miss."

She stood back to allow room for others to pay their respects to Alice, and when she was assured that her friend did not want for attention, Hannah withdrew from the crowd into a corner where she found an island of peace and privacy behind a tall potted palm.

She reached into her purse and brought out her mother's book of poetry where she kept the photograph of Neal Scott tucked between Wordsworth's *Lucy Gray* and *Ode to a Nightingale* by John Keats. Hannah looked into Neal's soulful eyes and conjured up his voice in her mind. Holding his photograph brought back the romantic weeks aboard the *Caprica*. The night of the storm when they had embraced and kissed in fear and desire.

With a racing heart, she looked at an envelope she had tucked in with the photograph. It had arrived that afternoon at the Australia Hotel with the daily post, just as Hannah, Alice, and Mrs. Guinness were getting ready to leave for town. Hannah had taken one look at the Perth postmark, and the familiar handwriting—she had written to Neal to inform him about her residential change from town to country, in the hopes that when the HMS *Borealis* docked, he would check for mail before setting sail for Adelaide— and she had wanted to open it at once. But this was Alice's night. Whatever Neal had to say, it could wait until after the performance. Hannah did not want to detract from Alice's special moment.

But now it was time to read the letter. Since he was long overdue arriving in Adelaide, she assumed it contained an explanation why, and with a new date for when she could expect to see him.

With trembling fingers, Hannah opened Neal's letter.

ADELAIDE
April, 1848

-15-

"And there we were, me and Paddy, God rest him, all alone with this mob of aborigines staring us down—"

When Liza Guinness saw the handsome stranger enter the front door of her hotel, to step in from the warm April sunshine and come striding across the modest lobby toward her, she forgot what she was going to say next. Forgot, in fact, who she was talking to and why. She quickly checked her hair to make sure it was up in its chignon and no strays.

Though a widow with two grown daughters, Liza Guinness still considered herself young and worked hard to keep herself so, with henna rinses, nightly facials, and an eye on her trim figure. And although she had run the Australia Hotel on this country road ten miles north of Adelaide for five years, she refused to "go bush," as so many women did after months in the rugged countryside so far from civilization—women who took to wearing divided skirts, simply because they rode horses in men's fashion instead of side-saddle, and who pinned their hair up any way that worked, and who wore men's bush hats and leather work gloves, and let the sun tan their faces. Liza Guinness always wore presentable day gowns, with fashionable drop-shoulders and wide, ruffled sleeves, and a crinoline modest enough to let her maneuver behind the hotel's front desk.

She was glad now that she kept up such practices, because the gentleman approaching the front desk with a charming smile was not only attractive but clearly well-to-do. He wore one of the new hats from Ecuador, made of white woven fibers with a black sweat band that were becoming all the rage as they were light and comfortable in hot summer months. The stranger's clothes were all white as well, and the jacket was made of linen, the sign of a man who could afford a personal valet.

Liza judged he was around twenty-six or twenty-seven and found herself wishing she were fourteen years younger. "What can I do for you, sir?" she asked in her most charming voice, while plump and matronly Edna Basset, with whom she had been gossiping, and who had come to the hotel for her mail, watched with interest.

He removed his hat to expose closely cropped dark brown hair, and looked around at the tidy lobby with plants, framed watercolors on the walls, and on the registry desk next to a vase of daisies, a handwritten sign that said, "Sleep fast, we need the beds."

He smiled. "I'm looking for Miss Hannah Conroy. My name is Neal Scott."

Two pairs of eyes widened. "Mr. Scott!" Liza enthused. "The American scientist? We've heard all about you, Mr. Scott, haven't we, Edna? But Miss Conroy said you wouldn't be arriving for at least a year."

"I know. There was a change of plans and no time to write ahead of time. Is Miss Conroy in?"

"She went to Barossa Valley."

His smile turned to a look of concern. "Do you know if she received my last message? I was here three weeks ago and was told I had just missed her. She was going to help with an influenza epidemic—"

"In Barossa Valley!" Liza said again in dismay. The German wine country was a good thirty miles away, with hills in between, so who knew when Hannah would be back? Liza turned toward the wall of cubby holes that held room keys, messages, bills, and mail. "Here," she said, retrieving a sealed envelope and handing it to him. "Is this it?"

He looked at the envelop he had sealed three weeks prior and his heart sank. Hannah did not know he was in Adelaide! "I'm afraid so."

"She should have been back by now," Liza said, replacing the envelope. "Can you wait for Miss Conroy? We have a lovely parlor, and we serve a variety of teas and cakes."

Neal glanced toward the open door where he saw a nicely furnished room that looked more like a parlor in someone's home than a public eatery. A few patrons sat on the sofas talking quietly, and an inviting fire roared at the hearth. It was so tempting ... "I'm afraid I can't stay. I leave Adelaide this afternoon."

"This afternoon!" Liza and Edna said in unison, both wishing to spend a bit of time with the intriguing American, and hoping to watch some romance blossom when Hannah returned. Life in the countryside could get monotonous. "We have heard that the epidemic has run its course," Liza said hopefully. "Which means Hannah is on her way home and could be here any minute. Just one cup of tea, Mr. Scott?"

"I'm sorry, but I'm meeting up with an expedition, and if I'm late, I know Sir Reginald will not wait for me."

Liza Guinness stared at this stranger who was the most exotic creature to ever cross her threshold—and the only American she had ever met. "Surely you don't mean Sir Reginald Oliphant?"

"The same."

"I have his books! I have read them all!" She turned to her friend with a glowing smile. "Fancy that, Edna. An *explorer* in my hotel." And Edna, who found herself wishing she was thirty years younger, returned the smile.

Neal consulted his pocket watch, then looked at the clock on the wall, then glanced back at the front door, shifted on his feet, frowned in thought and indecision, and finally said, "I'll just have to leave another message. Have you paper and pen?"

Mrs. Guinness loved romance, even when it was someone else's, and always helped it along when she could. She had heard all about the voyage on the *Caprica*, and had noted in particular that when Hannah spoke of the storm in which she and the American had almost died, her cheeks pinked and she cast her eyes down—classic signs, Liza thought, of a woman with a secret. It had been a shipboard romance, Liza was certain, and it thrilled her to think so. Especially now that she had laid eyes on the man himself instead of his flat, black and white photograph which, granted, showed an attractive young man but which did nothing for the exciting, flesh and blood male who stood before her now.

"Here you are, sir," Liza said, handing him a sheet of stationery and pointing to the pen in the inkwell.

.

As Hannah guided the buggy along the lane, drifting in and out of pools of shade and lazy autumn sunshine, she couldn't wait to get back to the hotel, which was just up ahead and around the bend. A hot bath, a cup of Liza Guinness's mint tea, and a nap would set the world right again. Solving the mystery of the influenza—which had appeared suddenly in Barossa Valley, followed a strange meandering course, striking some homesteads but skipping others, and then had vanished just as mysteriously—would have to wait for another day. Hannah was exhausted. Although she herself had not contracted the illness, helping to nurse so many of those stricken, in various farms and houses, had taken everything out of her.

She wondered if the mail had come. A letter from Alice perhaps, who was on tour with the Sam Glass Entertainment Troupe. With The Elysium such an astounding success, Sam was looking to open music halls in other cities, and the best way to gain backers and investors was to dazzle them with his best acts: two brothers who juggled flaming torches, a baritone who sang arias, a comic act involving cream pies and fire crackers, a sensational contortionist named Lady Godiva, and soloist singer Alice Star. They had gone first to Melbourne and were traveling on to Sydney after that. Hannah knew that Alice was going to win hearts everywhere she went, as she had in Adelaide where, in a short time, adoring citizens had begun to call her the "Australian Songbird."

Hannah almost hoped that there was no mail from Neal. Since his first letter back in November, he had written to Hannah regularly, giving her news and updates on the Oliphant expedition—"Soon to be launched!"—and entertaining her with stories of the people he was meeting and fascinating facts that he was learning: "Did you know, my dear Hannah, that kangaroos cannot walk backward?"

Five months ago, on the night of Alice's premier performance at The Elysium, Hannah had been disappointed to open Neal's letter and learn that he was not coming directly to Adelaide after all. When the HMS *Borealis* had docked in Fremantle, Neal had met acclaimed explorer Sir Reginald Oliphant, who was putting together a massive expedition from Perth to Adelaide and who had invited Neal to join him. "I am still coming to Adelaide, dear Hannah, but my journey will not be a mere two weeks by ship, but rather a slow and arduous—but exciting and thrilling!—trek across Unknown Territory."

Although they had expected to begin the trek in January, there had been one delay after another, keeping Neal in Perth. But if there was no letter waiting for Hannah today, it meant none had come during her three-week absence which could only mean that the expedition had finally launched and Neal was on his way to her.

Hannah did not like the idea that Neal would be in the middle of God-forsaken wilderness, surrounded by deadly snakes, wild dingoes, and hostile aborigines, nor did she relish the idea of hearing no word from him in a year. But Hannah had learned that dangers from native elements were part of a colonist's—and an explorer's—life in this new world, and that being separated from loved ones for long periods of time was just one more unique element of life in Australia. Men came out to the colonies to start up a business or a farm, and then they sent for their wives and children, often being reunited two or three years later. Mail took a year, with six months for a letter or parcel to travel to England, and six months for the reply.

So, which will it be? she asked herself as she neared familiar surroundings—the Basset farm on one side of the road, the Arbin chicken run on the other—a letter from Neal, or no letter?

A man on horseback appeared ahead in the lane, and as he drew near, he tipped his hat and said, "G'day, Miss Conroy."

Richard Lindsey and his wife were drovers who moved great mobs of sheep from stations in the north down to the docks and the slaughter houses. Whenever Hannah saw such men—rugged, tanned, fiercely independent— she was reminded of the outlaw Jamie O'Brien and her strange encounter with him in Lulu's garden. She wondered where he was. The wanted posters were still up, which meant he was still at large.

"Good day to you, Mr. Lindsey," Hannah called back. She had delivered Judith Lindsey's fifth baby.

Mary McKeeghan, true to her word, had spread Hannah's name around the district, and the calls had started coming in. Mostly it was to deliver babies, and while such endeavors were gratifying, Hannah continued to feel frustrated. There was so much more that she could do but wasn't being given the opportunity. In many cases, such as she had encountered in the influenza area, if a doctor wasn't available, people resorted to home remedies. When Hannah offered to help, they seemed baffled. She had gone to one house where she had heard that an entire family of twelve was down with influenza and struggling to take care of themselves. A harried neighbor had answered the door, and Hannah had handed the woman her card, offering to help. The woman had blinked at her and said, "Ain't nobody pregnant in here," and closed the door.

I am more than a midwife, Hannah wanted to say. She continued to expand her knowledge and skills. Hannah marveled at all the things she had discovered that one could do with eucalyptus: as an inhalant for chest ailments, a chest rub for the lungs, a liniment for sprains and sore muscles, and the gum could even be made into lozenges for sore throats. She was encountering illnesses and injuries never seen in England: centipede bites (treat with tobacco directly on the wound), snake bites (make cuts in the wound, suck venom out, then pack wound with potassium permanganate), and flea infestations in bedding (place a lamb in the bed before retiring, fleas will hop on).

She was just a few hundred yards from the Australia Hotel now, and every pore in her skin cried out for a bath. Hannah did not mind living in a hotel once again, as Liza Guinness's establishment was in the country and seemed more like home. However, she still wanted a place of her own and kept her eye out for properties for sale, hoping that she could save enough money at least to rent a little cottage. But every place she looked at paled in comparison to Seven Oaks.

Standing at the front desk of the Australia Hotel, Neal wrote, "My dear Hannah, I am sorry we missed. As I explained in my previous note, Sir Reginald could not find enough supplies and financial backers in Perth, and so he decided to come to Adelaide and launch an east-west expedition from here instead. I did not write to you as it was quicker to just come with Sir Reginald. My letter would have arrived the same time I did! I have spent the past three weeks gathering supplies and instruments, and hiring a wagon and an assistant, with frequent trips north to Sir Reginald's base camp. And now I must leave Adelaide today as the expedition departs in a few days and Sir Reginald will not wait for me. I expect to be back in less than a year, fate willing. Sir Reginald reckons that on good days we will make thirty miles, and on hard days maybe ten. And we'll be stopping to take photographs, explore the terrain, draw maps, and record information. Perth is thirteen-hundred miles away, we can reach it in six months, maybe less, which means I will be back before Christmas. Take care of yourself, my dear Hannah. I carry you in my heart."

As the handsome American in the white linen suit and Ecuador hat left the hotel, Liza Guinness called for her eldest daughter, Ruth, to watch the front desk, as she and Edna must hurry over to the feed store and bring Mrs. Gibney up-to-date on the latest events.

In the outer yard, Neal paused to look around, frustrated at the workings of fate that seemed determine to keep him and Hannah apart. Seeing no sign of her buggy, and deciding she must still be in Barossa Valley, he mounted his horse and took to the road southward toward Adelaide.

Hannah pulled into the side yard of the hotel, where a livery boy helped her with the rig. She was greeted in the lobby by young Ruth Guinness, who welcomed her back, giving Hannah her mail and a sealed envelope, saying, "Mum said this just came for you."

Thanking her, Hannah wearily climbed the stairs to her room, trying to decide if she should boil water for the bath first, or for tea. Setting down her carpetbag, she removed her bonnet and short cape. The she loosened her hair and shook it out, so that her black tresses fell over her shoulders and down her back. As she started to undo the buttons of her bodice, she sifted through her mail. *Two* letters from Alice. A friendly note from Ida Gilhooley, with whom Hannah had kept in touch. A notice from Mr. Krüger, the chemist in Adelaide, informing her of new inventory. And two envelopes that were Liza's own stationery.

Hannah frowned. No postmark or address on these two. Simply: *Miss Hannah Conroy.* When she realized whose handwriting it was, she tore open the second one—*"Mum said this just came for you"*—and as she read the first words, Hannah picked up her skirts and flew downstairs.

"The gentleman who left this," she said breathlessly to a startled Ruth Guinness, "where did he go?"

"I—"

Hannah turned and ran from the lobby, out the front door, where she shocked two new arrivals, flying past them, her long back hair streaming behind.

When she reached the road, she saw him up ahead, his horse going at a trot. "Neal!" she called.

He did not react.

Hannah took off at a run.

"Neal!" she cried. "Neal, *stop!*"

The chestnut mare continued its lazy trot while Hannah summoned every drop of strength from her fatigued body, shouting Neal's name, drawing the attention of men in the blacksmith hut, a pedestrian on the side of the road, walking with a sheep dog.

The distance between them was widening. And there was a bend in the road ahead. Neal would soon be around it and hidden by trees.

Hannah kept going. Stumbled. *"Neal!"*

He turned, stared for a moment, and then, wheeling his horse around, came back at a gallop, to jump down and sweep Hannah into his arms. "I thought—" she began.

His mouth was on hers as he drew her into a deep kiss. Hannah's arms went around his neck. Neal pulled her tightly to him. She held onto him with all her strength. The trees and the road vanished. They were on the *Caprica* again, falling in love, consumed with a brand new desire that was as painful as it was sweet.

Neal wanted to hold her forever and never stop. But he drew back. "Hannah, my God, Hannah."

"You're here," she said, and their lips came together again, in the middle of a dusty red-earth road, as they clung to each other in the same fierce desperation that had driven them to embrace in a storm that threatened to send them to watery graves. But this time there was no darkness, no cold ocean, just the golden Australian sunlight and their own heat.

Neal drew back again, this time taking a step away, to put Hannah at arm's length, and as he moved back, he saw that the top of her bodice was unbuttoned. He glimpsed the rise of creamy bosom and a hint of lace from her camisole—the top of her cleavage with dewy perspiration on the pale skin. He was rocked with desire. And then he saw something that made his face suddenly burn. The corner of a piece of linen with the initials NS embroidered there.

His handkerchief!

He fell back a step, stunned by the erotic power of such a discovery. She kept his handkerchief at her breast.

"I read your note," Hannah said breathlessly, pushing hair from her face, filling her eyes with the sight of him. "You're leaving *today?*"

"I have to go," he said in a thick voice, so intoxicated by the moment that he was oblivious of the livery boys standing at the side of the road gawking at the young woman with her hair shamelessly undone, the top of her bodice lying open to expose hidden treasure.

His handkerchief—

Neal still had her glove, exchanged for the handkerchief when they dropped anchor at Perth. Every time he had taken it out of his case and clasped it, as if clasping her hand, he had wondered if she held onto his handkerchief. Had he known at the time where she *kept* that little square of linen, he might have jumped ship and swum all the way to Adelaide.

They fell silent, looking into each other's eyes as the world, and reality, came back. "You really are leaving today?" she whispered again.

He saw the perspiration at her throat, on her high forehead, glittering on her upper lip and Neal thought: Sir Reginald be damned. "Maybe," he began. No. He had to go. "Hannah, I have an idea," he said suddenly, taking her by the shoulders so that the onlookers' jaws dropped. "I must go back into town and get the rest of my things. There's a wagon there that I've hired, and an assistant. But we will be coming back this way as we head north along Spencer Gulf. Come to Adelaide with me, and I will bring you back. It will give us an hour together, at least."

Hannah needed no persuasion. They hurried back to the hotel, past the boys who were disappointed that the risqué show was over. Hannah rushed upstairs to change her clothes, and Neal asked the youths to hitch a fresh horse to Miss Conroy's buggy and tether his own mare to the back of it.

While Neal paced impatiently in the lobby, with young Ruth Guinness staring dreamy-eyed at him, Liza and Edna returned, coming to a grinding halt when they saw Mr. Scott there. "We thought you had gone!"

"Oh, Mum," Ruth said giddily, "Hannah came back and they had the most *romantic* encounter in the road!"

"Ruth Ophelia Guinness, what a thing to say!" Liza cried. But her eyes sparked with interest, and her grin broadened. "How nice that you didn't miss Hannah after all, Mr. Scott."

Uncomfortable beneath the scrutiny of the three females, Neal was relieved to hear a door open and close on the floor above, and footsteps follow the upper hall, drawing near to the head of the stairs. He went to the bottom to greet her, and when he saw Hannah at the top, his heart rose in his throat.

She wore a pale pink gown with white lace cuffs and collar, a row of white buttons from throat to narrow waist. She had chosen not to wear the crinoline that gave women an unnatural bell shape, and Neal stared in awe. Although Hannah's long skirt was draped over many petticoats, the dress still gave her a more natural, womanly shape.

He recognized the exotic blue carpetbag from the *Caprica* and recalled that she said it held her most prized possessions. Had his handkerchief been moved to the bag, or was it still pressed against her breast, hidden beneath pale pink cotton, white buttons and a prim little lace collar? Desire flooded him. She was completely covered from head to foot to wrist, her hair tied up once again beneath a prim bonnet, and it was more erotic than if she stood naked at the top of the stairs.

Bidding good-bye to the ladies in the lobby, the couple departed in silence and, still not speaking, climbed into the little carriage with Neal taking the reins and spurring the horse to a trot.

Out on the country lane, the small, two-wheeled buggy with its protective leather hood and seat wide enough for only two people felt intimate. The sunlight created a somnolent heat while the hum of insects filled the air, joining the smell of the red dust and late-summer flowers. Hannah found the steady rhythmic rocking of the buggy to be arousing, especially with Neal at her side, his arm pressed against hers as he handled the reins. She couldn't speak. Her desire for him, the sweet aching that now consumed her, stopped the breath in her lungs. Neal looked so fetching in the white linen suit and white straw hat that nicely set off his new tan. She looked at the hands holding the reins, finely shaped with a dusting of brown hairs on the knuckles. *Masculine* hands.

Riding mutely at Hannah's side, Neal wanted to say something, wanted to voice the passion that gripped him, and he searched for eloquent words and poetry that would dazzle her. But he was so consumed with desire that he could barely breathe. Keeping his focus on the road ahead, the reins, the horse, he fought his impulse to stop the carriage and take Hannah into his arms and possess her completely right there and then, in the middle of trees, rolling green hills and sunshine.

Hannah finally found breath and voice. "Have you heard anything from Boston, any word about your mother?"

"Nothing so far," he said. Neal had written to his adoptive father, Josiah Scott, who had said he would make some inquiries. Neal had also sent inquiries to another lawyer, the hall of records, two newspaper archives, even a long time friend with whom he went to university—anything that would give him a lead on who had left him on Josiah Scott's doorstep. His friend had written back to say that the tear catcher bottle appeared to be a very exclusive and unique item, in that few glassmakers manufactured miniature bottles of emerald-green glass. The friend promised to keep looking.

Thinking of that now, Neal retrieved the tear catcher from his trouser pocket and held it out to Hannah, the glass flashing vivid green, the gold filigree shooting back sunlight. "I have a confession to make, Hannah. Ever since Josiah Scott sat me down years ago to tell me that I was a foundling, I had secretly clung to the belief that I wasn't rejected by my mother, that there *had* to be a reason why she gave me up. All those months at sea on the *Borealis*, with nothing but time and thoughts on my mind, I did a lot of internal examining. Changing this little vessel from an expensive perfume bottle to a tear catcher had a profound effect on me, Hannah. Thanks to you, I cannot believe now that my mother gave me up willingly."

"I'm glad," Hannah said, looking at Neal's profile. His handsome face, square and even-featured, seemed even more attractive from the side, with a straight nose over a thin-lipped mouth and firm jaw.

"I will keep writing letters home," he said, "contacting anyone I can think of who can shed light on the events of twenty-seven years ago, when Josiah Scott came home and found the cradle at his front door." And then *my dearest Hannah,* Neal added silently, *when I have the answers and know who I really am, I will ask for your hand in marriage.*

She gave the little glass bottle back to him. "What was it like on the *Borealis?*" she asked as a landscape of farm fields, pastures, and post-and-rail fences rolled by. Hannah had already read about the year-long adventure in the letters Neal had written while he was waiting for Sir Reginald to get the expedition launched, but Hannah needed his voice to fill the silence of longing and desire, to give the moment a semblance of normalcy.

"What was it like?" Neal murmured. He looked back five months to the day he disembarked from the survey vessel at Fremantle. He had hated to see it end. What an adventure! And yet, at the same time, something had happened....

Neal had looked toward the shore and to the distant horizon, and he had felt mysterious shifts and eddies within himself, as if something had been gently dislodged. Beyond the mountains lay the mysterious back country which men called the Outback. No one knew what lay out there. Maps of Australia showed coastlines in detail, with names, topographical features, and the gradual mushrooming of human settlements. But the middle was blank. It was like the blank spot inside himself, he thought. Neal had no idea where he came from, what his family name was, who his ancestors were. He felt tied to no one and to no place. Australia seemed like that to him, without identity until men uncovered its precious secrets. And when he had stepped ashore at Fremantle, he had felt the irresistible lure to be one of those men.

"We explored islands and estuaries," he said, "archipelagos and reefs. We sailed as far north as Port Hedland and as far south as Point Irwin. It was exciting but it was also frustrating being on the government ship and seeing the distant horizon, feeling something call to me, a big mystery in that vast unknown. When Sir Reginald offered me the chance to join his expedition, I jumped at it."

Neal grew animated. "It will be a scientific expedition, Hannah," he said, turning to look at her and flash a grin. "We will be measuring and quantifying, analyzing and recording everything we encounter. We will be opening up the continent for progress, for the telegraph and railway, so that someday one can travel from Sydney to Perth without taking a ship." He sighed and snapped the reins. "I would love for my adoptive father to experience this place. Josiah and I used to go hiking in the woods when I was young. He is a watercolorist. We would pack food and water, his easel and paints, and we would go trekking in the hills. Josiah would love this new country. Unfortunately, he is terrified of ships and ocean travel."

As he looked at her, Neal felt his heart do an aching tumble. And suddenly, he was wondering if it was possible for him to leave a day later. Could he travel at high speed and arrive in time for the launch of the

Barbara Wood

expedition? If I do, I can spend one more day—and one more night—with Hannah. "What about you? Tell me what you've been up to."

Hannah had written to him about her time with Dr. Davenport; her revelation in Kirkland's Emporium to go out into the countryside; meeting Mary McKeeghan; and moving into Liza Guinness's hotel. She had even told him about Alice, but not the precise circumstances of how they met. Hannah was still embarrassed about her naiveté and how her association with a bordello had almost ruined a good doctor's reputation.

Instead, she spoke of her new passion to own a place of her own. "Run a few sheep, raise medicinal herbs. A place that will still be here a hundred years from now. But it isn't turning out to be as easy as I had hoped. I am doing well as a midwife, but people hesitate to call me for any other help, even though I have assured them of my education and experience and competency. Once in a while, if the local doctor is miles away on another call, I will do in a pinch. But I am, in the end, just a midwife. But I won't give up. One way or another, I will have a place of my own."

Neal said nothing, but pondered this news with a troubled heart. How could he tell her that the restlessness that had caused him to leave Boston was continuing to grow within him? That the more mysteries he encountered, the more he needed to seek them out and solve them? His sojourn on the *Borealis* had not only *not* quenched his explorer's thirst, but had made him thirst for more. It worried him now to think that, in the seventeen months since they had said good-bye on the deck of the *Caprica*, they had both changed, their paths had continued to diverge until it suddenly frightened him now to think that, with Hannah determined to put down roots and he himself committed to further exploration, they could never hope to be together.

Unless one of them gave up his or her dream.

Neal had thought of asking Hannah to go exploring with him, to join Sir Reginald's expedition and wander the unknown heart of Australia at his side. And he suspected that Hannah wanted to ask *him* to stay with her, to buy some land, build a permanent home and become part of this new country. They could not do both.

"Tell me about the expedition," she said, seeing the sudden tension in Neal's neck and jaw, wondering what had caused it.

"We will be crossing the Nullarbor Plain," he said, "an area of flat, arid, and almost treeless country that lies to the west of Adelaide. It's very desolate, I hear. The word Nullarbor itself is Latin for 'no trees.' It's believed to have once been an enormous sea that is now dried up."

"Will the expedition be a dangerous one?" Hannah asked, not liking the sound of an enormous dried-up sea called *nullarbor*.

"It's a vital one and has to be done," Neal replied, leaving out the part about men going in and never coming out. "It isn't just an expedition of exploration, it's to survey and study the lay of the land for further expansion. Surveyors and geologists will be along, but what they need most is a good photographer. That will be me. But Sir Reginald is very experienced. He has written books about his adventures. My favorite describes a harrowing incident at the Khyber Pass. When the British invaded Afghanistan from India during the Afghan Wars, Sir Reginald was an advisor to the Army, and it was his quick thinking that saved the day. So, yes, it will be a dangerous journey, but I have every confidence in its leader."

Conversation died after that, as neither had the desire to talk when stronger passions governed them, and presently they were joining heavier traffic, and passing more buildings until they entered the city itself.

The Clifford Hotel on North Terrace, a posh street that faced the River Torrens and grassy parkland, was a three-storey building made of locally quarried bluestone and boasted twenty rooms with "dining and laundry services available." Neal guided the carriage to the rear yard, a busy enclave of stables and horses. Neal's newly hired assistant, Fintan, was there loading their wagon with supplies, Neal's instruments and photographic equipment.

When Neal introduced Hannah to Fintan, she could not help but stare. She had never seen so beautiful a youth, with large soulful eyes framed by the longest lashes she had ever seen on a male; a true cupid's mouth over a cleft chin; and inky black hair that grew out in extraordinary curls. He must melt every feminine heart he encountered, she thought. Yet when he tipped his hat and smiled, it was in a bashful way, and his cheeks flamed most endearingly. Hannah instantly liked him. She also thought it was too bad that Alice was away in Sydney. Fintan was about the same age, twenty-one she would guess, and it occurred to Hannah that they would get on famously.

"I just have to get my valise and pay my bill," Neal said as he took Hannah by the elbow and escorted her into the lobby which was small and tastefully appointed with horsehair furniture and potted plants. A fat-faced tabby cat slept in a sun-filled window.

Neal paused and looked into Hannah's eyes that made him think of morning mists. He took in the black hair that so perfectly framed her oval face, sweeping over her ears and up into a dainty bun that supported her bonnet. He wanted to sweep her into his arms and carry her upstairs, and leave Sir Reginald to fate. "I won't be a minute," he said.

"I'll wait right here," Hannah said, realizing it was a useless statement as what else could she do? But she had to say something to stop herself from blurting, "Take me upstairs."

Neal was down again in five minutes, carrying a leather valise and a handful of monetary notes which he gave to the desk clerk, with effusive thanks. They went around back where Fintan was checking the ropes on crates stenciled with warnings: DANGER! VOLATILE CHEMICALS. KEEP FROM HEAT.

Before they climbed into the buggy, Neal said impulsively, "Hannah, I want to show you something. It's a secret—not even Fintan has seen this. In fact, Sir Reginald didn't want me to have this information, but I wouldn't agree to go along unless he told me."

Her curiosity piqued, Hannah watched as Neal retrieved a map from his inside pocket and, unfolding it, said, "You've heard of Edward John Eyre?"

It was impossible to live in Adelaide for more than a few days without learning about the famous explorer who had opened up much of the unknown wilderness north of the city—and it was impossible to travel about the district without encountering streets, lakes, and mountains named Eyre.

"Eight years ago, in 1840," Neal explained, "Edward John Eyre set out from Fowler's Bay, which is here along the coast a couple hundred miles,"—he pointed to a coastal spot on the map west of Adelaide—"with a friend and three aboriginal men. When they reached Caiguna, two of the aborigines killed Eyre's friend and made off with the supplies. Eyre and the third aborigine, Wylie, continued on their journey, miraculously completing their crossing in June 1841, here, at Albany in the south, which as you can see is quite a distance from Perth.

"Sir Reginald is not going to follow Eyre's route, which tended to hug the coastline. He plans a much more ambitious one, farther north, deeper into the interior," and Neal traced a new route, from the top of Spencer Gulf, westward through big bold letters that said UNKNOWN TERRITORY, until his fingertip arrived at Perth on the west coast, thirteen hundred miles away. Hannah noticed, just eastward of Perth, a place marked *Galagandra*, circled in red. "Hannah, I am telling you this," Neal said as he folded the map and replaced it in his breast pocket, "because I want you to know where

I will be. But I ask you to tell no one else. Sir Reginald is adamant about keeping our route and destination a secret."

When he saw the worry on her face, he said gently, "Don't worry. Edward Eyre went in a party of five, ours numbers more than thirty. And Eyre made the mistake of relying on native guides, who ultimately betrayed him. We will have no native guides."

"But would they not be a help?" she asked in alarm.

"Sir Reginald has never trusted natives, ever since a nasty incident in the Sudan from which he barely escaped with his life. He believes natives have only one motive: to get the white man out of their territory."

With Fintan ahead driving the wagon, Neal and Hannah followed in the buggy. Tension grew between them. Neal's knuckles were white as he gripped the reins. Hannah clasped her gloved hands so tightly that her fingers hurt. Neal did not want to leave her. Hannah did not want him to go.

A mile from the Australia Hotel, as Fintan continued ahead in the wagon, Neal impulsively pulled the buggy off the road and, dropping the reins, swept Hannah into his arms.

They kissed without taking a breath, as if this were their last hour on earth. Neal snatched Hannah's bonnet away and drove his fingers into her hair. Hannah dug her fingers into his linen jacket. "I won't go," Neal said in a husky voice. "There will be other expeditions."

Yes! she thought deliriously. Stay with me. It will be heaven. "You have to go," Hannah said breathlessly. "You know that. It's your calling." Because if you miss this, and other expeditions do not come along, how long will it be before regret turns to resentment?

He cupped her face in his hands and looked into her mother-of-pearl eyes. "Then come with me, Hannah, on this great adventure! We are going to make historic discoveries!" But in the next instant he knew he couldn't ask her to come on a journey that was going to be fraught with danger. And it would be highly improper. If they were married …

With great reluctance, Neal took up the reins and goaded the horse into a trot, and presently the Australia Hotel came into view, where Fintan was chatting with the stable boys. As Neal helped Hannah down from the buggy, there were so many things wanted to say to her. *I will capture the wonders of Australia with my camera and lay them like treasure at your feet.*

"I can't leave you again, Hannah," he said quietly as they stood in the sunshine.

Hannah wanted him to take her into his arms once more, but they kept a respectable distance between themselves, as Liza Guinness and Edna Basset had come out to watch. "You must go, Neal, and I must stay. We are both called to things which we must do. And that is what will be your greatness. You will make wonderful discoveries. You will be in the history books."

"I didn't think it was going to be this hard."

"My father had a saying: most people are ready to carry the stool when there's a piano to be moved."

"A wise man," Neal murmured. There was so much more. He wanted to say, "I love you," he wanted to shout it, carve it in tree trunks, tell strangers on the street. But an old pain—perhaps two old pains, the first being his mother, the second Annabelle—stopped the words on his lips. Intellectually, he knew Hannah would never reject him, never hurt him. But living with the fear of it for so long had conditioned Neal to keep silent about his feelings. When I come back, he told himself, when I have proven my greatness to Hannah, as she predicts, then I will be free to shout it to the world that I am in love with Hannah Conroy.

She watched him ride off northward along the road that would take him past the farthest outlying farms and homesteads, beyond the boundaries of explored territory and into the mysterious Outback. Hannah trembled with fear and excitement. What was Neal going to find out there in the Great Unknown?

-16-

"So me and my mates are playing cards in Riordon's pub," Jamie O'Brien said as he tipped back in his chair and studied the cards in his hand. "When all of a sudden, Paddy Grady jumps up and says, 'Muldoon, yer a bloody cheater!'"

Jamie discarded a card, slipped the new one into his hand. "'Now Paddy,' says I," Jamie continued, his four companions listening. "'Faith, that's a terrible accusation. Have you any proof that Muldoon cheated?' 'I got proof,' says Paddy. 'Muldoon just discarded a three, and the hand I dealt him was a pair o' sevens, a ten, a deuce, and a queen!'"

The others laughed, but when Jamie put down his cards, fanning them out, their laughter turned to groans. O'Brien had won again. As the men threw down their cards and rose from the table, Jamie consulted his pocket watch. Five thirty. The pub would be closing in half an hour. In a few minutes there would be a rush at the bar for the "six o'clock swill."

As the others lined up for a last beer, Jamie discreetly pocketed the two cards he had had up his sleeve, just in case. Puffing on his long, thin cigar and nursing a whiskey while a fiddler played a lively Irish jig, Jamie surveyed the noisy patrons at tables and leaning on the bar. They were a familiar mob, even though he didn't know their names; he had seen their likes in every drinking establishment from Botany Bay to Fremantle. They were working-class types, the men who patronized this pub built of clapboard and spit—seamen and stevedores, dock laborers and itinerants. And except for Sal, the barmaid, there were no women.

There were no gentry either. The land surrounding Adelaide's river was mostly swamp, and so the city itself had been built six miles inland, requiring a carriage or horseback ride for anyone coming and going to Adelaide by ship. The harbor with its forest of masts and spars and rigging lay just down the road from this pub. Across the way, a modest wooden church was propped on posts over a swamp, with a sign that identified it as "St. Paul's-On-Piles."

It wasn't the worst pub Jamie had visited. He might not have seen the world, but he'd seen Australia. Ever since he escaped from a road gang four years prior, he'd been on the roam, moving from town to town, stopping at ports and settlements, finding work here and there, managing a few lucrative swindles, staying only long enough before his real name was known. He even got as far north as Port Hedland once, where he linked up with a pearling boat and lived a spell with the danger of getting eaten by sharks. Then he hitched a ride on a fishing vessel heading down to Carnarvon, working on the boat and getting paid at the end of it. From there he searched for gold in the Coonardoos, and when that didn't work, he joined a traveling circus. "Go a round with the Fighting Irishman," was the pitch outside the boxing tent. But the locals never won because Jamie was too tough and too fast for them.

As he counted his winnings, he entertained the two thoughts that had been foremost in his mind these days: buried treasure, and the pretty little midwife he'd encountered a year ago in Lulu Forchette's garden.

After that chance meeting, Jamie had left Adelaide when a swindle had gone bad and the mark had gone for the police. But now he was back and heading north into country no white man had ever seen, and the notion of finding the midwife had entered his mind.

She had not reacted when he had told her his name. Most women who had heard of Jamie couldn't resist hearing tales of his con games and how he relieved certain wealthy citizens of their money. Jamie didn't consider himself to be a real criminal. "An honest liar," was what he called himself. And he always assured the particular lady he was wooing that he lived by two strict rules: he never stole from anyone poorer than himself, and he never cheated anyone who didn't deserve it.

He thought now about the pretty midwife as she had stood in the moonlight, calm and poised as if they were at a church social. She had a forthright gaze. Honest. No guile or flirtation. No embarrassment, no apologies for being in a place where she should not have been. What would she think of his profession, the harmless swindles he pulled on self-important men who deserved to be bilked out of their money? Would she find his tales irresistible?

Jamie thought of the adventure he and his mates were about to undertake. "Plains of fire," the aborigines called it. A wilderness that was hotter than blazes where not even the blackfellah went. It would be nice to have a send-off in the company of the lady he had met in Lulu's garden. It could be interesting to have a little wager with himself, to see how long it would take for Miss Conroy to succumb to his charms.

"Hey!" came a shout from the bar. "Can't you read? The sign in the window says no dogs, women, or aborigines allowed!"

Jamie turned to see a black man, very old and dressed in rags, hovering uncertainly in the doorway. He was saying something and gesturing toward his open mouth.

"Ah, Bruce," came another voice, "the poor sod's hungry."

"I don't care! We got laws in this country. Can't give no liquor to an Abo. Go on, get out!"

The old man didn't move but held his hands out, pleading.

The one called Bruce, a dock worker with beefy shoulders and a red face, strode to the door and, towering over the white-haired black man, said, "Whatsa matter? You no speakie English?"

"Give'm food, boss," the old man said quietly.

"Give you food! Where do you think you are? Get a move on."

"Joseph plenty hungry."

"Joseph is it? So where's Mary?"

"Ah, Bruce," the fiddler called, having ceased his merry tune, "leave him alone."

"Gotta teach these people their place," Bruce said, reaching out and shoving the old man so that he stumbled and fell against the door jamb. "So whatsa matter?" Bruce continued, warming to his bullying, curling his large hands into fists.

"All right, mate, that's enough."

The big dock worker turned to see Jamie O'Brien standing there. "Stay outa this you God damn mick."

Jamie lowered his voice. "I think you oughta watch your language when there's ladies present."

"What!" barked Bruce, glancing toward the bar. "You mean Sal? Sal ain't no lady!"

In a move so quick no one saw it coming, the lean and wiry Jamie O'Brien had fat-bellied Bruce by the arm and was twisting it up against his back. Bruce gave a shout. "Yer breakin' me arm!"

"Apologize to Sal or I'll snap it right off."

"Ah," groaned the bigger man, "I'm sorry, Sal."

As Jamie pushed him out the door, sending Bruce tripping down the wooden sidewalk, Jamie called back to the pub's owner, "You oughta pay more attention to who you let into your establishment, Paddy. They'll attract flies." And everyone roared with laughter.

Jamie turned to the old aborigine who was still standing there. Joseph had cloud-white hair that made his black face seem blacker. He held his head high, and his chin jutted out beneath a long white beard. And from beneath a heavy brow ridge, deep-set brown eyes watched steadily. Jamie reckoned Joseph had been an esteemed elder in his day. "You don't want to be coming to places like this, old man," Jamie said. "It's not safe for you."

"Gottem no money, boss."

Jamie's heart went out to him. The elder had clearly been "detribalized"— he spoke pidgin English, wore cast-off clothes, and reeked of sly-grog gin. Jamie was seeing more and more like him. Lured by the white man's ways, they came to the towns where they lived in shacks on the fringes and caught white men's diseases and drank illegal liquor and eventually forgot the laws and customs of their own people.

Poor bastard, Jamie thought. He knew that when the aborigines saw the first white men come ashore sixty years ago, they thought the newcomers were spirits of dead ancestors, and so they welcomed them. When the white-skinned spirits did not understand the native language, and were ignorant of customs and culture, the aborigines thought death had wiped their memories. As the white men began to learn the aborigines' language, the natives believed the white-spirits were remembering their native tongue. It was not until too late that the natives realized these were not ancestral spirits at all but merely men.

"Go back to the mission, old man. They'll feed you there."

"Don't like mission, boss. Teach blackfellah Jesus, make him forget Dreamtime."

"Here you go, old man" Jamie said quietly, reaching into his pocket and pulling out a few shillings. "Get yourself something to eat. And go back to where you came from, if you can."

As he watched the old aborigine shamble away, Jamie recalled hearing someone say that it was being reckoned that the aborigines had been on this continent for thousands of years, possibly as many as thirty thousand. Jamie thought, fancy that. Thirty thousand years of living here, and then the white man comes, and sixty years later their way of life is all but gone.

A red-haired man came in then, short and scrawny, wearing a dusty black suit and a dusty black stovepipe hat, his freckled face bisected nearly in half by a scar left by a knife attack. "It's all set, boyo. I've found a bloke who'll outfit us and carry us up the gulf to the end."

"Change of plans, Mikey. We're going to make a stop in Adelaide."

Mike Maxberry stared at his friend and then shook his head. Judging by the cheeky grin on O'Brien's face, it must have something to do with a sheila.

-17-

Hannah had a baffling mystery on her hands.

As she threaded her way along the crowded sidewalk toward Victoria Square, she wondered how it was possible that not one of the final three formulas had turned out to be the correct one. She had been so certain that she would have the correct iodine preparation by now. Had she made a mistake along the way and now she must go over them all again? Or was it possible she did not have her father's complete notes?

Dodging carts and wagons and men on horseback, trying to keep her skirt out of the mud created by a recent autumn shower, Hannah recreated the events of that fateful night two years ago, when Luke Keen had come riding into their yard to tell them Lady Margaret was in labor. Hannah had been setting the table for supper, she recalled, and her father had been in his small laboratory, working on refining his iodine formula. They had dropped everything and had ridden off through the rain to help the baroness. What had her father done with his notes for that formula?

Hannah had been using the iodine preparation to wash her hands when she went on maternity calls—a few red drops in a basin of water—but now it was all gone, and without her rigid practice of antisepsis, there was a danger of infecting her patients. But in order to replenish her supply, Hannah needed to recreate her father's experiments until she found the right one. And so she had set up a small laboratory in her room at the Australia hotel, purchasing a few beakers, test tubes, measuring apparatus, a spirit lamp, and her father's microscope, brought from England.

When she began, shortly after Neal left for the expedition, Hannah was able to ignore many of the experimental trials because her father had noted next to the recipes: "Burns the skin," or "No effect on microbiotes." And as she knew the recipe called for iodine, she was able to set aside yet more of the formulas in the notebook. But in what quantities of iodine, and combined with what other chemicals, she did not know. And so she had worked these past four weeks, mixing and testing. And when she had reached the last of the recipes in the portfolio, she had not found the correct one.

Krüger Drugs & Chemicals Broker was located between a shop that sold canes, walking sticks, umbrellas and parasols, and a bakery that specialized in "German breads of all kinds." A small bell over the door jingled when Hannah entered.

Mr. Krüger's shop was crammed with chests of drawers and shelves stocked with bottles, pewter canisters, ointment boxes and apothecary jars—blue and white delftware labeled *sulphuric acid, spirits of lavender, castor oil*. On the long counter were a mortar and pestle with the Rx symbol of pharmacies everywhere, enormous transparent glass jars with leaches swimming in them, brass scales with weights neatly stacked, and two small statuettes of young men in ancient Christian robes: Saints Cosmas and Damien, twin brothers who were physicians and martyrs long ago.

Hans Krüger, a short round man with a shiny scalp, emerged from the rear of his shop, a smile instantly on his face when he saw Hannah.

"Ah Fraulein," he said expansively, remembering at the last minute the dinner napkin tucked under his chubby chin. As he slipped into his jacket and straightened his collar, Hannah detected the faint aroma of sausage and sauerkraut in the air.

"I have your order all ready," he said. Miss Conroy had been coming regularly into his shop to make purchases that were unusual for a lady: chlorine, lye, copper sulfate, ammonium compounds. Mr. Krüger had wondered if perhaps she was working on a new cleaning agent. Everyone was an inventor these days. Adelaide was full of people with new ideas, including a few ladies like Miss Conroy. Adelaide could be a dirty town, as trousers and skirts were the target of mud flying from horses' hooves, and ladies in particular lamented their inability to keep skirt hems clean as they were dragged across dusty streets covered in horse droppings. A good cleaning agent would make someone rich.

"Here you are," he said, and he held out the bottle containing a dark purple solid substance that would dissolve in water or alcohol. "How are the experiments going?" Such a surprise it had been, when he had politely asked during her last visit, what exactly she was working on—many people kept their projects and inventions a secret—and she had told him about a formula for medical antisepsis.

"I am having difficulty finding the right formula, Mr. Krüger. But I won't give up." Hannah spoke with a confidence that she did not feel. Having concocted and tested all of her father's iodine recipes, and having not found the right one, she faced the daunting task of doing it all again.

But she *had* to do it. In her nine months of serving the district around the Australia Hotel, Hannah had gained a reputation for being a "clean" midwife, with not a single infected case. It was the reason her practice was growing. She worried that without the iodine formula, her success rate, and her patients, might suffer.

As she slipped the bottle into her bag, she said, "Have you something for chapped hands?"

"Surely you are not testing the experimental formulas on yourself!"

"I'm afraid it's the only way I can judge that a formula is safe for a patient's skin."

He went to a cupboard and brought back a small jar. "I deal with strong chemicals, and I found that this cream helps."

Such a pretty young lady, he thought as Hannah paid for her purchase. There was a time when Mr. Krüger had wondered if he might introduce her to his son, a wine merchant just starting out and the same age as Miss Conroy. But as he had gotten to know her, Mr. Krüger had realized that, as charming as she was, and as much as he thought she might make a good daughter-in-law, the midwife from London was a little too smart and educated, and certainly too independent-minded to be happy spending the rest of her life in a kitchen.

As she left the chemist shop, Hannah looked across the busy street at the news kiosk. This was the real reason she had come into town. To see if there was news of the Oliphant Expedition.

Although Sir Reginald had tried to keep his great undertaking a secret, word had gotten out, and ambitious reporters had galloped with speed to the base camp near Iron Knob, arriving just as the great group of men, horses, and wagons was about to depart. They raced back to report to their respective newspapers, and a few of the more daring journalists hired boats to take them to Streaky Bay, where they hired fast horses, and galloped northward to catch the progress of the expedition that, according to headlines, was "DEFINITELY NOT FOLLOWING EYRE'S ROUTE."

At the newsstand, a giant map had been posted, with the expedition's movement thus far. Citizens were speculating on where Sir Reginald was headed, and wagers were being placed on the route and time of arrival. But it was a limited game as Sir Reginald's group would soon be beyond all communications and alone in the vast unknown heart of the continent.

Hannah looked for a break in the traffic before venturing across.

The newsagent's stand stood on a corner of Victoria Square, a grassy plaza dominated by a statue of the queen herself. The newsagent sold newspapers, magazines, penny gazettes and other periodicals, local and imported—*Punch*, *The Illustrated London News*, even *New York Monthly*

Magazine from America—as well as tobacco, pipes, cigarette papers, matches, confections, books and maps, candles, lanterns, and cheap tins of tea. A newly lettered sign declared in right red letters: "Direct from America. Pre-rolled cigarettes for modern ladies who wish to enjoy the pleasure formerly enjoyed only by men." To the newsagent's pleasant surprise, men were buying them, too.

Bertram Day, like most colonists, had endured a harrowing ten-month ocean voyage from his native Ireland to come to South Australia in search of a better life. He had arrived in Adelaide dirt poor and had supported himself at first by selling copies of an Adelaide newspaper on street corners. Then he had the idea to visit the docks each morning and purchase newspapers fresh off arriving ships, to turn around and sell the highly demanded *London Times* at a profit on the street. Mr. Day had then cobbled together a wooden stand in order to display his various periodicals, later adding walls and a roof, and expanding it to hold other goods to sell. He next came up with the idea of renting space on the walls of his stand, for advertising, and was clearing such a profit that Mr. Day had finally been able to afford to get married and now lived in a respectable cottage with a garden and a baby on the way. Everybody knew him and had a good word to say about him. Rumor had it that, back in England, Mr. Day had worked on a horse farm, mucking out stalls, as his father and grandfather had before him.

He was busy with customers, but he managed a smile as Hannah walked around his stand to get to the newspaper notices. She returned his smile. Mr. Day, Hannah had discovered, was a man of good humor. A sign on the wooden crossbeam above his head said, "Yesterday was the deadline for complaints." As she scanned the recently posted front pages, looking for word of Sir Reginald's progress, she was unaware of a certain ruffian watching her with a greedy eye.

His attention was upon her blue carpetbag.

It wasn't that the bag itself looked as if it were worth anything, but the way it bulged tempted the dirty-faced boy. And even though the lady herself wasn't dressed grandly, that was no indicator of anything. Folks got rich quickly in this corner of the world, and they found that those who flaunted it became targets, and so lots of rich people went out disguised. The carpetbag didn't fool him. It looked stuffed, and seemed to hang heavy on the lady's arm. He would reckon there was a wealth of treasure in it.

Hannah was both disappointed and relieved to find no news of Neal's expedition. Perhaps they had traveled too far now for reports—

She felt something bump against her and then yank her arm. "Pardon me," she said, and then she cried out as a ruffian snatched her carpetbag and headed into the park with it.

"Stop!" she cried, and started after him.

Five men went in pursuit, shouting after the boy to stop where he was, but he kept running, zig-zagging around pedestrians and horses, glancing back to send his pursuers a cheeky grin. His grin fell when he saw that one of those chasing him, a wiry fellow with quick sprint, was gaining.

And then the man grabbed the thief by the collar, yanking him off his feet, while onlookers cheered.

"Thank you," Hannah said to the stranger, her eyes on the carpetbag as he returned with the cursing lad.

The man pushed the boy toward Hannah and growled, "Apologize to the lady."

"I'm sorry," the kid grumbled, and then threw the bag at her, causing it to drop and fall open, its contents spilling out. And then the boy ran, shouting curses over his shoulder.

"I'll get this," the stranger said as he bent to help Hannah with her scattered things. But when he looked up, his eyes widened, his mouth lifting in a grin. "Faith …," he said. "It's the midwife, Hannah Conroy."

Hannah looked up, startled, and saw the familiar weathered face and craggy features, the pale blue eyes that squinted, creating creases at the corners. But she also saw now, in the sunlight, that Jamie O'Brien's nose looked as if it had been broken once, long ago. Not terribly crooked, but not arrow-straight either. She would not say it was a handsome face, yet attractive all the same, in an unconventional way. But it was the eyes that arrested her, as they seemed to watch her with a knowing look beneath the shadow of his hat brim.

As O'Brien helped gather up the medical instruments, bottles of medicines, bandages, paper and pen and ink, he thought: Hannah Conroy, the pretty little midwife he had come into town to find, and here she was!

"What's this?" he said as he picked up her stethoscope.

"It's for listening to the heart."

The smile turned cocky. "Can it tell if there is love in there?"

Hannah did not reply. She rose, straightened her skirt, and said, "Thank you again."

He said nothing as he offered a brash grin. Mr. O'Brien wore the same hat from their encounter in the garden, a wide-brimmed slouch hat made of brown felt with a black band around the crown. But this time his shirt was pale blue chambray, the sleeves rolled to the elbows, and over it, the same black waistcoat with silver buttons. At his waist, the fierce-looking knife sheathed to his belt.

He seemed in no hurry to accept her thank-you and leave. Pointing to her carpetbag, he said, "That's a lot of medical stuff for a midwife."

"My father was a doctor," she said. "These were his things. He taught me to use them." When she saw the amused glint in O'Brien's eye, she felt the need to add, "There is no reason why a woman cannot set a bone as well as any man."

The amusement faded in his eyes as his face took on another, unreadable expression. While people walked around them, ignoring the pair who blocked the path, and while Hannah examined the contents of her carpetbag, making sure everything was there and back in order, trying very had to pay no attention to the outlaw's scrutiny of her, O'Brien reconsidered his plan to persuade Miss Conroy to spend an evening with him.

Jamie O'Brien had known many women in his thirty-three years. He had loved them and left them and now could not recall a single one of their faces. But Hannah Conroy had remained clear and vivid in his mind from the night of their meeting in a rose garden. And now that she stood here in flesh and blood, on a busy street corner with May sunshine peeking through the clouds threatening to bring autumn rain, he realized that she wasn't like the others.

She held out her hand. "May I please have the stethoscope?"

"Here you are, Hannah Conroy." He handed her the instrument, and as she placed it in her carpetbag, slipping it down the side next to a set of medical scissors, she saw the corner of a piece of paper sticking up from a packet of curved suture needles. Wondering what it was, she pulled it out and found herself holding a receipt for shoe repair, from the cobbler on High Street in Bayfield. Turning it over, she received a shock.

In her father's handwriting, dated April 1846, a recipe was written:

5 g iodine
10 g potassium iodide
mix with 40 ml water and 40 ml alcohol

The final formula!

Her father must have placed it in his medical bag when Luke Keen had come to fetch them to Falconbridge Manor. Later, when Hannah had sold the cottage and packed up her things, she had rolled her father's instruments in a towel and had not seen the slip of paper among them.

"Pardon me, Mr. O'Brien, I must go. Thank you again for rescuing my bag."

Touching his finger to the wide brim of his bush hat, Jamie flashed her a grin, winked, and said, "I hope to do you another service again some day."

When she had walked away, Jamie went to the rear of the newsstand where his friend Michael Maxberry was smoking a cigarette and scanning a wall of news sheets.

"I want to know where that lady lives," he said, pointing to Hannah as she was swallowed by the crowd. Remembering that he had seen her come out of the chemist shop across the way, and thinking she might be a regular customer there, he said, "Nip across to that chemist shop, tell them your wife is in need of a midwife, someone recommended Miss Conroy, and you need to know where to find her."

"But we're about to leave town," Maxberry protested. "Gotta be well away before sundown."

"I want to know where she lives. I'll be paying her a visit when we come back rich men."

That was just like Jamie, Maxberry thought as he struck off across the street. One of these days his weakness for chasing skirt was going to get him into serious trouble.

-18-

"What the devil has gotten into those horses?" Sir Reginald Oliphant barked.

Neal looked up from his work. It was late afternoon, and the horses had been allowed to roam loose outside the camp, to graze on the local pale green saltbush. After sunset, they would be rounded up, tethered, and hobbled for the night. Neal noticed in the dying sunlight that the animals did seem jumpy.

"They're skittish about something," said Andy Mason, one of the horse wranglers. He looked up at the blue, cloudless sky and then surveyed the distant horizon, which was growing dark in the east, golden-orange in the west. Seeing nothing out of the ordinary—and a man could see for *miles* in this flat land—he rose from his chair and sauntered over the sand to take a look.

The expedition was camped two hundred thirty miles northwest of Adelaide, just beyond a God-forsaken spot Edward Eyre had named Iron Knob due to the substantial deposits of ironstone in the area—a dun-colored sandy wilderness dotted with scrub and the occasional stringy-bark tree, punctuated by queer mountain formations streaked brown and tan. Neal had examined the soil and, using a magnet, had determined that there were most likely heavy ore deposits beneath the surface. He reported this to Sir Reginald, who made a note that this might be a good place to recommend for future mining operations.

The members of the expedition sat in folding canvas chairs at tables that had been set with teapots, cups, and plates of sandwiches. Neat white tents, glowing in the declining sunshine, stood in a perfect circle around a roaring campfire over which a skinned kangaroo was being roasted. Within the tents were beds neatly made by trained attendants brought especially from England. Sir Reginald was known for exploring some of the world's most inhospitable regions, but he believed in taking British civility with him wherever he went.

As Neal watched the wrangler talk to the horses, calming them down, he wondered if he should bring his own three mares into the small roped-in compound they had erected for the animals. Turning his face to the West, he squinted over a landscape that was vast, barren, and forbidding. Was it his imagination, or had the temperature changed suddenly? And what was that muffled rumbling in the distance? A breeze had come up, causing the canvas walls of the tents to flap and make snapping sounds.

"Did you know," the leather-skinned explorer said as he poured tea into his cup, "that *sahara* is the Arabic word for desert?" Sir Reginald was in his sixties with ruddy skin, white hair and a bristly white moustache. He wore crisp white clothes and a spotless white pith helmet, and he looked to Neal more like a man watching a croquet match on a grassy lawn than one about to explore a dangerous and unknown desert.

"That would make it the Desert Desert then," Professor Williams, looking up from his journal, said.

"Indeed!" Sir Reginald went on to regale his companions with stories of his exploits up the Nile and in East Africa, the fierce savages he had battled, harems he had visited in Cairo, and hookah dens offering hasheesh. "You know, Mr. Scott, I've been to America many times. I have a fascination for your Indians. Had the good fortune to sojourn for a while among the Seminoles of New York. Amazing people."

Neal looked at him. "You mean the Seminoles of Florida, don't you?"

"Right you are, Mr. Scott, my mistake. Big place, America."

Neal returned to his work. He was examining rock samples he had collected, analyzing and cataloguing them, using a diamond to scratch each piece and then referring to a Mohs chart written in German as a guide to determine each sample's hardness: calcite—3; quartz—7. He weighed them on scales, measured them with a ruler and calipers, and then, in a notebook, drew sketches of each specimen with descriptions underneath. Neal had not yet been given the opportunity to take photographs, as Sir Reginald had kept the expedition moving. When the salty adventurer had been curt with the newspaper reporters who had followed them from Adelaide, Neal thought Sir Reginald seemed strangely determined to evade public attention. When Eyre's expedition set out eight years prior, a military band had played "God Save the Queen," and ladies with parasols had come to see them off. When Neal asked Sir Reginald about his curious desire for secrecy, Oliphant had quipped, "Publicity is vulgar."

Neal wasn't along for the fame. Whatever lay ahead, in territory never before explored by white men, he was confident he would be able to analyze and catalogue everything he found, just as he was doing with the rocks. He had brought along the very best scientific equipment: the finest binoculars of German craftsmanship, a Swiss pocket watch, a mariner's compass *and* a sextant, a barometer and instruments to calculate wind speed for weather predictions. And the tools of geology: magnifying glasses, picks, chisels, hammers, brushes, whisk broom, calipers, scales, jeweler's loupe, field notebook, bottles of acid, and water, sieves, trowels.

Neal had also brought along a portable writing kit crafted from light-weight wood that opened out into a lap desk complete with inkwell, storage for paper and envelopes, and a small built-in clock in the latest modern design. He planned to chronicle every inch of the journey, every second of every day. It was going to be the most accurately recorded wilderness expedition man had ever launched.

He thought of the expanse that lay before them, the Nullarbor Plain, which Eyre had described as "a hideous anomaly, a blot on the face of nature, the sort of place one gets into in bad dreams." But Neal was looking forward to uncovering its mysteries, and his companions seemed equally energized.

Besides Sir Reginald and himself, and Fintan Rorke, Neal's young assistant, the party was comprised of a surveyor; a cartographer; a botanist; a zoologist; three professional hunters; two cooks and stores-keepers; a wheelwright; horse wranglers; a few able-bodied men to carry firearms and keep an eye out for hostile natives; the English valets whose job it was to serve meals, make the beds, and carry out personal tasks for the men; and a military colonel whose purpose Neal surmised was to act as representative of the British Crown. There were no Frenchman, Germans, or Italians in the group as Sir Reginald did not trust foreigners.

Professor Williams, a gaunt man with an impressive gray beard splayed across his chest, was the zoologist. He had come to Australia to write a definitive text on the wildlife of the great southern continent, with chapters broken down into mammals, birds, reptiles, fish, and insects. The last chapter was reserved for aborigines, whom Williams hoped to observe in their natural habitats, recording their hunting and eating habits, mating rituals, rearing of the young, and defense of territories.

Colonel Enfield, the military representative, was in his late thirties and had hair so light blond that it was almost white, as were his brows and lashes and moustache. With his pinkish skin, the officer looked almost albino, and Neal wondered how he was going to survive beneath the desert sun. Enfield also had a habit of blinking too much, which indicated his eyesight might not be good.

Neal had not yet gotten a chance to get to know the others—John

Allen, the tracker and scout; Andy Mason, the horse wrangler; Billy Patton, the fat cook; and all the rest. And so because he was traveling with strangers, Neal had removed the emerald-glass tear catcher from its gold chain and replaced it on a sturdy leather thong so that he could wear it about his neck with the tiny bottle hidden beneath his shirt. It wasn't that he thought he was traveling with thieves, but the bottle and its gold looked a costly and tempting trinket, and he didn't want to wake up one morning to find it, and one of the other men, gone.

Neal had one other treasured memento that he kept on his person as well: Hannah's glove. Whenever he brought it out, to think of her, to keep their connection alive, it was as if he held Hannah's hand in his own.

As the wind began to pick up, requiring paperweights for the maps that had been laid out on the tables, Neal looked over at his young assistant, who was sitting in the deepening shade of a tent, whittling a piece of wood. Neal thought of Fintan Rorke as a youth, and yet, at twenty-one, Fintan was only six years younger than himself. It was the boyish looks, Neal thought, and his eager smile. When Neal had gone to a carpenter for special boxes to be made for his dangerous chemicals—transporting them over rugged terrain required extra strength and sturdiness—he had met a man with five apprentice sons, all competing to be a partner in their father's business. Fintan was in the middle, and when he heard Neal talk about the expedition, he had jumped in and asked if they could use an able carpenter along the trip. Neal had hired him, deciding that they could use someone handy at repairs, and Neal had liked the boy's initiative, speaking up instead of waiting to be asked. They had gotten along at once, as Fintan followed orders cheerily and seemed to possess the sort of sunny disposition that was going to be needed on the arduous trek.

The wind gusted, making Neal's paper flutter and sending sand flying across the ground. He called out to Fintan to see that their wagon was secure and the crates properly tied down. Every time they set up camp, Fintan always made sure the photographic chemicals were not near any heat or flame. Everyone in the party had been warned about the volatility of Neal's supplies and they avoided going near his wagon.

"Will do, Mr. Scott!" Fintan called back as he set aside the piece of wood he had been carving. "A waste of time," his father had always groused. "There's proper work to be done." Fintan was good at his carpentry craft, knew his way around saws and adzes and hammers. And he could do more than carve a bedpost, too. Fintan was good at fixing wagon wheels and axles, or cobbling together custom boxes and contraptions such as Mr. Scott the photographer needed. But that wasn't what Fintan wanted to do in life. He wanted to create *beauty* with wood and knife, because therein lay his God-given talent: the ability to take a homely little block of wood and make a rose of it, or a sleeping cat, or a butterfly.

Not that young Fintan ever expected his talent to amount to much, not when a living was to be earned and who would buy wooden knick-knacks that only gathered dust anyway? So he saved his whittling for his leisure time, and at that didn't show off his work. These rugged men of the world would no doubt have something to say about a boy who carved flowers! He didn't mind. Fintan knew he was as manly as the rest of them, and just as fond of the ladies. It was just that … he couldn't name it, could only feel a sense that there was something more to the world than money, women, and fame.

John Allen, the tracker who had come from England years ago and knew South Australia like a native, rose from his chair and stretched his lanky frame. "Let me tell you, Professor," he said to Williams, who had just made a comment about aborigines. "Three things you gotta watch out for in this country: snakes, dingoes, and abos. There's poisonous snakes all over the place here, and while dingoes look like ordinary dogs, they're as vicious and cunning as any dangerous beast found in Africa. But the biggest threat is from the abos. Don't let their sleepy looks fool you. They're sly and crafty, and they hate us. You'll feel the spear in your back before you see who threw it."

When Andy Mason, the red-haired horse wrangler, voiced the observation that this land belonged to the aborigines before the white man came, Allen retorted, "They weren't doing anything with the land. Just walked all over it. Didn't plant anything. Didn't build anything. So why should they care if we took it? You don't see them turning down our tobacco and whiskey. They don't have any culture, no writing, no alphabet. Didn't even invent the bow and arrow! Abos got no morals. Old men marry little girls eight years old. Husbands give their wives to strangers. They don't believe in God, they worship rocks and trees, they go about naked, and they're cannibals to boot."

Sudden rumbling in the distance caused everyone to turn toward the West, where the sun was almost gone. "Do you think a storm is coming?" Neal said, noticing dark clouds on the horizon that he could have sworn were not there moments ago. The weather had been peculiar all afternoon, with a strong but dry cold front crossing the area, preceded by hot, gusty northerly winds.

"Strange weather," Sir Reginald murmured. He realized that the temperature was rising, and then he saw what he thought at first were rain clouds rolling toward them from the West but then realized they were a dramatic red-brown dust cloud *rolling on the ground.* It looked like an enormous brown cliff, and it was racing straight toward them.

At *this* time of year? he thought in alarm as he shot to his feet. Oliphant knew that sandstorms typically occurred in spring. He was familiar with Sahara Desert *simooms,* and the *haboob* near Khartoum. He knew that a sandstorm moved whole sand dunes and completely change the face of the earth.

"Sandstorm!" he shouted, and began barking orders to gather the horses together, to tie down anything that was loose, to find shelter. "Turn your backs to it!" he shouted as the wind grew stronger.

"Jesus Christ," Colonel Enfield cried. "Where the hell did that cloud of dust come from?"

The red-brown wall was picking up speed, and as it grew in strength it grew in size until it was as tall as a mountain, and seemed to stretch from the southern horizon to the northern. The men fell silent as they stared in awe at the force of nature that was about to engulf them. And then they began to run.

"Scott!" Sir Reginald called out to Neal. "What the devil are you doing?" The crazy American had mounted his horse.

"We have to round up the animals!" Neal shouted, clamping his hat to his head as the wind now blew ferociously and his horse wheeled in a circle.

"You can't outrun this thing!" Sir Reginald's pith helmet flew off, and tents started to come loose from their stakes. Men ran frantically about, and horses galloped off in all directions. Within seconds, visibility plunged to a few feet. And then the sandstorm hit.

Neal covered his mouth from the choking dust and spurred his horse into a run.

"You crazy bastard!" Sir Reginald shouted after him.

But the horse was not fast enough. In minutes, Neal and his mare were swallowed up in a great, brown deadly cloud.

The hour was late. Hannah had stuffed cloth under the door in case her concoction created an odor that leaked out. She didn't want to alarm Liza

Guinness's other hotel guests. The room was cozy against the night. On the bed, her nightdress was laid out. On the table by the bed, beneath the glow of the oil lamp, Neal's photograph stood in a pewter frame. Next to it, the small ivory statuette of Hygeia.

Beyond her closed drapes, a strange wind howled in the trees. It had come up suddenly, rattling panes, sending gusts down the chimney, causing gates and doors on the outbuildings to slam open and shut. A devil wind, Hannah thought as she stood at the small work table Liza Guinness had had brought up from the kitchen and upon which Hannah had set beakers, test tubes, microscope, and spirit lamp. Listening to the wind, she thought of Neal in the wild, inhospitable wastes of Australia and was comforted by the thought that he was in the company of thirty men, with horses, rifles and pistols, and barrels of water. She prayed that he was enjoying his wonderful adventure and making important discoveries.

Addressing her task, she spooned out a measure of the solid iodine and weighed it on the small brass scales she had purchased from Mr. Krüger. She then ground it to a powder using a pestle in a mortar bowl. Hannah worked with careful movements by candlelight. "Iodine was first identified in 1811 and is extracted from seaweed," John Conroy had written. "Iodine's chemical properties are as yet unknown. The solubility of elementary iodine in water can be increased by the addition of potassium iodide. A tincture can be made, as iodine dissolves readily in alcohol."

She stirred the iodine into a liquid preparation and watched the emulsion turn dark purplish-red, a strong aroma rising up from the beaker. It smelled familiar. She cautiously dipped her finger into the solution and felt no stinging, no burning. She held it in there for several seconds, and when she brought her finger out, aside from purple discoloration, there was no ill effect on her skin.

Now came the step that would tell her if this was truly her father's perfected formula. Preparing a microscope slide with a drop of water in which she had rinsed her hands, she peered into the lens and saw the tiny creatures moving through the water. Then, using a pipette, she drew up some of the new iodine solution and placed a drop on the water.

Drawing in a breath, flexing her fingers, and sending a prayer to God, Hannah bent and looked into the microscope. She moved the candle around until sufficient light was shed on the glass slide. Then she adjusted the focus and—

The microbiotes were not moving.

The formula had killed them.

"Thank Heaven," Hannah whispered in relief. She had the formula again and could count on continuing to bring babies into the world without endangering them or their mothers with infection.

As she poured the new mixture in a small bottle, she thought of the strange workings of fate. Had she not had her bag snatched that afternoon, and had Mr. Jamie O'Brien not rescued it for her, she might never have found the note with the formula written on it.

The wind picked up outside, making shutters bang and tree limbs scrape the brick walls. Suddenly, her bedroom windows burst open, swinging inward on their creaking hinges, the curtains whipping about. Hannah rushed to close them. But as the wind stormed into her room, sending papers flying, blowing out candles, threatening to topple fragile lamps, Hannah found that the windows would not stay latched. She closed them, and the wind pushed them open again, and when Hannah felt the first cold drops of rain on her face, she knew a storm was coming.

She shut the windows once more, but as soon as she let go, they flew open. When a strong gust sent a lamp crashing to the floor—luckily it was not lit—Hannah remembered the key in the door lock. It also locked the windows. She ran to the door, seized the key, and ran back to the windows. Fighting wind, curtains, and swinging window frames, she managed to get them closed again and was able to turn the key in the latch before they blew back open.

As the wind raged outside while the windows remained shut, Hannah straightened the curtains and then stepped back to survey the damage to her room, thankful that she had remembered that the key locked both the door *and* the windows.

She froze. Feeling the cold iron key in her hand, she looked down at it, and was flung back to another windy night, two years ago. "This is the *key*, Hannah," her father had said with his dying breath as he had pressed the bottle of iodine in her hand.

Hannah gasped as the enormity of her discovery began to dawn on her. Could the iodine formula possibly be a *cure-all*? Was that what her father had been trying to say with his dying breath? Had he unwittingly opened the way for a whole new revolutionary form of medicine?

Hannah held her breath. She felt as if a doorway had suddenly opened, and on the other side lay an infinite number of possible paths. If her father had indeed invented a universal cure …

In rising excitement, Hannah had to curb her sudden eagerness to plunge ahead with new tests, new experiments. She knew that she must give this more thought, more analysis and examination, and then determine how best to proceed. She did not know where this discovery was going to take her, she knew only that she must pursue this unexpected change of events, step through that open doorway to follow those infinite paths wherever they might lead.

The sandstorm raged into the evening and most of the night, pinning Neal beneath an oilskin as he fought for breath and thought for sure he was being buried alive.

By the time the wind died down and the night was quiet again, Neal could not hear the shouts of men nearby, nor the sounds of horses. He found himself half-buried under a tarpaulin that had been carried on the storm from the camp, to slap against him like the errant sail of a ship. Neal hauled himself out of a sand dune that hadn't been there before, and staggered to his feet to look around. But all he saw was night blackness, for the stars were blotted out. He tried to call to his comrades but his throat was too parched to support a voice. Although badly shaken, Neal kept a level head. No doubt the other members of the expedition were nearby but, like him, were unable to shout. He recalled the many times his adoptive father had taken him wilderness hiking, Josiah Scott having a passion for painting watercolors of woods and waterfalls, and saying, "If we are ever separated, if you ever get lost, remember that the number one rule is to stay where you are." Neal and Sir Reginald's men would never find each other in this utter darkness, so he would stay where he was and assess the situation at daybreak. He curled back into the warm tarp and drifted into a deep sleep.

When light broke over the edge of the world, it pierced his eyes and pulled him back to consciousness. Shaking off the sand, Neal crawled out from under the oilskin and squinted with gritty eyes. The dawn sun cast golden light upon a queer landscape. Not a tree or bit of scrub remained. Reddish-orange sand drifts had been sculpted where none had been before.

Neal turned in a slow circle, not believing his eyes. Where were the horses? Where was the camp? Where were Sir Reginald and the others? He hadn't gone far on his horse when the sandstorm struck. Everyone should still be here, tents and wagons and horses.

And then he realized: they must have reconnoitered in the dark, collected everything by lantern light, and moved on. He saw not a single remnant of the impressive expedition that was to have taken him the thirteen hundred miles to Perth. Gone, too, were his scientific instruments and tools and aids, the modern technology that would have shown him the way.

And he knew why. When Sir Reginald had let slip a comment about the Seminoles of New York, and Neal had caught the error, he had seen a brief look on the older man's face that had been as good as a naked confession. Oliphant was a fraud. He had never lived with the Seminoles. Neal wondered if the old man had set foot outside England, even. It was the only explanation for why the others would pick up and sneak off under the cover of night, leaving him for dead! Reginald Oliphant was worried Neal would expose his secret.

And now Neal was alone in a vast, dry wilderness, with no sight of a single soul or beast from horizon to horizon. The sky was filled with a strange haze—sand particles high up in the atmosphere, his scientist's mind surmised—and so he could not pinpoint the sun, nor determine east, west, south or north. He had no compass or sextant, no food, and no water. And no hat to protect his head from the sun.

Finally he began to walk, stumbling along, putting one foot in front of the other, having no idea where his steps were taking him.

-19-

Although Michael Maxberry questioned his friend's judgment in sending for this sheila, Mikey did as Jamie asked. For one thing, Jamie was in a bad way, and for another, who else could he fetch? Not with Jamie O'Brien sporting a bounty on his head.

"Hannah Conroy won't turn me in to the coppers," Jamie had said through a haze of pain. "She'll make me right and none will be the wiser."

Mikey hoped so as he climbed the wooden steps of the Australia Hotel, because if she wouldn't come, or if she did run for a constable, then Jamie was a goner for sure.

Hearing the bell over the front door, Liza Guinness emerged from the back office, patting her hair to make sure it was up and tidy, and running her hands down her crinolined-skirt, likewise in attention to tidiness. You never knew who was going to come through the door, was Liza's philosophy.

Her smile broadened. The gentleman in the black jacket, black trousers, white shirt, and tall stovepipe hat was dusty and sweaty to be sure—weren't most of her patrons?—but he *was* a man and not half bad looking if you looked past the puckered scar that seemed to bisect his face. Pub brawl, Liza surmised as he approached the desk. Got the business end of a knife and lived to tell the tale. "Good morning, sir, want a room and a bath?" She turned the register around for him to sign.

"I'm looking for Hannah Conroy. I've been sent to fetch her. A mutual friend is hurt. North of here, on the road."

Her eyebrows arched. "Mutual friend?"

"Yeah, she knows him. They're good friends."

A man! And a *good* friend. "Mr. Scott?"

"Yeah, that's who. Mr. Scott."

Liza snapped her fingers to catch the attention of a maid who was watering the potted plants. "Trudie, run into the kitchen and tell Miss Conroy there's someone here to see her."

Jacko Jackson had come into the kitchen looking for gloves as his hand had gotten blistered while chopping wood. But when Ruth Guinness, who was smitten with the happy-go-lucky young man, had seen the terrible blister, she had sent for Hannah. Taking one look at the enormous, painful bubble on the heel of Jacko's palm, Hannah had insisted that it must be drained and covered.

While she worked, with Jacko sitting on a stool and Hannah in a kitchen chair, she explained to Ruth how it was done. Liza Guinness's daughter had expressed a keen interest in pursuing a career like Hannah's, saying that she fancied traveling around the district, helping people. Hannah had even taken the eighteen-year-old on some calls, an experiment that was proving beneficial to both as Hannah discovered that she enjoyed teaching, and Ruth was glad to get away from the hotel.

"To relieve blister pain," Hannah said, as Ruth watched closely, "drain the fluid while leaving the overlying skin intact. But first we will put some of this medicine on it."

"Why?" Ruth asked.

During her last trip into to town, Hannah had paid Mr. Krüger a visit and in the course of their conversation, as she had stocked up on supplies for her midwifery kit—camphor, willow bark, ammonium carbonate—she had mentioned her suspicion that the iodine formula might be a cure-all. Mr. Krüger had then shared with her a letter from his brother, a medical researcher back in Heidelberg, who had written about the recent discovery of a microscopic organism that had been named *bacterium*, after the Latin for "little staff," and the theory that bacteria might cause disease and infection. It was a radical idea embraced by few men of medicine and science, but the news thrilled Hannah because it meant that her father was right, and the more microbiotes that were discovered and identified, the closer medicine would get to conquering disease.

She voiced none of this to Ruth and Jacko, however, saying simply, "This medicine will make the blister heal faster."

Ruth had not inherited her mother's prettiness but was rather plain with a round face and short, turned-up nose. But her personality sparkled, and Hannah could tell that Jacko was flattered by the feminine attention.

She swabbed the blister with the iodine preparation and then sanitized a needle by dipping it into the iodine. "Aim near the blister's edge. Now let the fluid drain, but leave the overlying skin in place. Apply some more iodine to the blister, and we'll cover it with a bandage. In a few days, we will cut away all the dead skin and apply a fresh bandage."

"I thought you was supposed to pop a blister, peel off the skin, and leave the underneath exposed," Jacko said to Hannah, although he was smiling at Ruth.

"That is an old remedy that needs a good burial," Hannah replied as she gently cleansed the flattened blister without disturbing the collapsed film. Hannah had seen blisters get so infected that her father had had to amputate fingers and toes.

As Hannah showed Ruth how to properly bandage the hand, she thought of all the old remedies that were going to fall by the wayside as medical science made breakthroughs and advances. Before her revelation with the key, Hannah herself would not have thought to apply her father's compound to Jacko's blister. Even now, she was only guessing that the iodine would protect the hand from infection. This was an experiment. But she didn't tell Jacko or Ruth that.

On that windy night four days ago, Hannah had been excited to think that the iodine might be a cure-all. But then a new problem had settled in: how to prove it? She knew she needed to find ways to test the preparation, but how could she do it without causing harm? A blister was a far cry from conquering all the diseases that plagued humankind.

"Miss Conroy?" Trudie said from the doorway. "There's a gentleman asking for you."

She went into the lobby where Maxberry swept his stovepipe hat off his greasy hair and said, "Miss Conroy, a mutual friend is hurt and asking for you."

"Mutual friend?"

"Yeah. Mr. Scott."

Hannah gave him a skeptical look. "Mr. Scott is hundreds of miles from here."

He reddened. "Yeah, well, I figured the truth might not get you to come. It's Jamie O'Brien."

She stared at him. "Where is he?"

"Two days north of here, along the gulf. Got hurt bad. I'm to take you to him. Don't worry," Maxberry added quickly, "I brought my missus with me. Everything's proper. You won't be going off with a stranger."

"What happened?"

"He broke his leg, and it hurts like the devil."

"He needs a surgeon."

"Can't do that, miss, and I think you know why."

"Yes," she said, meeting his eyes. "I'll have the buggy hitched up."

"Carriages take too long, miss, we gotta move fast. By horseback. I got me own horse and took the liberty of hiring one for you. It ain't got no side saddle, though."

"Just let me get a few things."

Hannah hurried upstairs to fetch her carpetbag. She also picked up the leather satchel that she kept in readiness for overnight cases, as childbirth labor could sometimes last days. The satchel contained a hairbrush and comb, a bar of Pear's soap, toothpaste, rose scented cologne, handkerchiefs, wash cloth and towel, a spare candle and matches, clean stockings and fresh underdrawers. Finally, she took Neal's photograph from the nightstand and slipped it into the carpetbag.

At the last minute Hannah reached under her skirt to untie the whalebone crinoline, letting it drop to the floor. Then she collected her bonnet and cape, for the nights were growing cold, and she rushed downstairs where she found her impatient escort pacing to and fro.

Liza Guinness was at the front desk. "I don't know how long I'll be," Hannah said. "But don't worry."

Liza was used to Hannah being suddenly called away and then being gone for a spell. "Take your time, dear," she said, and punctuated it with a wink.

As Hannah and Maxberry went through the front door, Hannah looked back. "Why did she do that, I wonder?"

"I told her I was fetching you for a friend. She asked me if it was Mr. Scott, and I said yes. Well, I couldn't very well tell her the truth, could I?"

Hannah thought she should go back and set Liza straight, and then decided that it would be impossible to make Liza, with her active imagination, understand. Hannah could picture her friend, who possessed a flare for the dramatic, sending a militia after her.

Mr. Maxberry's horses were tethered to a hitching post in the yard, and Hannah received a mild shock. His "missus" was a native woman.

"Her name is Nampijinpa," Maxberry explained, "but we just call her Nan. She's a member of the Kaurna tribe, but she speaks English good. I think some missionaries got to her. She was wearing kangaroo skins when I first met up with her, but I managed to get her into a lady's dress."

Hannah could not guess Nan's age. She was very plump, with a broad grin that revealed missing teeth. Her hair was long and straight and as black as her skin. Hannah had never seen an aboriginal before, as they had all been rounded up years ago and moved to reserved lands.

Hanging her carpetbag and satchel from the pummel, Hannah accepted a lift from Maxberry with his fingers webbed, and managed as delicately as she could to get her leg over the other side of the saddle. Not since she was a girl had she ridden this way, and it felt, at first, very improper and unladylike. But then she thought of Mr. O'Brien lying in pain, and all thoughts of impropriety vanished.

-20-

"I have wonderful news for you, son," Josiah Scott said as he rested his arm on Neal's shoulders. "Your mother is here."

Neal sobbed with joy as he plodded across the limestone wasteland, nearly blind with sandy grit and brilliant sunshine. It had been four days since the sandstorm. He had lost his hat, and so he wore his white linen jacket draped over his head. He was thinking of the place on his map circled in red: Galagandra. When he had asked Sir Reginald the significance of it, Oliphant had said that some inland surveyors had reported abundant sweet water there. Neal knew the expedition was headed in that direction. If he could just get his bearings. But the map, along with absolutely every single other of his possessions—including Hannah's glove—was gone.

"You thought I was lost, didn't you, Mother?" Neal said out loud, speaking to no one but shimmering specters rising from the sand. He was aware that he was either dreaming or hallucinating, but he didn't try to shake it off because it was a pleasant fantasy, and he wondered where it would take him. Although vaguely aware that he was parched with thirst, that his lips were cracked and bleeding, and that there was nothing but scrub and sand and the occasional twisted limestone formation for as far as the eye could see, Neal was more sharply aware of his father's den back in Boston, with the law books, a world globe, an astrolabe, a bust of Aristotle.

He smiled at his adoptive father. Josiah Scott was a handsome man. Neal often wondered why he remained a bachelor. "Was it because of me, Father?" he asked the shimmering image of Josiah. "Were women not interested in marrying a man who already had a child—a bastard child at that? What a burden I must have been. But now that Mother is back, you can marry that nice widow lady who visits once a week to go over her property holdings with you."

Neal dragged the back of his hand across his blistered mouth. He squinted at a clump of mulga bushes and saw his mother standing among them. Her image wasn't as distinct as Josiah's. Her face was a blur, her gown plain and old fashioned, her hair done up in the ringlets mode of twenty-seven years ago. He was trying to reach her, but no matter how he kept his forward momentum going, she remained beyond his reach.

Neal sobbed. He was starving. He had tried to find food and water in this landscape that Edward Eyre had described as belonging in a nightmare. To no avail. A sick ache gripped his stomach. His legs screamed with pain. He had slept each night, curled in a ball, to dream of rescue and Hannah, only to waken to desolation with each dawn.

I'm going to die out here. I'm not even thirty years old. I should have asked Hannah to marry me. Why didn't I tell her I love her? She wouldn't reject me the way Annabelle did. The way my mother did. Hannah's different. The way she kissed me back, and held onto me ....

He forced himself to plod along as he kept a keen watch on the bleak terrain, looking this way and that. The sun played tricks on a man's eyes: it made the desert look as if it were dotted with silvery pools of water. The low mulga bushes stretched and widened in a bizarre optical illusion, the sunlight so distorting them at times that they resembled men.

He trudged on. An eagle soared once overhead, swooping down as if to inspect this stumbling intruder, and then it was gone, and Neal was alone again. He walked and walked, leaving his mother and adoptive father far behind. The horizon always stayed the same distance away, mocking him with shiny lakes of nonexistent water. By late afternoon he was feeling lightheaded. He tried to search for something edible, tried to find roots that contained moisture. A few witchetty grubs, perhaps. At a dried-up riverbed he dug frantically, hoping to come to water. But all was dry, bone-dust-thirsty dry.

He pushed on. His temples thrummed with pain. Even though it was May and winter was around the corner, the heat grew intense, baking down on him. He walked into the hot wind, and when the sun finally set, he welcomed it with relief. But his thirst was beyond anything he had ever known or imagined. And he was exhausted. He curled up against the slight rise of a sandy mound and, thinking of hungry dingoes and poisonous snakes, drifted off to sleep.

Neal awoke twice, startled by unidentifiable sounds. He shivered. Temperatures that made the Outback a cauldron during the day dropped to near freezing at night. He lay on his side shaking, teeth chattering, his eyes peering into the darkness as he imagined a circle of wild dogs closing in, or black men with spears.

When the sun came up, he welcomed it, and he trudged on. The pain in his head grew worse. He had stopped perspiring. His legs felt as if they were made of lead. Dehydration, he thought. Death by dehydration ...

In the late afternoon, with the coppery sun blazing in his face, as if daring the fragile human to survive yet another night, Neal suddenly heard a sound—a human sound. He stopped and listened, swaying unsteadily. He squinted through eyes so dry he could hardly blink. When he heard the sound again, he realized it was himself. He had been sobbing and didn't know it.

Neal was covered with insect bites now, and scratches from tramping through dead brush. His tongue was swollen. He throat closed up. But he kept walking. Ahead lay Sir Reginald's expedition, he was sure of it, with barrels of cool water and ointment for his sores and a pillow for his head. And once he had recovered, he was turning right back around for Adelaide and Hannah.

Neal passed the night in a sleep so deep that nothing woke him except, at last, the piercing rays of another new hot sun. At noon he fell, and it was some minutes before he could get up. He pushed on, fell again, got up and pushed on again. He grew delirious and started to laugh. He thought of his friend back home, Ernie Shalvoy, who had opened a photography studio in one of Boston's better neighborhoods. Ernie was mixing iodine with ammonia, and when he added it to the silver nitrate bath, the explosion blew the large front windows of the studio clear across Canal Street. Neal couldn't stop laughing at the thought of it.

Finally, with another coppery sun in his eyes, he slid to his knees and this time could not get up. His head was in so much pain that it felt as if it were going to explode like Ernie Shalvoy's studio. Neal toppled to the dirt and lay there, trying to think of a prayer. His pulse pounded so loudly in his ears that he did not hear whisperings nearby, and his eyes had been so nearly blinded by the sun that, just before he lost consciousness, he did not see the black shapes slowly gather around him, dark figures clutching spears, clubs, and boomerangs.

-21-

Hannah and her two companions had finally traveled beyond the farthest point she had ever journeyed from the Australia Hotel. It was new country, and exciting.

Before taking to the road, the trio had stopped at Gibney's Feed & Supplies, down the road from the Australia Hotel, and purchased flour, salt, dried strips of kangaroo meat, eggs, molasses, and whiskey. Now it was late afternoon. Adelaide, its suburbs, and farm country had fallen far behind. Spencer Gulf lay to their left, wide and peaceful with ships under sail on their way up to the isolated pastoral lands where men were growing rich on sheep. To the right lay hills and thick woods, and sometimes flatland where a courageous pioneering farmer was coaxing wheat out of the soil, and vineyards were laid out in luscious green patterns. Hannah saw more wildlife now. Instead of the occasional emu, flocks sprinted across her path, heads and necks forward on their great gray bodies, and instead of a lone kangaroo among the sheep, whole families beyond count now leapt in red-orange mobs. Overhead, the blue autumn sky was dotted with white puff-clouds, black cockatoos with brilliant pink or orange crests, wild ducks and flocks of geese, and, occasionally, a black swan with wings outspread.

Hannah thought: Neal came through here on his way to the expedition's base camp. In a year from now, when he returned, perhaps he would show her a photograph of this very view of Spencer Gulf, and Hannah would say, "I saw it with my own eyes!"

She and her traveling companions had exchanged not a single word since leaving Gibney's. Mr. Maxberry was a taciturn man who kept his eyes forward as they spurred their horses to a steady trot. Hannah wondered about the curious scar that bisected his face from forehead to chin. She was amazed he had survived the injury. Unfortunately, Mr. Maxberry could not hide his disfigurement with cosmetics and tiaras as Alice so successfully did.

Evening was coming on, and Maxberry brought his fatigued horse to a halt to announce that they would make camp for the night. While he went to collect wood and got a fire going, and Nan went down to the water's edge, carrying a long sharp stick, Hannah massaged her sore muscles and got busy mixing flour with water to be baked in the hot coals for bush-bread called damper. She was worried about Jamie O'Brien. "Broken leg, and it hurts like the devil." Extreme pain meant a serious injury. She wondered if it might be beyond her skills.

Nan came back to the camp, the hem of her wet skirt tucked into the waistband, her spear proudly bearing three large orange fish.

"Roughy," Maxberry said, taking the fish and gutting them with his knife before throwing them into a frying pan he had untied from his saddle. "They feed at night. Makes 'em easy targets for the likes of Nan. I've never been able to do it, but Nan has the skills of her people."

Hannah was curious about the aboriginal woman, and would have liked to ask questions. But she felt that might be impolite in Nan's culture, so she looked up at the stars, still finding them exotic after all this time. They were not the constellations of home. Instead of spotting the familiar Big Dipper, she saw the Southern Cross, a heavenly reminder of how far she had traveled.

Maxberry said nothing further as he cooked the orange roughy in the pan, his scarred face illuminated by the fire, while Nan tested the damper baking in the coals. While she waited to eat, Hannah brought Neal's photograph from her bag and privately looked at it by the fire and silently said to him: We are both dining beneath the stars.

They ate the fish plain, but to Hannah it was a banquet, she had been so hungry. To her surprise, however, no provision had been made for sleeping arrangements. She had to settle for curling up on the ground, bundling herself in her heavy cape. When Maxberry and Nan went to lie together on the other side of the fire, Hannah, who might have been shocked under different circumstances, thought, It's a different world.

She fell asleep with Neal in her thoughts, and awoke the next morning stiff and sore. After a breakfast of damper, molasses, and tea Hannah found a secluded spot in the shallows along the shore of Spencer Gulf where, lifting her skirts above the water, she bathed as best she could. And as she did, she saw majestic ships with billowing sails gliding along the wide, sparkling body of water.

Another day of nonstop travel followed. They kept the horses going for as long as they would hold up before camping. Finally, Hannah saw the faint outline of a mountain range off to the right. "Named for Flinders," Maxberry said as he climbed down from his horse and inspected the ground. It was noon, and Hannah was grateful for the respite. "They were supposed to be here!" Maxberry said in exasperation. "This is where I left them."

Hannah saw on the grassy ground the blackened firepit and evidence that a camp had been there. "He didn't stay and wait for us," Maxberry said. "They're moving north. Slower than us, I'd reckon, so we'll catch up."

Hannah wanted to ask why a man who was so seriously injured would dare to travel. What was so important up ahead that he had to keep moving despite a life-threatening wound? But she said nothing, knowing she would soon have her answers.

The next day, thirty miles up, they found another abandoned camp, but of more recent habitation, so that Maxberry said, "Probably tomorrow, the day after, we'll catch up with them."

It turned out to be the next day, when they reached the northernmost tip of Spence Gulf, and just a few miles beyond, in a region where no farms, no sheep stations were to be found, that they finally met up with the others.

The terrain had changed drastically. Here, Hannah realized, was the Outback. Farmland and rich pastures and verdant vineyards lay far behind as, before them, stretched the beginning of a scrubby desert, hilly in places, with clumps of gum trees here and there, and the occasional bushy mulga.

As they approached the camp of a few men and wagons and tents among stringy-bark trees on the sandy bank of a trickling creek, Hannah rode straight to a wagon that had been situated in the shade, with a group of men gathered around it. Hannah paid no attention to them as she had only Mr. O'Brien in mind. She found him among sacks of flour and potatoes and propped up against a water barrel. Jamie O'Brien was grinning at her from beneath the wide brim of his bush hat.

"Faith, I'm glad you came," he said. "I was afraid you wouldn't."

Hannah dismounted and walked stiffly to the wagon, thinking she would never get used to riding a horse the way men did. The first thing she noticed was his color: O'Brien face reminded her of ashes. Hannah noticed also that he was sweating and that he not so much grinned as grimaced in pain. Jamie's right lower leg had been splinted between two crooked branches. And it was a bad job.

Returning to her horse to fetch the blue carpetbag, Hannah came back to the wagon and said, "You should not have continued traveling, Mr. O'Brien. Nothing can be so important out here."

When he said nothing but tried to shift his weight, wincing, she said more gently, "Tell me what happened." She brought out her stethoscope and eyes widened among the onlookers—those who had never been to a doctor had no idea what they were looking at.

"We were loading water barrels," Maxberry said. He stood opposite Hannah on the other side of the wagon. "One of them slipped and landed on his leg. We splinted it. But then he insisted on riding his horse and broke the leg again."

"First of all," Hannah said, looking around at the bearded, dirty-faced men who seemed not to know what to do, "we need to remove this splint. It is useless." Whoever had done the job had not immobilized the ankle and the knee, so that O'Brien could move his broken leg freely. "We will need two straight planks. Take them from this wagon if you must. And would you please remove this splint?"

Two men stepped up and untied the rags that bound the useless splints to Jamie's lower leg.

"Remove his boot, please," Hannah said.

Maxberry glowered at her. "What for?"

"Just do it," Jamie said. He choked back the pain as Maxberry pulled the boot from his foot, and said in a tight voice, "Sorry for the socks."

His men laughed half-heartedly and watched as the lady unflinchingly pulled the grimy sock from Jamie's foot and then did a very strange thing. She removed her gloves and placed her fingertips on the curving part of the foot, halfway between the toes and the ankle. After a moment, she nodded in satisfaction and said, "You have a pulse. That is a good sign." She knew that standard practice in leg fractures was to check for a pulse at the groin as well, to be certain circulation was unimpeded, but in this case it was out of the question.

"I will manipulate the distal end and will need someone to hold his knee."

Maxberry volunteered.

"Please have the planks ready," she said to the other men, "and several rags for tying them in place." To Jamie she said, "Mr. O'Brien, I will be immobilizing your ankle and your knee with splints, which means you must keep your leg straight. Now, this might hurt a bit, but once the bone ends meet, the pain should subside."

Hannah positioned herself at the foot of the wagon, and as she pushed the pant leg up so that she could grasp the ankle, she was stunned to see thick bands of scar tissue encircling O'Brien's ankle. She realized they must have been caused by leg irons, and it was obvious his ankles had been rubbed raw many times, re-opening the wounds before they could completely heal.

And then she noticed something more alarming, something on the pant leg, midway on the shin. A bright red spot the size of a shilling.

Blood.

"Wait a moment," she said as calmly as she could to Mr. Maxberry, who had climbed into the wagon and knelt beside Jamie, ready to assist with the bone-setting.

Hannah opened her carpetbag and brought out sharp scissors with which she proceeded to cut the pant leg from the cuff to the knee.

The air was still and silent as everyone watched. Flies buzzed about, but no breeze rustled the dry leaves of the stringy-bark trees.

When the leg was exposed, Maxberry shouted, "Crikey!"

Hannah murmured, "Merciful Heaven."

And Jamie said, "What is it? Have you found gold down there?"

"Oh God," Maxberry said, "it's a bad break, boyo. Gone straight through the skin. Bone sticking out. When did that happen?"

"This morning," Jamie said. "I got down from the wagon and something didn't feel right."

"You broke your leg a *third time?*" Maxberry cried, and Hannah was shocked to see tears in the man's eyes.

She knew why. Compound fractures were always fatal. Any doctor would tell Mr. O'Brien that the only treatment at this point was amputation.

"Can you do it?" Maxberry asked Hannah.

"I have neither the tools nor the skill, Mr. Maxberry. You must take your friend back to Adelaide."

"No turning back," Jamie said. "Besides, what's losing a leg? I've still got another. Can you do it, Miss Conroy?" Blue eyes looked at her with frank honesty.

Hannah had assisted her father in an amputation when a Bayfield farmer had broken his tibia, and she tried now to recall exactly what he had done. "Compound fractures, where the bone protrudes through the skin," John Conroy had explained, "always results in gangrene and an infection so severe that it invades the entire body and kills the sufferer. The only prevention is to amputate at the knee and cauterize the wound with a firebrand so that the infection does not spread."

As his voice sounded softly in her ear, and O'Brien's men looked sad and lost—as a flock of ravens suddenly and noisily invaded a nearby gum tree—Hannah's focus moved away from amputation and fixed upon her father's words as she listened to them now with a fresh understanding.

At the time, it had not occurred to her to ask why infection could be prevented in the wound from an amputation but not the wound of a compound facture. But now that the question presented itself, she wondered, What is the difference?

Hannah had gone so silent that Maxberry gave her a sour look and said, "You ain't gonna faint on us, are you?"

She looked at him, an ugly man to be sure, but she saw pain and fear in his eyes as he knelt at his friend's side.

Hannah brought her eyes back to Jamie O'Brien, who was watching her with a devil-may-care smile on his lips. "No worries, Miss Conroy," he quipped. "This won't change my plans one bit. I reckon a man with one leg can be just as rich as a man with two. Besides, I was getting tired of putting boots on that foot."

Hannah studied the bloody wound, with broken bone ends glistening in the sun. Already, flies were buzzing about it. As she shooed them away and felt the weight of the sky upon her, the weight of the emotions of these men, as she studied the terrible situation and tried to think of what her father would do, or Dr. Applewhite, or Dr. Davenport—amputate, certainly—Hannah thought of the iodine compound in her bag.

Retrieving the small bottle of purple fluid, she felt her heart race. The formula had only been tested on normal skin, never in a raw wound (Jacko Jackson's blister hardly counted). It was a *hand-washing* solution. Her father had never mentioned applying it directly to torn flesh, or exposed bone! Mightn't this tincture also poison Jamie O'Brien's blood and kill him as surely as infection would?

Her fingers tightened around the bottle. What right had she to experiment on this man?

"Mr. Maxberry," she said. "Will you please change places with me?"

Maxberry jumped down and helped Hannah up into the wagon where she knelt next to Jamie O'Brien. As she started to uncork the bottle, Maxberry said, "What're you doing?"

"It's medicine," she said, suspecting he would not understand about microbiotes and antisepsis.

"You ain't making Jamie drink that."

"It's not to drink, it's for the wound."

"Let her do it, Mikey," Jamie gasped. "I trust her." He was having trouble breathing, Hannah noticed.

Hannah soaked her handkerchief with some of the tincture and then cautiously dabbed it on the bloody wound, washing it as well as she could. Instructing Mr. Maxberry to hold the ankle in mild traction, Hannah delicately manipulated the broken bone ends until they were realigned and back under the skin. With Michael Maxberry's eye upon her, and the wide eyes of the onlookers, Hannah stitched the wound with silk suture and a curved needle. The closure was neat and tidy, but the bandage proved a problem. Medical theory held that wounds were dirty, and so it didn't matter what one bandaged them with and that using anything other than dirty rags was a waste of good clean cloth. But, in keeping with her father's theory, Hannah decided to go against popular belief, and so she cut strips from her own petticoat and bandaged the wound with them, leaving her iodine-soaked handkerchief underneath.

The men strapped the boards to Jamie's leg and tied them securely, this time immobilizing ankle and knee. Hannah checked the pulse in his foot, and although fast and thready, it was there.

She looked at O'Brien. He had passed out.

"I'll take you back to the Australia Hotel now," Maxberry said.

Hannah looked toward the south, where unseen green fields and civilization beckoned. She scanned this forbidding wilderness that was a wasteland with a few trees and some scrub, hilly and full of flies. She espied a low range of hills to the west which, recalling Neal's expedition map, she knew were named the Baxter Range, and it lay north of a place Edward Eyre had named Iron Knob. Hannah thought of Neal, long gone with Sir Reginald's expedition, making wondrous discoveries and photographing them. Finally, looking at the injured leg she had just subjected to a highly experimental medicine, and knowing she had a responsibility to this man and to the outcome of her test, she said, "I will stay. I want to make sure Mr. O'Brien is all right."

"Suit yerself," Maxberry said, and then he addressed the others. "All right, you lot. We'll stay here the night and get a move on in the morning."

As they headed back to the camp, Hannah said to Maxberry, "You can't move Mr. O'Brien! He has to remain immobile for at least two weeks."

"Sorry, lady, but we have to keep a move on. Jamie himself'd be the first to say so. We've a long way to go yet."

For the first time, Hannah noticed the other wagons heaped with supplies, the horses and firearms. She estimated there were twelve, thirteen men, as well as Nan. "Where are we going?" Hannah asked.

Maxberry gestured in the direction of the northwest. "But," Hannah said in disbelief, "there is nothing out there."

He laughed and sauntered to the campfire where a billy can boiled over the flames.

Hannah turned her face into the wind, in the direction Mr. Maxberry had pointed. Northwest. Not the route Neal was taking, who was traveling west with Sir Reginald. They, at least, were holding to a parallel route to the coastline, should they need to resort to a ship in an emergency. Mike Maxberry had pointed to an unknown expanse that not even so seasoned an explorer as Sir Reginald Oliphant would dare to attempt.

What on earth could be out there that was worth risking Mr. O'Brien's life, *all* their lives?

-22-

Neal Scott awoke to a night of terror.

He was brought out of a black void by the chanting of voices, and as he slowly regained consciousness, the voices grew louder, and then his other senses woke up. There was a pungent aroma in the air, familiar and yet unidentifiable. And he was hot—very hot. But it was a moist heat, as if he were enveloped in steam. A foul taste filled his mouth, and his head throbbed. And the singing—it grew louder until he was finally able to open his eyes and see where it was coming from.

He stared in horror.

Black devils, their naked bodies painted with white stripes, were dancing crazily around a blazing fire. Others sat in a circle, hitting sticks together in a frenzied rhythm.

Neal realized in shock that he, too, was naked. And he was tied down. His back prickled. He lay on something strange—made of sticks, and he was hot and damp.

And then he realized: he lay over a pit.

Dear God, they are going to eat me!

Neal struggled against his bonds, but he was too weak. All he could do was lie helplessly in his restraints, like a sacrificial beast, and watch his captors perform a savage dance while Neal Scott, late of Boston, slowly cooked …

Blackness swallowed him as he sank back into the merciful void. And then he felt pain in the eyes. Sharp, like knives. And his mouth—so dry! The singing had stopped. Was this the moment they started carving him up? Weren't they going to wait until he was dead?

Wait! I am still alive!

Neal opened his eyes to bright, stabbing sunlight. He squinted until his sight adjusted to the daylight, and the sharp pain went away. He blinked up at a face looking down at him.

"How do you do, sir?"

Neal frowned in confusion. He was no longer tied over the roasting pit but lying on the ground under a shelter of branches. And beneath his bare skin he felt soft fur. He stared up at the face. She was smiling. "Jallara," she said, tapping her chest. "I, Jallara. How do you do, sir?"

Neal could only stare. Jallara was the most exotic girl he had ever seen. Although she was clearly aboriginal, her unusual features bespoke a mixed ancestry. Back in America, Neal had encountered people who were half African and white, and half Indian and white, but this girl was like none of those. She stood over him and she seemed tall, with long limbs. Her face was round with dimpled cheeks, thick black eyebrows above large black eyes, a soft nose and a sensuous mouth. Not exactly beautiful, but intriguing. Her skin was a dusky brown, her hair silky-long and black. She wore a strange costume, Neal noticed—a grass skirt that ended at her knees, and a loose covering above the waist that eluded identification. Was it a woven mesh tunic of some sort? A loose bodice, perhaps, made of the fibers of a white plant? Neal tried to get his eyes into focus when it struck him that it was no garment at all, but body paint, applied in lines and dots and swirls and with such density that it appeared to be a garment.

The girl was bare-breasted, and it so shocked him that a startled sound escaped his throat.

"Sick?" Jallara said in concern, dropping to her knees. "Pain?"

She smelled of animal fat, and her sudden closeness stopped the breath in his lungs. Jallara could be no older than seventeen. Her skin appeared to be smooth and supple, her eyes sparkled with dark lights, and when she smiled, twin dimples framed her lips so perfectly—

Neal turned his head, startled by his thoughts and his physical reaction to her presence.

He was further shocked when she slipped an arm under his neck and brought a possum-skin bag to his mouth. At the feel of the few drops of water, Neal immediately drank. At first he was aware only of the blessed water, cool and sweet, filling his mouth and running smoothly down his parched throat. And then he was aware of two bare breasts, firm and creamy brown, near his face.

His thirst slaked, Neal said, "Thank you," and then said, "You speak English."

Jallara's smile broadened to reveal strong white teeth. "How do you do, sir?"

Neal returned the smile. "*Limited* English, I see." As his head began to clear and he detected the delicious aroma of meat being cooked, as he stirred his limbs and found that he could prop himself up on an elbow, he shook his head to clear it, becoming aware that he was under a shelter that was part of a camp. He saw men, women, and children. He looked around the lively encampment of thirty or more aborigines—a makeshift settlement of lean-tos and shelters and campfires beside a water hole. The clan ranged in age from babes in arms to old gray beards, with the men engaged in making and repairing weapons, while the women nursed babies, crafted baskets and nets from string and fiber, and the children played with dingo puppies. Neal saw the leafy gum trees that stood at the water's edge—he knew they were ghost gums by the white trunks and peeling bark—with galahs and cockatoos in the branches, and on the ground, wildflowers and patches of grass. A veritable Garden of Eden in the midst of a barren wasteland.

"Where am I?" he asked.

Jallara frowned, as if struggling to recall words long-forgotten. Taking in the facial features that indicated possible white ancestry, Neal wondered if the girl had spent time at a Christian mission school, or possibly had lived on a cattle station. Finally she said, "You here, Thulan."

"Thulan? That's the name of this place?" Neal swept his gaze over the dusty boulders rising from the red sand, the few struggling gum trees beside the water hole, and beyond, vast desert as far as the eye could see.

She shook her head and tapped his chest. "You Thulan."

He frowned. "Why do you call me Thulan?"

"Thulan take us to you."

"What do you mean?"

She thought hard, searching for long-lost words. Then she said, "We hunt. We follow Thulan. He find you ... asleep ... eyes closed."

"Yes, I was unconscious."

"Thulan your spirit-guide. Maybe you walkabout. You Thulan Dreaming? He protect you."

"Neal Scott is my name," he said, tapping his chest. "I am Neal Scott."

She struggled with the words, but her native language did not seem to possess the letter *S*, and when it came out Neel-ah-kaht and seemed a struggle for her, Neal said, "Never mind, Thulan it will be," wondering what a *thulan* was, secretly hoping it wasn't something embarrassing or comical.

"We think you dead," she said. "Gum tree spirit save you."

"Gum tree?" And then he remembered the pit and the elusive smell. He realized now it had been the scent of eucalyptus leaves. The Aborigines had not been cooking him but treating him with the same sort of healing steam with which Josiah Scott had treated Neal's boyhood colds, using camphor and pennyroyal.

He rubbed his jaw and felt a young beard there. And then, remembering the rest of himself, quickly looked down and was relieved to see a gray kangaroo skin covering his loins. Perhaps it had been done because these people knew of white man's physical modesty—because the men in the camp, as far as Neal could see, did not cover their private parts—or maybe the kangaroo pelt was another stage of the cure.

"Where are my clothes?" he asked, and when Jallara did not seem to understand, he pantomimed until she nodded in understanding. Pointing to a large campfire, she pinched her nose and made a distasteful face.

Neal's eyebrows arched. "You burned them because they *smelled?*"

She nodded with a smile.

He looked down at his feet and saw in relief that he still wore shoes. Neal knew that his tender white man's feet were no match for this harsh terrain.

He sank back. "Thank you for saving my life, Jallara ... I don't know what happened to me ..." He rubbed his eyes. What *had* happened to him? His memory was foggy. There had been a sandstorm. And then he had wandered for days. Terrible thirst and hunger. But what was I doing out in the middle of nowhere?

He closed his eyes and tested his memory. "My name is Neal Scott," he murmured, "adopted son of Boston lawyer, Josiah Scott. My mother—or someone in her family, an angry patriarch most likely—left me on Josiah Scott's doorstep. I have a university degree in geology. I am a scientist and photographer. I am madly in love with a midwife named Hannah Conroy. I came to Australia to make discoveries and solve mysteries. I was part of an expedition ..."

Here, his memory grew hazy. He remembered faces of men around a campfire, one in particular, an older man, ruddy-faced and white-haired in a white pith helmet—

Sir Reginald Oliphant, famed explorer!

Neal breathed a sigh of relief. He had not lost his memory. He was just a bit foggy on the details. Dehydration affected the mind, he knew. Neal suspected that, in time, it would all would return.

And then he thought of Hannah. Saying good-bye at the Australia Hotel. The feel of her lips on his, her supple body in his arms ...

Exhaustion overcame him, and he drifted off into deep sleep. The next time he awoke it was late afternoon. Jallara was not there, but three fierce looking men gazed down at him from beneath heavy brows. They were black with wiry limbs and sinewy torsos, and yet they were old men, with white hair and long white beards. Their bodies were painted in white stripes, they carried spears and looked as if they had just materialized from an era long past. Their physical fitness impressed him.

Before Neal could speak, Jallara was there, kneeling next to him with the possum-skin water bag, and seedcakes formed into dark, round balls.

The three men squatted while Neal ate, and despite their ferocious appearance, they were friendly and smiled as they questioned him with Jallara translating. Neal had questions of his own. How long had he been with them, and where had they brought him? The answer, as nearly as he could figure, was days, and they were far from the place where they had found him.

The seedcakes were surprisingly delicious, but he could not eat much yet as his stomach had gone for too long without food. Neal was amazed at how weak he felt. Thanking Jallara for the meal, he sank back and looked up at her. "Where did you learn to speak English?"

She smiled. "Yes. English."

"Where? At a mission?"

She seemed not to understand. He thought a moment, then said, "Jesus," as that was the first word missionaries generally taught the natives. But she did not seem to understand that either. Then where had she picked up her English and her non-aboriginal blood?

The oldest of the three men who continued to sit with Neal—a black man with snow-white hair and beard, wearing animal teeth necklaces and a sliver of wood piercing his nasal septum—said something to Jallara, and she pointed to Neal's chest and said, "Thumimburee ask, what is?"

He looked down in surprise. It was still there! The emerald-glass tear catcher that he had disguised in a leather pouch and hid beneath his shirt in case it caught the interest of someone in the expedition. The aborigines hadn't removed it. And then he realized they must have thought it was personal magic, since they too wore necklaces bearing amulets with what he surmised were spiritual and mystical powers.

He managed to convey that it was a receptacle containing his mother's tears and the man named Thumimburee, through Jallara, said solemnly, "Very strong magic, Thulan."

That night the clan held a corroboree to celebrate the recovery of the white man they had found near death. The men and youths were adorned in feathers and bone, shells and animal teeth, their lithe bodies decorated with white paint, and they danced around a sturdy fire while the women and children clacked sticks together in rhythm.

They roasted a kangaroo and produced honey on the comb with wild fruit, all shared out, Neal observed from his twig shelter, in a complex system of priorities and taboos. There was no grabbing for food or fighting over it; portions were distributed according to a strict protocol that Neal had heard about during his time on the survey vessel out of Perth: the man who killed the kangaroo first gave servings to his own and his wife's parents, to his brothers, and to the men who had hunted with him. They in turn shared with their families, or with men to whom they owed a debt, sometimes leaving nothing for themselves. Neal knew that the boy who had caught a goanna could not eat it himself but had to give it to his parents, and a girl could only receive food from a man related to her by close kinship.

Jallara herself brought food to Neal, offering shyly the succulent slices of meat, bits of comb dripping with honey, and fat witchetty grubs roasted in the embers. He was ravenous and ate with such gusto that people stared, until he realized he was being rude, and slowed himself down. The only fluid the clan drank was water, but after his days of thirst, to Neal it was like the finest wine.

Every time he glanced Jallara's way, he found her watching him through the smoke and the sparks, her large, deep-set eyes fixed on him, and each time he felt a strange and shocking stirring deep within himself. He was intensely curious about her, drawn to her in an inexplicable way. Perhaps it was simply that she spoke English, making him feel at ease and less a stranger among these strange people. Or perhaps it was something deeper that he was not yet mentally fit to fathom.

He slept uneasily that night, waking up from nightmares in which he was lost in the wilderness. He lay in a sweat, staring up at the stars that peeked between dried brush and twigs, wondering where he was, to what place Jallara's people had carried him while he was unconscious. What had happened to Sir Reginald and the other members of the expedition? Were they dead? Neal thought of young Fintan Rorke, who whittled flowers out of wood, and prayed that they had survived. If they had, then surely Sir Reginald and his men were searching for him. Or had they given up the search by now and resumed their westward trek?

Or were they lost and wandering in this God-forsaken wilderness as he had been, but hadn't the luck to be found by aborigines?

The next morning the clan woke up to industriousness, with the men going off to hunt while the women foraged near the water hole. By afternoon they were back, the men with a kill, the women with grubs, roots, and the occasional lizard. They slept through the hottest part of the day, and then took up their never ending tasks of whittling spears, carving boomerangs, making stringy baskets, all the time laughing, singing, talking.

With the help of two boys, Neal was able to stand and shuffle to a place behind boulders to answer the call of nature. Now he had a better view of the terrain that surrounded this oasis, and all he saw was red sand, low lying orange hills, and spinifex—tall clumps of hummock-grass resembling giant startled porcupines.

He got a better look, too, at his exotic hosts. Although Neal had observed aborigines during his short time in Australia, he had never been in such close proximity to them. He had heard them referred to as "blacks," "savages," "natives," but Neal's scientist's mind looked at them in a different way. It occurred to him that the Australian Aborigines resembled no other people on earth. They were unlike black Africans, and certainly did not resemble the Polynesians, their closest geographical neighbors. The nearest that Neal had come to seeing someone with the same features was a guru from India, a turbaned mystic he had met in a Boston drawing room, a man whose heavy brow, wide nose, deep-set eyes, flowing hair and prodigious beard were similar to those he saw in this camp.

A memory suddenly came to him, long forgotten: Eight-year-old Neal exploring the world globe in Josiah Scott's study, looking at the continents and thinking how they resembled puzzle pieces. The eastern shore of South America looked as if it could fit neatly against the western shore of Africa, and the southern shore of Australia could fit neatly against Antarctica. When Neal later attended university and studied geology, he heard an intriguing new theory about continental drift. The theory was that, millions of years ago, only two huge land masses covered the earth before breaking up and drifting apart to form the continents that existed today.

Was this why Jallara's clan, with their hair that was wavy instead of tightly coiled or "frizzy," made him think of the Indian guru he had once met? Was it possible that somehow, long ago, a migration from the subcontinent of India led Jallara's distant ancestors to Australia?

As Neal watched Jallara's clan at their evening activities, other issues crowded into his mind. He thought of Hannah. Had she perhaps heard about the sandstorm? Did she think him dead? And what *did* happen after the sandstorm hit? As Neal searched his foggy memory, trying to find answers, he began to realize that something was bothering him, but he could not put a name to it.

Something vitally important. But what?

As he wrestled with his uncooperative memory, Neal watched the men groom one another around the campfire, using sharp stones to trim their hair. While the women and girls allowed their hair to grow below the shoulders, the men kept their curly hair cropped in a cloud around their heads. They also spent hours painting themselves, taking great care with the dots and lines that they applied in white pigment to their own and others' bodies.

Another night of fitful sleep as the importance of the elusive memory grew in Neal's mind. He was certain now that there was something very important he was supposed to remember. But what? Lying awake in the night, while his rescuers slept and snored, Neal kept going back to the days before the sandstorm, to see what it was he was supposed to remember. Had he promised to do something? Had he a specific task to carry out? Was he carrying a message to someone? If only he could remember!

He finally drifted off, only to awake suddenly and feel something warm and soft at his side. With a start, he sat up and saw Jallara lying there, fast asleep beneath his fur blanket. Neal was so shocked he couldn't speak. She lay on her side, facing away from him, her eyes closed, her shoulder rising and falling in gentle respiration. Neal scanned the camp. Everyone slept, including the dingoes. But what was going to happen come dawn? When daybreak shed light on him and this girl, was Thumimburee going to vent his fury? For surely some sort of taboo had been breached.

He looked at her more closely. Jallara slept with her hands folded beneath her head. In the moonlight, he saw that her face and torso paint was not smudged. Lifting the blanket, he saw with relief that her grass skirt was in place. In fact, nothing about her looked out of place, nothing untoward had happened while he slept, and it occurred to him that she had merely crawled in to keep him warm, for the night was bitterly cold, or perhaps she had heard him cry out in nightmares and came to bring him solace.

Strangely, she had that very effect on him because, as he lay back down, Neal felt comforted by her warm presence. It took him a while to cast off the disquieting after-effects of a bad dream, but he eventually drifted into dreamless slumber.

When he awoke, Jallara was offering him a possum-skin of water and warm seedcakes. As he looked into her black eyes and recalled how she had felt next to him during the night, Neal was suddenly gripped with the desire to repay these people for saving his life. While he was still unclear on the details of the sandstorm and its aftermath, he did know that if it weren't for Jallara and her family, he would be dead.

The solution came to him as he hobbled around the camp on weak legs, and paused at one point to support himself against a grass shelter. And the whole thing came tumbling down. An embarrassed Neal apologized profusely as two men helped him up, but they only laughed. The hut was reconstructed within minutes, and Neal realized he had found a way to repay Jallara and her people for saving his life.

This primitive clan that wore no clothes, owned no possessions, had no concept of money or wealth, did not read or write, hunted with sticks and lived in shelters that easily collapsed, were like Adam and Eve before the temptation in the Garden. Neal looked at their flimsy shelters and wondered why they didn't construct sturdier ones. And then he thought: They don't know how. As they didn't have hammers and nails, chisels and saws, it was no wonder. And why had they never invented the bow and arrow? Neal decided that he would show them. It would vastly improve their hunting, and with their hunting improved, their lifestyle would therefore improve. Neal would show them how to build stronger shelters and also how to plant seeds so that they could control their own crops all year round, instead of relying on scavenging.

Pleased with himself, he began his search for materials from which he could fashion a bow and arrow. And when his strength was restored, he would ask Jallara for her people's help in finding what was left of Sir Reginald and the expedition.

But how soon would that be? He was eager to get to work searching for survivors. Neal could walk on his own now; however, it was with a slow and limping gait, and he had to take care not to exert himself. His only clothing was the kangaroo pelt around his waist—and his shoes, thank goodness—and so he had to take care of his pale skin beneath the sun. He knew, therefore, that he was a long way from making an arduous trek across this wasteland. With that in mind, that he must build himself up, Neal made sure to eat every mouthful of food offered to him, and found that, after a while, he was acquiring a taste for it.

Jallara and the other females spent their day digging up thick, tuberous roots that grew around the water hole, which they called a *billabong*. When pounded into a mash, the tubers made a starchy food that tasted faintly like bitter potatoes. Saltbush, a green shrub that grew as a bush or a tree, and so-called because it could grow in saline conditions, produced tiny red flattened fruits that could be shaken off the bush and eaten. Spinifex grass produced seeds that were collected and ground to make seedcakes. The women of the clan made bread from scavenged grains, roots, and legumes.

And the flavor of witchetty grubs, once Neal got past the idea of what they were, was almond-like.

The men of the clan left each morning to hunt and returned each afternoon with birds and small game brought down by boomerangs and spears. When Neal noticed that they did not skin game first before cooking it, which a white man would have done, but rather roasted an animal in its hide, Neal asked Jallara if it was because of yet another sacred rule or taboo, and she replied with a grin, "Keep skin, keep good juice and fat."

To make the bow and arrow, he gathered reeds that grew along the billabong. The tall bamboo-like stems were highly prized for spears, and were also cut into short lengths to make necklaces, or to stick through the septum of the nose as an ornament. The leaves were used to make bags and baskets. And now they would be put to yet another use as Neal incorporated them into a newer sophisticated hunting weapon that he knew Thumimburee and the other men would welcome with gratitude.

As Neal searched the gum trees for young limbs that would make a good bow, he watched Jallara with the other girls and young women and wondered about her. What was her parentage? One of her parents was not an aborigine. Which one? And did she know both her parents, or was her story similar to his own, that she had no idea where she came from? Was she orphaned and perhaps left as a foundling like himself?

As she walked with him, Jallara asked, "You far from home, Thulan?" Her bare breasts continued to unsettle him. He tried to keep his eyes on the distant landscape of sand dunes, hills, and spinifex clumps. How to explain that he came from a culture that considered the sight of a lady's *ankle* shocking?

"Yes, I am far from home."

"You have wife?"

He thought of Hannah. "No, I do not have a wife."

"You far from your Dreaming, Thulan. Far from your spirit-powers. Who take care of the sacred places? Who dance for the spirit-powers to bring rain and possum and honey?"

"My father is taking care of things," he said.

She nodded in understanding as she dug into the earth and pulled out a fat, moist tuber. "When you leave?"

"When I have my strength back."

"No, Thulan. Whitefellah. When whitefellah leave?"

He stared at her. Was she serious? "You want to know when the white men are going to leave? *All* white men?"

She smiled and nodded. "Been here plenty long time now. Go home soon, yes?"

My God, he thought. You think all those white people filling up the towns and cities, spreading out with their farms and sheep stations and vineyards, their factories and mining operations—you think they are just *visiting?* "I do not know, Jallara," he said, suddenly filled with sadness.

The next morning, Neal awoke to discover an embarrassing infestation of fleas in his kangaroo skin loincloth, biting him and giving him misery. Jallara gestured to him to give her the fur. He had expected her to laugh, but she didn't and gave him a curious belt to wear temporarily, going around his waist with a large clump of dried grass to cover his manhood. He watched in perplexity as she draped the kangaroo pelt over a very busy anthill. Jallara smiled and said, "We wait."

By afternoon, Neal was astounded to find that the ants had swarmed the pelt and devoured all the fleas. Jallara brushed the ants off, gave the pelt a few firm shakes, and handed it back.

Neal had made the acquaintance of more clan members now. Allunga, a small nut-brown woman with a head of white hair whom Neal deduced was Jallara's grandmother. Burnu, a smiling youth of around eighteen who was forever staring at Neal, curious about the white stranger in their midst. Daku, Burnu's brother, and Jiwarli, their father who had a withered leg and walked with the aid of a forked stick. Their sister, Kiah, was a shy, giggly girl who seemed to be Jallara's best friend. And Yukulta, a young mother who was the clan's keeper of the dingoes. She suckled the puppies at her own breast, and slept with the dogs at night.

With each new dawn, Neal woke with two thoughts dominating his mind: the elusive memory that seemed very important, and Hannah. "I should have stayed in Adelaide," he murmured into the wind as he searched the gum trees for a sapling. "I should have stayed with Hannah. There will always be expeditions, but there is only one Hannah. If I had stayed with her, kept her close, married her, settled down with her—if I had stayed with Hannah I would not have been caught in a lethal sandstorm and then—"

He frowned. He was standing beneath a ghost gum, speckled sunlight dusting his sunburned shoulders. The girls and women were spread out on the plain, poking away with their digging sticks, rooting in spinifex clumps, chasing down rodents and lizards for dinner.

Neal repeated: "I would not have been caught in a lethal sandstorm and then.... My God," he whispered into the dry wind that never stopped blowing. "My God."

The elusive memory had come back.

Neal reached for the white-trunked tree to steady himself. The wilderness seemed to expand and contract before his eyes. The drone of flies grew louder. The sun sent piercing light through the overhead branches. Neal held his breath as the full force of the memory—and its meaning—washed over him.

I was caught in a lethal sandstorm and was left for dead.

All fog and haze vanished in an instant, and his mind snapped back into full recollection and crystal clarity. He remembered it all now: calling out in the night but finding no voice, deciding to stay beneath the protective tarpaulin to wait until dawn before searching for the others, waking at daybreak to find that they had moved on. They had not searched for him. He knew this because he had not gotten far when the sand cloud hit. The men would have all scattered but would have been in visual and shouting range afterward. Yet, when the dust settled and the sun came up, there had not been a scrap of tent, not a campfire ember left.

Sir Reginald had purposely abandoned Neal in the desert.

Because I caught him in a lie, Neal thought grimly. And if Sir Reginald never lived among the Seminoles, how fraudulent are the rest of his adventures? Enough for him to resort to murder to keep his secret safe.

-23-

It was time to leave the billabong.

As accurately as Neal could reckon, taking in his days with Jallara's people, his spell of unconsciousness prior to that, and the wandering after the sandstorm, it had been more than two weeks since Sir Reginald had left him for dead in the desert.

Neal had no idea where the billabong was located. Without a map or a sextant, or even just his pocket watch, Neal had no way of determining the longitude or latitude of his location. All he knew for sure was that while he remained here, stationery with the clan, Sir Reginald and the expedition continued their westward trek, getting further away.

And Neal had revenge in his heart.

"Can you take me south, to the coast?" he had asked Jallara the day before. Neal was no longer focused on making bows and arrows for the clan, or building sturdier shelters, teaching them the alphabet. He was now driven by something more primal. "The ocean? Big water in the south." Neal knew that if he could get to the Indian Ocean he could follow Edward Eyre's trail westward at least as far as Esperence, and from there strike north in the hopes of crossing Sir Reginald's path. Neal recalled Galagandra, circled in red on the map. He asked Jallara if she knew of it. She did not.

"Can you take me?" he had asked again, and through gestures and using basic words, he had finally gotten his point across. Jallara had had a private counsel with Thumimburee while Neal had watched anxiously. For the past few days, since his memory finally came back, Neal had been consumed with only one thought: to find Sir Reginald. To his relief, he had seen Thumimburee smile and nod agreement.

When Jallara came back and said, "We go," Neal had said, "When?"

Again she had frowned. So he put his hands together on the side of his head and closed his eyes to mimic sleep, followed by a hand sign imitating the rising of the sun. Jallara's face cleared and she held up her thumb, which he knew indicated the number one. "One day?" he said. "We leave tomorrow?"

"Yes, tomorrow, Thulan!"

Now it was dawn, today they were leaving the billabong. As Neal helped them take down their shelters and bundle the sticks to be carried on their backs, he vowed that once he made it to Perth, he would see to it that food, clothing, and medicines were brought back to Jallara and her people in a gesture of gratitude for saving his life.

Finally they were ready, thirty-three men, women, and children, their shelters reduced to bundles of sticks, the campfires doused, all sign of human habitation erased. Neal felt a little guilty for making them leave such a nice home. He had only asked for two guides to take him south, but Thumimburee seemed to think the whole clan had to go.

The clever-man held out his arms and, turning in a slow circle, chanted prayers. Jallara told Neal that Thumimburee was thanking the spirits of the billabong for giving them a good life there. He was also asking forgiveness from the spirits of the animals they had killed and eaten, and from the plants as well. It had something to do with balance, but which Neal did not quite understand.

But when Thumimburee and his clan started to walk northward, Neal said, "Wait, I said *south*."

"Come, Thulan!" Jallara called merrily. "Thumimburee say you friend, you come."

Neal stared at her. And then he realized that he had misunderstood. Jallara had not said they would take him wherever he wanted to go, but that *he* was welcome to go with *them*.

"But I have to go south!" he said, as the others continued walking, following Thumimburee who had spears, woomeras, and boomerangs tied to his back. "I have to find my expedition!"

Jallara stopped and turned and said, "We go this way."

"But why? I mean, what difference does it make where you go? There are no towns, no villages, no homes to visit. It seems to me your people can go anywhere they like."

"We follow songlines, Thulan."

He frowned. What were songlines? He saw no lines etched into the ground, no distinguishable landmarks.

He watched Thumimburee, tall and proud as he marched with a firm stride over the arid plain, leaving the billabong behind, children and dingoes running after him, with the hunters and women faithfully following. Then Neal squinted southward across a bleak and hostile expanse, wondering briefly if he could make it to the coast on his own. Knowing that he could not, Neal realized he had no choice but to go with them. He fell into step beside Jallara, thinking with dread that they were headed north, deeper into the unknown heart of the continent, farther from Hannah and civilization, in the opposite direction of Sir Reginald and the expedition.

-24-

"How do you feel, Mr. O'Brien?"

Jamie squinted up at Hannah as she sat silhouetted against the pale sun. They were riding in the back of the wagon, among the bags and barrels and crates of supplies, the wheels creaking in the late afternoon stillness. She had stayed by his side in the ten days since she had fixed his leg, from morning to night, watching him, caring for him. It was a nice feeling, Jamie thought. Unfortunately, she also would not let him step down from the wagon and help his mates search for opals, because that's why he had come out here. Jamie O'Brien was not a man to stay put. He was cursed with too much energy and the need for action. But Miss Conroy had not only elected to be his doctor but his jailer as well.

A pretty jailer though, he thought. Miss Conroy wore a gray gown with a matching gray bonnet, and her eyes were gray. Jamie had heard a word once, "nacreous," and he had never really understood it until now. It was a word invented just for Hannah Conroy, he decided, because she was not the gray of fog or colorlessness, but the gray of Irish mists and ancient castle keeps. And that black, black hair that beckoned to a man, *Come and explore.*

"I feel great," he replied with a grin.

"And how is your leg?"

"Which one?" The grin grew cheeky.

Hannah knew that his attitude was meant to deflect his fear. It had been four days since he had felt any pain, any sensation at all at the site of the wound. She studied Jamie O'Brien's face, shaded from the sun by the wide brim of his hat. He was not yet feverish, there was no excessive perspiration. But they both knew that the lack of pain was a serious sign. It meant that, beneath the bandage that had by now become grimy and covered in dust, gangrene was eating away at nerves and flesh, numbing the place where bone had broken through the skin. And gangrene was a certain death sentence from which not even amputation was a reprieve.

The bandage was to come off this evening and Hannah, like the others in Jamie's group, was tense with worry.

As the wagons creaked and groaned through the eerie afternoon stillness, with the only sound coming from the billy cans clanking on the pack horses, the sun slowly moved up the great china-blue sky, bleaching everything on the earth, taking away all the shade so that not even the occasional clumps of spinifex grass cast shadows. The terrain was other-worldly: a stony, tree-less desert of salt pans and sandstone flats, with bizarre cliffs and rock formations in the distance. A wasteland where, Hannah knew, nothing beyond stunted scrub would ever grow.

They had found little water, and even that had been salty. When they had climbed a steep rise in the terrain, from the summit they had seen a phenomenon that Edward Eyre had named Lake Torrens. But it only seemed to be water, as it was really a dry and glazed bed of where water had once lodged. To the northeast of Lake Torrens barren ranges continued tier after tier of rocky crags as far as the eye could reach.

It was a silent group that made slow progress northward, men trudging alongside the wagons or riding horseback, their clothes ragged and dusty, muskets slung on their backs. They had entered unknown territory where no white man had set foot, and it made Hannah remember something Captain Llewellyn had said on the *Caprica*, about a theory that God had created a second Garden of Eden somewhere in the world and that it might lie in the mysterious heart of Australia.

But this group was not searching for Eden or rumored lost cities or fabled inland seas. They were going in search of opal, Hannah had finally learned, and they were following Jamie because he had promised them riches. Not that he had anything certain to go by other than a very dubious a map and his own adventurous spirit. One of the men, Stinky Sam, had told Hannah that when Jamie was playing a game of cards that lasted three days, on a station west of Sydney, the final pot had contained shillings, pound notes, a man's gold ring, a lady's pearl necklace, the deed to a cattle run, and a map to an opal field.

Jamie had lost the game but had purchased the map from the winner, who doubted its authenticity anyway ("How can a place be mapped when it's a place no man has ever gone into and come out alive?"), but Jamie had been taken with the yellowed parchment and inked lines and Xs marked here and there. He had told his mates the aboriginal story of the Rainbow Serpent, how its body sparkled with flames of color and glittered like gemstones, and that it had laid beautiful eggs of a translucent stone that shot back rainbows of color. The mythical eggs, it was said, could be found in the continent's interior, somewhere north of Adelaide. Jamie had put two and two together and decided to launch a hunting party.

"The opals lay on the ground," Stinky Sam had told Hannah one evening over a dinner of potatoes, damper, and roasted emu bagged by Bluey Brown and his musket. "Beautiful chunks of frozen fire as big as your fist. Just there for the picking. We're all going to be rich."

Hannah had never seen an opal, although she had heard of them, the ones that came from Mexico and Europe. And as it was a rich, rare stone, she knew what drove these ragged men to follow Jamie O'Brien in blind faith—a group of mates drifting from one hope to another, picking up jobs here and there, drovers one season, shearers another, moving on when the mutual restlessness came over them, always believing Jamie that the end of the road lay just ahead.

They went by the nicknames Australians were so fond of: Blackie White; Abe Brown (called Bluey for no known reason); Charlie Olde, called Chilly because his initials spelled C Olde; Banger, who loved sausages; Tabby, who liked to take cat naps; and Ralph Gilchrist, whom they called Church because of the last syllable of his surname. There were also Roddy, Cyrus, and Elmo, three brothers who looked so much alike Hannah could not tell them apart.

They were men Jamie O'Brien had met over a pint and a game of two-up, in places with names like Geelong, Coonardoo, and Streaky Bay. And when O'Brien had his treasure map and his plan to hunt for opals, he had gone around to Geelong, Coonardoo, and Streaky Bay to gather up his band of adventurers, like Jesus calling his disciples, Hannah thought, each contributing what money he could for wagons, horses, and supplies, on the promise that when the treasure was found, it would be divided equally. Brothers Roddy, Cyrus, and Elmo were young bricklayers looking for excitement; Blackie White was a toothless blacksmith in his fifties; Banger had been a cook on a sheep station; Stinky Sam and Charlie Olde were stockmen on a cattle station where Jamie had worked one winter as a rouseabout; Ralph Gilchrist was a bullocky who had spent the better part of his life driving the great ox-drawn drays about the bush, taking supplies to farflung sheep stations and carting back mountains of wool. Bluey Brown and Tabby were axemen whose motto was "If it grows, cut it down," and they figured that, between them, they'd cleared a million acres of timber in their lives.

The only one not with them on this silent afternoon as the sun was turning to red-gold was Stinky Sam, who had gone off in search of opal, armed with a pickaxe, a lantern, and a canteen filled with whiskey. Stinky Sam got his nickname from working in a slaughterhouse outside of Hobart Town, where he had served time for pickpocketing back in Dublin.

Hannah looked out at the bleak landscape and thought, The earth has gone flat, as it was in the days before Columbus. The horizon was impossibly far away, and the sky so vast that Hannah felt as if she were back on the *Caprica*. It was late May—winter was coming, but the days were warm so that Hannah could only imagine the furnace this desert must be in the summer. At night, however, the temperature plunged, making everyone shiver and keep close to the fire. But they had brought tents and Hannah had one entirely to herself so that she had privacy.

As they made slow, steady progress each day, the men spread out in search of firewood and opals. It made Hannah think of Neal, and she wondered if this wilderness was similar to the land he was exploring

As the wagon creaked along, Jamie said, "Did I ever tell you, Miss Conroy, about this bloke I once knew, name of Fry? I was up Gundagai way one summer and I happened upon old Sammy Fry strolling through the town, looking for all the world like a down and out beggar—no socks, his pants held up with rope, a hole in his hat. 'See here, Mr. Fry,' I say. 'Everyone knows you've struck it rich with sheep. You own your own station now, yet you still go about looking like a shearer. Why don't you dress like the successful man you are?' And old Fry replies, 'Why should I? Everyone hereabouts knows who I am.'

"Well, wouldn't you know it, just a year later, I'm walking down one of the busiest streets in Sydney, and who should I run into but old Sammy Fry, dressed just as ragged as ever, but just as rich I had heard. 'See here, Mr. Fry,' I say again, 'you're in the big city now, you ought to dress better.' And old Sammy says, 'Why should I? Nobody hereabouts knows who I am.'"

Hannah smiled. She had discovered that Jamie O'Brien had a gift for storytelling and was a font of anecdotes, tales, myths, stories, and fables. The narratives rolled glibly off his tongue, and they were always entertaining.

"Ever hear of a bloke named Queenie MacPhail, Miss Conroy?"

"I don't believe I have, Mr. O'Brien."

He grinned and said, "Would you like to hear how Queenie got his name? I was droving up along the Murrumbidgee River, far from where most folks live, and met a farmer named MacPhail, and his religious wife. They invited me in for a bite to eat and told me their complaint. There weren't many churches in that area and MacPhail's wife was beginning to worry about their son, who was nine years old and had yet to be baptized.

Of course, that meant he also hadn't yet got a name, so they called him Boy. Mrs. MacPhail confessed to me that she was worried her boy might die and St. Peter wouldn't know who he was and wouldn't let him into Heaven. So I offered to ride about and fetch back a traveling preacher who could do the christening.

"We didn't know it, but the boy was listening at the keyhole as the MacPhails and I made arrangements with the preacher, and the boy got it into his head that christening must be like branding, because the preacher was talking of adding him to a flock. So the lad ran off, determined never to suffer a christening. We all ran after him, MacPhail, his wife, the preacher, and me, and the boy led us a merry chase, all over the farm and right back to the house where he dodged in and out of rooms like a Tasmanian devil. By the time his father collared him and Mrs. MacPhail screamed 'Give my boy a name!' the preacher was so rattled he dropped his baptism water.

"'Quick, woman!' shouted MacPhail, 'another bottle,' as he was about to lose hold of his son. She slapped the bottle into the preacher's hand and as the reverend splashed the liquid on young MacPhail's head, saying, 'I christen thee—' he saw the label on the bottle and shouted, 'Good Lord, it's Queen of the Highlands!' And to this day, Miss Conroy, old Queenie MacPhail boasts that he's the most baptized man on God's earth because it was done with good Scotch whiskey."

Hannah smiled and leaned forward to shift the flour sack at Jamie's back, as he was looking uncomfortable.

When Hannah had asked Jamie why he was going in search of opal, he had said, "I've never done it before. Life is short, Hannah. A man should taste everything he can." When she had asked, "What if you strike it rich? What will you do then?" He had quipped, "I never think that far ahead." In this way she had gotten to know more about the man in her care: Jamie O'Brien the carefree drifter who sometimes worked at honest labor, sometimes stole and cheated and lied, depending on his mood or the weather or the time of day. A man with a restless spirit and energy that couldn't be contained. Hannah had also discovered that Mr. O'Brien was a man used to ladies succumbing to his wit and his roguish charm.

What Hannah did not know was how Mr. O'Brien had come to be like this. She had yet to hear about his background, or what it was that had put him on the path of a lifetime of adventure outside the law.

Finally, up ahead, Maxberry raised his hand and the straggling party came to a weary halt. It was time to stop for the night and make camp.

And remove Jamie's bandage.

As usual, four men came to the back of the wagon to help O'Brien down for the night, his splinted leg making it impossible for him to walk even with a crutch. Hannah climbed down first, bringing her blue carpetbag with her. Her heart rose to her throat. She was dreading what was to happen next.

As Jamie hooked his arms around two sets of sturdy shoulders, he watched how dainty and ladylike Hannah went in search of some privacy, as if she were perusing flowers in a garden. His men went to great pains to see that she had all the privacy she needed. His men had also started combing their hair and watching their speech, and they made sure they didn't spit tobacco juice near her.

As the men unhitched the wagons and unsaddled the horses, letting them loose to graze on saltbush, Tabby got started on a fire while others gathered fuel and pitched tents, and Nan went off with her digging stick to hunt for goannas and geckos, Hannah made sure Jamie was comfortably situated with his back to a boulder, a bottle of water in his hands.

Then she retreated to the canvas tent that had been erected for her, and she sat cross-legged to stretch her aching back. She hurt all over. She was tired and hungry. More than anything, she craved a bath, but water was precious in this arid expanse and must be reserved for cooking and drinking. Jamie's men were foregoing baths and letting their beards grow. Even O'Brien himself, normally clean shaven, was sprouting a stubble-covered jaw.

The sun slipped behind the horizon, and the tent grew dark. Hannah lit her lantern and, as she did every night, brought out Neal's photograph. Smiling at the handsome face, she said, "I wonder if you have made any fabulous discoveries yet, if you have named mountains and rivers after yourself, if already your photographic plates carry fantastic sights never before seen by human eyes."

She fell silent, recalling their last day together, on the road to Kapunda, when they had kissed with such passion, and she had felt Neal's ardor to be as sharp as her own. Her desire for him had not diminished, she loved him as deeply as ever, and yet …

She lifted her eyes to the canvas wall and thought of the man who sat on the other side, a few yards away. Jamie O'Brien. What was it about him that seemed to have cast a spell on her? From that first night in Lulu Forchette's moonlit garden, Hannah had felt strangely enchanted by O'Brien. Every time she thought about him, and when she had encountered him again as the newsagent's kiosk, Hannah had felt an indescribable draw to him. She was attracted to him, and the attraction was growing. How was that possible? She was in love with Neal. She wanted to spend the rest of her life with him.

But she could not shake Jamie O'Brien's eyes from her thoughts, his rakish smile and slightly crooked nose, the way he scoffed at his injury and told humorous tales of drovers and shearers, or of the clever ways he relieved unwitting Poms of their shillings.

She returned to Neal's photograph. "I am afraid," she said softly to him while outside, men's shouts and laughter rose to the darkening sky, "that if Mr. O'Brien has gangrene, I blame myself. I think now that I acted too hastily in applying the iodine preparation. I had a suspicion that, if the iodine can kill microbiotes, it can also kill living flesh. Perhaps I should not have used it, for I fear now that while I might have succeeded in killing harmful microbiotes, I also killed the vessels and nerves that feed the tissues of Mr. O'Brien's wound. Dead flesh becomes gangrene, and I caused it."

"Hoy in there!" barked Michael Maxberry outside the tent. "Food's ready!"

Nan had speared some lizards, and Bluey Brown had managed to kill a lone wallaby with his trusty musket, so they had fresh meat for supper. But it was not a joyous meal. Whereas previous nights had been noisy eating affairs, filled with talk of what they were going to do with all the wealth they were going to find out here, tonight's supper was a quiet one as each man focused on the contents of his tin plate, shoulders hunched in the firelight, as if to deny the existence of the stars above, the vast desert around them, and the death of Jamie O'Brien's right leg.

Church asked about Stinky Sam, wondering out loud where "the old bugger" had gone off to, suddenly turning red and muttering an apology to Hannah.

"He's gotten lost," Maxberry said as he gave the fire a poke, sending sparks up to the stars.

Hannah wasn't hungry, and so she left the circle to check on her patient.

Jamie was sitting with legs stretched out, his back against one of the few boulders in the vicinity. Hannah sat next to him on the gritty ground, gathering her skirts under herself and drawing her shawl tightly about her shoulders. A hundred feet away, eleven men and one aboriginal woman sat huddled around a fire. The horses were tethered to the wagons where Maxberry and Church had strung a rope of pans and cutlery to sound an alarm in case dingoes came sniffing about, although it had been days since they had seen anything but the occasional kangaroo or wallaby.

"Mr. O'Brien, would you mind if we waited for morning to remove the bandage? I would prefer to inspect the wound in the sunlight."

"It's as good a time as any," he said with a smile.

"Are you worried?"

"About the gangrene?" He shook his head. "If I die tomorrow, I've had a good life. And if St. Peter doesn't let me through the pearly gates, then I'll just go round and slip through a hole in the fence." He absently rubbed the scars on his left wrist. "Won't be the first time I've stuck it to the authorities."

"Mr. Maxberry told me that you and he met on a road gang."

Jamie laughed softly. "I was out along the Snowy River when I met up with a bloke looking to buy kangaroo skins. I told him I had two hundred of them, fine red ones, ears and tails and all. I gave him a price, he agreed to it. I took the buyer's money, told him where to find the skins, and I rode off. The troopers caught up with me four days later. The magistrate accused me of malicious intent to defraud the other man. I defended myself by pointing out that the two hundred skins were where I said they would be. 'You failed to mention,' the magistrate said, 'that they were still on the kangaroos!'"

Jamie laughed again, and Hannah smiled.

"Unfortunately, he didn't have a sense of humor, not like when I was caught the year before, selling a horse. The buyer listened to my sales pitch, gave me fifty quid for the horse, and when he saw that it was a *clothes*-horse I'd sold him, he had me hauled before the magistrate who had a good sense of humor—and a bit of gin in him I would wager—as he cautioned the buyer to be more careful in the future. I was let go that time. But the kangaroos, they landed me in a chain gang where Mike and I worked a while before making a good escape in the middle of the night."

"So you admit you're a swindler."

"Only when I can't find dishonest work," he said with a wink, and Hannah wondered how a man who was about to lose his leg, possibly his life, could carry on a flirtation.

"Aren't you worried about your victims?"

"Most of them ask for it. You see that horse, the chestnut mare?" Jamie pointed into the darkness, and Hannah looked back to where the horses were tethered. "It was a race at Chester Downs. I'd won a few quid that day and would have gone home except I saw this fat braggart name of Barlow boasting about his champion racehorse. I looked the animal over and said I'd like to buy her. We haggled all afternoon and agreed to a swap of land for the horse. I gave Barlow a government deed to a hundred thousand acres up Kapunda way, and he gave me the mare. That was last week. I reckon by now he's tried to claim his land and has discovered the deed is a forgery."

"And it doesn't bother you?"

Jamie searched Hannah's face for signs of judgment and disapproval but found none. "The man's greed is what got him into trouble. Barlow knew that the land was worth much more than his horse. He thought *he* was swindling *me*. Hannah, I make offers that are too good to be true. An honest man would turn them down."

"Aren't you afraid Mr. Barlow will have you arrested?"

"He won't report me to the coppers. His kind don't like to look stupid. He'll cover the loss and keep his pride."

"You said he asked for it. What does that mean?"

"I choose my targets carefully, Hannah. Besides, Barlow reminded me of my father."

Jamie lifted his face and looked long and deep at the black sky. Then he brought his head down and, removing his hat, set it on the sand. Hannah saw how the night breeze played with his dark blond hair, growing long now about his neck. "My parents were among the first free settlers in New South Wales, grabbing up land and riding to success on the sheep's back, as the saying goes. I was the only one born in Australia. My parents came out with children, and then two were born ahead of me but they didn't thrive. I was the last, with my mother dying the following spring of a badly weakened constitution. It could have been a nice life, I suppose, but sudden wealth changed my father. He had worked another man's sheep farm back in Suffolk, so when he got his fifty-thousand acres, he gave our station the grand sounding name of The Grange and got rich running thousands of sheep on it, sturdy heavy-fleeced merinos. Long ago, he'd been a generous man, but money made him greedy, always wanting more, buying neighboring land from folk who couldn't meet their mortgages. My father covered his humble past by filling the house with expensive furniture, rugs from Turkey, even suits of armor imported from London. He put on the airs of a gentleman and demanded the same of his sons. My brothers complied, going to posh boarding schools, joining clubs in Sydney, wearing top hats and acting like proper English gentleman. But I was different. I was born here. I drew my first breath in the Australian air, and that set me apart from my family. Try though he did, my father couldn't turn me into one of them. I was wild. I couldn't stay put at a desk and a chalk slate. A succession of tutors came and went from The Grange, and my father took a rod to my backside more times than I care to count. When I turned fourteen, he decided to send me back to England, to go to school there and learn to be a gentleman. So I ran away. I packed a swag and hit the track and I've been on the move ever since."

"Have you ever been back?"

"Once, a few years ago. The old man had taken a new wife and sprouted a new crop of O'Briens. I went up the front steps, but he wouldn't let me in the house. Said he had disowned me and I was never to come back. My bounty poster at the time didn't have as long a list on it as it does now, petty crimes really, but he threatened to send for the troopers. He wasn't a total bastard, though. He gave me an hour's head start."

He looked at Hannah for a long moment, his eyes roving her face, taking in the dainty bonnet capping dark hair that was gathered in a knot at the nape of her neck. Out here in the rough and ready wilderness, he thought, and she still looks like a lady. "Let me give you a bit of Outback wisdom, Hannah."

She had never given him permission to address her by her first name, nor had he ever asked. But she did not protest.

"The trick in life, Hannah," he said, "is to cram everything into the moment. All your hours and days, all your pasts and futures. Compress then into *now*, and savor it like a rich man's feast."

"And live outside the law?"

He searched again for signs of judgment but found none. She was curious about him, he knew, and she deserved an answer. "I don't live *outside* the law, Hannah. I live by my own law, pure and simple. No toffee-nosed Pom in a white powdered wig twelve thousand miles away is going to tell Jamie O'Brien of the lower Murrimbidgee how to live."

He picked up the enamel cup that sat in the sand near his hat and, lifting it in a toast, took a sip. Hannah knew it was whiskey. O'Brien set the cup down and said with a sigh, "I feel sorry for the bloke who doesn't drink."

"Why?"

"Because when he wakes up in the morning, that's the best he's going to feel all day."

Jamie shifted his weight and winced.

"Pain?" Hannah asked in alarm, and hope.

"There's that one tie that's still bothering me. If you could loosen it a bit?"

Tension on the splint bindings had had to be adjusted over the days, first to accommodate swelling, and then to tightened the splints as the swelling had gone down. Hannah delicately picked at the knotted rag, and when the two ends fell away, she stared in horror.

In the light of the moon and the stars, Hannah saw a great black spot staining the bandage directly above the sutured wound. She closed her eyes. It *was* gangrene. The necrosis had seeped up through the bandage. There was no hope.

"Everything okay?" Jamie asked.

"I'm just re-tying it," she said, picking up the filthy ends of the rag with shaking hands and re-doing the knot, covering the horrific black spot.

Jamie rubbed his stubbled jaw and said, "Would you do me a favor, Hannah? Will you remove your bonnet? Just for tonight?" He added with a grin: "Call it a dying man's wish."

Hannah thought of the black spot on Jamie's bandage, thought about how everything was going to be different tomorrow, and so, reaching up, she removed the pins and then the bonnet, setting it aside on the sand.

"That's much better," Jamie said, his gaze brashly roving the hair that shone like jet in the moonlight. Then his eyes met hers and Hannah saw his pale blue irises reflect starlight and moonlight, and Hannah found herself thinking what an attractive man O'Brien was, and she realized she was falling under a strange spell. She rubbed her arms. Chill was seeping through the wool of her shawl, through the fabric of her dress, through her skin and flesh right into the marrow of her bones. She knew it had nothing to do with the cold night.

"I want to share some magic with you," he said. Jamie reached into his pants pocket and brought something out. "You will need to remove your glove for this."

Hannah did so, and was startled when Jamie placed something cool and smooth on her palm. "Feel that?" he said softly. "Like holding a cloud."

The opal was the size and shape of a robin's egg, smooth and soft. She turned the pale blue stone this way and that, catching moonlight and shooting back colors, and it made her think of Jamie O'Brien's eyes.

"Look into it, Hannah, move it about. Go into the heart of the stone and let the colors swirl around you, bring you in to where there is only peace and silence. Feel the colors embracing you. The stone is cool, the colors are bright. The aborigines believe opals are healing stones. They're the eggs laid by the Rainbow Serpent and they possess tremendous power to heal and to soothe."

Hannah was mesmerized by the stone, thinking it possessed the best characteristics of the most beautiful of gemstones: the fine sparkle of almandine, the shining purple of amethyst, the golden yellow of topaz, and the deep blue of sapphire. Now she understood Jamie's passion to find more.

As she started to hand it back to him, he said, "Keep it. As payment for leaving your comfortable hotel and coming out here to help me. Besides, we'll be finding plenty more." Then, looking into her eyes, he said, "Stay with me tonight, Hannah."

She went back to her tent to fetch two blankets, and settled next to Jamie, who made a place for her at his side with his arm outstretched so that it curled protectively around her shoulders when she leaned into him. Hannah spread the blankets over the two of them and, resting her head on his chest, lay for a long while listening to the steady beating of his heart.

Hannah closed her eyes, spilling tears onto the dusty fabric of his shirt. As he started to tell her a humorous Outback tale about a race and an old drover's horse, Hannah listened to Jamie's voice deep within his chest, and the rhythm of a strong, brash heart. And she thought that, under other circumstances, in another time, she could fall in love with this man.

-25-

Hannah woke once during the night and thought of going back to her tent, but she did not want O'Brien to wake up and find himself alone. And so she stayed with him until dawn, when the others awoke after a night of fitful sleep.

Breakfast was a dispirited affair of beef jerky, damper, and tea, and all they spoke of was that there was no sign of Stinky Sam who had gone off the day before. Finally, the men carried Jamie to the wagon where they laid him in the bed among the supplies.

As fresh sunlight broke over the flat, unforgiving desert, they gathered around the wagon, a tired, solemn group with shadowed eyes and the stoop of hopelessness in their shoulders. Hannah knelt at Jamie's side and, before removing the bandage, she took his right hand and placed in it the opal he had given her the night before, curling his fingers around the cool, smooth stone. Their eyes met, and he smiled in gratitude.

Hannah opened her carpetbag, and as she prepared to cut the blackened bandage, she mentally prepared herself for all possibilities. Having assisted her father in the management of many wounds, she was experienced with the various conditions of injured flesh: from angry red festerings, to foul sores oozing pus, to the black necrotic tissue of gangrene. She peeled back the dirty rag and poured water over the wound to rinse away the caked blood and pale yellow fluid that had accumulated beneath the bandage.

But when Jamie O'Brien's pale, injured shin was washed clean, Hannah froze. This was one possibility for which she had not been prepared.

The others also fell silent, mouths dropping open.

"Holy St. Hilda," said Ralph "Church" Gilchrist as he crossed himself.

"What is it?" cried Jamie. "It is worse than we thought?"

Hannah started to speak but could not find the words. It was Maxberry who said, "It's a miracle, boyo, and that's a fact."

Lifting up on his elbows, Jamie finally had the courage to look at his leg. Like everyone else, he stared in astonishment. "What happened?"

"Your wound, Mr. O'Brien," Hannah finally said, "appears to have completely healed."

Although the skin of his calf and shin was white and puckered, as expected, and although the wound itself, with two rows of neat black sutures, was stained purple, there was no sign of pus or infection, no drainage of any kind.

It explained why he had felt no pain, she realized. Not because of gangrene, but because the wound had *healed*.

And then she saw her handkerchief among the bandages, purple and ruined beyond saving—the dark purple iodine that had seeped into the outer bandage making her think gangrene lay beneath—and she had the answer.

Her father's formula.

Relief washed over her. And something else—a powerful, shuddering emotion that made her close her eyes and reach for the edge of the wagon. She swayed slightly, kneeling there next to Jamie O'Brien who was now laughing. The others were shouting and laughing, too, and throwing their hats into the air, with dirty-faced Tabby dancing a jig, and Bluey Brown shooting off his musket, and Nan grinning with gapped teeth. Hannah went quiet and still as she said prayer of thanks.

The sight of the clean wound astounded everyone, and they gathered around again to stare and comment. They had all seen bad wounds. Maxberry himself had nearly died from the wound that had festered on his face. Never had any of them seen anything so clean as this. There would hardly even be a scar.

Jamie said, "Faith, Hannah, you saved my life."

But she was thinking of something else. The iodine *was* a cure-all. As she was suddenly filled with excitement, wanting to hurry back to Adelaide and explore this astounding discovery—she would ask Mr. Maxberry to escort her back—the morning silence was broken by a shout. They turned to see Stinky Sam stumbling into camp. "Opals!" he cried, waving his arms. "I've found opals! *Millions* of 'em!"

-26-

The mountain had been calling to him for days.

Neal didn't know how he knew it, couldn't find the words to express exactly how the distant mountain beckoned. He knew only that he could not stop staring at the red-gold monolith that stood on the red desert like a sunset frozen in time. It was like no geologic formation he had ever seen. To Neal, mountains had jagged peaks, alpine forests, snow. This queer upthrusting of rock was roughly the shape of a bread loaf, with no apparent vegetation, no peaks, and no foothills or forests surrounding it. How on earth had it been formed? What strange gestation and birth had produced such a cryptic phenomenon?

As the two brothers Daku and Burnu, their black bodies painted white, torsos bent, with spear and woomera balanced in their hands, stealthily stalked an echidna, Neal—who was supposed to be ready with his boomerang should the spears miss their mark—stood mesmerized by the strange mountain. With the hot wind blowing against his face, Neal felt himself grow curiously detached. The mountain shimmered in the heat, it seemed to move, to breathe, as if some queer power were reaching out to him, to draw him toward itself. He wished he had his camera equipment. He wished he could capture the phenomenon on glass.

"Very sacred place," Jallara had said when the clan first arrived at this spot, days before. "First Beings live there in Dreamtime."

"People lived there?" he had asked. Neal thought he heard, on the wind, a low vibrating hum, like a tuning fork quivering in the lowest register. It was not something he detected through his ears, but rather it was something he *sensed*.

"Not people, Thulan. Creators."

Creators, Neal thought now as the hunters threw their spears and cried out in victory. What was causing the strange vibrations? Was it the force of subterranean steam or seismic activity? He wished he had his geological tools and scientific equipment. He would have liked to explore the jutting red rock—after all, he had come to Australia to unravel mysteries—but Jallara had warned him that the mountain was forbidden. "Very sacred, very taboo," Jallara had cautioned, saying that not even the clan's clever-man, Thumimburee, could walk on that ground.

Unfortunately, Jallara's words and warning only piqued Neal's curiosity. But as much as he would have loved to break away from the group and go exploring, he respected their laws and would abide by them.

Besides, there was something else he wished to explore, and it had nothing to do with geology. Nothing to do with the real world, in fact.

In the past five months, since leaving the billabong, the clan had experienced a death, two births, one girl's rite of passage, and two youths' rites of passage. For the death and births, Neal had been allowed to partake in the ceremonies. For the secret girl's ritual, he was banned, which he understood. But when he was barred from the manhood initiation of the two boys, Neal did not understood why until Jallara had explained that only males who had undergone initiation could participate. Disappointed, Neal had had to stay behind in the camp with the women and girls and young boys while the men had taken the two youths out into the wilderness for secret rites.

All through the night, as Neal had sat with Jallara at the campfire, as he had heard the faint twangs of Thumimburee's didgeridoo drift from the distance on the wind, his interest grew. And when the boys were brought back the next day, barely able to walk, Neal's curiosity had sharpened. Jallara had said it was a ritual of blood and pain. She had not exaggerated.

After the youths recovered, they had then gone on something called walkabout while the clan picked up camp and continued on their never-ending trek, leaving the initiates behind with only their spears. When the youths rejoined them a few days later, there was a happy corroboree to celebrate the boys' entry into manhood.

"So walkabout is a proof of manhood?" Neal had asked Jallara.

"They go to see spirits, Thulan. Get secret message."

Spirits, Neal had thought. Secret message. Like a vision quest. What had the boys seen? What messages had they received out there in the wilderness with only a spear and their wits? As it was taboo to speak of one's experience during walkabout, Neal could only guess. And his curiosity grew.

He woke up one morning to realize that he wanted to experience walkabout.

The more he thought about it, the more the idea excited him. What was it like to have a mystical experience, to have a spirit-guide send you a secret message? Was it even possible that an atheist like himself, who did not believe in any realm beyond the physical world that he could see and touch, could experience the mystical?

He had asked Jallara to present his request to Thumimburee who, to Neal's surprise, had readily agreed. The clever-man told Jallara that since *thulan* had led them to the dying man, that Thulan Dreaming watched over the stranger, then it was permissible for him to undergo the spiritual rites of blood and pain.

Even so, the final decision was not an easy one for Neal to make. He was still obsessed with finding Sir Reginald. Justice and retribution filled his thoughts day and night. When the clan had left the billabong, five months prior, and the clan had traveled north, Neal had been horrified. To his relief, however, they had soon turned to the west and had continued a westward trek since. Neal suspected that since they followed a track parallel to the expedition's, when the time came for Neal to leave the clan—which was soon—he had only to aim his steps southward and he would eventually meet up with Sir Reginald.

Neal was physically fit now, and ready for the trek. Thumimburee had offered to send three men with Neal, to take him across the plain to the point where he could continue on his own—where there was plentiful water, vegetation, and game. Neal was eager to go. The sooner he left this place, the sooner he would confront Sir Reginald and demand an accounting for his crime—the sooner, too, that Neal would arrive in Perth, and the sooner he would be back with Hannah. But if he chose to undergo the initiation rites, he would be here for days longer, perhaps even at the risk of missing Sir Reginald altogether, who might right now be in Perth or certainly very near. And then Neal's would-be murderer could catch the first ship back to England, and Neal might never catch the man who had left him in the desert to die.

He gazed across the plain at the red-gold mountain. He felt as if he had been divided into three men: one thirsting for revenge, the second yearning to be with his beloved, and the third a scientist who knew that this was a most extraordinary opportunity that would never come his way again.

What a paper he could write! The first white man to participate in the secret savage rites of a primitive people, deep in the heart of unexplored territory. What scientist worth his university diploma could pass this up? *I came here to explore mysteries. The world of spirits and the metaphysical is the greatest mystery of all.*

However, the experience was not without its risks. Jallara had warned Neal that sometimes youths who went walkabout never came back. Or sometimes the extreme tattooing—the first phase of the initiation—resulted in death due to the evil spirits of infection invading the wounds. And finally, although rarely, it sometimes happened that the secret message sent to the initiate by the spirits was so powerful, a message "Bigger than his head," that he died on the spot.

While his companions continued to search the barren landscape for prey, their keen eyes on the lookout for tracks, scat, and burrows—or, with luck, the overhead flight of a bird—Neal's eyes remained fixed on the taboo mountain

Once again he had the odd sensation that it was speaking to him. As if it were daring him to submit to the ancient rites of blood and pain, to let his blood run into the timeless sand beneath his feet, like countless generations of men before him. Not a paper, he thought suddenly. A book! One white man's extraordinary sojourn among a "lost" tribe of aborigines.

Hannah materialized before him, a transparent specter standing between himself and the red mountain. She was smiling, her hair hanging loose and free, her gloveless hands reaching for him. The desert was teasing him, playing tricks. And then he thought: No! There was a reason this spiritual place had brought Hannah to him, because it suddenly became clear to Neal that this was something that would make him worthy of Hannah. He could distinguish himself as a scientist by undergoing the secret initiation and then writing about it. A chronicle of his time with the Aborigines, as an anthropologist studying a clan untainted by contact with Europeans. It would be a sensation. His life with Jallara's clan would make news around the world, people would snap up his book, thirsty for descriptions of secret initiations. He could travel about and lecture. He would become famous.

And then he would ask for Hannah's hand in marriage.

As he broke the spell of the red-gold mountain and brought himself back to reality, Neal saw that the brothers Daku and Burnu had captured two echidnas and a gecko while he had stood staring off into the distance.

Neal felt a stab of guilt. In his five months with the clan, as he had gained strength and learned skills from his new companions, he had done his best to contribute to the food supply. His efforts to introduce the bow and arrow had been fruitless, and he had given up once he saw the phenomenal hunting skills of Thumimburee's men, using only spears and boomerangs. Neal's own initial efforts at spear, woomera, and boomerang had caused much laughter among the men, but determination to survive and to make his way back to Sir Reginald and revenge had turned him into a quick study.

His initial plan, before he set eyes on the mountain, had been to part ways with the clan tomorrow. Jallara's people were headed toward a tribal gathering of all the clans, called a *jindalee*. It was where, she had explained, the hundreds of members of the tribe renewed friendships, exchanged news and stories, strengthened clan ties, the clever-men sat in judgment of wrong doers and meted out punishment, laws and taboos were reinforced, babies were named and given protective spirits, the ancestors were honored, and girls found husbands. The *jindalee* was the reason, Neal knew now, why the clan had struck north after leaving the billabong, why they continued on the move instead of staying in one place.

But he would not be saying good-bye tomorrow after all. Eager to get back to camp now and inform Thumimburee that he wished to undergo the secret initiation, Neal fell into step with Burnu and Daku, who made fun of him in a friendly way—their stringy bark baskets were full of game, Neal's was empty. He saw Jallara up ahead, with the other women, on the perimeter of the camp they had set up among a cluster of boulders where a lone mulga tree grew and a well provided artesian water. She was engaged in the eternal search for roots and tubers, nuts and berries, insects and grubs.

Tall and long-limbed, her brown torso painted in white designs, her long wavy hair and grass skirt stirring in the wind, Jallara was like the taboo mountain. Exotic, mysterious, unexplored. And untouchable. Jallara was going to find a husband at the *jindalee*, join his clan, and travel away from this territory into that of her new family. Neal would never see her again.

He had been intrigued by her from the first moment he set eyes on her, and she had said, "How do you do, sir?" For a long time Neal did not understand why he was so taken with her. It was more than mere curiosity, more than a healthy man's natural reaction to her supple body and seductive breasts. And then the answer had come to him one afternoon as he had watched her sitting in the shade of a mulga tree, weaving a stringy bark basket. Jallara had been chatting and laughing with the other girls, and when she tossed her head and Neal had glimpsed light brown highlights in her black hair, reminding him that she was part European, it had occurred to him to wonder how her aboriginal mother or father had even *met* a white person, let alone be with them long enough to produce an offspring.

In his early days with the clan, Jallara did not have enough English to tell him her story, but over the weeks, as they spent time together, more of the language came back to her, remembered from her childhood. From what Neal could gather, Jallara's mother had married into another clan, whose territory shared a boundary with this one, and lay to the southeast. Somehow, her mother either left, or was taken by white men, and ended up working as a cook on an isolated cattle station. As near as Neal could determine, Jallara was about ten years old when she and her mother were either let go or ran away. "We walk, we walk, we walk. Following the sun. We sleep at Echidna Dreaming. We walk. Follow Rainbow Songline. We kill wallaby. We eat wallaby. We walk, we walk. Sleep at Possum Dreaming. Eat wallaby. We walk, we walk. Mother sick. We stop at Cockatoo Billabong, Place of Four Trees. Mother die. Jiwarli find me, bring me to mother's clan."

Here, then, was the root of his fascination with Jallara. Like himself, she was the product of parents from two worlds. While Jallara's case was racial and Neal's was that of social class, there was that strange bond. We are alike, she and I.

Jallara smiled as Thulan drew near. She had watched him enjoying the exhilaration of throwing the boomerang and seeing how far it would go, savoring the new strength in his body, the new skills he had learned during his time with her people. He still wore a fur pelt for modesty, and the shoes because of tender feet, but his torso was smeared with white paint to ward of insects and evil spirits, hunting weapons were strapped to his back. He was bearded, and his hair grew long. He looked like a hunter.

He made her think of her father, to wonder about him. Jallara had never given her father much thought, but this white man in their midst had made her start wondering. Who was he? How had her mother met the white man? Why did she not stay with *his* clan?

And what about Thulan? What had made him leave his clan to go walkabout in land far from his people? He had used words like "explore" and "open the way." Concepts she struggled to understand. She also wondered what sickness of the soul had driven him to perfect skills with spear and boomerang.

Jallara had watched him during his early lessons, and she had seen an obsession in Thulan's training. Long after the other hunters laid down their weapons, he kept practicing. He had driven himself to building his body. Jallara did not know why. When Thulan first woke from his deep sleep, the first days, he was cheerful and pleasant. And then he had changed. He had became serious and determined. He said he had remembered something. Jallara feared it was something bad because she sensed a sickness in Thulan's spirit.

She was curious about him, and fascinated by him. Even, in a way, attracted to him. But she knew he would not be with them for much longer, and that a new husband awaited her at the *jindalee*. But she was worried about Thulan and wished she could do something to heal the sickness in his soul. The sickness had a name: *yowu-yaraa*. Thulan would call it "anger."

She had slept with him at first, and then he had sent her away. This puzzled her. The nights were bitterly cold. In her family, husbands and wives slept together, children slept together, people even slept with the dingoes. It was necessary to keep warm, but also so that one was not alone when one walked in the dreams of sleep. But Thulan slept alone. Was this also part of his spirit-sickness?

"Jallara," Thulan said as he drew near. "Please tell Thumimburee that I have decided to be initiated into the clan."

-27-

The secret initiation consisted of three phases. Neal was familiar with the first two: tattooing and walkabout. The third remained a mystery as no one would talk about it. Yet another taboo in a world filled with taboos.

The ordeal began the night before the ritual, with Neal being separated from the main body of the camp to a place among the boulders where a pit had been dug and mulga leaves smoldered. He was told he must crouch over the smoky pit from dusk until dawn, without food or water, without falling sleep, while the men sat with him, chanting. With his knees bent, bracing himself between rocks, Neal held himself over the smoking pit until his knees screamed with pain and his spine felt as if it would crack. He had never known such agony, but he stayed there, determined to endure the torture for the sake of science.

At dawn, the men led him half a day's walk from the camp, away from the eyes and ears of the women and uninitiated boys. When they came to a cluster of dry boulders and clumps of spinifex, Daku collected the long grass blades, which when burned, gave off a pungent black smoke. The men chanted as they waited for nightfall. After the sun had gone down, Thumimburee untied his kangaroo-fur bundle and brought out two curious carved sticks, called *wirra*. Neal thought they were boomerangs, but they were not symmetrical, each having one long wing and one short one. The back side of the flat *wirra* were carved in symbols, and when Neal saw their undersides studded with rows of sharp thorns, he knew their purpose.

While one of the elders produced a didgeridoo and took his place on the ground, the others stood in a circle holding sticks. Neal was told to stand by the fire where Thumimburee gestured for him to remove the kangaroo loincloth. After Neal laid it in the sand, the clever-man then pointed to the small leather pouch that hung around Neal's neck. When Neal hesitated to removed the hidden emerald-glass tear catcher, Thumimburee made it understood that he only had to hang it down his back. The tattooing, Neal realized, was to be on his chest. And it was to be done while he was on his feet.

As Thumimburee commenced the sacred task, chanting as he did, and the hypnotic twang of the ancient didgeridoo filled the night, Neal tried to remain detached and objective, noting the steps of the ritual, the objects used, memorizing every detail of the rite for the scientific paper he was going to present to the prestigious Association of American Geologists and Naturalists. The paper was then going to be a chapter in his book.

Thumimburee placed the first of the long *wirra* on Neal's torso, to the right of the breastbone, its longest arm reaching Neal's waist while the short arm curved up and over his right pectoral muscle, ending at the shoulder. Applying an even and gentle pressure, so that the thorns were imbedded in Neal's skin, Thumimburee took a rock and began tapping the back of the *wirra*. At first, Neal felt only a pricking sensation, but as the thorns were driven into his flesh, he felt pain. The pain blossomed and spread as Thumimburee tapped the entire length of the *wirra*, from waist, up the chest and to the shoulder. The men chanted and banged their sticks together, while the didgeridoo sent out a song older than time, and sparks shot from the campfire to the stars.

Neal broke out in a sweat. He had not expected it to be this painful. Why couldn't he lie on his back while they did this? He was shocked to feel blood trickle down his bare thigh. Was he bleeding that much? He thought of hungry dingoes prowling in the night. As he clenched his fist and tried not to cry out, Thumimburee stopped the tapping and Neal relaxed an inch. But then the *wirra* was withdrawn and Neal could not help a groan of pain.

He was afraid to look down at himself, afraid that the sight of so much of his own blood might make him faint. Before he could chance even a glance, Thumimburee had the second *wirra* up against the left side of Neal's torso, and the piercing was repeated.

Despite the nighttime drop in temperature, Neal sweated profusely. He felt lightheaded. The pain more than doubled. And blood now trickled down his other leg.

And yet, through the red haze of incredible pain, Neal was suddenly filled with manly pride. Was this what it felt like to be a noble savage? He couldn't wait to record his experience on paper. He tried to imagine how he looked in the glow of the campfire, surrounded by primitive men banging sticks together. He pictured himself—the tall white man bravely submitting to a savage ritual, holding his head high, allowing no cries of pain to escape his throat. He wished he had his camera equipment, that young Fintan was there with the box and the tripod capturing the shocking scene. What a photograph it would make! It would go wonderfully as the frontispiece of his book—a taste for the reader of the sensational things to come.

When the left side was finished, he started to speak, but Thumimburee silenced him. Neal watched the clever-man drink from a possum-skin pouch, and was startled when he sprayed it on Neal's chest. Neal choked back a strangled cry. The liquid burned worse than fire. Gasping in pain, he looked down at himself and saw pale green water trickle over his raw wounds. It had a grassy smell. Three more times the clever-man took a mouthful of the plant juice and sprayed it on Neal's punctured flesh, and the burning intensified.

Thinking he couldn't take much more, praying that the ritual was over, Neal watched in horror as Thumimburee reached into a pouch and, bringing out a handful of red substance, smeared it over Neal's many puncture wounds. He watched by the light of the campfire as the red clay, mixed with his own red blood, was applied to his torso, and rubbed in with such vigor that he thought Thumimburee meant to skin him entirely.

Finally, when Neal thought his knees were going to give way, as he bit his tongue to keep from crying out, he felt helpful hands beneath his arms as the brothers Daku and Burnu eased him to the ground where he was given a skin of water and many congratulatory pats on the back. They spent the night in that spot, with men sitting watch, and the next morning they brought Neal back, to recuperate beneath the shade of the mulga tree.

It took two weeks for the tattoos to heal. After the initial pain subsided, itching set in, but Neal had to keep his hands away from the scabs covering his chest. But then the itching went away and the scabs began to fall off, leaving Neal's white torso covered in an astonishing pattern of dots rendered from the rust-red heart of Australia.

-28-

"What comes after walkabout?" Neal asked. "What is the third phase of the initiation?"

But Jallara held up her hand in a gesture that meant the topic was taboo, and so he could only pray that it wasn't something ghastly, like eating a live snake.

It was morning; the camp was bustling with celebration as everyone loved the pomp and excitement of walkabout. The boys threw boomerangs or chased one another, and the men stood around Neal giving him advice, pointing this way and that, gesturing, even though he didn't understand a word. They were all remembering their own walkabouts, years ago, and were giving him pointers. But for once Jallara wasn't translating. She was involved in the sacred ceremony of preparing the initiate for departure. While the women were painting his body and tying feathers in his hair and beard, Jallara placed a necklace of animal teeth over Neal's head, to rest on his newly tattooed chest and lie alongside the small leather pouch that held the emerald tear catcher.

"Do not eat *thulan*. He is your Dreaming spirit. Taboo to kill, taboo to eat." Neal had learned that *thulan* was their name for a lizard that the British colonists called Thorny Devil, and which Neal knew by the scientific name of *Moloch horridus*. Ten inches long with a flattened body and spiny skin, *thulan* had the ability to change its color and the pattern on its skin to match the ground it stood on. Neal had encountered many during his trek with the clan and thought the little beast both ugly and beautiful. The clan feasted on *thulan* regularly, but no pieces were ever served to Neal.

"Thulan has nothing to fear from me," he said with a smile. For once, Jallara did not smile back. Why was she being so solemn? Even her friend, giggly Kiah, was strangely somber. Neal wondered if it had something to do with the third ritual, the one after walkabout, and which was taboo to mention.

"When do I rejoin the group?" he asked when he was ready to go. He looked at the faces gathered around him—black-skinned with heavy brows and deep-set eyes, faces that he recognized as belonging to Allunga, Burnu and Daku, Jiwarli and Yukulta, people he had come to think of as friends.

"When it is proper time," Jallara said.

Neal frowned. "What do you mean? What time will that be?"

"Only Thulan know."

"You mean it's up to me to decide when to return?"

"Up to the spirits, Thulan. You receive vision, you come back."

He stared at her. He couldn't rejoin the clan until he had experienced a vision? Neal had assumed there was a prearranged time limit, such as seven days or by the next full moon. Or possibly when the initiate felt he had survived long enough. Neal had not anticipated this. How could he come back if he received no vision?

He was starting to wonder if he had taken on more than he could handle. When he had looked at the men's magnificent tattoos, and heard stories of walkabout, it had all seemed so manly and adventurous, the sort of tales white people in their parlors loved to read. He had not expected so much pain and sacrifice. Or risk to his life.

But he couldn't back out now. It would be cowardly. And what would he write in his book—what would he tell Hannah? It crossed his mind that he could invent a vision. But he knew he couldn't lie. This was a sacred ceremony. Even if it wasn't his own religion, he had to respect these people's beliefs.

He looked out at the ochre plain and considered the ordeal before him. Neal had snared his share of goannas and geckos, he had even knocked a big red kangaroo off its feet (although Daku and Burnu had had to finish the animal off). Neal knew how to track echidnas and burrowing rodents, how to start a fire, and how to find water. Since he doubted there would be any messages from the spirit world for Neal Scott of Boston, Massachusetts, as much as he might welcome a chance to experience it, he would have to choose his own time to rejoin the clan. Perhaps five days would seem reasonable. And he wouldn't have to lie. Since it was taboo to talk about one's secret spirit-message, no one would ask him for details, they would just assume he had visited the other world.

Finally, declaring him spiritually ready, they gave him a spear and a kangaroo fur blanket, and nothing else. Thumimburee said that if he did not come after the cycle of one moon, they would search for him, and bury him, for his long absence could only mean that he was dead.

Neal watched them tear down their shelters and tie the stick-bundles to their backs. They kicked out the fires and erased all traces of human habitation, as they had done in every camp since leaving the billabong, and then, without a backward glance at Neal, the clan struck off toward the west.

He watched them for a long time, observing the way the shimmering waves of desert heat distorted their figures and finally swallowed them. He knew they were only a few miles away, and yet he felt as if he were the last man on earth. The wind, without the flavoring of children's laughter and women's chatter, was empty and unsettling. It whistled through his long hair and beard as if to say: *We have you alone at last.*

Neal turned in a slow circle, looking at a landscape he had once thought bleak. He saw it now through different eyes. It was a land of colors. Ochre plains dotted with clumps of green spinifex were framed by dramatic red rocks, lavender mountains and brilliant blue skies. "We call this the Nullarbor," he had told Jallara one day.

"Why?"

"Because there is nothing here."

She had not understood, and at the time Neal had not known why. Couldn't she see the wasteland, the lack of striking topography, just blowing wind and dust? But now he understood. As they had trekked, Jallara had pointed out areas that held sacred meaning to her people: Anthill Dreaming, Dingo Songline, the place where Lizard-Spirit Ancestor created the first *thulan*. Neal was still not adept at distinguishing the features that identified such places, but he grasped the significance of what she was telling him: that this vast plain of twisted rock formations and buried water and stunted trees was criss-crossed with ancient ancestral tracks, and dotted with spots of religious and historical significance to the people who had lived here for thousands of years.

It was not an empty wasteland.

"Follow songlines," Jallara had said. "Look for places of Dreaming." But as hard as he looked now, Neal could not find these things, he had no idea of where to start even. Still, he decided as he hefted his spear and struck off in a direction opposite from the way the clan had gone, there was plenty for him to see here, and he might as well get started and not waste time. While serving on the HMV *Borealis* Neal had read books written by naturalists who had been among the early explorers to the continent, and so in the course of his first morning of walkabout he was proud of himself for being able identify much of the fauna he encountered. This desert was a naturalist's dream, and he wondered—dared hope, even—if he might stumble upon a species never before seen by white man and which he would have the honor of naming.

At noon, his stomach growled and he looked toward the cluster of boulders that had been the clan's home for the past few days. No one had said he could not remain there, as there was water and small game. But then it wouldn't be "walkabout." Neal presumed that the purpose of the ritual was to cover ground and wait for the spiritual revelations to come.

Nonetheless, hunger and rationalizing drove him to the old camp, where he drank from the artesian well and roasted a fat gecko. He slept through the hot afternoon, deciding he would take up wandering after sundown.

But when he awoke after sunset, he decided it would be best to stay here for the night and strike off in the morning. And so he sat with his back against the trunk of the lone acacia and looked up at the sky.

He was used to the stars by now, an astonishing brilliant canopy that one never saw above cities. As he listened for sounds of predatory creatures, Neal thought of his life up to this moment. He recalled his twelfth birthday when Josiah Scott had sat him down and said he was old enough to be told the truth, saying, "I am your adoptive father," showing Neal the cradle, the blanket, the emerald glass bottle he had thought once held perfume. Neal would never forget the tears that swam in Josiah's eyes that day, as if in telling the boy the truth, he was losing the son he had had for twelve years.

Neal thought about Hannah, as she had held onto him during the storm off the island of St. Helena, and again as she had clung to him on the dusty road in front of the Australia Hotel.

He turned his gaze to the monolithic mountain that burned red by day but turned a saturnine purple at night, and he drew the fur more tightly about himself. He knew it was October, but had no idea of the date. Strangely, he didn't care. There was a time when Neal had kept date and day and hour in his mind, the scientist conditioned to live by facts and external data. But his sojourn with the aborigines had shown him a different way to mark the passage of time, through the stars, the length of shadows, even his own internal rhythms.

And he had learned so much more. As Jallara's recollection of English had come back, and as Neal had become adept at understanding her gestures and inflections, and even a smattering of aboriginal words, he had discovered an intricate religious belief system. In the aboriginal worldview, every meaningful activity, event, or life process that occurred at a particular place left behind a vibrational residue in the earth. The land, its mountains, rocks, riverbeds, and waterholes, all echoed with vibrations from the events that had brought each place into creation.

It made Neal think of the rust-red mountain, now looming dark and sinister against the stars, and he wondered if the vibrations he had imagined emanating from it had begun long ago by the very cataclysmic geologic event that had created it.

Jallara also spoke of the Dreamtime which she said was the "time before time," when Ancestor Spirits came to Earth in human and other forms, to give the land, animals, and people their form and life as it was known today. Which was why, Jallara explained, the Ancestor Spirits and their powers were not gone but were present in the Dreamings seen all around.

It didn't make much sense to Neal, who had had little religious training. Josiah Scott had taken him to church on Sundays, but Neal had barely listened to the sermon from the pulpit. But one thing did make sense. With each day spent among Jallara's people, Neal came more and more to understand their close ties with the earth and with nature. He learned that the clan didn't feel separate from the scheme of things, that they didn't regard themselves as superior to animals or to water or rocks, but believed that they were all part of the complex web that had been spun at the beginning of creation, in the Dreamtime.

As he listened to rustling in the overhead branches of the mulga tree, wondering what kinds of birds or rodents were up there, Neal thought again of his gratitude to Jallara and her people for saving his life, and his desire to repay them somehow. He had abandoned the idea of showing them how to build sturdier shelters when he realized they needed light collapsible dwellings for their nomadic way of life. That was when he had hit upon the idea of reading and writing. Jallara's people possessed phenomenal memories. To listen to Thumimburee recite the clan's history was spellbinding. "We walk, we walk, we camp at Emu Songline. Hunt kangaroo. Three sleeps. We walk, we walk...." Some stories took hours in the telling, or days. Impressive, Neal thought, but it would still be better if they had a permanent record.

As he rolled himself up in the kangaroo pelt, wishing he had a few more as the cold was severe, he decided that once he reached Perth he would find a way to bring the alphabet back to Jallara's clan, and the tools of reading and writing.

He tossed and turned in fitful sleep. The silence was eerie. Neal had gotten used to hearing human sounds at night—snores, sighs, coughs—

even the sounds of copulating, which had unsettled him at first but which had become as natural a sound in the night as a baby's cry. Finally he drifted into dreams. Hannah was there, in quick flashes that he tried to grasp but could not. He dreamed that the clan had returned for him, and he was awash with relief. There was even a brief scenario with Sir Reginald in which Neal accused him of murder.

He awoke to bright sun slicing through the mulga branches. He drank his fill of the artesian water and then struck off. He wished he had a container to carry extra water with him, but he had learned where to find sources in this seemingly arid plain. When kangaroos needed water, they dug wells for themselves, sometimes as deep as three or four feet. Kangaroos were not in abundance in this area, but there were a few, and Jallara had shown Neal how to find these "kangaroo wells." For food he would do what the clan had done, hunt for roots and seeds, or bring down an animal with his spear. If he was lucky, he would find emu eggs which were green-shelled and ten times as big as a chicken's egg.

He turned his face into the hot wind and took one step away from the camp.

And then he stopped.

He felt it behind him, felt its heat and uncanny vibrations.

The mountain.

Neal turned and, as he looked at the monolith glowing golden in the morning sun, he finally faced a truth about himself: his decision to undergo initiation had nothing at all to do with scientific curiosity, or the desire to write a paper about the experience. It was an excuse, he realized now, to send him out there, on his own, so that he could come to terms with the mountain that, even now, continued to beckon.

Taboo or not, he had to uncover the mystery of the red mountain.

-29-

All through the morning and into the afternoon, Neal moved under a strange compulsion, his feet treading the sand as if under a spell of their own, drawing him closer to the monolith that had turned from golden to red. Even so, Neal could not accept that there were supernatural forces at work.

It is scientific curiosity, he told himself when he arrived at the base of the sheer cliff, and to prove his point he examined the rockface with an analytical eye, making mental notes: it is composed of a coarse-grained sandstone rich in quartz and feldspar. Uplifting and folding has resulted in vertical strata. The surface has been eroded. Weathering of iron-bearing minerals by the process of oxidation has given the outer surface a rusty color.

He wanted to reach out and touch the wall but was suddenly afraid. I have a university degree in geology. I am a scientist.

Yet he stood transfixed at the base of the towering mountain and felt the power of the red rock that was blinding in the sunlight. Was the mountain magnetic in some way?

No, Neal thought at last, feeling something inside himself capitulate to powers greater than he. There is no magnetism. No subterranean streams or seismic disturbance. There is nothing geological going on here, nothing that belongs to the physical world.

And suddenly he knew: that at some point in the past few days, unbeknownst to himself, Neal had changed from an objective scientist to a spiritually hungry man yearning for a message from the unseen world.

And if the spirits did send me a secret message, what would it be?

Although his brain reminded him that he had promised to respect the laws and taboos of Jallara's people, his heart heard the call of the spirits within the mountain. Once again, as if driven by a will other than his own, Neal's feet began walking, following the sandy base of the smooth cliff like a man searching for a doorway. He stepped over pebbles and cobbles, debris that had been washed down the rusty surface for millennia, and followed the jagged footprint of the monolith, the late afternoon sun blinding him, the heat pressing down on him. Sweating profusely, he removed his kangaroo fur loincloth and dropped it to the ground along with the fur blanket. He continued his exploration of the base of the mountain. Sweat dripped into his eyes. He ran a hand over his forehead and it came away soaked. Jallara's people always slept during the worst heat of the day. Neal knew he should be doing the same.

He lost his grip on the spear. It fell to the ground and he kept walking, the sun now behind him, so that he knew was going in a circle and that eventually he would arrive back at the place where he had started. Why was he doing this? What did he hope to find?

He had his answer when, glancing at the ground, he saw the thorny lizard in his path.

It seemed to pause, look up at him, and then it skittered on. Neal followed until the *thulan* appeared to suddenly vanish into the rock. But when Neal examined the surface, he was surprised to find space there. Eons ago, rock had broken away from the main body of the mountain, creating a narrow defile.

Neal slipped inside, and what he saw took his breath away. The slanting sun illuminated a cliff wall that rose smooth and majestic from the desert floor, curving at the top to form a queer overhang. It resembled an ocean breaker about to crash on shore, petrified in a forever cresting wave. His scientist's mind tried to identify the rock and its immense age, how it had been thrust up through the earth. But all he could think of was how beautiful the stone wave was with radiant orange and yellow strata in the red. It looked unreal.

And then he saw *them*.

People. Men and women. Children and animals. Symbols forming clouds and sun and moon. An endless parade of them, executed by different hands in different pigments, red, white, yellow and black. They marched across the face of the rock with long limbs and haloed heads, spears in their hands. Kangaroos in retreat. Babies nursing at breasts. A white-haired elder being laid on a burial mound. The chronology baffled him. Neal had learned that in Jallara's language there were no words for yesterday, today, or tomorrow. They never spoke of a future, although they did understand that a past lay behind them. They seemed to have no need for the concept of time, as they lived in the constant now. So how did that explain this chronicle? And then he knew. Each generation came to this rock wall and recorded their *now*, making this a string of "nows."

All these figures, walking, running or lying down, killing kangaroos or plucking up spinifex grass, were generations of one family. Jallara's clan. Neal imagined Thumimburee reciting the lengthy narrative as the family saw depictions of those who came before them. Here was the permanent record of people who Neal had thought needed an alphabet and writing tools.

As he continued to follow the mural, he saw fathers and sons, down through the ages. He reached out to a man leading a boy by the hand, both carrying boomerangs. A father teaching his son to hunt. Tears pricked Neal's eyes.

And suddenly, he was reminded of *other* tears. A memory from his boyhood, long forgotten. Nine-year-old Neal had come home early from school one day and had walked in on Josiah Scott, sitting in his study, weeping. Neal realized he must have suppressed the memory because it had embarrassed him—for a little boy to come upon the man he worshipped, and find him crying like a woman—but now the scene flashed back into his mind in vivid detail—Josiah Scott sitting at his desk clutching Neal's baby clothes and blanket and emerald-green tear catcher, and sobbing with all his heart.

For eighteen years, Neal had kept the shocking scene buried. He must have run from the house, although he had no recollection of that. It had frightened him to see his father sobbing so. Josiah Scott, who had been such a tower of strength to the boy, who knew everything and was a rock of such stability that the son had not known a moment of insecurity. Neal never brought it up, Josiah never knew that the boy had witnessed his moment of weakness, and Neal had never thought about it again.

Until now. It was strange that primitive stick figures painted on an ancient wall should dredge up that memory now. To what purpose?

With a lump in his throat, Neal resumed walking between the two walls of rock, the sun no longer beating down on him but continuing to illuminate figures that gradually became fantastical in appearance. He placed his hand on the wall and could have sworn he felt the mountain vibrate.

The air grew heavy, he heard a buzzing sound. The wall seemed to go on forever. The illustrations grew more primitive, less identifiable. Neal deduced by the alluvial erosion of the wall that these paintings were very old, perhaps thousands of years old. He was going back in time.

Jallara had explained about her ancestors, the First Ones, who came from the Rainbow Serpent, and she had pointed to the sky. Seeing the eons-old paintings overwhelmed him. The men became less human in appearance until, near the end, they reached enormous proportions and appeared to have round transparent bowls covering their heads and looked as if they were coming down from the sky. At the top edge of the mural, there were stars and what looked like flames. What *were* these beings? Creators, Jallara had called them.

Staring at the figures, Neal felt the air shift and change around him, as if the air pressure were dropping and rising.

And then, before his disbelieving eyes, the figures on the wall started to *move*.

Neal gave a cry and fell back. His mouth stretched in terror as he saw spindly black arms and legs move on the rocky surface, as one-dimensional creatures stretched and breathed and fleshed out. Neal stood frozen with horror as he watched the figures walk before his eyes, as if in some grotesque shadow play, and then suddenly arms shot out, seizing him, pulling him into the wall.

He screamed. He couldn't breathe. He was smothered in rock. Black figures with arms and legs like sticks danced around him. Flames came down from the sky. Neal saw impossibly tall men walking toward him, glass globes encasing their heads. He screamed again, but no sound came out. He was immobilized in the rock as the animals came to life, kangaroos with misshapen bodies and hawks swooping down with sharp talons. All around him, in the red atmosphere that was suffocating him, he saw frightening creatures swimming in the strata. Long-fingered hands reaching for him.

He ran. It was dream-like. His legs were sluggish. He felt hands holding him back. He fought to get away, to escape from the rock.

Help! screamed his silent voice. *Somebody help me!*

Suddenly, in the dense sediment and rock strata that imprisoned him, Neal saw a light coming toward him, glowing brighter as it drew near, and as it reached him, he saw that it was a beautiful woman—not a black-ink stick figure, but a flesh-and-blood woman with blond hair and white skin and a flowing white gown. She smiled at him for a moment, as her hair floated about her head, and then she leaned forward and whispered something in his ear. As Neal felt the dark figures begin to recede into the rock, the woman covered her face with her hands, and when she brought them away, Neal saw that they were filled with diamonds. Raising her arms, she let the diamonds rain down on Neal's upturned face, and where they touched his skin he felt pinprick sparks of life and joy.

In the next instant, he was out of the rock and in cool night air, blinking up at the night sky. He gasped for air, drawing in rasping breaths like a man just rescued from drowning. His eyes did not focus for a moment. He didn't know where he was. And then he saw Jallara looking down at him.

He blinked. She was kneeling at his side, and he saw the emerald glass tear catcher in her hand. She had broken the seal and sprinkled his mother's tears on his face.

Shaking and heaving for breath, he sat up, propping himself up on an elbow. Neal looked around in bewilderment and saw that he was no longer in the rocky gorge but a distance away from the sacred mountain.

"I find you," Jallara said, handing the now empty tear catcher to him. "You not wake. Spirits hold you. They keep you. I call, 'Thulan,' you not hear. You trapped in spirit world. I use mother's tears to give you birth again."

He frowned, shook his head to clear his mind. He must have run out of the mountain when he had thought he was running inside the wall, but he had remained trapped in the nightmare until—

"Jallara, I had the most astonishing vision!" he said, his respirations returning to normal, although his heart continued to race. "I don't know who she was, perhaps an angel. And she gave me a message."

"You must not tell me, Thulan."

"I *can* tell you, Jallara, because it is a wonderful thing, and it is something I should have known all along, and perhaps I did. She told me that Josiah Scott is my real father." He knew now that that was why the memory of the day in Josiah's study had been brought to the surface, why primitive stick-figure fathers and sons had wakened his memory, to tell him that what he had witnessed as a boy was not a moment of weakness after all, but his father's naked anguish.

Neal looked up at the stars as they peeped over the summit of the mountain. Then he looked at Jallara, her deep-set eyes filled with starlight. "I am not sure you understand all my words but I need to tell you. Josiah Scott is my real father, of this I have no doubt. I was not left on his doorstep, he took me because for whatever reason, my mother could not keep me. The day he sat me down, when I was twelve years old, and said I was old enough to know the truth, when he said he was my adoptive father, there were tears in his eyes, and I thought it was because he was speaking a painful truth. I know now that it was a painful *lie*. To protect my mother, I now believe. I was not a foundling, Jallara, but a love-child, and that is a very different thing. Josiah Scott and my mother were in love but were forbidden to marry. I also know now why he never married. He has been in love with her all these years. But ..."

"But what, Thulan?"

"If the lady who appeared to me in my vision was in fact my mother, does that mean she is dead?"

Jallara shook her head. "It mean the power in her tears save your life."

Neal struggled to stand up but found he was incredibly weak, so he stayed seated on the cool sand. Although he was naked and the night was cold, he felt no chill. And then he had another concern. "Jallara, you told me the mountain was taboo, but I had to come here. I couldn't stay away. Please forgive me if I have offended you or your ancestors. I suppose I will not be initiated into the clan now. In my defense, I followed a *thulan* in there."

To his surprise, she smiled. "You come because mountain call. Ancestors call. You one of us, Thulan."

He stared at her. "I was *supposed* to go in there?" He sighed and squinted up at the rising stone wall, backdropped by stars. "Does it have a name?"

"No name."

When I get back to civilization I will add No Name Mountain to the map of Australia. And then he thought, No, because then white men will come looking for it, desecrate it, and slap a name on it like Victoria or Albert. Maybe even plant a flag on top. Neal shuddered at the thought.

A breeze came up, cold and frosty, but all Neal was aware of was how it lifted Jallara's long wavy hair. "Jallara, did Thumimburee know what it was I would learn here?"

She shook her head. "Every vision different."

Neal thought about this. And then he realized that walkabout had nothing to do with survival, it had to do with spiritual revelations and self-knowledge.

"If I had not asked to be initiated into your clan," he said in awe, marveling at the mysterious workings of the unseen world, "I would not have come to this mountain, I would not have seen the ancestral wall, and I would not have realized that I do have a father and that I am someone's son." How would a scientist explain it, because no instruments, no clever tools or charts could analyze and measure and categorize his mystical experience. "The First Ones have converted me, Jallara. I now believe most definitely in the spirit world."

She shook her head and tapped his chest. "Thulan already believe in spirits. Always there."

He wondered if she was right. It did stand to reason that, if a man yearned to discover the existence of a spirit realm, then part of him must already believe. "I've learned something else about myself," he said quietly, his bones still aching as if he had truly been trapped inside rock. "I am arrogant."

She gave him a puzzled look. "Arro-gahnt?"

"I thought I had all the answers for your people, that I could miraculously create a better way of life for you by giving you bows and arrows and sturdier huts, when you have managed to live and survive here for thousands of years. That mural *is* your recorded history, is it not?"

She smiled. "Ancestors. First Beings. Thumimburee."

He nodded. The first and newest figure as one entered the stone wave was the current clever-man.

"I cannot believe now what I said to you when we left the billabong five months ago, about how it didn't matter where your people went because you had no towns, no homes to visit. I saw this as a white man's world. But it isn't. You have your own landmarks, your own places that call to you. We think of your people as aimless nomads, because we cannot see the songlines or the Dreaming places."

Neal had been so certain Jallara's people would regret leaving the plentiful waterhole. And then he had been stunned to find the clan arriving at hidden water deposits—holes in the limestone floor of the desert, covered with stones and brush, and filled with sweet water. He had thought he would tell them how to live, when they had sorted it out thousands of years ago. He smiled sheepishly. "It would be like having Thumimburee walk into my father's house on Beacon Street and tell us that our fireplace was wrong, that we did lighting wrong, that our beds were ridiculous, and then show us the *proper* way to live. I saw myself as the superior white man come to enlighten you. Whereas the truth is, you enlightened *me*."

Neal fell silent and stared at Jallara. His mind was clearing now, his body recovering from its ordeal. As the experience within the mountain began to recede and seem more like a dream than an actual occurrence, Neal returned to the present and to reality, and to suddenly wonder what Jallara was doing there.

"Why are you here? Does Thumimburee know you followed me?"

When she smiled demurely and looked at him from beneath thick black lashes, Neal's eyes widened. He noticed something different about Jallara. She was heavily costumed and decorated. He had never seen her this way. Feathers, many necklaces of seeds and bones and teeth. One necklace was fashioned from shells. Where had they found shells in the middle of a desert? "What—" he began. And then he knew. "*You're* the third ritual."

"First, pain," she said with a smile. "Second, spirit world. And now, manhood."

Although he was suddenly filled with sexual desire, he started to say, "We are not married. And I have promised myself to someone else." But he stopped. Jallara was not here for love or devotion or to take his heart from Hannah. Her presence with him at this sacred mountain had more to do with religion than carnal needs. Had she been chosen for the task because she was half white? Had she requested it? Or had she competed with the other girls and won? It didn't matter. The more he looked at her in the moonlight, looked deep into her exotic black eyes and saw her moist, smiling lips, the more he stopped questioning the moment.

Jallara reached into a pouch that hung from the belt of her grass skirt and brought out small green leaves that carried a pungent aroma. She pressed them to Neal's lips, and he tasted a bitterness that was not altogether unpleasant. She reached into another pouch and produced small red berries. Neal waited for her to feed them to him, but instead she pressed them against her neck, tilting her head and brushing her hair back as she squeezed the berries against her bare skin, sending juice running down to her shoulder. To Neal's surprise, she reached up and drew his head down so that his mouth met sweet berry pulp, and the mixture of the two flavors produced an unexpected delightful and erotic taste.

Jallara drew away from him and rose to her feet. She held out her arms and hummed as she executed a seductive dance in the moonlight. Neal was mesmerized by the swaying of her breasts, the supple undulating of her hips. When she reached behind and untied the belt of the grass skirt, to remove the rustling garment and toss it aside, Neal saw that she was completely naked. He groaned with desire.

When she finished her dance, her skin glowing with perspiration, Jallara knelt before him and gently pushed him back onto the sand. She leaned forward and swung her long hair back and forth over his erection. She ran her tongue lightly over the still-tender tattoos. Neal inhaled her earthy, musky scent and sent his hands exploring the hills and valleys of her mysterious landscape.

He reached up and pulled her down, moaning with excitement. She encircled in him her arms. He rolled her over so that Jallara lay on her back and he looked deep into her eyes as he caressed her breasts, nipples, and belly.

Jallara clasped him tightly to her and, with her warm moist lips against his ear, murmured in her melodic language words that sounded to Neal like water tumbling over stones.

When he entered her, and she wrapped her strong thighs around him to draw him deeper inside, Jallara looked up at the mountain that blotted out the stars, and she thought: What did you see in there, Thulan?

Jallara had never been inside the mountain. No female had, as it was taboo for them, and the men never spoke of it. She was envious, wishing she could experience what Thulan had. For the first time in her young life, Jallara wondered why men created secret places for themselves, forbidden to women. She thought about it as she held the white man in her arms, felt his hardness within her, felt his hot breath on her cheeks and neck. And something occurred to her that had never occurred to her before: Women already have their own secret places, and in them we create life.

Jallara groaned with pleasure. Thulan felt warm and strong in her arms as he pressed his lips to her hair, neck, shoulders. She felt dampness on her skin and realized that he was crying. Initiates often cried after their ordeal, because spirit-visions were powerful. Recalling that she had thought Thulan needed healing, and knowing that in a few days they would be saying good-by, she stroked his hair and whispered sweet words into his ear.

As he moved rhythmically inside her, Jallara smiled up to the stars and thanked the mountain spirit. The sickness had left Thulan's soul.

-30-

"Help! *Help!*"

Hannah snapped her head up. She listened. Had someone shouted for help? The constant howling wind in this bleak wasteland played tricks on the ears. She squinted into the afternoon glare and surveyed her surroundings—the red-sand desert was marred by twelve gaping holes with rubble mounds in between, giving the desolate plain the bizarre appearance of a field of giant moles.

Hannah was herself kneeling on one of the rubble heaps, called mullocks, sifting through sand and rock brought up from the mines. With a small curved pickax, she searched for gemstones overlooked by the miners underground. She had found several large opals—from pale blue to black opal with a heart of fire.

"Help! I've got a bloody cave-in here!"

Hannah shot to her feet. Which of the mine shafts had the call come from? She saw men running, and when they gathered around a crater and looked down into it, she realized that it was the mine being worked by Ralph "Church" Gilchrist, the bullock drover from up Toowoomba way. Since opal was only found underground, shafts had to be sunk and then tunnels dug parallel to the surface. From what Hannah surmised as she joined the others, Church's shaft was clear, it was his offshoot tunnel that had caved in.

"Are you all right, boyo?" Mike Maxberry shouted down.

A thin voice rose up: "Get me outa here. I've got ceiling coming down. If you need incentive, I'm clutching an opal the size of yer arse."

They had all arrived now, to stand at the rim of the crater and look down into the darkness. Charlie Olde cupped his mouth and shouted, "Church, you stupid sod, can you hear us? If you're dead, give a shout."

Hannah saw that although the men joked, fear was plain on their faces. So far, no one had been lost to a cave-in, but the threat was always there, and every morning that the men climbed down into their shafts, the thought stood on their minds loud and clear: Is today the day I get buried alive?

"I need the bucket!" Church shouted back.

Jamie O'Brien called for the windlass, a huge contraption requiring six men to haul it from another mine to Church's and stabilize it over the hole. Jamie's men had constructed it out of wagon planks and axles, and it consisted of a horizontal barrel supported on vertical posts and turned by two cranks so that the hoisting rope was wound around the barrel as the bucket went up and down. It was used for hauling rubble out as mines were dug. It made Hannah think of a giant wishing well.

As Jamie O'Brien helped to anchor the windlass and keep it level, he shouted, "We're lowering the bucket, Ralph. Can you clear your way out?"

O'Brien no longer needed a splint or crutches but was able to walk again, albeit it with a limp. And as he wrestled with the cumbersome windlass, Hannah was unable to keep her eyes off his wiry musculature. Jamie had removed his shirt so that his torso glowed with perspiration in the afternoon sun. And Hannah was flooded with sexual desire.

It frightened her, this ache for Jamie O'Brien that grew with each passing day. She was not in love with him. Her heart still belonged to Neal. But her body had a mind of its own.

The other night, over a supper of roasted goanna and damper, he had asked, "When are you going to call me Jamie?" Hannah had relied, "Although we are in the wilderness, Mr. O'Brien, we must maintain proper decorum. In fact, I believe we must do so *because* we are in the wilderness."

But she knew that calling him Mr. O'Brien had more to do with keeping a barrier between herself and this man to whom she was becoming frighteningly attracted. And because she suspected Jamie O'Brien felt the same way toward her—the way she would feel his eyes on her, the self-assured smile he would send her across a glowing campfire—she feared he might make an overture that she would not be able to resist.

Hannah pushed strands of hair from her face as she squinted in the late afternoon sunlight to watch the bucket go down into the narrow mine shaft that was wide enough for one man with a bit of elbow room. The wind in this desert blew relentlessly, night and day, hot and cold, north to south, east to west. Hannah was forever holding onto her skirts and taming her hair. She had lost her bonnet long ago, to watch it carried away on the wind.

But she was exhilarated. When the bandage came off Jamie's shin to reveal a clean wound, she had known that the iodine prevented infections in serious wounds such as compound fractures. What other miracles might the preparation perform? When Mike Maxberry had offered to escort her back to Adelaide, Hannah had thought of what she could do with the money, if opals were indeed as precious as Jamie O'Brien said—she could move out of the Australia Hotel and into a place of her own from which she could study and experiment, and widen her scope of learning. And help so many more people. She had thought, Neal is crossing the Nullarbor with Sir Reginald, Alice is touring the colonies with Sam Glass, and Liza Guinness thinks I am with Neal. No one would miss her, and so Hannah had said she would like to stay and hunt for opals.

After Jamie had bought his mysterious treasure map, he had discreetly chatted up experienced gold and gem hunters, called fossickers, to learn about opals, and based on what an old fossicker had told him, he knew they would have to sink holes and "gouge" for opals. So he and Maxberry had picked up equipment and supplies all over Adelaide, never too much from one place so as not to rouse suspicion and cause a "run." Jamie and his men had worked night and day in the spot Stinky Sam found, until the whole area became so pocked with holes, each with its own miner gouging away, that Nan had laughed and said, "*Kooba peedi*," which in her tongue meant "white men in holes." Jamie had taken his knife and etched onto one of the boulders, *Coober Pedy*.

At first, their finds had not been spectacular—small pieces of pale blue stone, and not exactly the "millions" a drunken Sam had reported—but Jamie and his men dreamed of great chunks of fiery gems such as they had heard of in legend, and so they had settled down to serious mining, creating a home of this bustling little settlement five hundred miles north of Adelaide and consisting of six tents, a horse corral, a twig and brush shed for working the opals, and an outhouse made of planks from one of the wagons and constructed by Blackie White, who had declared, "Dig the dunny deep the first time and you won't have to keep moving it." Although water had to be rationed, Hannah was able to hang out laundry. It hadn't been washed, but the wind and sunlight and sand seemed to whip the clothes clean.

And it wasn't all hardship and labor. Charlie Olde and Stinky Sam were so good with pistols that there was meat at almost every meal, and what those two former stockmen didn't catch, Nan got with her digging stick. The three carrot-topped brothers Roddy, Cyrus, and Elmo, bricklayers with whom Jamie had linked up in Botany Bay, and whom Hannah couldn't tell apart, provided evening musical entertainment—Roddy on the banjo, Cyrus with a fiddle, and Elmo whistling through his missing front teeth.

And there was always Jamie with his amazing store of Outback tales.

While everyone watched and waited as Jamie worked the windlass with Blackie White, and they waited for Church to dig himself out—and Hannah tried not to stare at Jamie's sweaty back and sinewy arms—a cooking aroma drifted their way. Nan was at one of the fires, roasting a fat goanna she had trapped and killed, cooking it in the skin aboriginal-style. Hannah didn't know Nan's story. No one did. Judging by the scars pitting her dark face, Nan had once had a severe case of pox, a white man's disease. Jamie said that Mike Maxberry didn't talk about the native woman he kept company with, saying simply that her entire clan had been wiped out by a chicken pox epidemic, with only Nan surviving. For some reason, she had attached herself to Mike and stayed with him since.

Nan didn't talk much, even though she knew English. But one thing Hannah had heard the aboriginal woman say was that this area of the outback was called Plains of Fire by the aborigines. A wilderness that, in the summer, was hotter than blazes where "not even blackfellah goes."

This was the source of what had been troubling Hannah on this sunny spring afternoon in September as she had noodled on mullocks for overlooked opals: her growing fear that these men were so gripped with opal fever that they would not abandon these fields when the time came. And that time, blazing summer, was coming soon.

Suddenly a muffled roar was heard underground.

The men exchanged fearful glances.

"Church!" Jamie called down. "You still there?"

They listened, but all they heard was the whistling wind.

"I'm going down," Jamie said.

"And lose you, too?" Maxberry shouted. "Boyo, it's suicide going down there. Ralph is buried!"

Jamie climbed over the side and, using the handholds and footholds gouged into the stone wall of the shaft, slipped his right foot into the bucket, gripped the rope and said, "Lower me."

Roddy the carrot-topped bricklayer took over for Jamie and cranked the handles with Blackie White. They waited in anxious silence as the winch creaked Jamie O'Brien down into the abyss, his dark-blond head swallowed by darkness. They heard a thud at the bottom, and then the hurried clearing of rocks and stones, heavy breathing, and the occasional, "Hang on, Church, I'm coming."

Hannah bit her lip. Only last week Jamie had wondered out loud if the men were sinking shafts too close together, possibly creating a dangerous situation by destabilizing this patch of desert. As sounds drifted up from the bottom of the hole, but no sound coming from Ralph Gilchrist, Hannah looked toward the distant horizon, across the hundreds of miles of flat windswept desolation, and thought, No one knows where we are.

Finally: "Got him!" And as Roddy and Blackie strained at the windlass, hoisting Ralph up the shaft, hands reached out, ready to grab him.

Ralph was covered in blood from a head wound. Hannah was immediately at his side as the men laid their friend on the ground. He was fully awake, Hannah could see, and in a great deal of pain. The cave-in had pelted him with rocks and stones that had cut him all over.

The men joked with Ralph to lift his spirits. And Ralph, himself grinning, roared, "Quit yer laughing, you lot. This ain't as funny as it looks!"

But when Hannah saw Ralph Gilchrist grimace, revealing his teeth, she received a shock. "Merciful Heaven," she whispered.

She stood and, suddenly shaken, said, "Will you please carry him to his tent? I shall look after him there."

Jamie climbed up and out of the mine shaft, to the cheers of his friends, but Hannah was too stunned to congratulate him on a brave deed.

The opal hunters didn't know it, but they suddenly had a very serious and deadly situation on their hands.

-31-

When Hannah finished seeing to Ralph Gilchrist's wounds, none of which were life threatening, she came out of the tent to find that night had fallen and the men were gathered around the main campfire. Stinky Sam was digging biscuits out of the embers while Nan was skinning the goanna and dropping juicy chunks of lizard meat onto the men's tin plates. Hannah watched them pass around a canvas water bag, drinking freely.

She was worried about their dwindling water supply. Scant winter rains had come through, keeping the barrels full, and Nan was adept at digging in dry creek beds and sucking up brackish water through a reed. But a rainless summer was coming. While there was enough water now for men and horses, soon it would be all gone. Hannah had held back some of the precious water as an eye wash, because of the constant threat of a conjunctivitis called "sandy blight," but even that would not last long.

And now they had an even bigger worry. She glanced back into the tent where Ralph Gilchrist lay moaning. He hadn't long to live, and it had nothing to do with the cave-in.

Hannah lifted her face to the cold wind. The air felt different this evening, strange. Was rain coming? But no clouds covered the bright, frosty stars.

She looked at Jamie O'Brien at the campfire, noting that he had changed into a fresh shirt, one that he had hung on a line to let the wind and sand blast it clean. Over it, the familiar black leather vest with silver buttons. And while he had to forgo shaving because of water restrictions, Jamie kept his dark blond beard clipped short and his hair trimmed at the collar.

As she looked at the other men's faces illuminated in the fire's glow, while they ate and laughed and talked, Hannah thought what a close-knit fraternity it was. It was the mateship peculiar to the Outback, she knew, where danger was so rife that many times the only thing between a man and certain death was the friend riding at his side.

So the problem of convincing these men to abandon the opal fields, that it was a matter of life or death, lay with Mr. O'Brien. Hannah knew that if she could convince *him* to leave, the others would follow.

As Jamie told a story, he kept his eyes on Hannah, standing outside the tent Ralph Gilchrist shared with Tabby and Bluey Brown. She had a worried look on her face. Was Church all right? Hannah was a sight, Jamie thought with a rush of sexual yearning. Her gown had seen better days, and wisps of hair hung loose about her face. But she was still every inch the lady.

Hannah Conroy occupied Jamie's thoughts night and day. He dreamed about her. As he toiled away in his mine, chipping at the sandstone, he wondered what it would be like to hold her, to kiss her. After years of chasing skirts and enjoying amorous conquests, Jamie thought himself immune to love. Had not even come close.

Until now.

Now he knew where the songs and poems came from, about love and romance and eternal faithfulness. He had thought they were just fanciful notions and words composed by lovesick young men. Jamie wished now that he himself had the gift for poetry and lyric, because simply thinking, "I love this woman," sounded inadequate and far from his true feelings.

"You always tell the story wrong, Jamie," Charlie Olde teased. "The dog that sat on the tucker box. The way I heard it, the word wasn't *sat*."

As the others laughed, Jamie growled, "Watch your language," and suddenly seeing Hannah standing there, Charlie blushed fiercely and apologized to her. But Hannah wasn't offended. Jamie O'Brien's tales fascinated her.

As colorful as he was, however, Hannah realized that Jamie didn't know much beyond Australia or his own experience. He'd been around and seen a lot, but when she made mention, perhaps, of Keats or Byron, he didn't know what she was talking about. He knew nothing of history or science, and his knowledge of geography, outside of Australia, was scant. "Never been to England. I hear it rains a lot." Jamie O'Brien's smarts lay in his foxy quick-thinking brain, craftily tricking other men, and staying one step ahead of the law.

She could not help comparing him to Neal, which she knew was not fair, but there it was all the same. Neal, who was book-smart and educated, a gentleman with a thirst for knowledge, for solving mysteries, a man of honesty and integrity and with whom she had once thought she was going to die.

How was it possible to be attracted to two men at once, and men so different from each other? Perhaps it *was* possible, if the emotions themselves were different, too. Her love for Neal ran deep and sure, and made her toss and turn in restless dreams. Her feelings for Jamie were less sure, less definable, and more immediate. He felt forbidden to her, and therefore exciting. Not love, perhaps, but desire. Definitely desire.

Hannah always looked forward to evenings at the campfire—in the company of men who were shy and polite with her, who watched their language and called her Miss Conroy—beneath a vast starry sky, listening to Jamie O'Brien's stories. She thought what beautiful ballads they would make, and she imagined Alice singing them on a stage to a spellbound audience. Jamie spun colorful tales of drovers and sheepmen, soldiers and outlaws, of immoral women and saintly wives, of explorers and adventures, swagmen and bushrangers, natives who went walkabout, and men who drank and gambled and gave up their lives to pursue elusive dreams. Jamie told of Aborigines named Pingjim and Joe, and mountains called Karra Karra and Wellington, of towns with ancient names and names that were new, like Gundagai and Victoria. And he boasted about his own swindles, taking money from gullible men, selling land that didn't exist, making off with the horses and wagons of Her Majesty's troops, all told in a wry tone with a cheeky grin.

Hannah joined the group at the campfire, trying to think of how to break the latest news to him.

"You think that's funny, miss," one of the three carrot-topped brothers said with a mouth full of food, "you shoulda been with us the day Jamie here was approached by a toffee-nosed Pom fresh off the boat. The bloke said he'd heard about a curious animal we have here, a kind of bear that lives in trees. So Jamie tells the Pom it's called a Drop Bear. They are called that, says Jamie, because they drop out of gum trees and suck the eyeballs out of anyone walking underneath. The Pom said he really wanted to see one, so Jamie tells him he can protect himself by rubbing dog urine on his head before he goes out walking."

"You know, Miss Conroy," Blackie White said, as if competing for her attention, "after I first met Jamie up Brisbane way, I took him home and my mother said he hadn't the manners of a pig. But I stuck up for him and said he did."

"Hey, Jamie," Tabby the axeman said, "did ya tell Miss Conroy about the time you boxed a kangaroo?"

Jamie grinned and said to Hannah, "Yeah, I did box a kangaroo, but I let her win. She had a joey in her pouch."

As the others laughed, Hannah quietly said, "Mr. O'Brien, may I have a word with you, please?"

They went to the opal shed—four wagon axles supporting a twig and brush roof—where a makeshift table had been constructed of planks and barrels, upon which were spread the finds from all the shafts: chunks of sandstone embedded with luscious opal of all the colors of the rainbow. A king's ransom.

When Jamie was sure they were out of the hearing of the others, he turned to Hannah and said, "So how's Church is doing?"

"His injuries are minor."

"Thank God. When I saw all that blood, it had me worried."

Jamie wore no hat so that his hair, the color of antique gold, Hannah thought, was stirred by the evening wind. But there was enough light from a flickering lantern to make his eyes shine blue like the opals on the table. Without other people around them, with just the silence of the night and the stars above, Hannah felt suddenly nervous. He stood very close to her. He smiled, crinkling the corners of his eyes.

"Mr. O'Brien, we have a serious situation on our hands. The very thing that I feared has happened. Ralph Gilchrist has scurvy."

When he didn't react, she added, "You would know it as the Barcoo rot."

His eyes widened. "Are you sure?"

"He has bleeding gums. It is the first sign. His condition will get worse."

"How did he get it?"

"Scurvy is caused by a diet deficiency. Months of eating nothing but meat and biscuits."

He rubbed his jaw. "Then how come the rest of us don't have it?"

"We all will eventually, it is only a matter of time. Before Mr. Maxberry fetched me from the Australia Hotel, I was eating fruit and vegetables. My body most likely still has a store of the necessary acidic juice that prevents scurvy. I am guessing that in the months before you and your men departed Adelaide, you all ate properly. Mr. Gilchrist clearly did not. His diet was already deficient, so he is the first to show the symptoms. But I assure you, Mr. O'Brien, if we do not head back for Adelaide at once, we shall all come down with it."

"How serious is this scurvy?"

"It is fatal in every case."

Jamie frowned. "Don't you have any medicine for it?"

"Scurvy isn't like illnesses that are accompanied by fever. It is a disease of nutritional lack. Unless he gets proper food—fruit and vegetables—he will die. As will we all, Mr. O'Brien, if we stay out here much longer. If you don't want to go to Adelaide, then at least get your men to the head of Spencer Gulf, where there is fresh water and vegetation."

The wind picked up, rustling the brush over their heads and making the support poles sway and creak. A few strands of Hannah's hair had come loose from the chignon, to whip across her cheek. Jamie resisted the impulse to reach up and sweep it back.

"It's not that simple, Hannah." He ran his fingers through his thick hair. "They gave up their jobs, they pulled up stakes, they left wives and sweethearts behind. And they promised them they'd come home rich."

"We have opals," she said, gesturing to the generous spread on the table.

"Not enough, not split twelve ways.

"They can have my share."

"And they can have mine, too, but it's still not enough. They put their life savings into buying the wagons and horses and all the supplies and tools.

"They'll want their money back and more. You've seen how these men work, how driven they are. With each little bit of opal they find, they are that much more obsessed with finding more."

When she started to protest, Jamie said, "Hannah, these men are more than casual mates. When Mike and I escaped from the road gang and the police launched a manhunt for us, I went straight to these blokes for help. They gave us a hiding place and food and steered the police in the wrong direction. I owe these men my life, so when I came into the treasure map and knew I was onto something good, I wanted to share it with men who had saved my life."

The wind gusted, and Hannah had to hold her skirts down. "If it is about repaying a debt, Mr. O'Brien, you can repay them now by saving *their* lives."

"But it's like this: yes, Ralph's come down with the scurvy, but there's no sign of it in the rest of us. They won't leave while they're still feeling healthy, and I'm not sure I want to make them. Look at young Charlie there," Jamie said, pointing to the youngest in the group at the campfire. "I met him up Murrumburrah way ten years ago. This was long before I was put to work on a chain gang. I was free in those days, and on the road looking for shearing work when I found this boy in a field digging a hole. He was crying because he was burying his brother. So I set my swag down and finished digging the grave and then covered up his brother. Charlie told me he was all alone in the world. He was fifteen, I was twenty-three, so I invited him to join me, and we ended up at Bunyip cattle station where he got a job as a stockman working under Stinky Sam, whom I'd already made friends with the year before. Six years later, those two hid Mike and me and gave us food and lied to the police who came looking for us. That was at great risk to themselves, because harboring us would get them prison for sure. I've promised to make them rich men, and I can't go back on my promise."

Jamie fell silent and studied his calloused hands, while the wind gusted around him and Hannah, and the men at the campfire jumped out of the way of flying sparks. "Ralph Gilchrist," he said softly, "was being waylaid by bushrangers when I met him on the road. I joined the fray, and together we sent them running. But for me, Church would have died or been left crippled, so he gave me a summer's work and a good life droving bullocks. I've a special friendship with each of those men, Hannah, and I won't let them down."

She thought about this, and something occurred to her. Ever since he told her that he had run away from home, Hannah had thought of him as a man without a family. And yet it was not so. Jamie O'Brien had a very close-knit family. She had never thought that family could be more than flesh and blood. But she thought now of her own close friendships with Alice and Liza Guinness, and she realized that she regarded them as family. It startled her. The night her father died, Hannah had seen herself as being alone in the world. But, like with Jamie, it was not so.

Before she could try another attempt at persuasion, a sudden bright light illuminated the sky, followed by a deafening crack.

"What—" Jamie snapped around in the direction of the flash just as a second bright light burst against the dark night. He and Hannah stared in shock at the streaks of blinding white appearing suddenly and branching from the sky to the ground.

"Hoy! A storm is coming!" shouted Blackie White as the men jumped up from the campfire. "And it's coming *fast!*"

As they now saw monstrous black clouds materializing out of the night, billowing toward them, the men dropped their plates and frantically ran around to all the empty barrels in the camp, upending them to catch rain water.

Another blinding flash as more lightning forked down, striking the opal shed and setting it on fire. Great forks of white light streaked down from the black sky, filling the air with a burning smell. Hannah's skin tingled. She felt the hairs rise on the back of her neck. The bolts came quickly now, racing along the flat plain toward the vulnerable camp, hot-white branches striking the ground five, ten, fifteen times at once. It was as if the whole desert had suddenly been electrified. The thunder was deafening.

"We have to get into the mines!" Jamie shouted. "We're not safe out here! Somebody get Church!"

Roddy and his two brothers ran into Ralph Gilchrist's tent and came out with him by arms and legs.

The wind was furious now, the lightning on the leading edge of a gust front where the new storm was forming. Rain was a miracle and a blessing on this parched land, but the swords of fire that split the sky and sparked the earth were terrifying in their brilliance and intensity, the thunder cracking so loud that it seemed the sky was splitting open.

Jamie O'Brien took Hannah by the wrist and ran with her. "Down here!" he shouted as, all around, the rest of the men headed for the mine shafts.

"Hurry, Hannah! I'm right behind you!"

"What about the horses?"

"There's nothing we can do for them. Hurry!"

She descended, groping for the handholds gouged into the stone wall, getting her feet caught in her petticoats. She saw Mike Maxberry send Nan down a nearby shaft, their silhouettes eerie against a sudden fork of lighting. Hannah thought they had been struck, but then she saw Mike climb over the rim shaft after Nan.

When Hannah was halfway down, she looked up, but Jamie wasn't descending. "Mr. O'Brien!" she called. *"Jamie!"*

He appeared briefly. "I have to help the others." And then he was gone.

When Hannah reached the bottom, she turned her face upward to watch anxiously for Jamie. Lightning forked and struck the ground, illuminating the night with a brilliance brighter than day. In between lightning bursts, the mine shaft was plunged into the deepest blackness Hannah had ever known. She heard men shouting. She smelled smoke and sulphur.

And then there he was, lowering himself into the crater. She watched Jamie clamber down, while above, white light flashed in the night and thunder cracked and roared.

"Everybody's down the shafts," he said breathlessly as he neared her.

Thunder rumbled and the ground shook. Hannah thought of Ralph Gilchrist's cave-in.

"We'll be all right down here," Jamie said when he reached the bottom. By the light of a lightning flash, he found a wall torch, which all the mines were equipped with and, striking a match, lit the tarred tip. The flame cast light on a narrow tunnel with rough stone walls. Hannah saw chisels and small pickaxes on the floor. When she saw the blanket, she realized they had chosen Tabby's mine, where he liked to take cat naps.

The tunnel was narrow, with the ceiling just inches above their heads, and it didn't stretch far underground, about twelve feet Hannah reckoned. It might have felt like a grave, but cool air wafted down the shaft, the torch flame flickered, and Hannah could hear the storm above.

"Might as well make ourselves comfortable," Jamie said as he took Hannah's hand and helped her down to the floor littered with sandstone chips.

"What if rain comes down the shaft?" Hannah asked, as he sat next to her, their backs to the wall.

"I'll keep an eye out. For now it's the lightning we have to worry about."

Hannah watched shadows dance on the wall opposite. She was able to stretch her legs before her, but there was little room beyond that. Jamie's nearness made her heart race.

She needed to talk. "Mr. O'Brien, when I came out of Church's tent, you made Tabby apologize to me for something he said about a dog that sat on a tucker box?"

Jamie laughed softly while, above them, lightning streaked down from the sky and burned the desert floor with a fiery fork. He looked at Hannah, sitting so close to him her arm was pressed against his. This close, and in the glow of the torch on the wall, he saw the fine details of her face, the arched brows, the thick lashes framing irises the color of doves. Her complexion had warmed in the past months. Hannah Conroy was no longer pale but glowed with a healthy Outback tan. He shuddered with desire. "Do you know the story?"

She shook her head. His nearness made it suddenly impossible to breathe. Hannah struggled with her feelings, fought down the rising desire in her body, the ache that was both familiar and new.

"It's an old story," he said. Jamie sat with his knees bent, his wrists casually propped on them, a relaxed posture that hid the inner turmoil of his emotions. "It goes back to the early days of exploration in New South Wales. They were hard and hazardous times with supplies and stores having to be transported along makeshift tracks over rough terrain by bullock teams. Sometimes the wagons would get bogged down and the bullocky would have to go in search of help. The story is about the bullocky's dog guarding its master's tuckerbox—where the drover's food is stored—while he was away seeking help."

Jamie turned to Hannah, his eyes meeting hers. "It was a summer of droving, and my team got bogged down nine miles south of Gundagai. After trials and troubles, when I got back, old Prince was still there, guarding my tucker box. But he'd starved to death doing it, because he wouldn't roam from the treasure he was meant to guard. Starved to death guarding a box of food. I buried old Prince in that tucker box he'd sat on for so long."

"It's a sad story," Hannah said.

"That's why Tabby had to make a joke. Men don't like to cry in front of their mates, so they say the word wasn't *sat* on the tucker box."

Hannah looked at Jamie for a moment, and when she caught the meaning, she smiled.

"You should write your stories down, Mr. O'Brien," she said quietly, the breath trapped in her lungs, her chest tight with desire. She had secretly pledged herself to Neal, counted the days until they would be together again. But here was this man, rugged and sunburnt, as colorful as the tales he told, and living by a curious code that mixed honor with crime. Hannah wanted to be held by him, wanted to experience the excitement and exoticness of Jamie O'Brien.

"Don't know that I can sit still long enough to write things down," he said. He kept his eyes on her, watching the gray irises reflect the flickering torchlight. "You know, a few minutes ago, when I went to help the others and you called out to me, you called me Jamie."

"Did I?" Hannah whispered.

Jamie wondered, if he were to kiss her right now, would she kiss him back, and would they keep kissing until the storm passed?

In the past, when a woman took his fancy, Jamie had no trouble wooing and courting her until they were both blissfully enjoying the pleasures of a bed. He had no qualms about kissing and saying farewell afterward. Not that he was without feelings. Jamie always made sure a woman didn't surrender her heart to him, that she was of like mind when it came to having a sporting romp, no strings attached. And when he picked up his swag and hit the road, he always made sure that he left the woman with a smile on her face.

But Hannah was different. As much as he would like to take her into his arms right now—burned for it, in fact—and as much as he knew it would leave him with the memory of a lifetime, it didn't seem right. And for the first time in Jamie's checkered life, the word "marriage" came into his mind.

The moment stretched as the storm rolled over them, sending cold wind gusts down the shaft, and flashes of bright light. The tunnel had become intimate. Hannah tore her eyes away from Jamie's and, clearing her throat, said, "How can I convince your men to return to Spencer Gulf before they come down with scurvy?"

Before he could reply, Hannah added, "I know what the men say about me, that I am just a midwife so what do I know? I have heard it before. But I did fix your leg, did I not? You, at least, Mr. O'Brien, know that I have skills and learning beyond midwifery."

He gave her a long, considering look and then said, "And how is that, I wonder? How does a lady learn things that only men know?"

She told him about her father, how she had helped him with his patients, how he had taught her everything he knew, and the things she had learned since. "I know what I am talking about in regard to the threat of scurvy."

"I don't doubt it."

"It is frustrating, Mr. O'Brien.

He watched her pink, moist lips. "What is?"

"All I want do is make sick people well."

"Sounds easy enough."

"For a man, yes. Women are limited."

"And who is it that's limiting you?"

Hannah was held in his opal-blue eyes for several heart beats. Then she looked up at the rough-hewn ceiling of the tunnel. The thunder had rolled on and could be heard in the distance. The lightning had stopped. "Listen," she said. "It's raining."

"We can't go up just yet. Not until we're sure about the lightning. I'll keep an eye on the shaft, make sure no rain floods us out. It's going to get very cold down here, Hannah." Jamie reached for Tabby's blanket and handed it to her. "Bundle up in this."

Hannah spread the itchy blanket over the two of them as they sat with their backs to the wall. The temperature was dropping, but the glow from the flickering torch created the illusion of cozy intimacy. Listening to the gentle sound of the whispering rain, Jamie put his arm around Hannah, holding her tight. She leaned into him. Jamie O'Brien smelled of dust and sweat, his body was as hard as the rock that sheltered them. As Hannah felt his warmth permeate the fabric of her gown, she thought of the stories at the campfire, the things he had said about the men he had brought to this desolate place, their deep bonds, their unique, shared history, and Hannah thought about her attraction to this man, that it stemmed in part from his being Australian. Jamie O'Brien was born here. His soul had received its generating spark from this ancient land, tying him to the red earth and gum trees in a way no immigrant could be.

Hannah desperately wanted to be with him, to be part of Jamie O'Brien as surely as she wanted to be part of Australia, to belong to them both. But her heart still yearned for the man who had held her and kissed her as the *Caprica* teetered on the edge of certain doom. Bonds of love and shared experience connected her to Neal Scott in a way no other person could understand.

She wanted to be with Neal. But at the same time ...

Jamie was thinking of the woman sheltered beneath his arm. He knew it would be easy to kiss her, hold her, and take her now. But he felt strange shiftings and changes within himself, new feelings, and an unaccustomed stab of conscience.

He needed to think.

Withdrawing from the warmth of Hannah and the blanket, Jamie went to station himself at the base of the shaft while the rain whispered above. He had never looked inside himself. He knew the lay of Australia's land, but his own inner landscape was unknown to him. It didn't profit a man, he always believed, to examine things too closely, especially himself. Live for each day and don't ask questions, was Jamie O'Brien's rule.

But now he was looking back over his life and seeing things with a new eye. *Had* he always had his mate's best interests at heart? Jamie had always believed himself to be a generous man, even when cheating at cards because he always shared the winnings with his mates. But all the larks were his idea and his friends just went along. It hadn't occurred to him to say, "What do *you* think, Bluey?"

He thought of Hannah, who was having a strange effect on him. She wasn't like the Bible-thumpers who stood outside pubs to hand tracts to the men stumbling out. She didn't seem disapproving of him at all. But she made him think about his own mother, whom he hadn't thought about in years. What if she had lived? Would his life have gone differently? Where would that gentle, taming influence have led him? Was that what Hannah Conroy was doing to him now? Jamie enjoyed his life on the roam, stopping where he felt like it, moving on when the horizon called, sometimes working at honest labor, sometimes dealing from the bottom of the deck.

Hannah hadn't judged him, but Jamie was now judging himself. And as he revisited his life, his actions, as he weighed his deeds and motives—as his conscience, asleep all these years, woke up—the most astonishing revelation illuminated Jamie's mind. That, maybe it wasn't up to him to punish the greedy men of the world just because his own father had been greedy.

Clearing his throat, Jamie turned to Hannah and said, "I'll talk to my men. I'll tell them about the scurvy, and if they agree, we can all leave tomorrow."

Tomorrow … "You'll see me before Christmas," Neal had said back in April. Now it was October. Christmas was just weeks away. Was he already back in Adelaide, looking for her, worrying Liza Guinness now that she knew Hannah hadn't gone off with him?

"Thank you," she whispered. And watched Jamie climb up the mine shaft, to disappear into the night above.

-32-

When Hannah awoke, dawn was breaking, and once she was out of the mine and in the bracing cold air, she saw that the rain had left puddles and ponds, with puffy clouds reflected in them. The world smelled fresh and new again.

Like a child's schoolroom slate, clean and brand new and waiting to be written upon, Hannah thought as she stretched her aching muscles. She was spellbound at the sight of this breathtakingly beautiful landscape. She had witnessed many sunrises at this fantastical place the men had nicknamed Coober Pedy, but she had seen it as a barren, lifeless, and colorless wasteland. But now, as golden rays of sunlight swept over the desert, illuminating ancient rock formations and the more recently man-made craters and rock mounds, she saw that the desert sparkled, as if blanketed in jewels. Salt pans glittered with rainbow-colored mineral deposits. The sky luminesced like mother of pearl. Birds carved pathways in the sky above. Hannah saw small lizards and burrowing rodents appear as if by magic from the sand. She knew that, soon, flowers would bloom here, if only briefly. And the wind gusted fresh and pure, bringing the promise is a new day and new starts.

Suddenly, Hannah was thinking of people she had met: Lulu Forchette, whose name surely was false, living in luxury, and Mr. Day, the prosperous newsagent on Victoria Square, who would be mucking out horses' stalls had he stayed in England, and Alice Starky, now called Star, from kitchen maid to golden-throated darling of a music hall stage. She thought of a man named Gladstone who came into Kirkland's Emporium one day, a barber-dentist who had the audacity to call himself "Doctor" and whose office on Hindley Street was always busy, his dental chairs constantly occupied, with patients waiting.

"Who's restricting you?" Jamie O'Brien had asked down in the mine.

And Hannah was now able to reply: I am.

At the Australia Hotel and Seven Oaks sheep station, in Dr. Davenport's office and Lulu Forchette's parlor, everywhere Hannah had gone, she had handed out a card that identified herself as Miss Hannah Conroy, trained midwife.

I told people who and what I was. *But what if I say I am something else?*

She turned toward the camp, where the others were now straggling in, marveling that the tents were still standing and only the roof of the opal shed had burned leaving the stones still there, intact. Hannah looked for Jamie and found him at the burned opal shed, sifting through cinders with Mike Maxberry. When he raised his head and saw her, he dropped what he was doing and came running. "I was just going to go down and fetch you, Hannah. Are you all right?"

"I could not be better, Mr. O'Brien." She hugged herself in the chilly dawn, no longer fighting her desire for this colorful Outback man, but embracing her unique love for him, relishing it, not knowing where it would lead or what tomorrow held, knowing only that, suddenly, the future sparkled.

What if I say I am something else ....

"Hannah," he said, touching her arm. "Talk to the men about the scurvy. Ask them if they want to go back. I'll go along with whatever they decide."

"Thank you," she said, marveling at the way his dark gold hair caught the dawn. "I will look in on Mr. Gilchrist now."

After making sure Ralph was comfortable, Hannah went to her own tent and was relieved to find that her things inside were dry. She freshened up, and when she came out, saw some of the men pouring tea from a billy over the fire, and chowing down on biscuits while they all spoke at once about the electrical storm. Banger and Tabby were rounding up the horses that, miraculously, had survived the night. Mike Maxberry and Jamie O'Brien were still brushing off and inspecting the gemstones in the charred shed.

Hannah joined the others at the campfire, where they said "Good morning," and asked how she was doing, did she get through the night all right in Tabby's mine, and how was Church this morning. Accepting a cup of tea from Nan, Hannah addressed the men, who listened politely.

As she told them about Church's scurvy, how serious it was, and that they were all going to come down with it—speaking to the men with authority—Hannah felt new strength within her. "Who's restricting you?" Jamie had asked, and when Hannah had finally, honestly replied, *I am*, she had discovered a fundamental truth.

We are who we say we are. I told people I was a midwife, thus restricting myself. I cannot blame others for placing me in the very pigeonhole that I created! But the world has been washed clean like a slate, and I can write anything on it that I wish.

"So you see, gentlemen," she concluded, "we must return south, at least to the head of Spencer Gulf, as soon as possible."

When she saw their blank faces, she added, "I know you all have thought of me as a midwife. But I am more than that, I am a health practitioner. And therefore, I know what I am talking about."

Roddy wrinkled his freckled nose. "What's that? What did she say?"

"She's a healthy something," his brother Cyrus replied.

"I am a health practitioner," Hannah repeated.

Blackie White scrubbed his beard. "Never heard of it."

"Health *what?*" said Maxberry.

"It means," Jamie said as he came striding up, "that the lady knows what she's talking about."

"What's a health practitioner?" asked Bluey Brown, the axeman who knew about doctors and barber-dentists but nothing more.

"It means that if Hannah says we leave, then we leave. Get started packing up, you lot, we're going back."

"She ain't a doctor," argued Mike Maxberry, who was so covered in soot and cinders that his hands were as black as Nan's.

"She's a *lady* doctor," Jamie said. "And believe it when she says we're all going to lose our teeth and die scurvy deaths. Besides, a fierce summer's coming, and we've found enough opal to set ourselves up on our own land. So start packing up."

They hurried away, all secretly pleased to be getting out of this desolate place and anxious to start spending money. Maxberry scratched his head, looking back over his shoulder with a dubious expression on his face. Was she right about the Barcoo rot? He ran a finger over his gums and felt his first loosened tooth.

Jamie turned to Hannah and grinned at her with deep creases at the corners of his eyes. "Health practitioner, is it? It's for sure no one can tell you you're not what you say you are. And you get to make up the rules. And now, Miss Practitioner, I've a brilliant idea to share with you …"

He took her by the elbow and walked her over the damp ground to the blackened remnants of the opal shed. "Something's changed in me, Hannah. I went down that shaft last night one man and came up another. I want to end my wandering life. I want to stop cheating and stealing. Settle down, if you know what I mean."

"But what about the police?"

"I can clear my name. I'll have enough money from the opals to pay fines and bribe judges. I can get that wanted poster taken down and my good name polished clean. No more Jamie O'Brien the gyp artist."

And the minute we get back to Adelaide, he added silently, I'm going to give you the biggest and most expensive wedding ring our opals will buy.

-33-

Jallara had a wonderful secret.

In the days since her night with Thulan at the sacred mountain, the Moon Spirit had not visited her, and so her monthly sequestration from the rest of the clan, as all menstruating females must practice, had not taken place. A new life had begun in her belly. The clan was going to be thrilled. Thulan's child meant that Thulan himself would be with them forever, which meant saying good-bye to him would not be as painful.

She did not tell him. Jallara knew that white men held peculiar ideas about children, especially boys, saying, "He is mine," when everyone knew that a child belonged to the clan. If she were to tell him, he might decide to stay with them and therefore not continue on to his own Dreaming, or he might want to take her and the child with him to the white man's world. It was best he did not know.

A hot sun beat down on the thirty-three aborigines and lone white man as they spoke a sad farewell. It was time for the clan to strike north and meet the other clans at the *jindalee*. This time, Jallara knew she would have no trouble finding a husband, not like in past when she had been passed over because she wasn't beautiful. This time, men wouldn't mind her lighter skin because her pregnancy would be proof of her fecundity, and that was more important than looks.

She gave Neal a special spirit-stone, gray and smooth, that fit in the palm of his hand. It was carved with mystical symbols, and she said it would protect him throughout his life.

As Neal accepted it, slipping the small stone into the leather pouch that held the empty tear catcher, he thought of Jallara's mixed blood, wondered whether her mother had been with a white man by choice or had been forced. It made him think of the Merriwethers, well-intentioned missionaries who had declared their desire to bring Jesus to the aborigines.

"Jallara," he said with passion, "take your people far from here. More white men will come this way. A road will be laid. They say the railway will come, it will bisect your land and cross the songlines. The telegraph will come through here, and towns will spring up. Your way of life will be destroyed."

She smiled, not knowing what roads and railways and telegraphs were. "We cannot do different from what the First Ones taught us, Thulan. We cannot go from here."

And so Neal knew that they were doomed.

It was time to go. He had lived with Jallara's clan for six months. A lifetime.

With Daku and Burnu to keep him company and lead the way, Neal lifted his hand in a gesture of farewell, and struck off toward the west, where he would cross unknown land in search of the man who had left him to die.

"If I have to take one more bite of lizard, I'm going to hang myself from a tree—if we can find a bloody tree!"

No one paid attention to Billy Patton's grousing. As much as he complained about the food—and he was the expedition's cook, after all—he managed to tuck away a few helpings every night.

The camp wasn't as orderly and pristine as it had been six months prior, just north of Iron Knob when Sir Reginald had insisted upon daily inspections, spit-polish shines, and a regimented schedule. A challenging trek over hundreds of miles of wilderness, braving sand and wind and freak rain, not to mention dingoes and snakes, water rationing, and now this intense heat, had taken its toll. The tents were grimy and tattered, and so were the men.

But now that they were nearing their goal—a shining beacon called Galagandra—their spirits were lifting. Only young Fintan Rorke remained disheartened. He had taken to eating alone and keeping to himself, whittling creations out of whatever wood he could find, and brooding over the death of Mr. Scott. They should have stayed and searched for him. Fintan would never forgive Sir Reginald for that.

But despite keeping to himself, Fintan had become a vital member of the expedition. As wagons had gotten stuck, as axles and wheels had broken, Fintan's skills had been called upon over and over until his name was the first called whenever anything needed to be repaired. He didn't mind. It was what he had signed up for, and he was on a grand adventure. But he was sorry about Mr. Scott, and hated having to turn over all that fine camera equipment and scientific instruments to Sir Reginald when they reached Perth. Somehow, he didn't think it was what Mr. Scott would have wanted.

"Hey!" shouted John Allen, shooting to his feet. "We've got Abos!"

Everyone turned to squint in the noon sunlight, and when they saw the black men approaching, carrying spears, they reached for their guns.

But one of the natives raised his arm and shouted, "Don't shoot, I am Neal Scott!"

As the white men looked at each other in astonishment, and then ran to welcome their long lost comrade, Neal's two companions touched his arms and murmured farewells. There was sadness in their eyes as they turned and started back over the distance they had covered.

Neal watched Daku and Burnu deliver themselves into the ancient desert and then found himself at the center of a genuinely happy reception. "We thought you were dead, mate!"

"Aborigines found me," Neal said, searching the camp for Sir Reginald. "They saved my life."

"You've been living with Abos all this time? You'll have some stories to tell!" Their eyes bugged out at the sight of his chest tattoo. When they drew close to get a better look, Neal fell back a step. The men stunk!

As Neal was brought into the camp, the men all talking at once, and he recognized their faces, he realized that no one was missing. And then he saw the horses in the makeshift paddock, including the chestnut mare he had been riding when the sandstorm struck.

Fintan pushed through and unabashedly threw his arms around Neal. "Thank God!" cried the twenty-one-year-old.

Neal smiled. "It's a nice welcome, Mr. Rorke."

Fintan drew back and ran his sleeve under his nose. Like the others, his thick black hair had grown long, but there was only a sparse, downy beard on his jaw. "Your things are all here, sir. I never even opened your trunk. Everything's as you left it."

"Thank you," Neal said, thinking of Hannah's glove, and feeling an intense need to hold it in his hand.

With tears glistening in his large soulful eyes, Fintan said quietly, "I wanted to stay behind, Mr. Scott. When Sir Reginald said we were to get moving and it wasn't even daylight yet, after the sandstorm blew past, I said we had to stay and look for you. He told me I was welcome to, but that he was taking the wagon and the horses."

"It's all right, Fintan," Neal said, his eyes on Oliphant's tent where the others said their leader was napping. "You couldn't have done otherwise."

"But I kept all your equipment and chemicals safe. Nothing blew up. And I wouldn't let the men touch any of it. Your camera is still in perfect working order."

Bringing himself back to his young assistant, Neal said, "I'm going to start tomorrow, taking pictures. We still have a ways to go before we reach Perth. There will be some beautiful landscape to photograph."

Sir Reginald came out of his tent then, as ruddy-complexioned as ever, in white shirt and shorts, his hair and beard both white and flowing. "My God, is it Mr. Scott?" he boomed, and strode toward Neal with outstretched hands.

But Neal kept one hand on his spear, the other casually at his side.

The walrus moustache fluffed out as the older man said with bluster, "We thought we'd never see you again! And look at you! Gone native, I see. By God, you'll have stories to tell!"

"For a while there," Neal said quietly, his eyes steady on Sir Reginald, "I didn't think I would see any of you again. It looks as though the expedition is a success so far."

"Indeed it is! Haven't run into any natives though, not like you. We're looking to find Galagandra next where there is supposed to be plenty of sweet water. Come, come, sit down. You must be hungry. I say, that's an impressive tattoo. You must tell us how you got it."

As Neal was led to the circle at the campfire, surrounded by cheerful fellows filled with congratulations, he decided not to confront Sir Reginald until they arrived at Perth and Neal had conducted a discreet investigation. When he had proof of his suspicions that the man was a fake, he would make it public.

He wondered if Oliphant had an inkling of what he suspected. And if, between here and Perth, he should, what would the man do? They were still far from civilization, far from any white settlement. Neal knew he had to be careful. Oliphant had already left him for dead once. He might do a better job of it next time.

-34-

When the Australia Hotel came into view, Hannah cried out with joy.

Although it was not officially summer, November's heat bore down on the weary group as they followed the dusty road in their wagons and on horseback. It had been a long, hot trek back from the opal fields. Poor Ralph Gilchrist had not survived. They had buried him in the wasteland just north of the tip of Spencer Gulf. And then Nan left them. The day before they had reached the head of Spencer Gulf, they had encountered a group of aborigines, standing at a distance, watching. The next morning, Nan was gone. When they neared the Kapunda copper mines, the three brothers, Cyrus, Elmo, and Roddy, also left, saying they had quite liked the mining life and would seek their fortune here.

And so it was a smaller band that made its way to the Australia Hotel, with visions of clean beds, hot baths, and meals served on a table.

They saw at once that something was wrong. As they drew near, with Hannah riding next to Jamie in the wagon while he handled the reins, she saw no carriages or horses tethered to the hitching post. The whole property was strangely quiet—no stable boys, no goats bleating, no chickens scratching in the dust. The buildings had a neglected air about them, and as Hannah and Jamie climbed the wooden steps to the front door, they sensed that the establishment had been deserted for some time.

"What happened?" Hannah murmured in alarm as she tried the door to find it locked. She peered through the grimy windows and saw Liza's furniture still in place, even with some newspapers yellowing on an entry table. Behind the front desk, one of Liza's humorous signs—"If you want breakfast in bed, sleep in the kitchen"—dangled on a nail.

Returning to the dusty road where, it seemed, a lifetime ago, she had kissed Neal good-bye, Hannah received another shock. The few establishments that had sprung up around the hotel—Gibney's Feed & Supplies, Edna Basset's dry goods store, and the blacksmith—were likewise boarded up and deserted.

Hannah tried not to panic. Surely there was a reasonable explanation. But as she climbed back into the wagon next to Jamie, she felt a terrible fear in the pit of her stomach—some sort of illness must have come through here, taking the lives of people she had known.

"Liza," she said before her throat tightened. Had Alice been a victim, too? Mary McKeeghan at Seven Oaks?

Dear God, Neal—

They rode in silence after that, and as they neared the outskirts of Adelaide, with traffic becoming thicker and homesteads closer together, they passed Lulu Forchette's house. Hannah was surprised to see children playing in the yard, clothes flapping on a line, a young woman sweeping the porch steps. Hannah saw the vegetable garden, the horses in the stable. It was clear that a family had moved in. But the rose garden was gone, and that made her a little sad. But she was also relieved to see that whatever had happened back at the Australia Hotel had not come this far.

At her side, Jamie was thinking the same thing. He also wondered where that poor dingo had gone to, losing his hunting territory.

Adelaide seemed strangely quiet, and Hannah wondered if they had miscalculated and today was Sunday. But saloons were open, so it was not the Sabbath. And yet, traffic seemed lighter, with fewer pedestrians in the streets. And then she noticed the vacancy signs in the hotels.

Had the contagion that had taken Liza and the others made it to the town?

Hannah decided that as soon as they were done at the jeweler's, she would go straight to the Post Office to see if Neal had left her a message. She prayed he had not yet returned to Adelaide.

Jamie drew the wagon up in front of Grootenboer's Jewelers on Flinders Street. While he tethered the horses to the hitching post, the others dismounted, wiping their sweating brows and saying they wanted their money as soon as possible because they were going in search of a bath, a big dinner, and some female companionship. And Hannah scanned the brick wall next to Grootenboer's, plastered with newspapers. She anxiously searched for headlines about the Oliphant expedition arriving in Perth, to see if they had arrived in the six months Neal had estimated, after which it was but a two-week voyage back by sea. But there was nothing.

And then she saw something that made her freeze. A wanted poster with a face on it!

And it was unmistakably Jamie O'Brien. The new engraving process that had begun with the *London Illustrated News* had finally made its way to these far-flung colonies, and the police were using it as a crime-fighting weapon.

"Jamie," she called quietly, and when he turned, she beckoned him to the wall.

"What is it—" he began, but when his eye caught on the poster, a dark look came over his face. Someone had been able to describe him well enough to an artist that the engraving was a remarkable likeness. But more alarming than that was a new offense that had been added to his crimes: horse theft.

"So the bloke at the race course reported the swindle after all," Jamie said. He looked at Hannah. "I don't know if I've enough money to buy myself out of this one. Horse stealing is a hanging offense."

Hannah knew the rest. That there would be no more safely walking the streets for Jamie, going into any place he felt like, no more confidence games, no more being at liberty to live his life outside the law.

Telling Maxberry to stay outside with the others, Jamie entered the jeweler's shop with a handkerchief held to his mouth to partially hide his face. Hannah went in with him.

A chubby, white-haired gentleman sat on a tall stool behind the counter. As soon as the two customers walked in, he stood and said, "Welcome, welcome, how can I be of service?" in a thick Dutch accent.

Men in dirty and ragged clothes, with beards and sunburns, were a common sight in Adelaide, as gold-hunters, explorers, cattle- and sheep-drovers frequently plodded into town in search of a bath, a clean bed and a fresh beginning. One could never tell by a man's looks how much wealth he had, and so Mr. Grootenboer, like other Adelaide merchants, treated Jamie and Hannah with as much respect as if they had arrived by elegant carriage.

Keeping the handkerchief to his mouth, as if to cough the last of Outback dust from his lungs, Jamie said, "We found these," and dropped a few rocks on the counter top. It had been decided ahead of time that they would sell the opals all around town, not just at one place.

Mr. Grootenboer picked up one of the sandstone rocks that had a bit of shiny blue on one side. "Opals! This doesn't look volcanic," the Dutchman said with interest. "What was the topography where you found these?"

Jamie described the area without being specific, and the man's bushy brows shot up. "Opal in sandstone? I didn't know it was possible. Let me take a look."

Mr. Grootenboer wore a long chain around his neck, at the end of which hung a jeweler's loupe—a monocle with an extra-thick lens for inspecting gemstones. Holding the lens before his right eye, he brought each stone up for close examination, making sounds in his throat while Jamie and Hannah waited.

Finally, Mr. Grootenboer said, "These stones are very rough and need to be cut. I have not the expertise in this skill, you understand. I would have to send the stones to a lapidary in Sydney. Opal is a soft gemstone, relatively speaking, and so care must be taken in grinding off the outer sandstone. And then there is the polishing and shaping ..." He sighed and set the last stone down. "It would be at great cost to me, and I do not know what profit I can make. Nonetheless, I can takes these off your hands for, say, five shillings."

"How about this one?" Jamie said, and he handed Mr. Grootenboer a much larger chunk of sandstone with a heart that shone black at first, but then bright red, yellow, and orange when turned to the light.

While they waited for Mr. Grootenboer to carry out his inspection, Hannah looked around the small shop and saw the Help Wanted sign in his window: "Man Only." She had seen other Help Wanted signs during their ride into town, all of them specifying men only. Had there been some sort of illness that afflicted only men? Then where were Liza Guinness and her daughters?

The moment stretched as Mr. Grootenboer studied the larger stone through his glass, until he suddenly gasped in astonishment. Letting the loupe drop, he cleared his throat, pursed his lips, and appeared to be controlling his excitement. "I can pay you a good price for this, sir," he said. And then he leaned forward and murmured, "I can pay you an even *better* price if you tell me where you found it."

"Mr. Grootenboer," Hannah said with a look of curiosity on her face. She had noticed an extraordinary amount of gold watches for sale in the shop. They weren't new, some even appeared to be quite old. When she asked about them, Mr. Grootenboer blinked at her owlishly and said, "Haven't you *heard?*"

"Heard what?"

"Gold has been discovered in California."

Hannah and Jamie exchanged a puzzled look. "Where is California?" Jamie asked.

"It is a territory in America. Gold was found there a few months ago— nuggets the size of a man's fist, just lying on the ground. Many men have left Adelaide to go to California to get rich. They sell me their possessions for the price of passage."

Outside in the hot sun, Jamie shared the money from Mr. Grootenboer with the others with the promise that he would continue to sell the opals and dole out the profits. Of course, now he would have to work with more care, with his likeness plastered all over town.

"Hannah, I know of a place where me and the boys can lay low, but what about you? Where will you be? How can I find you?"

Hannah had expected to be staying at the Australia Hotel. Now she would have to find lodgings. But first it was a trip to the Post Office. When she and Neal had parted back in April, they had devised a plan to connect with each other when he returned. The central Post Office, where they could leave letters "in general care." "I am going to see if my friend Alice is back in town. She would have been at the Australia Hotel, but she might be somewhere else now. I can find out at The Elysium Music Hall. And for now, until I find somewhere to stay, that would be the best place to send me a message."

They looked at each other on the hot, dusty sidewalk as people stepped around them. The air was filled with the drone of flies and the odor of horse droppings, but Hannah and Jamie were aware of nothing except each other. There was so much each wanted to say, but now was not the time. And … something had changed. Hannah didn't know what exactly. The new bounty poster had come as a shock. The police threat was now very serious.

And also, now that they were back in the city, things felt different. Hannah had ties here, another life, and the prospect of Neal in her near future. She was momentarily caught off balance. Where did Jamie O'Brien fit in?

"We have to go," he said quietly, watching her from beneath the broad rim of his dusty bush hat. Jamie had also sensed a change. "I'll send you word when all the opals are converted into cash."

She watched him go, riding the horse he had purchased with a forged deed while Blackie White took the wagon. As they disappeared down the busy street, Hannah was reminded of the night a man materialized out of the darkness to save her from a savage dog. She was filled with that same sense now, that Jamie O'Brien had sprung from Australia's red earth to walk a while in her life, like a mythic being, drawn from gum trees and cockatoos and the Rainbow Serpent, only to leave her again and return to the land that sired him.

-35-

There was no letter waiting for her at the Post Office, so she surmised that Neal was still in Perth, for surely they had made it by now. But just in case, she would write to him in care of the authorities in Perth who were sure to give it to him when the expedition arrived with great fanfare and celebration. She didn't want Neal going to the Australia Hotel and receive the same shock she did.

The front doors of the Elysium Music Hall stood open to the heat of the day, music pouring out onto the sidewalk. As Hannah stepped into the relative coolness, a large burly man with arms like hams and wearing a striped waistcoat blocked her way. "We're closed until this evening. No one's allowed during rehearsal."

"Is Miss Alice Star here?" Hannah asked, trying to peer around him into the theater where acrobats were tumbling on the stage.

"Who wants to know?" he said.

"I'm a friend."

"You and half of Adelaide," he said.

"Please tell her Hannah Conroy has come to visit."

A moment later, she heard her name called out in a familiar voice. "Hannah!"

Alice burst into the theater lobby to take her startled friend into a tight embrace. "We were so worried! We had no idea where you went! Liza said you were with Mr. Scott. Did you join the expedition? Have you been to Perth?"

Alice drew back, her eyes the color of cornflowers wide with amazement. "Hannah, your tanned! You've been in the sun! Tell me what—"

Hannah laughed. "Alice, let me catch my breath." She was amazed at the change in her friend. Gone was the shy girl who had worked for Lulu Forchette. The touring and singing on so many stages had brought out Alice's natural sparkle and charisma. She exuded self-confidence. She was also physically beautiful. The scars were so well hidden, the eyebrow painted on so perfectly, and her hair arranged so artfully that one would never suspect the deformity underneath.

"Alice, you act like a woman in love."

"I am in love—with the theater, with audiences, with singing." In a more somber tone Alice said, "But I am not in love with a man, and I doubt I ever will be. But I do have admirers now, and I am satisfied with that."

Hannah marveled at the beautiful gown of green and orange silk, dropped shoulders edged with lace, wide, flouncy sleeves and an adorable cap set on her blond hair at a tilt. Alice Star was a vision of the very latest in fashion.

"But never mind me! We were so worried about you, Hannah!"

"It's a long story. What do you know about Liza Guinness? The hotel is closed up."

Alice explained how she had returned to the Australia Hotel, to rest after the hectic tour of the colonies—to great acclaim, she added with no false modesty—and learned that Liza had met and fallen in love with a drover. When they heard of the gold strike in America, Liza's new beau wanted to go. So they got married and took the first ship to a place called San Francisco. "Liza left a letter for you, Hannah, and I have all your things, your clothes and trunk, even the little statuette of Hygeia.

"Oh Hannah!" Alice said, hugging her again. "I am so happy to see you. Where are you staying?"

"I don't know yet. I have only just returned to town."

"Then you will come and stay with me. I've rented a lovely house. It even has a housekeeper and servants. Imagine!"

-36-

Three notes arrived at the Elysium from Jamie O'Brien, telling Hannah that he found it necessary to move around and stay hidden, but that the opals were bringing good money and that he would soon have plans for a new life. He added that she was in his thoughts and in his heart, and that it tore him apart to be in the same town with her and not be able to see her.

The final note came precisely two weeks after they had said good-bye in front of Grootenboer's Jewelers. He asked to meet her outside of town on an old logging road that led to nowhere. As the location was not far from Lulu's, Hannah had no trouble finding it. They met in the late afternoon, in the privacy of a stand of gum trees where the dusty ground offered a patch of grass beside a trickling creek.

Jamie was already there, his horse a few feet away, grazing. As Hannah brought her buggy to a halt, she felt her heart rise in her throat, as she knew they had come here to say good-bye. Jamie wore clean clothes and even wore a new bush hat, but he had kept the beard, Hannah noticed, although it much more nicely clipped and shaped than when she last saw him. She assumed he kept it as a disguise, and she thought the golden blond an attractive contrast to his darkly weathered skin.

Jamie went to help Hannah down from the buggy, and as he neared her he saw that the change he had first sensed outside of Grootenboer's was now complete. Hannah was a city person again, and a proper lady, from her silk bonnet tied beneath her chin, to the crinolined gown of silk the color of early corn. Her face still bore the tan from the Outback, but he knew it would fade in time as she protected her complexion beneath hats and parasols. And her hands, too, would eventually go soft and smooth again, erasing all evidence of her time as an opal hunter.

He removed his hat as he looked down at her with eyes, though he smiled, that were filled with sadness. "Me and Mikey," he said without preamble, "have to leave."

"I know."

Shafts of golden sunlight pierced the overhead branches, while the drone of insects filled the air.

"We're going to California. We have signed on as deck hands on the *Southern Cross*. The captains of private vessels have discovered that they can have their pick of crews and don't have to pay a cent in wage as all the men want is to get to California—men whose names the captains don't ask, as long as they are strong and able to go up in the rigging."

"It must be hard for you to leave Australia," she said.

"I feel a thirst for far off places. I thought I could settle down and change my ways, but the call of adventure is hard to ignore. I have never sailed across an ocean, Hannah, I have never visited a foreign land. It's time I expanded my horizons." He grinned. "And think of all those rich pigeons in California, waiting to be plucked."

He reached inside his pocket and pulled out a roll of bank notes. "This is your share of the opal money."

"This is too much!" It must have been hundreds of pounds.

"We don't have to pay for passage, and just need some money to get us started on a gold claim. The others have all gone home—Bluey Brown, Tabby, Charlie Olde and the rest, back to where I first rounded them up, going home richer men and with big smiles on their faces. But they chipped in, so this is from all of us. We want you to have a good start in Australia. My mates have a soft spot for you, Hannah. I think they all fell in love with you."

He paused, his manner growing somber. "I want to ask you to come with me, Hannah, but it wouldn't be fair to you, and I don't think you would say yes. You came to Australia to accomplish great things. Maybe someday I'll come back and see they've put a statue of you in Victoria Square."

Her eyes filled with tears.

"I have something else for you." He gave her a small book bound in black leather with silver embossing. The word Diary was stamped on the cover. She opened it and saw a cramped hand in pencil, every page filled. "It's my stories," Jamie said. "I'm giving them to you."

Hannah was speechless as she flipped through the pages and saw the stories of Queenie MacPhail, the dog on the tucker box, and all the rest.

"But you should take these with you to California, Jamie!"

"The stories are yours now, Hannah, they don't belong to me any more. I reckon I'll be collecting a whole new bunch of tales in California. Stories about gold fossickers and a whole new country."

He stepped closer. "Go ahead with your dream, Hannah. Be a health practitioner. Make your own rules. Let your hands work miracles. You saved my life. You can save others. Be a healer, Hannah." His voice broke. "My

God, I love you, Hannah Conroy. And I know that if I live to be a hundred, I will never love a woman as I have loved you."

He pulled her into his arms and kissed her hard.

As Hannah hooked an arm around his neck and returned the kiss, leaning into him, tears stinging her eyes, she thought that Jamie O'Brien, for all his boasting that he was a true Australian, that here was where he belonged, he was in fact a man without a home.

He stepped back and released her once and for all. "I'll come back someday. You'll see. I'll come back to you, Hannah."

She watched him mount his horse and ride off through the trees, southward in the direction of the docks from where, in the morning, a ship named the *Southern Cross* was setting sail for a place called California.

-37-

"My God, man, did they turn you into a savage like themselves?" Sir Reginald did not bother to hide his contempt. It rankled him the way the American refused to act like a decent human being. Two weeks with the expedition now, and he still refused to put clothes on.

Neal said nothing but continued to turn the lizard on the spit over his fire. I'm a savage? he thought. I'm not the one who stinks to high heaven.

With water scant and needing to be rationed, the members of the expedition had abandoned all attention to personal hygiene. And despite the intense December heat, they still went about fully dressed so that their filthy clothes smelled. They had ceased bothering with dental care, too, and they were constantly scratching flea and lice bites. Neal had not returned to European clothing on purpose, so that his sweat could evaporate. He protected his skin from insects with paint made from pulverized rocks and plant juice. And he took care of his teeth the way Jallara's people did, with fine twigs and eucalyptus leaves.

He knew he was a queer sight, a half-naked white man wearing a fur loincloth as he stood at his camera tripod, giving instructions to young Fintan. Neal knew that Sir Reginald disapproved. The contempt went both ways. Neal had looked at Sir Reginald's expedition map with disgust. The men had named places after themselves, as was their right as the so-called discoverers: Mason's Creek, Allen's Hill, Mount Williams. Neal saw now where he had traveled with Jallara's clan, in an area of the map that was blank, with the word "Unknown" stamped on it. But Neal saw names there: Ant Dreaming, Dingo Songline, No Name Mountain. He wondered what the real names were of the places these white men had christened after themselves.

They had finally reached Galagandra, the place where they were to have found an abundance of sweet water. So far, none had been found. It was a region of salt-lakes and sandplains covered with desert oaks and mulgas, impossibly flat from horizon to horizon with only the occasional hill here and there. The expedition was camped alongside a dry creek bed where spindly trees struggled to survive. Further up, a cluster of boulders taller than a man abutted the foot of a homely red hill no more than a thousand feet in elevation and covered in scrubby brush.

Tracker John Allen had taken two scouts with him earlier that morning to explore the source of the creek, which no doubt overflowed its shallow banks the few times it rained out here. That would make the soil in this area alluvial, the silt run-off being carried down from the hill to the plain, and rich in quartz. Neal knew this because Sir Reginald had asked him to analyze the local soil, although to what purpose Neal had no idea.

Sir Reginald got up from the campfire and glowered at his expedition geologist. He couldn't put into words what exactly rankled him about Scott's behavior. The tattoos in particular unsettled him. Six rows of red dots rising from below the navel, up along either side of the sternum, over the pectorals and gracing the shoulders. It was a cicatrix both fabulous and disturbing. The older man could only imagine the pain endured. What else had gone on during the savage rites? Neal wouldn't talk about it, saying it was taboo. As if the laws of the natives had any credibility in a white man's world. And what the devil did he carry in that leather pouch about his neck?

Oliphant paused as he watched the American roast a lizard in aboriginal fashion, unskinned. Since the day he had suddenly walked out of the desert in kangaroo fur and carrying a spear, and in the days of trekking since, Neal had made no mention of the sandstorm and its aftermath. He had been strangely quiet, not at all the cheerful and loquacious fellow he had been before the sandstorm. Had something sinister been done to him during his six months with the savages? Or did the cause lie closer to home?

Does he suspect the truth about me?

"Put some clothes on, man," Oliphant barked as he turned on his heel to walk away.

Neal ignored him. The reunion with his white colleagues had not turned out to be such a happy affair after all. The men were constantly asking him about the sexual practices of Jallara's clan, asking him if he had tasted "black velvet." And Professor Williams was wanting to pick Neal's brain for his book on wildlife. What could he tell him? How the aborigines celebrated when a baby was born, or how they mourned when someone died—just like white people did. They weren't a subject for a book on *animals*. Neal thought of the nights around the campfire, listening to the resonant twang of Thumimburee's didgeridoo and the soft melodic voice of Jallara as she explained to Neal how songs came down from the spirit-powers of the Dreamtime and how playing such songs spun a web of continuity between the people and their Dreaming, in a succession of creation, uncreation, and recreation.

He touched the small leather pouch on his chest and felt the smooth magic stone inside. "Very strong spirit-power, Thulan," Jallara had said with a glowing smile. "Spirit-power take care of Thulan while he follow his songline."

He also thought of the emerald glass tear catcher, empty now. *My mother's tears brought me back from the spirit world.* In the days since his experience at the rock wall, Neal had examined his vision. The truth was obvious to him now. Looking back: Josiah's constant boastings of his adoptive son's many achievements, the holidays in the mountains, the birthday parties, giving the boy whatever he asked for. Neal had assumed it was to make up for his lack of having a real father, that Josiah had gone overboard in compensation, when in retrospect it was all the actions of a truly doting father.

Neal looked across the camp to where young Fintan was taking care of their horses. In the days since being reunited with the expedition, Neal and his assistant had captured some beautiful images of the Australian outback. Astounding rock formations. A lone tree in the middle of a vast plain. A rainbow that went straight up in the air like a column. Neal wanted his father to see them, wanted Josiah to know about his son's accomplishments. *I lived with a tribe of Aborigines, Father. I survived on my own in the desert. I underwent a secret initiation. And I have preserved the beauty and soul of Australia on my photographic plates—sights that no white man has ever seen.*

As he turned the goanna on the roasting spit, the morning silence was broken by a shout. John Allen calling out, "Gold, I've found gold!"

Everyone jumped up and ran, breakfast forgotten.

Neal followed and found the men near the giant boulders on their hands and knees, frantically digging in the dry red soil while Sir Reginald watched with a smug grin on his face.

"We came here for *gold?*" Neal said.

"That's right, and gold we've found."

Neal stared at the white-haired man. "You never said anything about gold."

"The fewer who knew it the better." Oliphant reached into the pocket of his baggy shorts and brought out his fist. Opening it, he exposed a bright, shining nugget. "Its history is spotty, but a bloke in Perth told me about escaped convicts. This nugget somehow made it back to civilization and I bought it for fifty pounds and one word: Galagandra."

"So this whole expedition was a sham," Neal said.

As he watched Billy Patton and Andy Mason and Colonel Enfield—even the sedate Professor Williams—dig into the red soil in the shadow of stunted mulga and gum trees, Sir Reginald said, "I couldn't very well let the truth be known, now could I? Have a stampede on my hands. Just a trusted few."

Neal watched the unsettling display for a moment—the men seemed to have gone out of their minds—when his eye caught on something that made his blood suddenly run cold.

On the boulders: stick figures painted in black pigment.

"My God," he whispered. "This is a sacred site. Sir Reginald, you have to get these men out of here."

Oliphant made a dismissive gesture.

"If the local tribe gets wind of us—"

"Then we'll buy this place from them. Give them whatever they want."

"This is a sacred site, they won't sell it!" Neal looked around nervously. With Sir Reginald's men on their hands and knees, unaware, vulnerable, it would take but a swift, surprise attack, and the whole lot would be wiped out.

He looked back at the camp, a hundred feet away, and saw Fintan hurriedly unpacking Neal's tripod. Rorke was a very able assistant, Neal thought in strange detachment. He had learned when to assemble the photographic equipment, and he knew that this was going to be a historic moment to be captured. Neal also noted that Fintan wasn't interested in digging for gold.

Neal turned in a slow circle, taking in the red plain, the few trees lining the creek bed, the boulders, and hill. How was he going to persuade these gold-hungry men to get out of here?

And then: up above, on the crest of the hill, a silhouette against the sky.

"Sir Reginald," Neal said softly.

And in that moment, fat Billy Patton shot to his feet, hand in the air, shouting, "I found a nugget! I found a—" His voice was stilled by a spear shooting through his chest. He looked startled and then fell over dead.

Neal spun around. It was not the man on the hill who had thrown the spear. Now he saw them, five aborigines, arms raised, spears in hand as they came running.

Neal seized Oliphant by his shirt. "Get these men out of here!"

Sir Reginald looked at the aborigines. His color drained. "You know these people, Scott. Talk to them. Show them your tribal tattoo."

"I don't know them!" Jallara's clan had encountered other groups, some friendly, some hostile, speaking different dialects. Neal knew from the rock paintings that these people were different from Jallara's tribe; they would speak another language. His tattoo might only get him killed.

The natives were now between the white men and the camp, their unearthly cries rising to the sky. Their spears flew and landed with deadly accuracy. Andy Mason, the horse wrangler, clasped one in his stomach as if to pull it out, before he fell over dead. The other men scrambled for the safety of the boulders—the sacred site of their attackers.

"No!" Neal shouted as the natives closed in on the trapped men. He turned to Oliphant. "Do something!"

"I ... I don't know—"

"The Khyber Pass! The ambush! You managed to get them all out. How did you do it?"

"Well, you see, I never—"

Neal released him with a shove. "You made it up. *You made it all up!*"

The ruddy complexion paled. "I'm afraid you've found me out. I never was at the Khyber Pass."

"You're a fraud! That's why you left me for dead! You knew I had found out your dirty little secret. Have you been *anywhere* in the world?"

Sir Reginald was speechless with fear. He blinked in the direction of the aborigines, where more had suddenly materialized, all running toward his men with spears.

Neal spun around, thinking of the rifles back at the camp. More were dead now—Colonel Enfield, John Allen.

As he started toward the camp, Sir Reginald grabbed his arm and said, "I will pay you a thousand pounds to get me to Perth."

Pulling the hand from his arm, Neal ran back to the camp.

Sir Reginald made a dash to where the horses were tied up, seized a chestnut mare and, hauling himself up, riding bareback, galloped off. Neal turned and watched in horror as a boomerang went spinning through the air, catching the Englishman on the neck to send him toppling from his horse. A mob of aborigines was immediately upon him. Sir Reginald's screams rose to the sky as clubs rained down on him.

Neal was frantic. More aborigines had appeared. There were perhaps fifty now. Where were they coming from? It was going to be a slaughter. He knew that fire wouldn't scare them off, and rifles wouldn't be enough. And then he thought: Explosions.

He searched for young Rorke and found him crouched behind a wagon, firing his rifle, but shaking so badly that he missed his marks.

"Fintan!" Neal called, and the young man came running, his face the color of clay.

"We'll drive them off with chemical explosions. Help me get the wagon rolling."

"But Mr. Scott, the plates, all the pictures you've taken."

There was no time to empty the wagon. As the attack continued at the boulders, with a few of the white men firing pistols, killing aborigines, Neal and Fintan pushed the wagon loaded with photographic supplies along the creek until it rolled on its own. As it neared the aborigines, Neal lifted a fire brand from the campfire and threw it onto the crates. It took but seconds. Huge fireballs erupted. The deafening chemical explosions spewed dense black clouds into the air, and sent the aborigines scattering in all directions. As the nearby trees burst into flame, Fintan stared in horror, thinking of the shattered glass plates—the astounding rock formations, the lone tree, the rainbow—all gone.

The survivors came running back to the camp, bleeding and hurt. Seven lay dead with spears in their chests.

"Brilliant!" Professor Williams said to Neal. Blood trickled down his forehead. "Where is Sir Reginald?" And then he saw the broken body next to the horse.

Neal scanned the area. The natives had vanished. But he knew it wasn't over. He had to muster the men, get them and the horses away from here. He squinted through the smoke at the boulders. Was there time to bury the dead?

Another man came staggering out of the smoke just then with a dazed grin on his face. Despite a blood stain on his shirt that was spreading, he waved his fist, showing off the large gold nugget he had found. "There's more! Just lying on the ground to be picked up."

As the men ran back to the site of the slaughter, Neal tried to stop them. "Wait! The explosions aren't over! Those trees are on fire. There are more chemicals to be ignited."

But the greed for gold was too much. The men rushed in. Neal watched as the trees caught fire, branches dripping with flame, about to drop on the remaining unexploded crates.

While the men scrambled on their knees in the red earth.

He hesitated for only a second and then plunged through the smoke, reaching for arms and legs. Fintan followed, delivering himself into the intense heat and black cloud. A large mulga bush burst into flame. It shot sparks at the wagon, igniting the last of the chemicals—a lethal formula of highly toxic potassium cyanide that was used as a fixing agent in photography.

It exploded in fire and poisonous gas, engulfing Neal and Fintan, their cries rising to the smoke-filled sky.

-38-

"There! How does it look?"

As Hannah stepped back to admire her handiwork, she dabbed her forehead with a handkerchief. It seemed strange to be decorating a Christmas tree on such a hot day.

"The candles will look lovely," Alice said, "once they are all lit."

Hannah had moved back into town not only because the Australia Hotel was closed, but also because, during her absence, a new doctor had arrived in the district and was receiving calls from people who had once been Hannah's patients. So she had chosen a small two-storey house in a newer part of Adelaide, away from where the established doctors had their offices, and had created a private residence upstairs, with the ground floor made into an office, waiting room, and small laboratory and dispensary.

She had been here for four weeks, with her brass shingle hanging on a post by the sidewalk—*Miss Hannah Conroy, Health Practitioner Trained in London, Specializing in Women & Children & Midwifery*—but she had yet to attract a single patient. Hannah was not discouraged. She had placed ads in newspapers, had put up notices all around town, and had even gone around to establishments, as "Dr." Gladstone the barber-dentist had done, handing out her calling card and informing local merchants of her new practice. She knew that people just needed time to adjust to a new specialty, and to accept her.

Just as she knew that Neal would be knocking at her door any day now.

Six weeks ago, she had said farewell to Jamie O'Brien on the old logging road. He was on his way to California, and she would cherish his memory forever. Hannah had left a letter at the post office should Neal go there after discovering that the Australia Hotel was closed. She had also posted a notice for him on Mr. Day's public message board. He had said he would be back by Christmas, which was just two days away.

"I have to get back to the Elysium and rehearse for tonight's Christmas show. You will be there?" Alice was drawing bigger crowds than ever, now that she had toured the colonies and drawn rave reviews.

"I wouldn't miss it," Hannah said, giving her exuberant friend a hug. "Thanks for the help with the tree."

She saw Alice to the door, and as she closed it, spotted the newspaper her housekeeper had purchased during the morning shopping, folded neatly on the entry table.

Hannah picked it up and opened it out. The front page headline read: OLIPHANT EXPEDITION PERISHES IN DESERT. Underneath, the report began: *There are No Survivors of the Noble but ill-fated Expedition.*

The floor tilted. Hannah reached for the wall to steady herself. She suddenly couldn't breathe.

Services were held at St. George's Church in Perth with Lieutenant Governor McNair delivering the eulogy for the thirty-two Brave Men who departed from Adelaide nine months ago under the leadership of Sir Reginald ...

It was a moment before Hannah realized she was hearing a knock at the front door. Mrs. Sparrow, the housekeeper, appeared from the back, in her tidy dress and white apron, and went to answer it.

A woman with two children stood on the threshold. Behind her, in the street, the carriage of a wealthy family waited at the curb. "Is this the house of the lady practitioner?" the woman asked.

Mrs. Sparrow stepped aside and the visitor came in. When Mrs. Sparrow introduced Hannah as the practitioner, the woman said, "Timothy can't stop coughing, and Lucy has an awful rash." The finely dressed woman lowered her voice and, unaware of Miss Conroy's unusual paleness, said, "And I have a private problem myself. To tell the truth, it's nice to have a lady to go to about these things. Doctors don't understand, do they?"

MELBOURNE

November 1852

-39-

She was here again, the intriguing young woman who had caught his eye.

Sir Marcus had finally learned her name, Miss Hannah Conroy, and as he conferred with Dr. Soames, he watched the young lady's progress across the hospital lobby and up the stairs to the floor above. He was intensely curious about her.

She had been here before, each time looking very much out of place. After all, a hospital was, by definition, an institution for people who could neither afford to pay a doctor to come to their home nor to pay someone to take care of them. Visitors to Melbourne's Victoria Hospital were generally of the lower class, usually ragged, a few even drunk and rowdy. Which was what made the attractive young lady—always well dressed with gloves and a bonnet, and a dainty parasol hooked over her arm, clearly a woman of breeding and gentility—appear so out of place. Sir Marcus Iverson, distinguished director of the hospital with a private practice of his own in the better part of town, could only surmise that the young lady in the pale yellow gown and looking not a bit wilted in the November heat, was here out of Christian charity.

But she carried a leather satchel, which intrigued him all the more.

As she reached the top of the stairs, Hannah paused to press a handkerchief to her throat. Summer seemed to have arrived before its time. Or perhaps the perspiration was due to her excitement at having found her dream home in the country at last.

Hannah currently had a residence off busy Collins Street, living upstairs with an office downstairs, where patients visited five mornings a week. She had brought Mrs. Sparrow, her housekeeper in Adelaide, with her, and had hired two maids. Now she was thinking of hiring an assistant to help her with patients, as she had once assisted Dr. Davenport. From the moment Hannah had decided, that miraculous dawn at Coober Pedy, that she would refer to herself as a health practitioner, her road had taken an upward turn. Not only were women crowding into her waiting room, they were inviting her into a popular social circle as well. Many of her patients were wealthy; many had become her friends.

But many were also poor, as Hannah did not discriminate, and Nellie Turner was one, presenting herself at Hannah's office a month ago, asking Hannah to be her midwife when the time came. But when Hannah returned home this morning from a visit to patients in the countryside, she had been told that Nellie had gone into premature labor and had been taken by friends to Victoria Hospital.

That was why she was here, to make sure Nellie was all right after giving birth. And as she made her way down the rows of patient beds in the female ward, Hannah thought of the beautiful property she had encountered on the road to Bendigo. A clover farm that also ran a few sheep and cattle, with a handsome homestead that compared with Seven Oaks. Hannah had stopped her carriage and looked out over the paddocks and green fields and had known at once she must have it. The name of the farm, carved in wood over the gate, was Brookdale, and a "For Sale" sign was tacked to a pole. From a neighbor Hannah had learned that the owner's name was Charlie Swanswick and that he was eager to sell. The only problem was, Charlie was up in the goldfields, with thousands of other men, and no way to find him. There had already been two other parties making inquiries, the neighbor said, so if she was interested, Hannah had better hurry up and find Charlie.

As soon as she finished checking on Nellie Turner, Hannah was going to find an agent to go north, locate Charlie Swanswick, and make an offer on the property.

She passed between two rows of beds, twenty to each side of the room, occupied by patients suffering from dysentery, pneumonia, influenza, and broken bones. Since it was the responsibility of family and friends to see that a patient was fed, bathed, and nursed back to health, the ward was a noisy place, with children running about while husbands fretted over wives and mothers fussed over daughters. The only hired person on the ward was a plump woman in a long gray dress with a white mob cap covering her hair as she swished a wet mop over the floor. Hospital attendants had little to do with the patients other than emptying chamber pots.

As Hannah neared the bed at the end of the row, she was surprised that Nellie's baby wasn't tucked into the bed with her. "Hello, Nellie," Hannah said quietly and she slipped off her gloves and rested her hand on the young woman's forehead. The patient, with eyes closed, did not respond. To Hannah's shock, Nellie's forehead burned with fever.

She counted Nellie's racing pulse and then drew the blankets down to gently palpate Nellie's abdomen, causing the girl to moan.

Hannah froze. Nellie was exhibiting the classic symptoms of childbed fever. How was that possible? Hannah was suddenly thrown back to the night her mother, Louisa, lay burning with fever, two days after giving birth to Hannah's baby brother. John Conroy had worked night and day to save them, only to lose them both to a disease that had no known cause, no cure, and that was fatal in every case.

She turned to the attendant and said, "Please fetch Dr. Iverson. He's downstairs, in the main lobby."

Hannah reached into her bag for her stethoscope, saying, "There, there," as she placed the bell to Nellie's chest and listened. The labored breathing was another unmistakable sign of childbed fever.

"My dear madam, what do you think you are doing?"

Hannah straightened and saw that Marcus Iverson had arrived at the bedside, a dignified gentleman of around fifty, tall, imposing. He was the director of the two-storey, eighty-bed hospital, and despite his sometimes severe bearing and aloof manner, was known for his kindness and compassion. Hannah had noticed that he always took the time to reassure the patient with a gentle touch, a word of comfort. In London, she had seen doctors make rounds and not even acknowledge the person in the bed.

Hannah also liked the fact that Dr. Iverson always wore a clean frock coat, trousers, and white shirt when he made rounds, and insisted his medical staff do the same, even though it was contrary to popular practice. Marcus Iverson's other revolutionary ideas included emptying bedpans more than once a day, feeding patients who had no family and friends to bring meals, and changing the sheets between bed occupancies.

Hannah removed her stethoscope and said, "Mrs. Turner has a high fever and severe abdominal pain."

Sir Marcus gave Hannah an arch look. "And what is your authority here?"

"I am a midwife. I was to deliver Mrs. Turner's child, but I was away in the country."

Sir Marcus pursed his lips as he absorbed this unexpected information—Miss Conroy resembled no midwife he had ever seen—then he addressed the patient. As Dr. Iverson laid a gentle hand on Nellie's forehead, keeping his expression impassive, her eyes snapped open, wide with terror. "Am I going to die, sir?" Nellie asked in a tremulous voice.

"Not at all," he said, patting her shoulder and turning away. He addressed Hannah. "You believe this is a case of childbed fever?"

Hannah folded her stethoscope into her bag. When she had redefined her profession from midwife to health practitioner, she had retired the blue carpet bag and replaced it with a handsome leather satchel. "I believe that is what we have here, doctor, and as you know it is highly contagious."

Giving her a brief, puzzled look, he nodded, sharing her concern over this unexpected turn. The patient had been healthy the day before. What had happened since then?

To the ward attendant, he said, "Instruct Mrs. Butterfield to prepare chlorine sheets and arrange to have bellows brought in and a boy to operate them."

Hannah knew that hanging sheets soaked in chlorine around an infected patient, and filling the air with pungent fumigating smoke, were the standard practice for fighting infectious fevers. Nonetheless, she reached into her bag and brought out a small bottle of her iodine preparation. "Dr. Iverson, might I ask you to instruct your doctors to wash their hands in this before they examine the other patients? Especially if they see to Nellie first."

"Why?"

"As an extra precaution, in case the fever is not spread through the air but on human hands."

He looked at the small bottle, finding himself more aware of the slender hand that held it than the medicine itself, taking note that there was no wedding band. "What is it?"

"An iodine solution that I have made myself. It is a mild antiseptic."

Strange talk from such a lovely young lady, Iverson thought. "I am not convinced that hand washing has any significant impact, negative or positive, on a person's health," he said. "But I have read the recent literature from Europe, and some put forth a good argument for the so-called germ theory. And as you say, extra precaution cannot hurt. However, I cannot subject my staff to an unknown formula that, for all I know, will cause the flesh to fall off their fingers. But I *will* order a basin of chlorinated water to be placed at the entry of the ward."

He paused, giving Hannah a frank study, suddenly realizing that she seemed familiar to him, as if they had met before, then he said, "I am curious. Might I ask how you know about childbed fever?"

Hannah handed him her card. He lifted an eyebrow as he read it.

"Health practitioner? What exactly does a 'health practitioner' *do*, Miss Conroy?"

Hannah thought Sir Marcus handsome in a severe way—*patrician* was the word that came to mind—and when he lifted his eyebrow in that manner, he reminded her of Lord Falconbridge. "I deliver babies," she said, "but I also manage wounds, dispense medicines, give advice on health and hygiene, and instruct families in how to take care of their loved ones who are sick."

His dark eyes scrutinized her. There was that nagging feeling again that they had met before. "And what is your training?"

Hannah had learned how to offer a professional presentation of herself. Whereas she would have once said, "My father was a doctor," she now replied, "I apprenticed with my father, who was a medical doctor. I trained at a London Hospital. I assisted a ship's surgeon for six months. And in Adelaide, I was a medical assistant to a prominent physician."

Iverson gave her a thoughtful look. Miss Conroy did not look like a flimflam artist or a charlatan. She had seemed to know how to properly use a binaural stethoscope, and she *had* correctly diagnosed childbed fever.

He didn't know what to make of her. Sir Marcus was fifty-two years old and considered himself a man of the world. And yet never in all his experience had an unescorted lady boldly introduced herself to him, offering her card! But, according to her *curriculum vitae*, for want of a better term, she was a professional woman, in a league by herself, and he was both baffled and intrigued. Miss Conroy was attractive, in her mid twenties, and unmarried. Calling herself a health practitioner, showing resourcefulness and courage. A young lady with a head on her shoulders. And who was somehow familiar to him. "I beg your pardon," he said, "but have we met?"

"We have. It was at the home of Blanche Sinclair, last year, a fête that she held for a charitable cause."

"Yes, I remember now. Forgive me." Sir Marcus was astonished with himself. When he had decided to put Blanche Sinclair out of his mind, apparently he had put her friends out of his mind as well. But that meeting, last year, at Blanche's residence came back to him now, and his first impressions of Miss Conroy as being an attractive young lady, friendly but reserved, and that he had sensed a curious sadness about her, as if she had just lost something or someone dear to her.

"Will you be attending the charity ball tonight, Dr. Iverson, at Addison's Hotel?" Hannah asked.

Sir Marcus had received Blanche's invitation and had immediately thrown it away, having no intention of attending her charity ball tonight, or any other event that Mrs. Sinclair might put on. Not after what happened a year ago. But now, with the charming Miss Conroy smiling at him in what looked like such an inviting way ...

"If my schedule allows," he said, recalling the old expression about cutting one's nose off to spite one's face. It would be foolish to deny himself the pleasure of this young lady's friendship because of his ill feelings toward Blanche Sinclair.

Sir Marcus found himself, in the next moment, thinking of the amateur rowing competition that was going to take place on the Yarra River next month. It would be Melbourne's first sweep-oared regatta and was to be modeled after the Henley Regatta held annually on the Thames. He wondered if Miss Conroy would like to accompany him and share a picnic lunch on the river's bank.

As he slipped her card into his pocket, Sir Marcus said, "You understand, Miss Conroy, that Nellie is now a patient of this hospital. She is no longer your charge, so I will have to ask you not to disturb her or interfere with my staff in any way."

"May I ask where the baby is?"

"Nellie was unable to nurse last night, so her neighbor, who was visiting, took the baby to be wetnursed by her daughter. I bid you a good day, Miss Conroy," he said, and could not help watch as she walked down the length of the noisy ward, could not help thinking what a fine figure she cut ...

Outside on the wooden sidewalk, Hannah paused to collect herself beneath the spring sunshine. It was November, flowers were in bloom, and summer was coming. But now a dark cloud hung over her. How on earth had poor Nellie contracted the deadly childbed fever?

Hannah had left her small carriage in front of the hospital, the horse tethered to a hitching post. She paused to look back at Victoria Hospital as horses clip-clopped past in the dusty street.

The hospital was really just a substantial stone house with two wards: male and female. There was no surgical theater, just a bench kept out of sight and out of hearing of the wards. The kitchen and laundry were outbuildings. There was a downstairs room for treating walk-in patients, an office where records were kept, and Dr. Iverson's office. Lighting was by candles and oil lamps, water was drawn from a well, solid waste was deposited in an open cess-pit in the rear.

The building stood in the middle of vacant land covered in brush and tree stumps, but the government had recently increased the land grant so that the scrubby grounds stretched through to Russell Street, and now the vacant lot was being leveled for landscaping, with plans for the building of a bathhouse for the patients. There was even talk of installing gas lighting by 1856.

Although having a hospital for the poor was a noble achievement—all credit to Sir Marcus Iverson—it still wasn't the answer to the many ills that plagued crowded Melbourne. In the sixteen months since the discovery of gold in the north, the city had been inundated by a massive influx of immigrants from all over the world, all coming to seek their fortune. The result of such uncontrolled overcrowding was outbreaks of disease.

The little statue of Hygeia that Dr. Davenport had given Hannah stood prominently on her fireplace mantel, a reminder that the daughter of the god Aesculapius was the goddess of hygiene, and therefore the goddess who *prevented* disease. It was Hannah's dream to write and publish a comprehensive home health manual and educate people in hygiene, nutrition, safety, proper nursing care. She had collected an impressive body of her own learning, and wanted to share it with others. All the things she had learned from Dr. Applewhite, Dr. Davenport—even Lulu Forchette ("For chronic abdominal gas, a daily cup of buttermilk does the trick.")—and in her travels around the countryside, would go into the book. But so far, Hannah had not found the time to even begin such a major undertaking. Along with her demanding practice, she was still searching for the answer to the mystery of her father's dying words. Hannah had assumed he had meant the iodine preparation was a universal cure-all. But in the past four years, she had discovered that it was not so.

She looked up and down the street, congested with carriages and men on horseback, the stage coach from Sydney, the overland postal coach from Adelaide. The day was warm. Reaching into her bag, she brought out a folded handkerchief with which to pat her forehead, but when she saw the initials, she stopped. This was not a handkerchief to be used but carried as a cherished memento.

"Don't you get lonely?" her friend Blanche had once asked, and Hannah knew she was referring to male companionship. But Hannah wasn't interested in a man, not with the loss of Neal still felt too sharply.

The day of the headline about the expedition perishing in the desert, Hannah had gone around to newspaper offices for further details. But they only knew the sketchy story that had arrived via travelers from Western Australia. Hannah had then written to the colonial authorities in Perth, to receive the insupportable response that Sir Reginald and his entire company had been slaughtered by hostile aborigines. "A lone survivor," the report had said, "made it to Perth, one Archie Tice, a surveyor with the expedition. He took a horse when hostilities broke out and, galloping away, had looked back and seen horrific fiery explosions, killing all. Mr. Tice barely made it to a Christian mission in the Outback to report on what happened, and then he himself succumbed to the extreme exposure he had suffered."

"There you are!"

Hannah turned to see her friend, Blanche Sinclair, draw up in an elegant barouche pulled by two horses. A groom sat next to the liveried driver, and a young lady in a maid's costume sat opposite Mrs. Sinclair as they rode with the top down. A little on the plump side, with shiny red-brown hair swept up under the latest style bonnet, Blanche was thirty but her deeply dimpled cheeks and a chin that narrowed to a point made her look younger. Blanche was immensely rich, her husband having made smart investments in copper and silver, shipping and wool. His death from a fall had left her well provided for. Blanche managed her inheritance with fine business acumen, knew how to spot fortune hunters, and had more friends, Hannah often thought, than Australia had gum trees.

"I've just been to your house," Blanche said from beneath the shade of her pink parasol. "Mrs. Sparrow said you came in from the country this morning and that you went straight out again. I thought you didn't like to put your patients in the hospital."

"I don't. Her friends brought her here."

"You look worried, Hannah. Is your patient going to be all right?"

"I suspect she has childbed fever, and yes, I am very worried. But Dr. Iverson is taking the proper precautions. I pray it doesn't spread."

Blanche's eyes flew open. "You spoke with Marcus?"

Hannah caught the look of sudden hope in Blanche's eyes and, knowing how her friend felt about the distinguished doctor, wished she had something more positive to report. "He didn't recognize me at first. Of course, this is the first time I've spoken with Dr. Iverson since he and I met at your house last year. When I reminded him of that meeting, he remembered me."

Color rose in Blanche's cheeks. "Did he say anything about tonight's ball?" In the past year, Blanche had sent Marcus Iverson invitations to several events she had organized, and he had responded with regrets to each. She was beginning to despair of ever mending the rift she had unwittingly caused in their friendship, for she still had very deep feelings for Sir Marcus.

Blanche glanced toward the hospital entrance, and Hannah saw both fear and longing in her eyes. Then Blanche brightened her smile and said, "The tickets to tonight's gala are sold out. Thanks to dear Alice. Everyone wants to hear her sing."

"She is more than happy to put on a private performance. It is for a good cause, after all."

Four years ago, after receiving the news of Neal's death, Hannah had thrown herself into her work, finding solace and escape in studying medical texts. When she had exhausted Adelaide's limited resources, she had made the decision to leave that small city and move to Sydney. At the same time, Alice had begun to feel the limitations of Mr. Glass's music hall, finding in herself the need to share her music and joy with larger audiences. And so together the two friends had decided to make new lives for themselves elsewhere (and as luck would have it, Sam Glass was happy to let Alice out of her contract as he was having an affair with a trapeze artist who performed on stage in little more than tights and a ruffled corset, and who had declared that there could only be one star performer at the Elysium). And so together, Alice and Hannah had left Adelaide in search of bigger dreams, but when they had fallen in love with Melbourne during their ship's one-day layover, they had decided to stay.

Alice now sang for packed audiences at the Queen's Theatre on the southwest corner of Queen and Little Bourke Streets. Her nickname, "Australian Songbird," earned in Adelaide, had followed her to Melbourne, where she was the toast of the town.

"Will you be escorted tonight, Hannah?"

"I will be coming alone."

Blanche shook her head in friendly exasperation. "Only you, darling, could pull it off. A lady going about on her own!" But Blanche was secretly impressed, and proud of her friend's accomplishments.

When Hannah first arrived in Melbourne, she had put notices in newspapers and on public boards all around town, had given her card to doctors and chemists, but patients had been slow to come. And then she had thought: women spread information through word of mouth rather than the printed word. And so she had gone out and introduced herself to seamstresses, hairdressers, and hat makers, handing them her card and informing them of her services. Blanche Sinclair had learned about Hannah from the woman who monogrammed her handkerchiefs. And she had come to Hannah's office trembling, frightened, with nowhere else to turn—one of the wealthiest women in the colonies, turning in desperation to a stranger who called herself a health practitioner.

Blanche had been bathing one morning and discovered a lump in her right breast. She had gone at once to her regular doctor, a man who didn't even touch her but had asked her to describe the lump to him. After she had done so, he had gravely pronounced that the breast must be amputated. Two more doctors delivered the same diagnosis and bad news, once again without touching her, for that would have been highly improper. And then Blanche had heard of a lady practitioner who specialized in women's problems and was surprised when Miss Conroy had said, "We must determine what the lump consists of."

Disrobing to her camisole, Blanche had reclined on an examining table. Hannah had first delicately probed the lump with her fingertips, rolling it around, saying, "Does this hurt? How about now?" Finally she had said, "I do not believe it is cancer. Freely mobile lumps like this are usually benign. Those that are fixed and ill-defined tend to be malignant. However, there is a further test, to make sure."

Using a thin metal tube sharpened at one end, which Hannah called a trocar, and attached to a slender rubber hose, she had gently inserted it into the skin. Although it had been painful, Blanche had borne the discomfort because the test hadn't lasted long. A dose of laudanum first, and then brief insertion. Almost at once Miss Conroy had said, "It is not cancer. It is a cyst. This straw-colored fluid that I removed from the lump is proof." After the cyst was drained and the wound bandaged, Blanche dressed while Hannah gave her a prescription for laudanum and explained, "Please keep an eye for infection, although I disinfected my instruments."

That was three years ago, and they had been friends since.

Blanche's endless praise of Melbourne's new "doctress" resulted in more patients than Hannah could handle. And she had learned that it wasn't just healing skills they sought. There was the fact that she was a woman with none of the mortifying embarrassment one had with a male doctor. Hannah's touch was light and gentle, they all declared, unlike some male physicians who could be quite ham-fisted.

"By the way," Blanche said now, "there's been a last-minute addition to our showing tonight. Cecily has discovered another artist."

Hannah smiled. Cecily Aldridge collected artists the way other people collected art.

"This one is a *photographer*. An American. Newly arrived in Melbourne, and Cecily persuaded him to exhibit ten of his pieces tonight. She says his work is absolutely brilliant and that we should raise considerable funds through sales of his works."

"American?" Hannah said, suddenly hearing a pounding in her ears. "Do"—she struggled for breath—"do you know his name?"

"I met him just now, hanging his pictures at Addison's. His name is Neal Scott, and he is new to Melbourne as he has just recently arrived from Sydney with his fiancée."

-40-

Blanche Sinclair wrung her hands nervously, praying that her charity ball went successfully. Praying also that Dr. Marcus Iverson decided to come.

The gala event took place at the new Addison's Hotel on Collins Street, a four-storey building of local bluestone, with a façade of columns and arches and large plate glass windows. Addison's boasted two hundred rooms, a ballroom, a barbershop and four restaurants, and tonight was its official opening. Blanche had approached the wealthy owner with an intriguing proposal: that he celebrate the launch of his grand establishment—the biggest hostelry in Melbourne—with a social event put on for raising funds for an orphanage. The best and richest of Melbourne society would attend, Blanche had assured him, and think of the poor motherless children.

Suspecting that giving her rich friends a glimpse into the new hotel might not be enough, she hit upon the idea of an art show, featuring Melbourne's established and promising artists. With the addition of champagne, a string quartet and a solo performance by Alice Star, Blanche was certain they would raise enough funds to begin construction on a new orphanage.

Up and down the street, lamplighters with their familiar long poles were going about the business of lighting the candles in street lamps, each glass globe giving off a comfortable glow against the night. The front of Addison's had been decorated with additional lanterns, and bright light spilled from the large plate glass windows as elegantly dressed people arrived in fancy carriages and walked two by two through the brightly lit entrance of the hotel. Although a few gentlemen arrived alone, and some ladies arrived in pairs or groups, only one lady stepped down from her carriage and walked along the red carpet unescorted. But everyone knew Hannah Conroy, and so they were not surprised.

The lobby had been converted into an art gallery, with paintings displayed on walls and easels. A string quartet played Mozart, while footmen in livery moved through the crowd with glasses of champagne and platters of hors d'oeuvres. Overhead, chandeliers burned with a hundred candles, and silver candelabras had been placed on shelves and tables, making the lobby glow and glitter. The women's gowns were the colors of the rainbow, shining like butterflies in silks and satins, with sparkling gems at their throats, while the men wore black or gray, with starched shirts and polished shoes.

Seeing her friend step through the tall glass doors, Blanche came up with hands outstretched. "You look lovely, Hannah." Blanche was pleased to see that her friend had taken her advice and used the services of the best dress designer in town. Hannah's off-shoulder gown of cream-colored satin and edged in pink lace showed exquisite taste.

"Everyone is here," Blanche with satisfaction, herself wearing a stunning gown of deep purple that offset her violet eyes. "The Governor sent his regrets, but that was to be expected. His wife is here, and she has her eye on a painting that will bring in a hundred pounds."

Hannah handed her cape to a maid and searched the crowd for a particular face. She could not recall when she had been so nervous, excited, and afraid all at once.

After her encounter with Blanche outside the hospital that afternoon, she had come straight to Addison's Hotel, where finishing touches were being done for tonight's gala. Blanche had said she left Mr. Scott here, but Hannah was told he had just left. She had gone home to go through the two weeks' worth of mail and messages waiting for her, to see if Neal had left one. Hannah's housekeeper, Mrs. Sparrow, confirmed that an American gentleman had indeed paid a visit, and had left a note. "I pray you are the Hannah Conroy," Neal had written, "with whom I spent six months at sea on a ship called the *Caprica*."

Hannah had no idea where Neal lived, or how to find him, and so she had had to endure the agonizing hours until she would see him at tonight's charity event.

"And the American photographer?" she asked, her heart racing. Hannah had to raise her voice to be heard over the roar of conversation and laughter that rose to the high ceiling. "Is he here?"

"Mr. Scott said he had to step out but that he would be right back," Blanche said, her eyes darting anxiously toward the main entrance. Was Marcus going to come? If he did, Blanche decided she would take him aside and explain about what happened that day a year ago, why she could not agree to organize his hospital tour.

Suddenly, there he was, handing his opera cape and top hat to one of the attendants. Blanche was thrilled to see him, and he looked exceptionally distinguished in black cutaway coat and tails, the silver in his black hair catching the light from the chandeliers. Blanche felt a jolt of sexual desire and realized that her feelings for him had not diminished in the year since he had stopped being friendly toward her. She could pinpoint the exact moment when his attitude, after two years of being a dear friend (although there had been no romantic overtures), had changed to one of cold aloofness. She knew how devoted Sir Marcus was to his hospital, that it was his life. But how could she tell him that the very sight of the building put knots in her stomach and chilled her to the bone? She had not expected his reaction afterward, when she had turned down his request that she organize a fund-raising tour of his hospital. It had surprised her when the invitations to picnics and horse races stopped. And by the time she realized the reason, she didn't know how to fix it.

Dr. Iverson came through the crowd and walked right up to Blanche and Hannah, and while Blanche's heart raced in utter delight to see him, it was Hannah whom he addressed. "It is nice to see you again, Miss Conroy."

"Thank you," Hannah said. "Dr. Iverson, what is Nellie Turner's condition?"

"Come now!" Blanche said, stepping between them, dismayed by the way Marcus ignored her. Blanche was further upset by the way he looked at Hannah. She felt pain rush through her, but she kept up her smile to cover the deep hurt. "No business talk tonight. Marcus, let me introduce you to our artists."

"I should be delighted, Mrs. Sinclair, but in a moment, please." Marcus Iverson was appalled at the rush of desire he felt by Blanche's nearness. She had proven herself to be less than a friend, but while his mind knew this, his heart said something else. He only had himself to blame. After his wife died, he had thought he could never love another woman. For a long time he devoted himself to medicine and his hospital. And then Blanche Sinclair's husband died, and Marcus found himself wishing to comfort her. She was, after all, young and attractive, with a delightful personality, well read and educated, and generous. He started taking her for carriage rides and picnics and they became very good friends, after a respectable mourning period. There had even come a time when he had wondered if they had a future together.

And then he had asked her to organize a charity tour of his hospital to raise funds for a new wing—with Blanche Sinclair chairing the event, the donations were guaranteed—but to his shock she declined with the thinnest of excuses. Showing her true colors, he had decided, proving to be only a shallow friend.

A carriage drew up outside just then, pulled by four plumed horses and drawing everyone's attention. Two footmen opened the door and assisted the passengers to the wooden sidewalk—a young lady, and older woman, and a middle-aged man—all attired in fine evening dress. The fourth passenger, Miss Alice Star, stepped into the glow of the lights in a stunning white gown and white velvet cape trimmed in white fur, with tall egret feathers rising from a diamond tiara in her golden blond hair. Alice was one of the highest paid performers in Melbourne, second only to famed Shakespearean actor Donald Craig.

Doormen opened the hotel's doors, and as Alice swept under the chandelier, everyone applauded. She paused dramatically, returned the salute with a stage bow, and then handed off her cape and told her three escorts to go and enjoy themselves. Hannah watched as a circle of admirers formed around Alice. At twenty-five, her figure had filled out into womanly curves. She was more confident and radiant than ever, with no sign of the timid maid Hannah had met in Adelaide almost six years ago.

Excusing herself from the circle, Alice glided toward Hannah. "Is it true? Neal is alive? I almost fainted when I read your note. Have you seen him yet? Where is he?"

"I am told he stepped out and will be back."

"Have you seen his work yet?" Although Alice had never met Neal, she had heard a great deal about him from Hannah, had seen his photograph, and had witnessed the depth of Hannah's grief when she received news of his death. But now! He was alive!

After a polite exchange with Dr. Iverson and Blanche, both of whom moved off in different directions, Alice threaded her arm through Hannah's and, as they made their way through the glittering crowd, said, "I am bursting with joy for you, Hannah. I don't know how you can be so calm."

"Alice," Hannah said as they walked past easels displaying paintings of varying styles and subjects, the artists at the center of attention. "Neal is engaged to be married."

Alice stopped and stared at her. Now she saw how pale her friend was, saw the dampness in Hannah's eyes, and how her lower lip trembled. "You can't be serious!"

Hannah spoke with barely controlled emotion. "I have now had the information confirmed by others. Neal opened his new studio last week, and already everyone is clambering to have him take their photographic portraits, and a few were not shy about asking after his marital status."

"Oh, Hannah," Alice said, her joy turning to sharp disappointment. "I am so sorry. How could that happen?"

Hannah tried to speak objectively, but it was a struggle to hold herself together. "Well, it *has* been four and a half years since we last saw each other. A lot can happen in that time. Certainly a lot has changed in my own life. Here we are," she said as they arrived at a section of wall hung with large photographs in beautiful frames. A sign identified them as being the work of "Neal Scott, Photographer."

Hannah and Alice stared in wide-eyed wonder. While the other artists had chosen to depict Australian city or rural scenes—sheep shearing, horse races, ships in harbors—the American photographer had ventured into the world that lay beyond the last outpost of civilization, capturing images of wonders that most people would never see. And Neal's photographs of the Outback were more than mere pictures, they were works of art.

With tear-filled eyes, Hannah looked from one to another, taking in the mountains, rock formations, tree-less plains. She sensed a spiritual power emanate from the images. How had he managed, with glass and paper and a few chemicals, to invoke the sheer immensity of the Australian landscape? One in particular captivated her: On the right and left edges, leafy eucalyptus trees seemed to lean away from one another, giving the illusion of curtains opening upon a theatrical stage, and in the distance an awesome rock, ancient and massive, rose up from the flat desert. Neal had so expertly composed the picture that it was as if he knew there was an audience standing behind him and his camera. He had captured an incalculable volume of luminous space, filled it with incandescent light, and turned it into a stunning display of radiant wonder. By a clever trick—the bottom of the photograph had been cropped so that there was no hint of ground where a bulky tripod and human being had stood—Neal created the illusion that the observer of the vista were drifting in space. Hannah was taken aback. This was spatial experience on a breathtaking scale. Neal magically drew his audience into the scene, allowing them to float through golden light and across ancient land.

It made her heart swell with love for him, and an aching desire to tell him in person how deeply his work affected her. And then the remembered the fiancée and pain shot through her.

"Notice the frame, Hannah," Alice said quietly.

Struggling for composure, Hannah tore her eyes from the image and inspected the wooden framework. At first it looked like a fanciful pattern surrounding the photograph, but when she looked more closely, she saw miniature flowers carved into the wood, and trees, tiny woodland creatures, even a waterfall!

"Alice," she said, "it looks like the frame around that painting your secret admirer gave to you."

"Yes, it does," Alice said, suddenly excited.

It had started a month ago. Alice had been performing nightly at the theater, plus weekend matinees, and while she was used to seeing regulars in the audience, one in particular had caught her attention. At first she wasn't sure why he especially caught her notice until she realized that he always sat in the same seat near the back, in shadow, and that at the end of each show, he would leave instead of trying to see her backstage, or wait in the alley at the stage door like the others (which was why Alice never went out without at least three escorts). Alice was also used to receiving lavish gifts and flowers, but in every case the giver identified himself. A week ago, a package had been delivered to her dressing room with no card from the admirer. The package contained a watercolor by a local artist—black swans on the Yarra River—but when Alice saw the exquisitely carved wooden frame—miniature birds and butterflies—she realized that it was the frame, not the painting, that was the gift. And as the gift had been given anonymously, she had wondered if it had come from the mysterious man who sat in shadow.

"I wonder if he is here, tonight!" Alice said suddenly. "These beautiful frames are every bit works of art as the photographs. It makes sense that the man who carved them would be here, doesn't it?"

Hannah saw a spark of interest in her friend's eye that she had never seen before. Alice did not lack for admirers, but she wasn't interested in being courted. She had told Hannah that men were not in love with her but with her façade, with an illusion, and she knew that once the make-up was washed off, the hairpiece and tiara removed, their dream would be dashed, and she would be left humiliated. Yet there was something unique about this particular admirer. Why was he hiding his identity? Why did he come to every performance and yet not step forward to introduce himself? It might only be a game, but Hannah saw that Alice was intrigued.

"Miss Star," Blanche said, coming up in a rustle of silk and petticoats, her deeply dimpled cheeks flushed, her narrow pointed chin shiny with excitement. "We're ready for you."

Alice hesitated, placing a hand on Hannah's arm to ask softly, "Are you all right? Shall I stay with you?" When Hannah assured her that she was all right, Alice took her place in the center of the lobby, beneath the chandelier, and waited graciously while everyone quieted down. When the air was so still that only the occasional sputter of an oil lamp was heard,

Alice cleared her throat, clasped her hands at her waist, drew in a deep breath, and began to sing.

> *I dreamt I dwelt in marble halls*
> *With vassals and serfs at my side,*
> *And of all who assembled within those walls*
> *That I was the hope and the pride.*
> *I had riches all too great to count*
> *And a high ancestral name.*

The audience was instantly hers. Without musical accompaniment, with only her angelic looks and golden voice, Alice Star, née Starky, who had once mopped floors in an Adelaide whorehouse, so captured her audience that it was as if she sang to a collection of statues. And she sang so sweetly that no one would guess Alice's painful secret, that only Hannah knew: that although she was the toast of Melbourne, and lived in a beautiful home with servants and a carriage, Alice Star was a very lonely woman.

As Hannah watched with pride, never ceasing to be amazed at her friend's ease of enchantment, she saw the hotel's front door, on the other side of Alice, open and swing closed as two people entered. They stopped when they heard the singing, and waited politely in opera cape and cloak, top hat and bonnet.

The woman of the pair, young, slender, an emerald green gown glimpsed beneath her cloak, kept her eyes on Alice. But the man with her, top hat still on his head, allowed his eyes to rove the room until they came to a rest upon Hannah.

She nearly cried out. She wanted to run to him, deliver herself into his arms, and thank him for being alive. But she had to remain where she was, while Alice sang and Neal stood by the front door, his eyes fixed on Hannah.

Blanche, standing at Hannah's side, inclined her head slightly and whispered, "So that's where Mr. Scott disappeared to. He went to fetch his fiancée."

> *But I also dreamt which charmed me most*
> *That you loved me still the same*
> *That you loved me*
> *You loved me still the same,*
> *That you loved me*
> *You loved me still the same.*

Hannah was in agony as Alice sang and no one could move. Memories washed over her, from the *Caprica*, from the dusty road in front of the Australia Hotel. Intense longing returned, and a sweet, painful ache.

Neal was very handsome in a smart black cut-away coat with tails over black trousers, a starched white shirt, and white cravat. His brown hair was longer than when she had seen him last, and she noticed a natural curl over his white collar. He was clean shaven, although his sideburns were fashionably long.

She thought of their kiss, their moment of lovemaking in the carriage, the feel and taste of him. She did not think she could endure the agony of this reunion, being introduced to the beautiful creature in the emerald gown.

Hannah was wondering if she could invent an excuse to leave—a patient needing her—when Alice's song came to an end. There was a moment of silence as the audience realized it had been released from the spell, and then came the applause and shouts of "Brava!"

The quartet started up again, conversation resumed, and people gathered around Alice to praise her. Neal removed his cape and hat and handed them to one of the maids. Hannah saw him murmur something to the young lady in green, who nodded with a smile, and then he wasted no time in crossing the vast lobby to where Hannah stood.

Speechless with emotion, she reached for him, arms extended, slipping her gloved hands into his. They were in the midst of a sea of noisy humanity, yet Hannah was aware of only one other person. "Neal, I thought you were dead." He was tanned, and there were new creases on his face. He smelled of familiar shaving soap. "What happened?"

"Hannah, I am so sorry. I have been trying to find you. I knew you would have seen the news story, that you thought I was dead."

He told her briefly about Galagandra, the attack, and the chemical explosions, but he omitted mention of the sandstorm, Sir Reginald's treachery, and his sojourn with Jallara's clan. This was not the time or place. "I didn't know it, but when the natives attacked, one man, a surveyor named Archie Tice, managed to ride as far as an aboriginal mission where he told them he got about half a mile away when he heard the explosions and looked back to see the black clouds. He told the missionaries it was a massacre, and then he himself died a few days later of an infected spear wound. It was the missionaries who reported the sad fate of the expedition to the authorities in Perth. They didn't know that Fintan and I survived."

"Fintan!" Hannah said, remembering the handsome youth back in Adelaide.

"After the smoke cleared, we found our camp still intact, with horses, food, and water. It took me three days to bury the dead. I guess the explosions frightened the aborigines because they never came back. Fintan was injured. We were out there for weeks before fossickers found us and took us to the same aboriginal mission where a Christian couple much like the Merriwethers nursed us back to health. Hannah, it was a year before we returned to Perth. We had had no idea that our story had been reported in the meantime!"

"Why didn't you set them straight?"

"I started to, and then I realized that someone sharp enough would realize we had been out there for gold, and Galagandra would be overrun with gold seekers. Luckily, Archie never said anything about us discovering gold. It was sacred land, Hannah, I couldn't do that. Fintan and I went to Adelaide as soon as we could. I searched all over for you. I knew you thought I was dead. But I thought I would find you! I went to the Australia Hotel, but it was under new ownership. I went to Seven Oaks, and the McKeeghans had no idea where you were. Finally, I did get information on your whereabouts, that you had gone to Sydney."

She swallowed painfully. "I didn't think to leave you a message at the Adelaide post office, or on Mr. Day's public board. I thought you were dead!"

She tried not to search the crowd for the young woman in green. She wanted to ask Neal about her, to hear her name, to hear the details of how they met. But at the same time ... Hannah did not want to know any of this. She knew he would tell her everything in time, but for the moment all she could think of was that Neal was truly alive.

Hannah was vaguely aware of space being cleared in the vast lobby, and couples taking up a waltz. Aromas drifted on the air as a buffet table was set, bringing delicious aromas of roast beef and spring lamb from the hotel kitchen. The lobby was hot and noisy, people passing by murmured, "Good evening, Miss Conroy," but Hannah was aware of none of these.

"I only got your note this afternoon," she said. "I have been out in the country, visiting patients. But why did you ask if I was the same Hannah Conroy who had sailed on the *Caprica*?"

He laughed softly. "You wouldn't believe how many women share your name. In Sydney, I put up notices on public boards and adverts in newspapers. I checked with hospitals, doctors, chemist shops, other midwives. I even offered a reward for information on your whereabouts. I followed two leads to Hannah Conroy, both taking me far off the track into the Outback, only to find very different Hannah Conroys. Finally, I decided to try my luck in Melbourne. I sent Fintan ahead to find a studio for us, while I came the overland route with my equipment and supplies." He added with a smile, "I don't trust ships."

Hannah saw changes in Neal. He seemed more subdued, not as brash as he had been when he had started out on the expedition with his scientific instruments. She wondered what had happened to him during his journey through the wilderness. Even physically, he was different—the closely cropped hair now grew long and curled loosely around his ears. His skin was tan, with lines at the eyes and framing his mouth. Strangely, the sun-wrinkles did not make him look older but wiser. Hannah looked at the photographs displayed on the wall and wondered if it was Australia itself that had wrought the changes.

She also wondered about the fiancée, her name, how they met. But she was afraid to ask.

"But look at you, Hannah," Neal said softly. "You are obviously doing well. I take it you are a success as a midwife?"

"I have had to make some adjustments," she said, reaching into her small bag and bringing out her card. "I had difficulty getting established at first, and I blamed society. And then one day I realized that it wasn't society that was confining me to a narrowly defined role, I was doing it to myself. Once I redefined my role in life, success followed."

Hannah had changed, he thought as he looked at the card, and it was more than a mere re-titling of her occupation. When they first met, more than six years ago, he had thought of her as a girl. Now she was a woman. On the *Caprica* she had had only a vague idea of her direction. Now she was in charge of her destiny.

"I say, are you the photographer, sir?"

Neal turned, blinked. "I beg your pardon?"

A whiskered gentleman with a portly belly and red cheeks said, "That picture up there, can you tell me where it was taken? I've never seen anything like it." Hannah recognized the man as Mr. Beechworth, a wealthy entrepreneur who had recently formed Melbourne's first railway company.

Blanche materialized at that moment to say, "Did you know the bidding has reached fifty pounds on that piece, Mr. Beechworth? If you want it, you must enter your bid right away. The auction will close soon."

Blanche looked at Neal for a long moment, and then at Hannah. She knew there had been someone in Hannah's past, a gentleman with whom Hannah had sailed from England. But there had been few details, little of the story, only that he was the reason Hannah was not interested in being introduced to eligible gentlemen in Melbourne. And now, as she led Mr. Beechworth to the auction table, she wondered if this intriguing American might be the mysterious someone from Hannah's past ...

Across the crowded lobby, Dr. Marcus Iverson watched the pair at the photographic exhibition.

He had observed Miss Conroy and the American for the past few minutes, noting in their body language an ease and familiarity that denoted friendship, yet at times a tension and nervousness that might indicate deeper and more intimate sentiments not yet requited. Sir Marcus was surprised to feel a stab of jealousy, an emotion he had not experienced since the days when his beloved Caroline had been the belle of many balls and the center of male attention.

He decided to pay his respects to the American photographer who had donated his time and presence for such a deserving cause.

They were standing a little closer than decorum called for, Sir Marcus thought as he neared Miss Conroy and Mr. Scott. And the way their eyes were locked, the way the gentleman touched Hannah's arm, as if the world did not exist—

Sir Marcus was nonplussed by his feelings. All he could think was that Hannah Conroy reminded him somehow of his own cherished Caroline, who had died of typhoid. Caroline had been a widely read, highly educated woman with opinions of her own, and while he had not always agreed with her, he had enjoyed their debates. Sir Marcus did not deny that he admired smart women, found such minds very attractive in fact, and suspected that there were far more intelligent women in the world than they themselves let on.

"Hello again, Miss Conroy," he said.

After Hannah conducted an introduction, Sir Marcus turned to Neal, extending his hand. "A pleasure to meet you, sir."

While the two men spoke for a moment about photography, Hannah espied Neal's fiancée across the lobby, stunning red-hair shining beneath the chandeliers. Hannah could see what Neal saw in the young lady. But it hurt. Hannah felt sick. She had grieved for him, mentally laid him to rest, only to have him stride back into her life in all his power and virility—to lose him all over again to another woman. It was more than she could bear. And she did not want to be introduced to the fiancée. Not yet. She wasn't ready.

Dr. Iverson addressed Hannah. "I am afraid I must leave this delightful event," he began, and suddenly an idea came to him. "When I left the hospital this afternoon, there was a new case of childbed fever."

"Oh no!"

Sir Marcus cleared his throat, a little ashamed at his obvious ploy to break up the tête-à-tête, and not sure why he had done it. But he was also pleased that it had worked, because Miss Conroy said, "Perhaps, Doctor, I should pay a visit to Nellie Turner?"

Unaware that Hannah's eyes were on a woman in green coming their way, Sir Marcus said, "That would be a good idea, Miss Conroy, and I should welcome your opinion on the new case. Shall I meet you at the front doors?"

When Sir Marcus left, Hannah said, "Neal, I really must go, and people are going to want to talk to you about your photography."

"Hannah we have to talk," he said quickly. "Tomorrow morning. The very first thing. My studio?"

"Tomorrow is my morning to staff the Quaker Meeting House for the distribution of clothing to the poor. But I am available in the afternoon."

She slipped her gloved hand into his, her heart rising in her throat at his touch. "I want to hear everything you have been doing," she said, dreading to hear about the fiancée, "and I shall tell you a rather extraordinary story in return."

Alice was standing near the entrance, chatting with friends, when she saw Hannah retrieve her cape and leave with Dr. Iverson. She watched the carriage drive off, and then she turned her attention to the crowded lobby, where she saw Neal Scott at the far end, surrounded by well-wishers and people with questions about his pictures.

Then he did a curious thing. Holding up his hand, he said something to Blanche, and left the group to stride to a plain door that led off one side of the hotel registration desk. A sign on the door said, "Private." Alice watched as Neal went in and emerged a moment later, returning to the table where the auction bids were being taken.

Alice returned her attention to the plain door and gave it some thought. What was behind the door, and what had it to do with Mr. Scott?

Excusing herself from her companions, she threaded her way through the crowd to the registration desk, with people congratulating her along the way. When she reached the door, she placed her hand on the doorknob and looked around to make sure no one saw, and then she quickly opened the door, slipped inside, and closed it behind herself.

A dimly lit supply room lay before her, with shelves stocked with boxed stationery and fresh linens, empty flower vases, and clean spittoons. But in the center of the floor stood large wooden crates with FRAGILE stenciled on the sides, and a mound of straw packing in between. Alice heard rustling from behind tall cabinets, and then someone whistling. Footsteps sounded on the stone floor, and presently a man came from the back, carrying a ball of twine and a pair of scissors. He wore no jacket over his trousers, his shirtsleeves were rolled up, suspenders curving over his broad shoulders.

He stopped short, the whistling silenced. "Hello!" he said with a smile.

"Hello," Alice replied, her diamond tiara glinting in the light of the flickering oil lamps. She could not help staring at the handsome young man. The cleft in his chin and the cupid's-bow mouth brought to mind a portrait she had seen of the poet Lord Byron. This young man was graced with the same long-lashed soulful eyes and luxuriant wavy hair.

Alice glanced at the crates with *Neal Scott Photography* stenciled on the lids and realized that they must be for transporting the framed photographs. "I am going to guess that you gave me a gift, sir," Alice said, feeling a strange fluttering in her stomach. "A framed watercolor."

When he blushed, Alice thought: He does not know how beautiful he is. The term Black Irish came to mind, those dark-haired folk in a red-headed population who were said to be the descendants of survivors of the Spanish Armada.

"Guilty of being your secret admirer," he said, and extended his hand. "Fintan Rorke at your service."

They shook hands, and Fintan held hers a moment longer than was necessary, black eyes delving hers.

"You know, Mr. Scott's photographs are beautiful," Alice said. "And they deserve to be sold for a lot of money. But I secretly believe it is the frames that people are really paying so much for. You carved them, didn't you, Mr. Rorke? You carved the one that was brought to my dressing room a week ago. I am very pleased to meet you."

"The pleasure is all mine," he said, and the small cluttered room suddenly became intimate, personal. The breath caught in Alice's throat.

"I wonder, Mr. Rorke," she said, "if you wouldn't think me too forward to invite you to come to the theater tomorrow night and be my guest backstage after the performance."

Fintan couldn't take his eyes off this angelic vision he had fallen in love with during the very first performance he had attended, a month ago. He had come ahead to Melbourne to find a place for Neal to set up a studio, and one afternoon had decided to take in a show that everyone was talking about. It took only one song from this ethereal creature, and Fintan Rorke was in love. He had gone to every performance since, to sit in the dark and adore her. He had even been so bold as to send her a gift, anonymously, to let her know that her beauty inspired yet more beauty.

"I shall be delighted and honored to accept your invitation, Miss Star."

The door swung open and light poured in. "Alice, there you are!" Blanche said. "I've been looking all over for you. The Governor's wife would like to thank you personally for your performance tonight."

"I'll be right there." She held out her hand. "Until tomorrow night, Mr. Rorke?"

He clasped her hand and she felt strength in the fingers, felt his warmth permeate the fabric of her white glove. With dark eyes holding her captive, Fintan said in a low voice, "Tomorrow night, my dear Miss Star."

Hannah was suspended in golden light. She floated in the air, wondering how it was she could fly. And then she realized Neal was holding her, his strong arms around her as he held her tightly to him, his lips pressed against her neck.

Radiant luminescence embraced them. Strange, towering trees surrounded them. In the silence, Hannah heard only the synchronous beating of their hearts. She felt Neal's bare skin beneath her hands. When had they removed their clothes? Her own skin burned with fire. Neal's kisses seared each spot they touched. When his mouth met hers, Hannah felt fireworks ignite within her. Her passion expanded to the sky. Sexual desire filled her with a delicious ache.

"I love you, Hannah," Neal murmured as his hands explored her body.

"Never let me go," she whispered as her flesh came alive beneath his touch. She closed her eyes. "Yes, yes ... *now* ..."

Hannah's eyes snapped open. She stared up at the dark ceiling, wondering where the light had gone, where Neal had gone. And then she realized she was alone in her bed, and that dawn had not yet broken. Her heart was racing, and her night clothes clung to her damp skin. Some time during the night she had kicked the bedding to the floor. Her legs were bare. She had never felt so hot.

Summer is coming, she told herself as she sat up and swung her feet over the side of the bed. She could barely breathe. There was no wind, no breeze. No way to cool off.

Going to the window, she parted the drapes and looked out at a street that never really slept. It was dark out, yet horses clip-clopped by, men loitered beneath glowing street lights. Loud voices rose nearby on the humid air. Hannah looked at the clock over her fireplace, on the mantelpiece where Hygeia stood in an eternal pose. It was five AM.

She had never known such physical desire.

He is engaged to be married.

Donning her robe, Hannah lit a lamp on her desk and put a tea kettle on to boil. While her apartment, on the floor above her office, had a full kitchen, she didn't want to disturb Mrs. Sparrow, who occupied a room at the end of the hall, so Hannah occasionally made tea in her bedroom using a spirit lamp. As she scooped tea leaves into a ceramic pot, she thought about her dream. It had been astonishingly real, causing emotions and feelings that she had buried when she had mentally laid Neal to rest, to flare up brighter and hotter than before.

He had come back into her life, only to be leaving it.

Neal had wanted to see her first thing this morning. Hannah was thankful she had a legitimate excuse to put off their reunion. Every Wednesday, she and Blanche helped with the distribution of donated clothing to the poor at the Quaker Meeting Hall on Russell Street. The busy task would keep her occupied until noon, keep her thoughts focused on the needs of others instead of her own anguish.

How was she going to survive in the same city as Neal, knowing he was with that other woman, loving that other woman, sleeping with her, giving himself to her? Hannah's throat was so tight with pain, she could barely swallow her tea.

She forced herself to focus on other matters, particularly the baffling case of Nellie Turner. Last night, after the gala at Addison's Hotel, Hannah had gone to the hospital with Dr. Iverson to find that Nellie's condition had worsened. And now two more maternity patients burned with the fever.

How was the contagion being spread? Where had it originated in the first place?

The tea was hot and sweet as it went down her throat. She closed her eyes. When was Neal's wedding date?

Blanche Sinclair lived in the northern suburb of Carlton, on Drummond Street, a broad avenue lined with European elms, where Melbourne's moneyed families of lawyers, doctors, men in government lived. A quiet, elegant neighborhood of polished brass plaques, butlers in white gloves, and rear entrances for deliveries. Her fourteen-room mansion was surrounded by perfect lawns and flowerbeds, and in the rear, a carriage house with stables for the horses.

It was a short ride from her mansion to the Quaker Meeting House, and she was accompanied by a maid who cradled a bundled of used clothing in her lap. Out of deference to her Quaker friends, Blanche wore a plain gray gown without ruffled sleeves or lace, and a modest cap covering her thick red-brown hair. Upon arriving, she sent her driver away with instructions to return at noon, and began supervising the unloading of sacks of donated clothing that had been brought to the rear of the Meeting House by wagons and carriages.

As she worked, Blanche could not stop reliving the events of the night before—Marcus arriving at the ball, making her hopes soar, only to treat her coolly and focus his attention on Hannah. At the time, Blanche had been hurt. Now she was angry.

Although she knew how much Marcus's hospital meant to him, and that he had been counting on her to organize the charity tour to raise funds, it seemed to her now an overreaction on his part when she declined the project. Overnight, they had gone from being warm and close friends to coldly polite strangers.

No matter, she thought now as she swallowed back her emotions and directed her energy toward organizing the volunteers inside the hall. Clocks cannot be turned back, nor the past recaptured and mistakes avoided. What's done is done.

Although the doors of a Quaker Meeting House are never locked, the large crowd gathering on the sidewalk called for members of the congregation to keep the doors closed and ask people to wait patiently and in an orderly line. Hannah was allowed through, and once inside, as she removed her bonnet, she surveyed the temporary tables heaped with the donations of generous citizens. She saw Blanche giving instructions to the other ladies: "Shoes and boots on this table, please, Myrtle. Skirts and bodices here. Winifred, please fold those shirts into neat stacks."

When she saw Hannah, Blanche set down the box of handkerchiefs she had been carrying and hurried toward her friend with outstretched hands. "Hannah! There you are! You poor dear! I was so dismayed when I read your letter. Are you all right?"

Among the morning's messages and calling cards and post that had arrived at Blanche's residence was a note from Hannah containing the astonishing news that the American photographer at last night's event was the man Hannah had been in love with and had thought dead the past few years.

"I shall be all right," Hannah said as she removed her gloves and bonnet.

"Why don't you go and see him right now? I can handle this."

But Hannah wasn't ready. Part of her was eager to run to Neal, to fly into arms and drink in his warmth and strength, to dispel once and for all his "death." But a greater part of her was afraid. She was not ready to hear about the fiancée. "There is a large crowd this morning," she said. The numbers of poor and needy in Melbourne were growing alarmingly as immigrants continued to pour into the city in answer to the call of gold.

"Do you want to talk about it?" Blanche said quietly, out of the hearing of the other ladies.

"Thank you, Blanche," Hannah said with a grateful smile. "But I would rather not."

As Hannah went to a tall, podium-desk where a ledger lay open, with a quill in an inkwell, Blanche recalled the way Marcus had looked at her the night before. Blanche had felt a stab of jealousy at the time, and she tried not to be jealous now. After all, Hannah was not interested in Marcus, and was, in fact, wrestling with her own demons—discovering that the man she so desperately loved and thought lost forever was not only alive but marrying someone else!

Retrieving the box of handkerchiefs, Blanche began sorting through them, her hands snapping this way and that. Hannah looked up from the ledger, where they kept a record of inventory and dispersal, and said quietly, "You're upset about Sir Marcus, aren't you?"

"Oh, Hannah, what a pair you and I make. Why does love have to be so complicated, and so painful? He came to my event and then ignored me. I think he's punishing me."

Hannah waited until Winifred Bromfield had picked up a bag of stockings and then returned to the table of boots and shoes. "Blanche, I saw something in Sir Marcus's eyes when you weren't looking. He still bears a fondness for you, I am sure of it. And I would wager he wishes the friendship were restored."

"Then he should say something."

"I imagine he is too proud," Hannah said, keeping her voice low and watching the other ladies as they prepared to hand out clothing. "Perhaps you should make the first overture."

As she watched her friend sort through the handkerchiefs, not doing a very tidy job, Hannah added, "You and Marcus had such a wonderful relationship. Everyone speculated that you might even get married. It's such a shame to give that up over a misunderstanding."

Hannah was surprised to see tears in Blanche's violet eyes when she turned and said, "It's because of my fear! I am positively crippled by it. Hannah," Blanche said, lowering her voice, "ever since that terrible experience I told you about, the one I had when I was a child, my fear of hospitals has been so deeply rooted in my nature that it is something I can never overcome. It is irrational, I know. And I have tried. When Marcus held the charity tour of his hospital, when you were away in the north district visiting farms, I dressed for the occasion and went in my Brougham. But as soon as I stepped to the sidewalk, my heart began to race, my mouth ran dry, and I broke out in perspiration. I could not move. I could not bring myself to join the others who were going up the hospital steps and through the front door. Hannah, this sounds strange, but I was in the grip of panic. And so I turned around and went home."

Hannah laid a hand on her friend's arm. "You need to tell him that."

"I don't know how. And anyway," Blanche stiffened her shoulders and tilted her chin, "maybe it's for the best, about Marcus and me. Not every woman needs a man. And there *are* other things in life."

Blanche Sinclair had come out from England eleven years prior, a bride of nineteen. Her husband, Oliver, had been well-to-do at the time and had tripled his fortune in Australia until his premature death at the age of thirty-eight when he had been thrown from a wild horse. In their seven years together, there had been no babies. Blanche wondered if she was barren. It didn't matter. She had never felt a longing to have children; she had not even created a nursery when Oliver had had their mansion built. Blanche's yearnings lay elsewhere. Although where, she did not know.

All she knew was that she wanted to *do* something. She wanted purpose. Blanche envied her two friends who enjoyed careers: Alice, who had the stage, and Hannah, the healing profession. When Blanche had asked them how they had known what they wanted to do in life, Alice had replied that singing came from her soul, that without it she would die, and Hannah had said that for as far back as she could remember, she had wanted to follow in her father's footsteps. Blanche had never known such personal passion, had never known a "calling."

She knew that she enjoyed a reputation for being one of Melbourne's busiest society matrons. Just last night at the ball, Mrs. Beechworth had declared, "Mrs. Sinclair, I don't know where you find the energy for all your projects!" Blanche had smiled. What the other lady did not know was that it was not enough, and that the more Blanche filled her time, the emptier her hours were.

But she refused to sit back and wait for her life's purpose to present itself. She opened up to new experiences—taking up archery, sculpting, collecting seashells—searching for her calling, as if it lay just around the next corner. As she once half-joked to Hannah, "I have a burning desire to have a burning desire."

She had made the mistake of expressing this dream to her brother back in England, who had written in reply, "You are restless, dear Blanche, because you are lonely. You need a husband. And as you seem to have proven yourself unable to have children, I suggest you find a respectable widower with children of his own and take over their care as soon as possible. Now that Father is gone, it is my responsibility to see that you are properly situated. If you cannot find a husband, then I suggest you return home to England. Mary and I shall make room in our house for you, and you can help raise your nieces and nephews."

Blanche had kept her personal feelings from him after that. Why did the answer to every woman's problems have to be a *man*? Even women with husbands and children could desire something else in their lives. Blanche's best friend, Martha Barlow-Smith, had five children but left them in the care of governesses and nannies while she pursued her interest painting watercolors.

But … was that a calling, Blanche wondered for the first time, or was it just a hobby? Did Martha have a passion, a *need* to paint, or was it a diversion from house and children?

Blanche was the president of the Melbourne Ladies' Benevolent Society, a group comprised of more than forty women of wealth and social standing, most of whom had families. She had never thought about it before, but she realized now that the members' husbands did not object to their wives' outside activities as long as the households ran smoothly and the children were taken care of. And none of the women received a salary. It seemed that, as long as the wife was not being *paid*, work was permissible, but earning a wage was beneath them.

How she envied Hannah, who not only plied a busy medical practice but had published a book as well, a collection of stories she had inherited from a man named Jamie O'Brien. She had had them published in a book called *This Golden Land: True Tales and Lore of Our Southern Land*—a tome filled with stories human and tragic, about drovers and sheepmen and aborigines. And Hannah was now planning a *second* book, a health manual for people who lived in rural places where doctors were scarce.

What was it like to know where one's talent lay? How did a woman find her niche in this world?

To Blanche's surprise, her fear of hospitals jumped into her mind and, for the first time, she did not see the fear as just an impediment to mending

Barbara Wood

her rift with Marcus Iverson. Suddenly she was wondering if such a crippling phobia was, in fact, impeding her ability to find her true calling.

It was such a new and astonishing notion that Blanche stood at the sorting table with hands frozen over the handkerchiefs, her eyes fixed ahead. She thought of Hannah and Alice, who had both overcome personal obstacles, fears and challenges, to be where they were today. Was that what Blanche must do? Face her fears?

She felt a small thrill of excitement. Perhaps a solution was to be had after all! And it might even lead to mending her friendship with Marcus Iverson. Then she frowned. How was she to do it? Facing a fear was one thing. Overcoming it, quite another.

-42-

Neal's new studio was part of a row of bluestone buildings that had gone up in the past year, and it consisted of the shop in the front, the photographic studio next door, called a "glass house" as it had a transparent roof to admit sunlight, and a dark room in the rear. Neal had said that he lived in the apartment above the shop.

In the warm afternoon sunshine, with carriages and horses passing by in the dusty street, Hannah paused on the wooden sidewalk and read the gold lettering above the window: *Neal Scott—Photographic Studio.* Underneath, a smaller sign said, "Now! Through a revolutionary new process, shorter sitting time! Perfect for infants, children, and folks with tremors! Our fine pictures take only fifteen seconds of exposure instead of the twelve minutes other photographers require. Now you can smile for your portrait."

With a racing heart, she entered the shop and found it tastefully decorated with portraits of women in wide crinolines, men standing stiffly in frock coats and top hats, and children with solemn faces. Many were framed in the same beautifully carved frames she had seen last night at the gala. Hannah looked around for Neal.

After leaving the Quaker meeting hall, she had gone home to bathe and change into fresh clothes (and had found a note from Alice, excitedly reporting that, last night at the gala, Fintan Rorke had turned out to be her secret admirer). From there Hannah had paid a brief call on a patient who was eight months pregnant, and now she was at Neal's studio, a jumble of emotions. Fear clashed with desire. Joy did battle with sadness. Hannah wanted to hear every detail of his life from when they parted in front of the Australia Hotel. But she was sick at heart to know she must also hear about a bride to be.

Hannah saw a small brass bell on the counter and was wondering if she should ring it when a curtain parted at the back of the shop and a young man emerged.

"Mr. Rorke," Hannah said, recognizing him. "It is a pleasure to see you again."

"And you as well, Miss Conroy," he said with vigor. "Neal's in the darkroom. He'll be out in a minute. He's been watching for you all day."

Hannah saw a new maturity in Fintan Rorke. His face was less "pretty" and more arresting. But he still had the endearing trait of blushing when he smiled.

"Please come this way," he said, taking her by the elbow and leading Hannah into a most extraordinary setting. This was the photographic studio, he explained, and it was currently decorated as an outdoor scene. Palm trees grew out of stone urns, flowers stood in vases. Beneath a glass ceiling, soft diffuse sunlight touched every leaf and petal. There was a bronze sundial, a marble birdbath, and a garden trellis draped in blossoming vines. Hannah felt as if she were in a fantasy world.

Fintan invited her to sit on a white wicker bench that was embraced by potted ferns and small, fragrant trees, as if she sat in a city park or in a greenhouse. "I'm afraid I must go," he said. "But Neal will be with you directly."

She watched him leave, wondering if he was on his way to see Alice. Fintan was dressed in a fine suit of clothes and what looked like a brand new bowler hat on his head. The spring in his step was unmistakable.

Hannah brought her attention back to the extraordinary studio which was a tranquil setting. But she was not soothed. Besides her anxiety over having to hear about Neal's fiancée, Hannah was thinking of the land agent she had contacted yesterday afternoon and whom she had hired to locate Charlie Swanswick, the owner of Brookdale Farm. She was anxious to hear from him. With so many overnight millionaires returning from the gold fields, choice properties were being snapped up. She prayed Mr. Samson Jones reached Swanswick before other interested buyers did.

Also on her mind was Nellie Turner and the two new maternity patients with childbed fever at the hospital. Where had the contagion come from, and how was it being spread?

The darkroom door opened and Neal emerged, and all thoughts, all worries vanished from Hannah's mind. He was dressed in shirtsleeves and black trousers, suspenders rising like exclamation points up and over his shoulders. And he had never looked more handsome.

"Hannah!" he cried. He reached her in three strides. She rose from the garden bench and before she could speak, he swept her into his arms and kissed her on the mouth.

Tears stung her eyes. She inhaled scents that were familiar yet also exciting—his shaving soap and hair cream. She pressed against the hard body, put her hands on the broad chest and shoulders, relished the masculine strength that made her feel helpless and feminine, and flooded her with desire.

The kiss was long and deep, and would have gone on forever but Hannah had to draw back and look up into his eyes. "Neal, we cannot do this."

"Why not?"

"We must think of your fiancée."

He frowned. "Fiancée?"

"My friend Blanche Sinclair told me that you had just recently come from Sydney with—"

"Oh! No, Hannah. When Mrs. Sinclair asked me what brought me to Melbourne, I told her I had come here to get married."

"But the young lady who accompanied you to the gala last night ... in the green dress."

He searched his memory. "Oh! You mean the lady who walked through the door when I did. Hannah, I have no idea who she was."

"But I saw you say something to her before you came over."

"I did? Probably, 'Enjoy the evening,' to be polite. We arrived at the entrance at the same time, I opened the door and let her go in ahead of me. That, dear Hannah, is the beginning and ending of my relationship with the young lady in green."

Neal fell silent and looked into her eyes, where he saw currents of emotions. His own being was flooded with intense feelings. He had dreamed of this moment for so long, had fantasized its many varied scenarios, that it hardly seemed real.

Neal was speechless at the sight of her. The memory of last evening flashed in his mind, what a vision Hannah had been! Her neck and shoulders had been bare, and the top of her bosom, her skin so pale and smooth, it had been difficult to tell where skin ended and white satin began. He remembered the last time he had glimpsed her bosom, that afternoon in front of the Australia Hotel, and it had rocked him to see his handkerchief tucked in such an intimate place. "Hannah, my God, Hannah," he whispered. He filled his mouth with her name, filled his eyes with every detail of her, from the shiny black wings of hair swept over her ears into a chignon in the back, to a single fleck of black in the gray iris of her right eye.

"Hannah, please sit down," he finally said in a tight voice.

When she was seated on the garden bench, looking up at him perplexity, breathlessly giddy and still stunned by the revelation that there was no fiancée after all, Neal said, "I've rehearsed this moment so many times, and now all words escape me." Lowering himself to one knee and taking her hands into his, he said, "Hannah Conroy, I have never loved a woman as I love you. You stole my heart six years ago, on the *Caprica*. I knew then, when we parted company at Perth, that I wanted to spend the rest of my life with you." Releasing her hands, he reached into his trouser pocket and brought out a small box. Lifting the lid, he exposed a diamond ring to the sunlight that streamed through the glass ceiling. "Will you marry me, Hannah? I promise to care for you and love you and respect you for all my days. Without you I am but a shadow of a man. You and I are two volumes of one book. You complete me, Hannah Conroy. Please say you will be my wife."

She could barely find breath to say, "Yes."

With a cry of joy, Neal swept Hannah up into his arms and, with his lips on hers, carried her to the stairs.

The carriage came to a halt beneath the glow of a street lamp, and the lone passenger alighted without the usual assistance from his coachman. Dr. Iverson was both annoyed and in a hurry. His young colleague, Dr. Soames, had sent an urgent summons to the hospital without saying why. Sir Marcus had been enjoying a dinner party with the Lieutenant Governor and other colonial officials, and so it was with a great show of impatience that he swept into the deserted lobby of Victoria Hospital and, without removing his cape or top hat, hurried up the stairs to the women's ward.

Lanterns and candles created pools of light along the length of the room where women slept or moaned or breathed with difficulty. At once, the pungent smell of the chlorine-soaked sheets met his nostrils, a sign that the air was being properly disinfected. When he reached the far end, he found Dr. Soames bent over a bed, taking a patient's pulse.

Edward Soames was a careful and methodical physician, Oxford educated, St. Bart's trained. Tending toward plumpness, he had a round, boyish face, with frizzy red-gold hair and spectacles that pinched his nose. A soft-spoken man who expressed genuine concern for his patients, but possessing, Iverson thought, the tendency toward alarmism that was often seen in young doctors.

"What is the emergency?" Iverson asked, looking around and seeing nothing that had warranted being called from an important dinner. The woman Soames was seeing to was not even Dr. Iverson's patient.

They had divided the ward, with each doctor overseeing one row of twenty beds. Maternity patients and gynecological patients were under Iverson's care; all other injuries and ailments were Soames's purview.

"It's another case of childbed fever, sir," the younger doctor said quietly.

Sir Marcus's sharp eyes went up and down the row of beds where his own patients slept. "When did we admit another maternity case? I gave strict orders we were to admit no more until the fever was contained."

"That's just it, sir," Soames said, laying the patient's arm on the sheet and giving her hand a reassuring pat. "This is Molly Higgins," he said of the sleeping patient. "A fifty-year-old washer woman who presented yesterday with a dislocated shoulder."

"And?"

Dr. Soames' hazel eyes widened. "She has childbed fever."

"That's not possible," Iverson said dismissively.

"I thought so too, sir, but I have been watching her closely. She was fine yesterday but began to exhibit the signs around noon. Now, there is no doubt."

Dr. Iverson removed his gloves and went to the patient's side. He counted her pulse, felt her forehead, and bent to listen to her chest. "Rapid pulse," he murmured, "fever and congested lungs." When he gently pressed her abdomen, she moaned in her sleep. "Could be something else," he said, but with doubt in his tone.

"Check under her nightgown, sir. The discharge is unmistakable."

Sir Marcus did, and his face went white. "How is it possible?" he said, stepping away from the bed and beckoning to the female ward attendant. "Childbed fever only afflicts postpartum women."

"Apparently not."

"Dear God," Sir Marcus whispered. There were forty women in this ward. Were they *all* going to come down with the fatal fever? The answer had to be in the bad air. If, as Miss Conroy asserted, the infection was carried on the doctor's hands, how had that happened in this particular instance? Dr. Soames had never touched the maternity cases, nor had Dr. Iverson touched the patients on the side of the ward, and he had certainly never been near Molly Higgins. "Clearly the miasma has spread somehow from one side of the ward to the other. We must maintain vigilance in keeping the infected air away from these patients." To the attendant he gave orders that chlorine sheets were to be placed around Molly Higgins's bed and to see that all windows remained closed and locked.

"Pray that this is just a fluke, Soames," he added with a mouth that had suddenly run dry.

Hannah lay in the crook of Neal's arm, tracing a fingertip over the lines of tattooed red dots on his chest. She listened in lazy joy as he talked softly. Hannah had never been so in love, had never felt so alive and so full of purpose.

She had long dreamed of this moment but had never imagined that physical lovemaking brought such pleasure, such delirium, and such desire for more. She lay naked beneath the sheets, and he lay next to her, the bedroom in a soft glow from a single oil lamp. Outside, voices drifted up from the street, the sound of horses' hooves filled the night. For Neal and Hannah, however, the outside world did not exist. They were deliciously tired from their intimate expression of love and desire. And now in a moment that Hannah thought of as soft and glowing, Neal was telling her a fantastical yarn about a girl named Jallara and her Aboriginal clan.

"An amazing thing," he said as he stroked Hannah's long hair that had come undone and streamed down her back. "They are the healthiest, most robust people I've ever met. They have very little illness. I think it's because of their nomadic lifestyle. They are constantly on the move, going to fresh grounds and fresh water."

Neal had decided not to mention Sir Reginald abandoning him after the sandstorm, that Oliphant had in fact been a fraud, his famous books based only on other men's books and hearsay, with a bit of fiction mixed in. No good could come of sullying a dead man's name, and Neal wanted to focus on the positive aspects of his experience.

Throwing off the blanket, he got out of bed and crossed to the window, where moonlight streamed in, allowing Hannah to feast her eyes on Neal's muscular body. He watched horses and carriages go by on the street below, where even a few pedestrians were still abroad, moving in and out of the glow of street lights. "It's hard to believe," he said quietly, "that just seventeen years ago, there wasn't even a village here. Did you know, Hannah, that John Batman bought all this land from the aborigines? He gave them blankets, clothes, tomahawks, and fifty pounds of flour. I wonder if they were aware of what they were signing away. And now the original inhabitants are either living in Christian missions or on a government reserve."

"Wouldn't they prefer to live freely in the Outback?"

"That isn't their ancestral territory. Melbourne is, and although they no longer have access to their sacred places, they are staying close by. I honestly think, Hannah, that some of them believe the white man will one day pick up and leave."

He turned to look at her across the moonlit bedroom. "Hannah, during my time in the Nullarbor, I experienced what I believe was a spiritual revelation. It came to me that Josiah Scott is my real father. I don't know how I knew it, but there was no doubt in my heart that I had not been left on his doorstep."

She sat up in bed. "But Neal, that's wonderful news! Have you written to him about this?"

"I gave it a great deal of thought and decided to respect his wishes. For whatever his reasons, my father chose not to tell me the truth about my mother and himself. When I left Boston for England eight years ago, when we said good-bye, that was his opportunity to tell me the secret he had kept all those years. But he chose to remain silent, and I will respect that."

"What do you think happened inside the mountain?" Hannah asked as she marveled over the small round scars on his torso, straight and curved lines that created an astonishing pattern of red design on his white skin.

"I don't know. All I can say is that the experience had a profound affect on me. I went into the Nullarbor expecting to measure and quantify and categorize everything I found. Instead, I came out thinking that there are some mysteries that can never be explained by science. The initiation did something to me, Hannah. It's hard to describe. I was made part of this land. My blood ran into the red earth while black men chanted prayers older than time. I went walkabout and found myself inside a red mountain. I belong here, Hannah. And perhaps that is another reason I am going to leave my current relationship with my father as it is. That was another life. *This* is my life now. But I need to know more about my new home. I need to go out and explore and capture Australia on glass. And there is more," he added softly. "I am no longer an atheist, but it is not something I fully understand and I need to explore that, too."

Hannah said, "You left Adelaide as a worshiper of the future, but came back in love with the past."

She slipped out of bed and joined him at the window, where they were concealed by curtains. Hannah was unashamed of her nakedness, relishing the freedom from clothing, the feel of the night air on her skin, and then Neal's hands touching her in places that ignited flames of desire. She pressed herself to him, and they kissed long and deep.

She laid her head on his chest and said, "Your experience in the Outback was a lot like my own with Jamie O'Brien and his men. It is as though we went through it together."

"We did. In spirit."

He looked long and searchingly, filling his eyes with every detail of her face as his hands explored her back. "We have both changed, Hannah my darling. You are now a health practitioner with an office and patients. And you did it on your own. The aborigines would say it was your Dreaming to be a healer. They would say that you are following your songline."

He kissed her again, deeply, shuddering with desire but also with a new and overwhelming emotion. "I thought I knew what love was," he said as he kissed her cheeks, her neck, her shoulder. "But oh my dearest Hannah, words escape me." He traced the curve of her jaw with a fingertip as he said, "I never want to leave your side. I had planned to travel north tomorrow, to a place beyond Bendigo. During my trip overland from Sydney, I ran into an old fossicker who told me about a sacred aboriginal site he had discovered last year. A curious formation of giant boulders in the forest north of Bendigo. He explored underground caves there and came across very old aboriginal art. Hundreds, perhaps thousands of hand prints on the walls, painted centuries ago, and some so high up they are beyond the reach of a normal man. When I expressed interest in seeing it, he said I had better hurry as he had stumbled upon a quartz reef near the cave and he said that once word of it got out, the area would be invaded by gold hunters."

"Then you must go," Hannah said.

"I can't leave you now that I have found you."

"Neal, we have had an outbreak of fever at the hospital. It began with my patient. I must go there tomorrow morning and help Dr. Iverson to keep it from spreading. Go to the Cave of the Hands and bring back beautiful pictures for all of Melbourne to see."

As Neal gathered her to him and kissed her again, Hannah heard her own words and felt a stab of doubt. Neal must go out into the wilderness, she thought, and I must stay where there are people. How can we possibly live together? When would we see each other? And where would we live? I could not live above a photography studio. I need an office to see patients. And Neal cannot live above a midwife's office, with patients calling for me at all hours.

As Neal enveloped her in a moment of warmth and love and desire, Hannah tried to suppress the questions that suddenly haunted her. Could two people, following such different paths, create a life together?

-43-

Fintan Rorke could barely contain his excitement as he approached Miss Star's dressing room at the Queen's Theater. As he had worked in his studio all day, sculpting a picture frame, delicately coaxing rosebuds and miniature starlings out of the wood, Fintan had thought of nothing but Alice Star and their brief encounter at Addison's Hotel the night before. He had stood there in the lamp light, twine and scissors forgotten in his hand, spellbound by the sparkle and enchantment Miss Star had brought into the musty room. She had invited him to come backstage after tonight's performance, and now here he was, wearing his best black frock coat and silk top hat, a small package in his hands.

He had something important to say to her.

Fintan knocked and a gray-haired woman opened the door. She wore a maroon satin gown with white lace cuffs and collar, and a white lace cap on her head. She smiled warmly and said, "You must be Mr. Rorke. Please come in."

Removing his hat, Fintan stepped through the door and into a theatrical world. He saw the rack of gowns and capes, the stands displaying bonnets, crowns and tiaras, the mirrored dressing table littered with bottles and jars, brushes and pencils—a performer's dressing room. But what met his senses was the glitter and sparkle of Alice Star's private world, the crystal chimney lamps encasing flickering flames, the fragrance of myriad flowers from bouquets in vases and baskets, the feminine sound of petticoats rustling.

Alice herself was still wearing the white Grecian gown from her performance, the Empire waist accentuating her breasts. A stole of transparent white gauze was settled on her shoulders, like a cloud, Fintan thought, and a rush of sexual desire shot through him.

Alice welcomed him with outstretched hands. "Thank you for coming, Mr. Rorke. Permit me to introduce my dear friend and companion, Mrs. Lawrence. Margaret has been with me since my days at the Elysium in Adelaide."

He took the woman's gloved hand. "Mrs. Lawrence, I recall seeing you at the gala last evening."

The older woman smiled brightly at the handsome young man, pleased that Alice was entertaining so refined a gentleman, and one with an artistic reputation. She retired to the one chair in the cluttered dressing room that wasn't strewn with clothes and assumed a watchful pose.

"Mr. Rorke, may I offer you some champagne?"

He glanced at Mrs. Lawrence, who sat primly observant, hands clasped in her lap, maroon skirts billowing around her, and he knew that etiquette had to be observed. Since he and Alice had only met the night before, and at that had not been properly introduced, Fintan knew that he was not to stay long, not on their first social engagement, and in Alice's private dressing room.

"I came to give you something, Miss Star," he said, and he handed her the small gift wrapped in a blue silk handkerchief.

Alice delicately picked at the knot and drew the silk away to reveal an exquisitely carved bird nesting in her hand. She gasped. The detail was astounding, down to the fluffy breast feathers, miniscule beak nostrils, and the long delicate tail. The piece had not been painted. Mr. Rorke had left it in the natural walnut color of the wood from which it had been carved, and it struck Alice as being all the more lifelike. She could almost see the plump breast rise and fall with little bird respirations.

"It's called a Splendid Fairy-Wren," Fintan said, "an Australian songbird, and she has a beautiful, rich warbling call."

As Alice cradled the enchanting creature in the palm of her hand, she pictured Fintan as he must have looked as he worked at his craft, his head bent, a curl of black hair falling on his forehead. She saw the concentration in his dark eyes, his hands manipulating the small sculpting knife—hands that would seem too large for so tiny and delicate a task.

She was at a loss for words. Fintan Rorke could have placed emeralds and rubies in her hand, and they would have been valueless compared to this.

"I don't plan to be a frame maker forever," Fintan said quietly, overcome by the look in her eyes as she stared at his humble work. "My dream is to be a sculptor and produce art."

She looked at him with wide, blue eyes. "But Mr. Rorke, your picture frames *are* art!"

"But I want to do more," he said. "I would like to sculpt people. I would love to capture *your* beauty, Miss Star," he added with a blush, "in mahogany or teak, to last forever." He fell silent then, and the moment stretched while they heard voices in the corridor beyond and felt Mrs. Lawrence's eyes on them. Fintan cleared his throat and glanced at Alice's chaperone.

"Margaret," Alice said, reaching for a crystal carafe. "Be a dear and refill this with water, please."

Mrs. Lawrence rose and took the decanter but gave the gentleman caller a significant look. "I shall be right back," she said, leaving the door ajar.

"Margaret is very protective of my reputation," Alice said.

"It's understandable. You must have a legion of admirers."

"She approves of you, though, I can tell."

"I want to tell you something, Miss Star," he said quickly, as if afraid of losing his courage. "When Neal Scott and I were in the Nullarbor, we were victims of a terrible tragedy …"

"Yes, I know. Galagandra," she said gently. "Hannah and I read about it in the newspapers. How awful it must have been for you."

Fintan glanced toward the door and the deserted corridor beyond. Returning his gaze to Alice, where he saw compassion in her clear blue eyes, he said, "Neal and I tried to save those men, but in the end we could only save ourselves. I suffered from nightmares for months afterward, and although the terrifying dreams have ceased, I am still not over what happened there, perhaps I never will be. But when I first attended one of your performances, my dear Miss Star, a month ago, I watched an angel in white standing in a glowing column of light. I heard silken threads of voice unfurl over the hushed audience, and I felt a most unexpected balm wash over me. Miss Star, for the first time since the tragedy at Galagandra, I knew a moment of solace."

He paused, holding her eyes with his, then he said, "I have attended every performance since, and each time I have left the theater feeling less troubled than when I went in. I have come to believe, Miss Star, that the grace of God and His healing power lies in your voice."

Alice did not know what to say. A mere "Thank you," was inadequate. Deeply moved, she could only part her lips and look up at him as he stood over her, taller, looking down at her with black eyes burning with passion. The breath caught in her throat. Her skin suddenly felt as if it were on fire. She thought of Fintan's hands as they coaxed a songbird from inanimate wood, and suddenly wanted to feel them on her body, coaxing love and desire from flesh that had never known the intimate touch of a man.

Margaret Lawrence appeared in the doorway at that moment, crystal carafe in hand, and a look on her face that said she had returned just in time. Alice and Mr. Rorke stood so close together one could barely see light between them. He had placed a hand on Alice's bare arm. His handsome head was bent. For a brief instant, recalling her own youth and days of courtship, Mrs. Lawrence thought of turning around and leaving them alone.

But Alice had an image to uphold. As a singer—a stage performer—she must be more vigilant than ordinary women. Her virtue had to be protected.

"Here you are, dear!" she said, placing the decanter on the dressing table. "My goodness, look at the hour."

Fintan stepped back. "May I pay a call on you again, Miss Star? Or perhaps we could visit the new botanic gardens?"

"I would like that," Alice said, offering him her hand. "By the way, Mr. Rorke, may I ask why you always sit in that shadowy corner of the theater?"

He grinned. "Because there I feel as if I am the only one in the audience, and that I have you all to myself."

Seating his top hat on his thick black hair, Fintan gave Alice one last lingering look, then he bade both ladies good night and left.

As she watched him go, Alice marveled at the strange new emotions that flooded her, exciting and marvelous, and as she held the memory of his nearness in her mind, she was unaware that her right hand had fluttered up in a defensive gesture to the side of her face, where scars lay carefully hidden.

-44-

Edward Soames stood at the front door of his residence, as he did every morning, and kissed his wife and four children good-bye. First, six-year-old Winston, then four-year-old Harold, next two-year-old Charles, and finally Lucy his wife, and little Anna, a baby in her arms—bestowing each with a tender kiss on the lips.

It was his habit to walk to his office, but this morning Dr. Soames hailed a hansom cab. He was feeling out of sorts and a little tired. The cab did not get far before Soames found that his breathing had become labored, and so he redirected the driver to Victoria Hospital, where he would have Dr. Iverson listen to his chest. It was probably nothing, but one could never be too cautious.

Hannah stared at the empty basin and wondered why it had not been refilled.

She looked around the noisy hospital ward where women were gathered at bedsides, nursing sick loved ones, coaxing them to drink the tea, eat the bread, take the medicine that the doctor ordered. Although it was not the ward attendants' duty to care for the patients, it *was* their responsibility to see that the hand-washing basins were kept filled with chlorinated water. And Hannah had arrived that morning to find all four basins dry.

Wondering where the attendants were—there were chamber pots to be emptied as well, and water pitchers to be filled—Hannah left the ward and went down the stairs.

Earlier, just before dawn, Neal had taken Hannah home in his own carriage, worried what people would think if they saw her leaving his apartment at such an improper hour. Hannah hadn't minded. They were engaged to be married, and she was blissfully in love. After kissing Neal good-bye, she had watched him drive off, wishing she could stay with him. But she was needed at the hospital, and Neal needed to pack his photography wagon for his trip to the Cave of the Hands. He had said he would come by her home at noon, to say good-bye.

Hannah looked into the noisy men's ward, where the beds were filled with patients recovering from injuries, gunshot and knife wounds, amputations, and lung ailments—all being cared for by wives, mothers, and daughters who clustered around the beds of their menfolk with food, pillows, and words of encouragement. She recognized old Dr. Kennedy bandaging a patient's head. While Dr. Soames and Dr. Iverson were the only two permanent doctors on staff, various Melbourne physicians and surgeons enjoyed privileges at the eighty-bed facility, and Hannah was acquainted with many of them.

Finding no attendants, she went to Dr. Iverson's office. It opened off the main lobby and was filled with bookcases, anatomical charts, a skeleton on a stand, desk and chair, and a tall, glass-fronted cabinet displaying instruments, rolls of bandages, and bottles and jars of ointments and medicines. On the other side of the office was a door that Hannah knew led to a small chamber that held a cot and a washbasin. Dr. Iverson sometimes slept there when he had a critical patient and did not want to make the trip home to his house in the northern suburbs.

The door opened, and he came out. Dressed in his usual meticulous frock coat and starched shirt, Sir Marcus carried a stethoscope and had a worried look on his face. "Miss Conroy, what can I do for you?" Night before last, when he and Miss Conroy had left the gala at Addison's, Dr. Iverson had found himself enjoying the young lady's company in the carriage. They had spoken of medical matters—she had astounded him with her knowledge in that field—and when they visited the patients in the female ward, Miss Conroy had comported herself in such a professional manner that he had thought she was as good as any man.

"I cannot find any ward attendants, Doctor."

"I know," he said. "They've run off."

"Run off?"

"Mrs. Chapelle has come down with childbed fever. The attendants ran away in fear."

"Mrs. Chapelle! But she came in with a broken foot. Dr. Iverson, how are the non-maternity cases becoming infected?"

"I do not know, Miss Conroy, and the situation has suddenly gotten worse. Dr. Soames is exhibiting the signs and symptoms of the contagion."

Hannah stared at him. "That's not possible," she whispered.

"Come with me."

Hannah was shocked to find Dr. Soames lying on the cot in his shirt and trousers, shoes removed, coat and hat hung on the nearby rack. His eyes were closed, his faced flushed and feverish.

"I have given him a sedative," Iverson said quietly. "We shall let him sleep."

They stepped out, closing the door. "Dr. Iverson, how can Dr. Soames have a woman's disease? Childbed fever is an infection of the uterus."

"I don't know." He rubbed his forehead. "I cannot, of course, be certain that it *is* childbed fever. It might be something else entirely. But with two more non-maternity patients contracting the illness, Miss Conroy, I think it best that we keep Dr. Soames here for now."

Iverson strode to the wall of books and perused the titles. "I believe we have an emergency on our hands, and I must get to the bottom of it as soon as possible or the situation will turn into something dire. I pray that the answer is somewhere in these texts."

But Hannah had another idea.

She pointed to a spot on Neal's map and said, "Here is Brookdale Farm."

They were standing on the front steps of her residence off Collins Street, a red brick building with a shiny brass plaque beside the front door that said, *Hannah Conroy, Licensed Midwife and Health Practitioner.* It was noon, and Neal had come to say good-bye.

He noted the spot, halfway between Melbourne and the Bendigo goldfields, and then folded the map into his pocket. "I will be sure to stop and take a look around." The warm breeze stirred an errant strand of Hannah's hair. Neal reached up and gently swept it behind her ear.

Hannah felt her chest tighten. Neal's touch, his nearness, the details of his face filled her with immense desire. But they were standing in broad daylight on a busy street. She struggled to maintain decorum. "If you encounter Mr. Samson Jones, the land agent, please remind him that I am anxious to sign an agreement with Mr. Swanswick as soon as possible."

Neal was going on the trip alone, traveling with his photographic equipment in a one-horse wagon, with a spare horse tethered to the back. He had said he did not know how long he would be gone, and Hannah could not help thinking that this was how it was going to be when they were married, the many farewells with Neal heading into the unknown.

"I will," he said quietly, looking into her eyes. Although Neal was eager to be on his way and exploring the Cave of the Hands, and although Hannah was anxious to get back to the hospital, neither could move, neither could be the first to say, "Good-bye." After all this time, Hannah thinking Neal dead, Neal desperately searching for Hannah—finding each other at last to spend the night making love and making plans, it was time for their paths to separate once again.

But there was more. Hannah had returned from her morning at the hospital with alarming news. A deadly contagion had broken out and was spreading unchecked. Even one of the doctors had been stricken. Neal wanted to stay. What if Hannah fell ill? But she insisted he go, reach the Cave of Hands before the gold hunters did.

Hannah, too, was thinking of the hospital and the terrible danger that lurked there. She was filled with a sense of dark foreboding. An unstoppable and fatal illness in Melbourne, and now Neal was leaving her once again. But she did not let him see the anxiety that had her in a grip, did not confess her fear over their unknown future.

Neal reached behind his neck and untied a leather knot that rested there. He had had a small hole drilled in the top of the stone talisman Jallara had given him, to suspend it at the end of slender leather thong. He removed it now and placed it over Hannah's head, tying the thong at the nape of her neck so that the stone lay on the lace collar of her gown, at the hollow of her throat.

"Powerful magic," he said. "It will protect you as you follow your songline." He kissed her, holding her tight, whispering a blessing in her ear, and then he climbed into the wagon and guided the horse into the street.

Hannah watched him go. It took all her willpower not to call him back.

Hurrying inside her house, she wrote two hasty notes to Alice and Blanche, with whom she had a luncheon engagement. "Please forgive me but I cannot make our appointment today. There is an emergency at the hospital. The ward attendants became frightened of an outbreak of contagion and have left. Dr. Iverson will need my help. I do not know when I shall next be free. The situation is becoming dire."

Asking Mrs. Sparrow to see that the notes were delivered, Hannah donned her bonnet and light cape, picked up her leather medical bag and a satchel holding personal items, and, informing her housekeeper that she might not be back for a day or two, struck off in the direction of Victoria Hospital, her heart tight in her chest.

-46-

Leaving her cape and bonnet and personal bag in the downstairs cloakroom, Hannah went first to the women's ward to check on Nellie Turner.

The bed was empty and had been stripped to its mattress.

Hannah looked down the length of the ward, which was now broken up by chlorine-soaked sheets hanging between beds, and saw two more vacancies—both had been maternity cases.

She found Dr. Iverson in the men's ward, where he was bent over an older gentleman who was coughing violently. To the white-haired wife who sat beside the bed, Sir Marcus said, "Continue to give him the tea, as strong as he can take it. We must break up that congestion."

When Iverson saw Hannah, he folded the stethoscope into his trouser pocket and escorted her away from the ward.

"Nellie Turner—" Hannah began.

"I am sorry, Miss Conroy. She passed away an hour ago."

"And the other two?"

"They have succumbed as well."

Hannah noticed new shadows under his eyes. He was also without his usual dignified frock coat but stood in shirtsleeves and suspenders, which surprised Hannah. "And how is Dr. Soames?"

"About the same. I sent for his wife. She is with him right now, while the children are in the care of their nanny." Dr. Iverson glanced down at Hannah's throat and noticed the engraved stone that lay there—definitely primitive and curiously out of place, he thought—then he looked at Hannah and added, "I have not said anything to Mrs. Soames about childbed fever, as I am praying that it is a mild influenza or a bronchial condition."

"Have any of the ward attendants returned?"

"I am afraid not. And, Miss Conroy, there are three more non-maternity cases. But Dr. Kennedy has gone for help. The problem, of course, is with the visitors. They don't understand the concept of infection and antisepsis. The confounded women keep opening the windows, causing the bad air to circulate."

"Dr. Iverson, may we speak privately in your office? There is something I must show you."

They crossed the lobby, where visitors came and went bearing blankets and food baskets. It was an unpretentious entry, with a tile floor and unadorned walls, a few chairs for outpatients. Dr. Iverson had not come to Australia to get rich but to realize a dream: to create a modern, progressive hospital that would become a model institution to be imitated around the world. This was something he could not have done in England, where he felt that the old ways were too entrenched for a man of vision. His first task when he had established himself in Melbourne had been to call a public meeting in which to lay the groundwork for a charitably-operated hospital. Funds were raised from among prominent businessmen and wealthy landowners—Blanche Sinclair had been particularly generous—a building site was purchased on the corner of Elizabeth and Bourke streets, and in March of 1846, the foundation stone was laid for Victoria Hospital.

Many speeches were made that day, in a grand and pompous ceremony for which all the citizens turned out, and Sir Marcus Iverson's words received a deafening cheer when he said, "From this day forward, hospitals will no longer be institutions where the sick go to die, but where they go to get well."

He wished his late wife were there to see the institution he had created in this new land. Blueprints of Victoria Hospital showed future expansions, innovations—a laboratory for research, even a children's wing, which was already under construction. On the grounds surrounding the main building, flower beds were being planted, and a handsome pavilion was planned for the benefit of convalescing patients.

All going according to plan, Dr. Iverson thought as they entered his office. But everything was now threatened by this mysterious and unstoppable contagion.

"Dr. Iverson," Hannah said when they entered his office, "I believe I know the cause of the contagion, and therefore a way to prevent it from spreading further."

He listened with interest as she told him her father's story, concluding with, "He found this microbiote in a sample of my mother's blood. He believes it is what causes childbed fever." Hannah opened her father's portfolio and arranged his notes on the desk for Sir Marcus to see.

Iverson picked up the pencil sketch of what looked like twined strands of berries. He read the label underneath, *streptococcus*, and thought it an apt name, as it was Greek for "twisted chains of spheres." He was also intrigued by the idea of microscopically analyzing a patient's blood to determine a diagnosis. He had never heard of such a practice. "Are you suggesting we follow your father's example by examining blood?" Dr. Iverson was proud of the wood and brass microscope he displayed in his office. Although he found little use for it, he thought the instrument lent a progressive air to the surroundings.

"I suggest we give it a try," Hannah said.

They went upstairs to the women's ward, where they discreetly collected specimens from the childbed fever patients. Returning to his office, Hannah demonstrated a remarkable aptitude for handling a microscope, placing each glass slide, adjusting the focus, moving the mirror until it caught the light. She examined each piece and then stepped aside for Dr. Iverson to take a look.

The streptococcus microbiote was evident in all samples of the infected patients, and absent in specimens taken from patients who did not have childbed fever.

"Remarkable," he murmured. Then he straightened with a thoughtful frown. Saying nothing to Hannah, he selected a clean slide from the box, pricked his finger, and allowed a small drop to fall onto the glass. Adjusting the eyepiece and reflective mirror, he examined his own sample and nodded, satisfied. "The microbiote is not evident in my own blood. I had to be certain. And so the question is, how did the microbe get into these people's bloodstreams? Was it breathed in from the air? If so, why aren't others infected? What made these particular people susceptible? Or if the germ is, as you say, Miss Conroy, transported—"

He stopped, and Hannah guessed by the way he suddenly glanced at the door to the small sleeping room, he had remembered Dr. Soames.

With a grave tone, Dr. Iverson said, "This will confirm it for us," and he selected a fresh slide and disappeared briefly into the room. When he emerged, saying something over his shoulder to Mrs. Soames, and returned to the microscope, Hannah felt her stomach tighten.

She held her breath as Dr. Iverson placed the glass under the lens, made adjustments, and then took a long silent look at his young colleague's blood.

Dr. Iverson closed his eyes and straightened. "The streptococcus is evident."

The moment stretched as neither spoke, and street sounds drifted in through the open window. From the women's floor above came the sound of a concertina. Visitors entertaining a bedridden loved one.

Finally, the rigid-backed and dignified Sir Marcus released a ragged sigh and said, "And you say your father's iodine formula kills these microbiotes?"

"On human hands and objects," Hannah replied, thinking of poor Mrs. Soames holding vigil at the bedside of a husband who, unbeknownst to her, had not long to live. "Unfortunately," she added, as she watched a large, noisy family climb the stairs to the female ward, a big yellow dog following them, "the iodine only *prevents* the spread of the contagion. It is not a cure. And we still do not know the source. How did Nellie Turner become infected in the first place? Until we have the answer to that, I fear that fresh cases will continue to break out."

"We will proceed one step at a time," Marcus Iverson said resolutely, rubbing his stubbled jaw. "I will see that basins of the iodine-water are placed at both entrances to the female ward and will instruct physicians to periodically rinse their hands in the solution."

But Hannah was thinking of the visitors and how to keep them from spreading the contagion. It would be impossible to tell every individual to wash his or her hands, especially if they visited more than one patient, as many often did. Written signs would be of little help, as most of these people were illiterate.

And yet Dr. Iverson couldn't bar them from the hospital, for who would then take care of the patients?

As Blanche's carriage neared the hospital, she felt the familiar symptoms— tight stomach, damp palms, dry mouth, and racing pulse. At her side, her best friend Martha Barlow-Smith was unaware of the panic that had suddenly gripped Blanche.

The two women rode through the afternoon sunshine as if on a casual Sunday outing instead of an errand of mercy and urgency. In the carriage ahead, Alice rode with her companion, Margaret Lawrence, and when they drew to a halt in front of the hospital, Alice and Margaret stepped to the wooden sidewalk, carrying hampers of food and clothing. But when Blanche's carriage pulled up and Martha collected her things and stepped down to the street, Blanche could not move. She looked up at the double doors of the institution's entrance and froze in fear. Martha gave her a questioning look. This visit was Blanche's idea. As soon as she had received Hannah's note about the hospital attendants running off, she had known they must go to Hannah's aid. "Are you coming, dear?" Mrs. Barlow-Smith asked.

"Yes, please go on ahead—" The breath stopped in Blanche's lungs.

Staring at the formidable entrance of bluestone and tall wooden doors inlaid with lead-paned windows, Blanche thought: It's just a building. But horrific visions flashed in her mind, random, rapid-fire, non-cohesive. She had been seven years old at the time and had accompanied her mother to a hospital in London on an errand of charity, bringing food and clothing to patients who had no one to take care of them. In the crowded lobby, young Blanche had somehow gotten separated from her mother, and had ended up wandering hallways searching for her, stumbling upon terrible sights of which her child's mind had no comprehension—emaciated bodies, too much blood, corpses—until her own screams had joined those of the afflicted. She remembered someone picking her up, and then her mother's arms were around her. Blanche had tried through the years to wash the poison from her mind, but that day came back in full force now as she looked up at Marcus Iverson's precious hospital.

I cannot do this.

And then, as she watched Alice and Margaret and Martha boldly mount the steps with their parcels for the needy, Blanche thought: I am never going to know what I am truly capable of doing until I overcome my fears.

Stiffening her spine, she drew in a steadying breath and stepped down from the carriage. With great effort she followed the others up the steps, one at a time, praying for courage, praying that she would not faint. When she reached the top, and her friends went through the doors, Blanche became rooted to the spot and could not follow.

Performing acts of charity was one of Blanche's most cherished tenets, a personal belief that had been inculcated in her at a young age. Her mother had been famous for her philanthropy and selfless generosity. And Blanche had always prided herself in carrying on that tradition. But she realized now, as she stood facing her greatest fear, that it was easy being charitable when it involved putting on dances and picnics and art shows. But had she ever truly been charitable? Because now she was faced with a test of true charity—going to those who were suffering inside this building and helping them in their time of need.

Thinking of her mother, and thinking of her own dream to find her purpose in life—thinking also of Marcus Iverson who deserved an explanation of why she had never set foot inside the hospital he so loved—

Blanche drew in another deep, bracing breath and, squaring her shoulders, reached out and placed her hand on the door.

Hannah was about to collect her father's notes and the slides when she glanced into the lobby and saw a familiar face come through the hospital's front doors.

"Alice!" she cried.

Hannah ran to her friend and was further surprised to see Margaret Lawrence come through the door behind her. "What are you two doing here?"

"We *four*," Alice corrected as Martha Barlow-Smith stepped through the double doors and behind her, to Hannah's shock, Blanche. "When we got your message canceling lunch," Alice said, "saying that you were alone with all these patients, Blanche and I knew we had to do something to help. Margaret and Martha insisted upon coming with us."

Dr. Iverson emerged from his office at that moment and stared across the lobby at the four visitors. He recognized Alice and her companion, Margaret. Standing with them was Martha Barlow-Smith, a full-figured society matron whose corset stays always creaked beneath her bodice. And then he saw the fourth member of the group.

Blanche seemed to be hanging back at the door as she glanced this way and that, her hand pressed to her bosom. Was she ill? Marcus strode across the lobby and as he drew near, saw that she was white-faced and breathing rapidly. "Mrs. Sinclair," he said, "Blanche, is something wrong?" He gave her companions a puzzled look.

"They have come to help," Hannah explained.

He scrutinized Blanche. "You do not look well," he said, taking her elbow. "Come into my office."

Blanche could barely breathe. This hospital smelled the same as the one of years ago—the stench of smoke, chlorine, vomit. A patient was hobbling by on crutches, and another sat with his arm bound in a sling. The same visitors with the same food baskets were here. And from where she stood, Blanche could glimpse into the men's ward where she saw the same rows of beds occupied by the same broken, emaciated, ailing bodies.

She started to swoon. When she felt a strong grip on her arm, she looked down at the hand that steadied her. Lifting her eyes, she saw a handsome face etched with worry and genuine concern framed by black hair with silver at the temples.

Marcus.

She blinked. Blanche had never seen him in shirtsleeves. Gone was the impeccable frock coat, and his tie was undone. Shadow covered his jaw. It alarmed her, because it spoke of the gravity of the situation here in the hospital. But in the next instant she was reassured and comforted by the way he looked, for it meant he was giving singular attention to what must be done here, with no thought to himself.

"I'm sorry," she whispered, pressing her hand to her forehead.

"Come to my office," he said gently, and then said to Hannah, "Please see to our visitors."

Inside Iverson's office, Blanche struggled to pull herself together. When Marcus offered her brandy, she declined it, and when he suggested she sit down, Blanche remained standing and said, "Marcus, I am mortally terrified of hospitals! There. I have said it."

"A lot of people are afraid of hospitals," he said in a reassuring tone. "It is nothing to be ashamed of."

"But my fear runs deep. It cripples me."

He waited, dark eyes filled with expectation and concern. But no disappointment, Blanche was relieved to see. No disapproval or silent recrimination. Remaining on her feet, struggling for strength and composure, she related the incident from her childhood, ending with, "That is why I could not organize your charity tour. I could not set foot inside your hospital once it was occupied by patients. I feel so cowardly."

He stepped closer and said in a low voice, "And yet you are here now, aren't you?"

"I am not being very brave about it."

He smiled. "It isn't bravery if you aren't afraid."

"Marcus, I should have been honest with you, but it sounded so foolish, and I didn't want you to think badly of me, what with your hospital being so important to you. I made such a mess of things. Marcus, I had no idea I offended you by declining to take on the charity tour. I didn't think that my being involved was so important."

"It was. You have a gift for organizing things, and I knew I would have had a successful event with you chairing it." He placed his hands on her arms and a thrill went through her. Suddenly the office was warm and intimate, the hospital and its horrors miles away. "Blanche, I have acted the fool! I told myself that I was affronted by your refusal to help me and my hospital, but the plain truth is that I learned the next day you had agreed to help Clarence Beechworth raise public support for his railway and I was infuriated. It was old-fashioned male jealousy, plain and simple. I have treated you cruelly and abominably. I don't know how you can ever forgive me."

"I should have told you the truth about my fear," she said, breathless at his nearness, the feel of his hands on her arms. Marcus stood a head taller, looking down at her with burning dark eyes, his black hair shining in the lamplight. Blanche thought she was going to swoon again, but this time for a different reason.

"And I should have pursued the issue," he said with passion, "but pride kept me from asking you precisely why you would not organize my event." He lowered his voice, his hands tightening on her arms. "I have missed our friendship, my dear Blanche. I have missed *you*."

"Oh Marcus," she whispered, giddy with desire.

He brought his face close to hers. "I realize now, my dear, that it was more than just having the most capable hostess in Melbourne organizing the event. I wanted *you* to be part of my hospital. I wanted you at my side as I showed off my great achievement. But you are here now."

"Yes I am," she whispered, captivated by his eyes. "And I shall stay."

He frowned. "Perhaps you should go home. You almost fainted."

"I am regaining my composure." And indeed she was. As the initial onslaught of sensations and memories began to subside, she felt strength return to her body and soul. She also felt Marcus's touch, the power of his voice, revitalize her. "The first step was the hardest. That was the one that I had to get past. From now on it will get easier, I am certain of it."

"You are an amazing woman, Blanche Sinclair," he murmured, wishing they were in another place, another time. "But now we must get to work."

"Tell me what to do."

-47-

"Alice! Alice, *where are you?*"

She snapped her head up, Blanche and Martha spun around, and a few of the patients cried out. They turned toward the doorway at the end of the ward where they heard heavy footfall running up the stairs. Who was making such a commotion at this late hour?

When a young man burst in, wearing an evening frock coat and a top hat—a very handsome young man, many noted as he rushed down the length of the ward—the patients drew blankets up to their chins, and visitors in the aisle got out of his way.

Fintan shouted again for Alice.

She stepped out of a cubicle formed by three hanging sheets where she had been feeding a patient.

"There you are!" he said, and seized her by the arms, looking her up and down. "Are you all right? Are you sick? Are you hurt?"

Before Alice could respond, Blanche Sinclair stepped forward and said crisply, "Young man, you are frightening the patients."

"Oh! Sorry," he said quickly, blushing and collecting himself. "Miss Star, they told me at the theater that you were in the hospital."

"I'm helping out."

He gave her a puzzled look and then finally noticed the others who stood around him. He recognized Margaret Lawrence, Alice's lady's companion, and he knew Blanche Sinclair from the gala at Addison's. The fourth was also clearly a lady, although he did not know her name. What was strange about Alice and her friends was their attire. They wore homely aprons over their gowns, their sleeves were rolled up to expose bare arms, and each of the ladies had her hair gathered up in a the sort of scarf scullery maids wore.

Aware of other eyes watching him, Fintan gave closer look to his surroundings, now that the panic of thinking Alice was hurt or ill had passed, and in the light of lanterns and candles, he saw the rows of beds occupied by women, and women in the coarse dresses shawls of the lower classes, sitting at bedsides, offering cups of water, brushing patients' hair.

The atmosphere was hazy, thick with pungent smells, and illuminated by the glows of lamps and candles.

Fintan had never been inside a hospital. And as he realized he was the only man among so many females, he was suddenly self-conscious.

Alice took his arm. "Come with me, Mr. Rorke," she said. "I shall explain." To Mrs. Lawrence, Alice added, "I shall be all right, Margaret, we won't go far."

As they entered the corridor at the end of the ward, Alice turned and said, "Mr. Rorke, you should leave. There is contagion here."

"Ah, that explains it."

"Explains what?"

"I don't want to alarm you, but there is a crowd gathering out front of the hospital, people demanding to know if their loved ones are safe here. Dr. Iverson is trying to reassure them, but they seem agitated."

"All the more reason for you to leave. Please," Alice added with a hand on his arm.

Fintan's look darkened. "All the more reason for me to *stay*."

When Alice saw visitors staring at them, she said, "Let us get some air."

She took him downstairs and through a rear door that led into blessed fresh night air. Fintan could not believe the pungent smells in the ward. He had thought his throat would close forever. As Alice explained that what he had smelled was chlorine, and that the four friends had come to help Hannah during a crisis at the hospital, she and Fintan followed a narrow gravel walk that was illuminated by moonlight and the occasional glow from sparsely placed garden lanterns. They could see where a grid of flowerbeds had been laid out, with blooming shrubs sitting in sack cloth bags, waiting to be planted.

Alice told Fintan about the work she had been doing since arriving at the hospital that afternoon. "I have never nursed the sick before, and so I had no idea of what to do. Hannah showed us."

Fintan only half listened. He had been thinking about Alice all day, had been looking forward to seeing her again at the theater. And then when he had been told that she was at Victoria Hospital—

He had not understood the depths of his feelings for her until that moment. His angel hurt or sick, or possibly worse. It was unthinkable. But now she was all right, not sick at all, but performing charitable works, an angel truly, he thought in relief as he walked at her side. And he would stay, too, in case the crowd in front of the hospital decided to get unruly.

They paused on the path, and Fintan looked at her to say, "It's an admirable thing you are doing here, Alice Star."

She looked up into deep black eyes and felt her heart flutter. Fintan Rorke moved her in ways no man ever had. Was it his physical beauty? His endearing shyness? His gift for creating beauty out of prosaic wood? Or his tragic tale of Galagandra? It is all of that and more, she thought. Fintan is so many things, so many aspects.

And Alice yearned to explore them all.

"It's not just me. Blanche confessed that she has had a mortal fear of hospitals all her life. You should have seen her this afternoon, Fintan. Just stepping through the front doors took great courage. And then going up to the ward, facing the patients. Blanche has been bravely battling her fear all evening. In fact, when Hannah said the ward attendants had run off, it was Blanche's idea that we come and help. Especially as Hannah is helping Dr. Iverson to determine the cause of the fever."

"I thought bad air caused fever," Fintan said, wanting to speak of other things. Wanting to touch her, take her into his arms.

"There's talk that the hospital was built on sacred aboriginal ground, and that it's haunted. They say that the hospital is cursed and that's why there is an outbreak of contagion. I don't believe it of course, but the ward attendants were Irish, and you know how superstitious *they* can be." Alice cast him a playful smile as she said this.

Fintan returned the smile, and then he grew serious. "You are even more beautiful in the moonlight, dear Alice. I cannot understand why you are not married. Or is there someone in your life and you don't make it public knowledge?"

"There is no one," she said, breathless at his unexpected presence— Fintan had been in her thoughts all day. How tall and elegant he was in his frock coat (although he had left the top hat in the hospital). "For a long time I convinced myself that my singing career was my life, that I didn't need a husband or children, that I could live without romantic love. It was easy to convince myself of this, Mr. Rorke, because no man ever stole my heart." She added silently: until now.

"Why would you want to convince yourself of such a thing? It sounds terribly lonely."

"There is something you must know." Reaching into the waistband of her skirt, she drew out a handkerchief. While Fintan watched in puzzlement, with the night wind whispering around them in the garden, rustling the branches and leaves of newly planted elm trees, Alice rubbed the linen over her right eye. She then folded the handkerchief and wiped it up and down her cheek and temple, back to her right ear. Then she faced him, giving him a good view of her face in the light of a garden lantern, and said. "Do you wish to see more?"

His thick black brows came together. "More of what?"

"Fintan, I am showing you my real face, something no one else sees." She held out the handkerchief. "This is a façade."

He looked down. "All I see is a very clean handkerchief."

Alice brought the handkerchief closer to her face and saw, in the moonlight, an unblemished square of linen.

"The make-up probably wore off," Fintan said with a smile, "while you were working in that very warm building. No doubt you wiped your face a few times."

She stared up at him. She *had* dabbed her face with a towel, not thinking that her carefully placed cosmetics were coming off.

"Alice," he said, taking her by the shoulders. "Last night in your dressing room, while we talked, I noticed you kept bringing your hand up to the side of your face. It was as if you were trying to hide something."

"I haven't done that in years!"

"It made me wonder. I looked more closely and realized your make-up was concealing something. And that was when I understood the truth about your singing, why it moves so many hearts. I realized that you don't sing from your throat, Alice, but from your soul. You don't just sing lyrics or musical notes, you sing your own pain. And I wondered if perhaps what you are hiding here," he said as he tenderly touched her temple and cheek, "is a personal anguish."

She spoke quickly, while she had the courage, about the fire at the farm, the rescue that disfigured her face, being on the streets, her life with Lulu Forchette—"But I was never with the customers, I never even sang for them."—until it was all out and Fintan Rorke was the second person in the world to know Alice's secret.

"It makes sense now, dear Alice. This is what you are singing about. And your audience hears this. They feel that you are singing directly to them, each man and woman thinks that your voice touches just them and no one else. You reach into their sorrows, Alice, you touch their fears and bring them peace, because most of us have a Lulu Forchette or a Galagandra in our lives. It is a wonderful and powerful gift that you have."

He laid a hand on her cheek and said, "Did you truly think I would leave you once I saw this?"

She looked into his eyes and understood a new truth. "No," she said.

Alice realized now that she had thought at first that she was testing Fintan, to see if his feelings for her could withstand her hidden scars. But now she realized it wasn't Fintan she had doubted, but herself. All the new self-confidence she had gained since her first audition at Sam Glass's music hall had been an illusion, built upon a foundation of cosmetics, hairpieces, and tiaras. Alice had never put her new self-confidence to a test. But now she had, and she had learned a truth about herself. That her self-confidence was genuine. The scars didn't matter any more. She no longer had anything to hide.

Fintan cupped her face in his hands and said, "Alice, you are a very pretty woman. Has no one ever told you that? Your eyes are captivating. I have never seen such a shade of blue. This lovely nose and delicate mouth. You are so much more than a few hidden scars. You have a face that is the envy of many women."

"Oh, Fintan," she said.

"Dearest Alice," he whispered, placing his hand at the back of her head.

She lifted her face to his and met his kiss with tears—her first kiss, a perfect kiss.

Fintan drew back and said with passion, "You inspire me to want to create beautiful things, Alice Star. I will carve your loveliness out of the finest wood God has created, and it will last for eternity, testament to my undying love for you."

They came together again in a deep kiss, bodies entwined in the moonlight, casting a single shadow on the garden path. And as they explored their new love and desire, and expressed it with their bodies, Fintan and Alice were unaware of ghosts moving nearby in the shadows—the "haunts" of this sacred ground who paid no attention to the lovers in the garden.

Stark white apparitions that moved on silent feet, their bodies spectral in the moonlight, as they advanced upon the stone building with hands clutching boomerangs and woomeras, and deadly spears.

Suddenly aware that they were not alone, Fintan and Alice drew apart and stared at the mysterious procession that walked by, an eerily silent parade of tall, thin-limbed people with skin as black as the night, their bodies glowing with white paint. Adorned with feathers and stones, animal teeth and beads, the aborigines seemed to have stepped out of another world, another time. They marched with their eyes set resolutely forward, ignoring or unaware of the young white couple who looked on with goose-flesh. Alice had never seen tribal natives before, except in pictures, and she saw now that mere pictures did not do them justice. There was a supernatural power in the dark, ancient flesh and deeply set eyes that peered from beneath heavy brows. Their silence was unsettling, their steady march to the front of the hospital, disquieting, for what on earth were they doing here?

Remembering the crowd of anxious white people gathered in front of the hospital, and what Alice had said about this ground being under an aboriginal curse, Fintan said, "This can't be good. We had better get back and warn the others."

-48-

Brookdale Farm was exactly as Hannah had described it, down to the last loving detail.

Neal filled his eyes with the majestic vista of the Outback station that stretched away in every direction, over rolling hills and flat fields, beneath the endless blue sky and mid-day sun. He listened to the wind, inhaled the fragrance of eucalyptus and he was sent back to a billabong in the middle of red sand and low lying orange hills. He saw the white-barked ghost gums of Brookdale and saw other ghost gums shedding silver leaves onto that distant billabong's surface. He thought of Burnu and Daku and recalled the taste of kangaroo meat. He heard Thumimburee's didgeridoo and remembered ancestral figures painted on a rust-colored wall.

Her name was Jallara, and she was the very soul of this land.

Hannah's book, *This Golden Land*, authored by "an Outback son," came to mind. I must photograph this place, Neal thought as he walked around the property that still displayed a For Sale sign. I must photograph others like it, along with the rivers and mountains mentioned in Hannah's stories—the paddocks and fields and shearing sheds. We can re-publish the tales with accompanying pictures, to truly bring Australia to life.

As he gazed at the house with the steeply gabled roof, the deep verandah wrapping around all four sides, he pictured the photographic studio inside, the dark room, the entry hall hung with his photographs. He imagined Hannah's private office—next to the nursery, perhaps, so she could be near the children. She would write her health manuals here. It would be *home.*

Station hands were tending the sheep and horses, men were working the fields, but Neal saw no sign of the land agent, Samson Jones, and assumed he was up at the goldfields, tracking down Brookdale's owner, Charlie Swanswick. Neal briefly wondered if he should take a detour and search for Swanswick himself.

He thought about the Cave of the Hands. He should have been there by now. But his wagon wheel had hit a pothole in the road, breaking the axle. Neal had managed to repair it but had camped overnight rather than try to navigate the unpredictable road in the dark. And then he had wanted to stop at Brookdale Farm and look the property over. As he was wondering if he should take a few days and search for Charlie Swanswick, but thinking that he had already wasted precious time getting to the caves, he heard a horse approaching along the tree-lined lane.

"Hoy, there!" the rider called out.

Neal stepped away from his wagon and waved in friendly greeting.

The stranger brought his horse to a halt and said, "Am I on the right road to Bendigo?"

Neal noticed that the man packed a bedroll behind his saddle, with a pick and a shovel tucked inside. "Just keep heading north. You'll come to the first camps by sundown."

"Thanks, mate."

As the man started to ride off, Neal said, "I was about to boil some tea, if you'd care to join me."

"Thanks, but I'm in a hurry. I heard that diggers are heading for a cave formation north of the goldfields, where the woods begin. There's rumors of rich quartz formations. Have to get there as soon as possible before there's nothing left." He eyed the supplies in Neal's wagon. "So where are you headed for? Don't look like mining equipment to me."

Neal was traveling with the latest photographic equipment from Germany, lenses and plates designed to take exposures in dark places, using something called flash powder. I am headed, Neal thought, to the very caves that you and the diggers are about to destroy. "I go about photographing sacred aboriginal sites."

The man rubbed his nose and laughed. "Now that's ironic. You driving all this way to take photographs of aborigines and there's a mob of them in Melbourne right now."

Neal stared at the man. "Natives in the city? I didn't think that happened any more."

"It doesn't. They know to stay away. But this lot looks wild, like they came from deep in the Outback. Ferocious looking. Maybe a hundred of them, all carrying weapons and demanding their sacred land back."

Galagandra flashed in his mind. "Where?" he said. "What sacred land?"

"The hospital."

"Victoria Hospital?"

"That's the one. Got the place surrounded from what I hear. Threatening to burn the place down with everyone inside. I gotta get going. Good luck with your pictures."

Without further thought to the sacred cave and the destructive diggers, Neal quickly steered his wagon through the gate of Brookdale Farm and stationed it under a group of shade trees. Unhitching the horse from the wagon to allow it to graze, he mounted his saddled horse and hoped that his crates and supplies couldn't be seen from the road. But if it all got stolen, it didn't matter. He had to ride back to Melbourne as fast as he could.

Hannah was in danger.

-49-

"I don't like the look of that mob," Dr. Iverson said to Fintan as they peered through the glass-paned doors of the hospital's main entrance. He guessed that nearly a hundred people had gathered out front while the late afternoon sun dipped behind Melbourne's tallest buildings.

As word of contagion and death spread through the city, citizens with friends and loved ones in Victoria Hospital had come out of concern. Dr. Iverson had allowed them in for orderly visits, cautioning them not to touch anything, and to visit only those who did not have the fever. He had then taken turns with Dr. Kennedy to periodically go outside and reassure the crowd, who refused to leave, that everything was under control.

But the unexpected arrival of the aborigines had upset things, reminding people of the legend that this land was cursed, causing panic. The way the natives just sat staring at the hospital, their naked bodies covered in white paint, the savageness of their appearance—the crowd had begun to grow nervous.

Fintan eyed the aborigines in the deepening dusk. It was an eerie scene. The twenty or so natives, males and females, ranging in age from adolescence to old age, sat on the grassy lawn that stretched from the street to the steps of the hospital. They had not moved since taking a position there during the night, their faces set toward the two-story building. They looked menacing as they held spears and boomerangs, with the primitive designs painted on their bodies, giving them a formidable aspect. "What do you suppose they are waiting for?"

"I do not know, Mr. Rorke." Iverson had tried speaking with the natives, with no success. Dr. Abe Kennedy, who had served two years at a Christian Aboriginal mission, had also tried, to no avail.

But Marcus Iverson had more to worry about than the strange visit by the natives. Three fresh cases of childbed fever had broken out—in the men's ward! He didn't understand it. He had established rules to make sure the contagion wasn't carried out of the women's ward, and Blanche Sinclair, with her natural talent for taking control of situations, had enforced the rules to the letter. The only conclusion Iverson could draw was that the three men had been exposed to the same contaminant as the initial case, Nellie Turner. But what?

He and Miss Conroy had spent every moment searching for the source, collecting specimens from water, linens, food, and inspecting them under microscopes. The microbe had to be carried on objects, possibly even the doctors' hands, because if the contagion were in the air, why had none of the volunteers or visitors or physicians come down with it? The fever appeared to strike only people who were already patients.

And what do three male patients have in common with a post-partum maternity case, a woman with a dislocated shoulder, and another woman with a broken foot?

And with Edward Soames who, under the watchful eye of his devoted wife, was now dying of the deadly disease.

If we do not find the source soon, Iverson thought in cold fear, the contagion might spread to the city, and we will have a massive, deadly epidemic on our hands.

When he saw several people marching up the hospital steps, no doubt more family members worried about the safety of their loved ones, Sir Marcus said, "I'd better go and have a word."

With the new cases in the men's ward, he had had to take drastic action. In order to contain the spread of infection, he had locked down the hospital, allowing only the barest number of visitors inside. No children or animals, and only such visitors as complied with the rules. Some insisted on visiting every patient in the ward, touching them, offering them bites of food that had already been sampled by other patients. Going up and down, spreading the contagion, and refusing to wash their hands.

"You should rest, Sir Marcus," Blanche said, staying him with a hand on his arm. She and her friends had converted the small children's wing, still under construction, into private quarters away from visitors and patients. Fresh beds and linens had been brought in, so that the volunteers and physicians could retire periodically to rest. But there were now twelve cases of childbed fever, and a constant round-the-clock vigil was required to keep the contagion from spreading further. Dr. Iverson would not allow himself the luxury of even a nap.

He gave Blanche an appreciative smile. Not only was she keeping her deeply ingrained fears at bay, she was doing an impressive job of organizing the female ward, delegating tasks, seeing to the efficient running of things. Although Blanche knew nothing about medicine or health care, she was a quick study. One lesson from Miss Conroy in how to turn patients every two hours to prevent bedsores, and Blanche was not only teaching the other ladies but establishing teams and times for the task.

Blanche also supervised the families and friends of the patients, giving them instructions on washing their hands, telling them what they could and could not do. And because Blanche was a lady of obvious high station, and because she spoke with authority, the visitors deferred to her.

He looked at the deeply dimpled cheeks and a chin that narrowed daintily to a point, the almond-shaped eyes the color of violets, and wished current circumstances were different. How he had missed her this past year! And how desperately he wished to make it up to her.

"I will go with you, sir," Fintan said, thinking that it was a lot of people for Dr. Iverson to handle.

"I welcome your help, son," Iverson said as he donned his black frock coat and went out to face a growing mob that held lamps and lanterns against the darkening day. To those he met on the steps, he said, "Please, go home. Your loved ones and friends are safe in my hospital. I promise you they are receiving the best care. We have lady volunteers in there now."

"We heard this place is cursed!" said one man. "We heard it's plague and it's going to spread to the city."

"There is no plague here. It is a specific fever that affects only a small portion of the population, and we are searching for a cause and a cure at this very moment."

"Then how come a doctor's got the sickness?" asked another. "Doctors ain't supposed to get sick."

"It's the blacks' fault!" blurted a third, and a chorus of worried voices joined him.

"Please," Iverson said. "The natives have nothing to do with this. The fever broke out before they even came—"

"Still, this used to be their land. They poisoned it!"

"They're using witchcraft!"

Before Iverson could say another word, a commotion broke out at the back of the crowd, people being pushed aside as newcomers shoved their way through. Iverson saw two bearded men come running toward him, jackets and trousers covered in dust, their bush hats sweat-stained and battered. "Where's my Nellie?" cried the shorter of the two as they reached the steps. He had long black hair in need of a trim, and bushy whiskers—the unmistakable characteristics of a man just arrived from the goldfields. He shot up the steps and seized Iverson by the lapels. "Where's my Nellie?" he cried in Sir Marcus's face.

Fintan stepped up and wrenched the man's hands from Iverson's jacket, and he saw a face distorted with grief, a beard soaked in tears. A young man, with eyes bespeaking pain and bewilderment.

Straightening his jacket while Fintan restrained the distraught man, Sir Marcus said in a gentle tone, "Sir, please tell me who you are and I shall—"

"I'm Joe Turner and I came home from the fields to find a neighbor wet nursing my newborn son. My brother here," he jerked a thumb at his companion, who also looked distraught, "Graham here, he says my Nellie is dead. That you killed her. But I don't believe it. I want to see my wife!"

Iverson stared at the two men and thought, Nellie Turner?

Then he remembered. She had died the day before.

He reached out to put a hand on Turner's arm. "If you will come inside with me, Mr. Turner. You've had a shock."

"Are you taking me to see Nellie?" Wide hazel eyes begged silently. "I don't mean no disrespect, sir, but we have to baptize the baby. We're christening him Michael after Nellie's father. But I can't do it without Nellie. Please, can she come home now?"

Sir Marcus exchanged a glance with Fintan, and then surveyed the crowd which he saw now had grown tighter, with everyone drawing near to hear what the two newcomers were upset about. "Really, sir," he said in a low voice. "It's best if we talk inside."

Turner wrenched his arm free. "I don't want to talk, I want to see Nellie!" His voice broke, and the pain of it seemed to roll out over the heads of those at the bottom of the steps.

"They won't let me see *my* wife either!" came a shrill cry from the crowd, and it was joined an instant later by another: "I've been waiting since noon to see my sister, and they won't let me in."

Everyone turned to an older woman with a paisley shawl over her head. "She came in with a broken ankle and now they say I can't see her! What if she's dead? What are they hiding from us?"

Shouts and yells rose to the sky, as everyone demanded to know what was going on inside the hospital, why were the aborigines here, were they all going to come down with the plague?

"I say we just go on in!" shouted a man in front, who was very large with arms as thick as fireplace logs. "They can't stop us!"

"I cannot allow you to do this," Sir Marcus said in a calm, authoritative voice that disguised his own fear. If this mob were to decide to storm the hospital ...

Joe Turner suddenly bolted for the double doors, his brother on his heels, and men began to surge up the steps.

"Stop him," Sir Marcus said, and Fintan reached the doors first, barring the way. On the other side of the glass, he heard someone hastily turn the keys in the locks.

"I just want to see my Nellie," Turner said with imploring eyes. "I just want to know she's all right. Our baby is so small—he is so tiny—he needs his Mum—"

Turner broke down again, sobbing into his hands.

"I want to take my sister out of the hospital!" cried another man.

Everson recognized who had spoken. A chimney sweep who came daily to visit. "My good sir, your sister needs to remain in traction. If she is moved, her hip will break anew, and she will never walk again."

"Better than dying of the plague!"

Shouts of agreement and fear joined him, and those in front surged toward the steps again, shouting about the deaths of loved ones, sisters and mothers who had gone into the hospital for a broken foot or dislocated shoulder, now lying in pine boxes.

"We'll break the bloody doors down!"

Sir Marcus and Fintan looked on in horror as a sea of enraged men began to sweep up the steps like an unstoppable tidal wave.

"Hold on there!" came a shout. Those inside the hospital, watching through the glass panes of the main doors, saw Neal Scott on horseback appear at the far edge of the throng. Jumping down from his horse, he sprinted around and pushed his way through to the steps. "What's going on, Doctor?" he asked breathlessly when he reached the top.

Someone shouted, "There's plague in the hospital, and we've come to take our loved ones out before they die."

"Mr. Scott, we cannot let any patients leave," Iverson said quietly, "the fever will spread to the city."

Neal turned to the men who were advancing up the steps, hands curled into fists. "Listen to me. There's no need for violence. Remember, this is a hospital. There are sick people inside."

"You stay out of this," growled the man with thick arms. "Have you lost anyone in this hospital? Has someone you loved died?"

"No," Neal said cautiously, his eye on the men as they edged closer, "but my bride-to-be is in there, and I wouldn't let her stay in there if I didn't think it was safe."

"Bride-to-be ain't the same as a wife," another man grumbled.

Neal surveyed the scene, felt the tension in the air, saw the angry looks of those nearest and who seemed intent on storming the hospital. He glanced at the natives and realized that the stranger on the road outside of Brookdale Farm had exaggerated. These aborigines weren't a mob of a hundred, and they did not have the place surrounded. They also did not seem intent upon burning the hospital down. A curious bunch, Neal thought. Not all of them were tribal. The younger ones wore girls' dresses or boys' trousers and shirts. From a mission, he supposed.

"We got a right to protect our families!" the thick-set man shouted, and the crowd shouted their agreement.

Another yelled, "Come on, let's break the bloody doors down!"

Iverson murmured to Neal, "We haven't the manpower to stop them."

"Look!" Fintan said, pointing. Marcus and Neal turned to see several men running around the side of the building. In the next instant, Joe Turner and his brother flew down the steps after them.

"Is there a back way in, Doctor?" Neal asked, imagining the mayhem should those men get inside.

"Yes, and it's unlocked. The keys are in my office. Mr. Scott, we should send for the police."

"I'm afraid there isn't time."

Their eyes met. "You go, Doctor," Neal said. "Fintan, you take off after that bunch. See if you can find help. Hospital attendants, visitors, *anybody*. I'll hold these men off."

Neal turned to the crowd and held up his hands. "Listen to me! There isn't room inside for all of you. And you will only end up frightening the patients."

"We have a right to go inside!"

"Very well," Neal said, squaring off with the angry chimney sweep. "You want to check on loved ones, reassure yourselves they don't have the fever? Is that right?"

"Damn right, mate!"

"So you really believe there is contagion in this building."

"Plague!" shouted several at once.

"And you're willing to infect yourselves? On purpose?" He flung out his right arm and pointed at the entrance, where bluestone columns stood majestically on either side of the doors. "You will deliberately walk through there and expose yourselves to whatever lethal sickness lies on the other side?" He then pointed to one of the men nearest him. "You, sir! How many children do you have?"

The man made a face. "What does that matter?"

"Because that's how many mouths will go hungry if you cross that threshold and become infected."

Neal leveled his gaze at those nearest him, and then he shouted over their heads, his voice carrying above the crowd so that those gathered under a glowing street light could hear: "How many of you men are willing to make widows of your wives? How many of you women are ready to leave orphans behind? How many of you don't want to live to see Christmas?"

This gave them pause, as they looked at one another, exchanging uncertain glances, murmuring sudden doubts and indecision.

"Does this make sense to you?" Neal pressed. "The doctors in this hospital know what they are doing."

"No they don't!"

"Doctors don't know a bloody thing!"

"All right," Neal said. "Yes, there is fever here, but it is being contained, and the other patients are being protected from it."

"Then why can't we go in?"

"Because you will spread the contagion."

But then someone on the steps remembered overhearing what the American had said about a bride-to-be. "You have a lady in there!" he shouted. "A woman you're going to marry. And you said you weren't worried that she was inside. And there's lady volunteers, you said. What about *them*? Ain't they spreading it?"

"Yeah," echoed another man. "And ain't *they* got husbands and kids?"

"You can't have it both ways, mate," the chimney sweep snarled. "Either it's safe in there or it's not."

"You know what I think?" shouted a burly man with the red nose and bloodshot eyes of a heavy drinker. "I think they don't know what's going on in there. I think they're lyin' to us, and as for me, I'm taking my brother out. He just has a broken leg. I can take care of him at home, which I shoulda done in the first place."

They surged up the steps, and Neal braced himself for a fight.

At that moment, the front doors opened, and Dr. Iverson emerged, to much jeering and hissing from the crowd. "I got to the back door just in time," he said to Neal. "I don't know how long it will be before they seize a piece of lumber and use it as a battering ram. We have to find a way to control this mob."

Fintan returned from the back of the building, Joe and Graham Turner with him.

The main door opened again, and Hannah came out into the night. "Neal! I didn't know you were here. Someone told me that—" And then she saw the Turner brothers. "You must be Joe Turner," she said, going to the younger of the bearded men. "Someone told me you were here. I am Hannah Conroy, I knew your wife."

"You're the midwife," he said, running his sleeve under his nose. "Nellie wrote to me about you. She said you were very kind to her. Is she all right? May I see her now?"

"I am so sorry," Hannah said softly, laying a hand on his shoulder. "Nellie did not survive."

Turner started to sob anew. Hannah's heart went out to him. Despite the manly beard, Hannah saw that Joe Turner was very young, barely more than a baby himself, she thought. "Mr. Turner," she said gently, "Nellie didn't suffer. She went peacefully." Hannah hated to lie, but sometimes it was necessary for another person's peace of mind. Even her father, a steadfast Quaker who believed in truth above all, occasionally spun a small fiction for grieving family members.

"Did ya hear that?" shouted one of the men on the steps, turning to face the crowd. "They killed his wife! Poor woman came in to have a baby and she perished of the plague! We won't let that happen to *our* wives!"

Hannah stepped forward, raising her hands. "Please, everyone stay calm! We have things under control." She moved into the light of a lantern, her white bodice glowing, her dark skirt like a cloud about her legs. The white lace cap on her dark hair was transformed into a soft halo. She stood tall, poised and confidant, and for an instant, all eyes were on her, voices quelled, the night filled with an uneasy silence.

And then the men on the steps decided they had delayed the rescue of their sisters, mothers, fathers, and children from the hospital long enough, and they started for the doors.

Just then, to everyone's surprise, the aborigines rose to their feet, and the crowd fell back in fear.

Neal frowned at the natives, saw their eyes, their unreadable faces, and then looked at Hannah. "That's strange," he murmured. "They are looking at *you*."

"Me!" she said. And then Hannah saw that that he was right. Twenty pairs of deep-set eyes, shadowed and piercing, were fixed on her. "But why?"

"I don't know. You are the first person they have reacted to."

Shouting erupted. The throng flowed and ebbed like a turbulent sea. "They're going to kill us!" "We'll all be slaughtered!"

One of the men on the steps rushed up, but Neal caught him and wrestled him back. "Outa the way!" the man grunted. "They ain't satisfied with putting a curse on us and killing us with plague. Now they're going to send spears through us."

Fintan ran to Neal's aid, and together they restrained the man. Iverson raised his arms for silence, but he received only a dull roar. He spoke over it, as loudly as he could without revealing his own fear: "We have nothing to be afraid of from the natives! If they had wanted to kill us, they would have done so by now. Allow us to ask them what they want, and then perhaps they will go away."

"I say we kill 'em!" came a shout from the crowd, followed by a bone-chilling chorus of agreement.

Neal said, "Stay here, Hannah. I'm going to try talking to them."

All eyes turned upon Neal as he cautiously approached the group. The natives had risen in unison, yet Neal had not heard any of them speak. Who had given the command? He drew near with conflicting feelings: fear, as he remembered the massacre at Galagandra, but also admiration and respect, as he thought of Jallara and her people. He sized them up—the white-haired elders adorned with paint and necklaces and feathers—then asked in English, "Which of you is the leader?"

Lamps and candles in the hospital windows shed light over the scene, and the white paint made the natives look like other-worldly specters. They were so like Jallara's people, Neal thought, and yet not.

When he received no response, he decided to try a few words in Jallara's dialect, phrases taught to him by Thumimburee that were used only among men. To Neal's surprise, a white-haired elder turned to face him. The onlookers shifted and murmured among themselves, fists tightening, ready to defend their fellow white man.

When Neal repeated the phrase, a girl stepped forward, wearing a plain dress and barefooted. Her black hair was long and silky, like Jallara's. "Hello, sir, I am Miriam. We do not speak your tongue."

He looked into her round face and deep-set black eyes, and thought, But it did the trick. This old fellow knew I had spoken a dialect of native language.

"I would like to speak to your chief, Miriam. Can you help me?"

"My father's father is chief. I speak English. I say what father's father say."

Neal respectfully addressed the elder as he spoke through the girl, "Why have your people come to this place?"

Miriam spoke to her grandfather and translated his reply. "He say he cannot talk to white man about this. It is sacred. Taboo."

Neal thought for a moment, taking the measure of the elder who stood before him with white hair and a long white beard, dark eyes peering out from a layer of thick white paint. "Why did you stand up when the white woman came out of the building?" He gestured toward Hannah but received only silence and an impassive expression.

He decided on another tack. "What is the Dreaming of this place?"

When Miriam translated, the chief gave Neal a look of curiosity. As he responded, and Miriam translated, the old man watched Neal carefully. "Crocodile Dreaming," she said, and Neal nodded in understanding.

Tapping his chest, said, "I am Thulan."

But the word meant nothing to the elder, so Neal said to Miriam, "Tell your father's father that my Dreamtime spirit is a lizard the white men call thorny devil. Do you know the word for that?"

She nodded with enthusiasm and spoke to the elder, whose thick brows lifted in surprise.

Encouraged, Neal unbuttoned his shirt and exposed his chest, allowing the chief a long look at his tattoos. Sounds of surprise erupted from the crowd of white men. They talked among themselves, speculating on this unexpected turn—had the American been captured and tortured by natives?—while the leader of the aborigines studied the white man who had undergone a secret aboriginal initiation rite.

The elder finally spoke, exotic syllables tumbling from his lips, familiar to Neal and yet foreign, for this dialect sounded like Jallara's. Miriam said, "He ask if you go walkabout."

"I did. I went walkabout in the great wilderness in the west. Spirits spoke to me in a vision."

When Miriam translated, her grandfather stood silently for a long moment, the night wind lifting his long white beard to expose the scars of his own initiation scars, incised in his skin long ago. He stared at Neal, dark eyes beneath heavy brows unreadable.

Finally he nodded in satisfaction and spoke, and Miriam translated. "My father's father say this sacred ground, and sacred ground is sick. Crocodile spirit very unhappy. We come for healing ritual. But white men must go away. Taboo to watch."

Neal surveyed the onlookers who wore modern jackets and trousers, bowler hats and tweed caps, the women in long dresses and shawls—people from another world who would have no understanding of what was going on here. But he knew it would be impossible to tell them to leave. If anything, mistrust and suspicion about a secret Aboriginal ritual would only make them stay all the more.

"You tell men go away," Miriam repeated. "Cannot cure sickness with white man here."

Neal studied the situation—aborigines protecting their sacred ground, frightened and angry white men thinking the natives had made their loved ones sick.

When the chief and his people shifted their attention away from Neal, he looked over his shoulder and saw that once again they were watching Hannah.

"Why," Neal began, "does the white woman interest you—" But he was interrupted by the appearance of an old aboriginal woman, pushing her way through, speaking to the chief and making him step respectfully away.

She was small and bent, her long white hair coarse and wavy and growing over her shoulders and down her back. Her aged body, painted white and draped in necklaces of teeth, feathers, and nuts, was plump. When she spoke, revealed strong white teeth. And yet Neal guessed by the wrinkled face and curve of her back that she was very old.

She spoke rapidly, and Miriam said, "White woman must come here."

"Why?"

When he received no answer, Neal looked back at Hannah who, guessing that she was needed, went down the steps to stand at Neal's side. Another rumble went through the crowd of white people—a nervous, jittery sound. Light from lanterns and torches illuminated faces strained with fear. What did the blacks want with a white woman?

Neal saw that the old aboriginal woman's gaze was fixed on the magic stone around Hannah's neck, lying at the base of her throat. The old woman then glanced at Neal, the white man with tribal tattoos, and then again at the white woman with a native talisman around her neck, and she seemed to be arriving at a decision.

"Neal," Hannah said quietly, "what is this all about?"

Miriam spoke up. "Crocodile Spirit speak to Papunya in a dream. Tell her to come and heal the land."

Hannah turned to the girl, whom she judged to be around fifteen. A small Christian cross on a string lay on her chest. "Papunya?"

"Papunya is clan clever-woman. She is my mother's mother's mother."

Hannah addressed Papunya: "Yes, there is sickness here, and we cannot find the cause or cure. Can you help us?"

After Miriam translated, the old woman turned away and took a large wooden bowl from another native woman. The bowl appeared to have been carved from a single block of wood, and she showed Hannah the contents, with Miriam explaining: "These sacred objects come from this place long time ago. Now we bring them back. Land needs these sacred things. We heal the land, we send away sickness with sacred objects that the land knows."

Hannah saw feathers, bones, stones, dried leaves, clumps of earth.

Papunya placed the bowl on the ground by Hannah's feet and then received another object from the other native woman: a tall wooden staff carved with intricate designs, from the tip of which objects were suspended on strings—a bird's beak, a crocodile tooth, a scarlet feather, a strip of withered snake skin, and a cluster of dried seed pods. As Papunya lifted her eyes to the large brick edifice that covered her sacred ground, Hannah saw no sorrow in the dark eyes, no anger, no perplexity. The clever-woman seemed to be sizing up the situation, as if trying to find a place in her world for this strange intrusion.

She then looked at Hannah, enigmatic eyes peering from beneath a heavy brow ridge. She spoke, and Miriam said, "Papunya ask who are you, what is your Dreaming."

"My Dreaming?" Hannah exchanged a glance with Neal and said, "I am a midwife and a healer."

Papunya closed her eyes for a long moment, and when she finally spoke, Miriam said, "Papunya say you seek hidden knowledge. Very important healing knowledge. You think it is lost but it is only hidden. And it is nearby."

Neal said to Hannah, "Do you know what she is she talking about?"

"I have no idea."

Papunya lifted the tall wooden staff and leveled it at the hospital, its mystical objects clicking together as she pointed and spoke.

"In there," Miriam said. "What you seek is in there. Crocodile spirit say you find hidden knowledge. *You* heal sacred land."

"I'm sorry, I still do not understand."

Miriam held a brief exchange with the clever-woman, then said, "Cannot say more. Taboo to speak of the dead."

"The dead? Who? I don't—"

"Burn the place down!" came a shout from the crowd, and a brick suddenly sailed through the air, breaking through one of the front windows with a crash. When screams came from within, Fintan banged on the doors and was allowed inside, the doors locking behind him.

The crowd surged, like a living entity, and as men and women pushed and shouted, incited by the rising tension and mistrust of the natives, and fed up with their demands not being met, Hannah quickly said to Miriam, "Please tell me what you are talking about. Who are the dead you cannot speak of?"

When Miriam's deep, black eyes stared back, Hannah said, "Are you talking about those who have died here in this hospital?"

Miriam did not reply. Hannah looked from the girl to the old woman, trying to read their faces but finding only impassive expressions. Suddenly, Hannah heard a voice from the past, her father saying, "I must tell thee the truth about thy mother's death ... I should have spoken long ago.... The letter explains ... but it is hidden ... find it ..."

"Neal," Hannah said suddenly. "I think I know what Papunya is talking about. But I have to go back inside."

"I'll go with you."

"No, you stay here. Protect these people. If I am right, then I have a way to put an end to this."

To the volatile crowd of white people, Hannah said in a clear, ringing voice, "Please stay calm. I will be able to answer all your questions in a moment."

She hurried up the steps, where Dr. Iverson was staunchly guarding the doors, and when she entered the foyer, saw women huddled against the far wall, with Alice and Fintan assuring them they were safe. Blanche stood over the broken glass, calmly asking Margaret Lawrence to please fetch a broom and a dustpan, and then suggesting to her friend Martha that she take the other women up to the female ward to settle the patients who were certain to have heard the crash.

Hannah hurried through to the new children's wing which was still in wood framing, with the walls only recently installed so that the long dormitory-style room smelled of sawdust and fresh pine. Quickly retrieving her leather medical bag, she took it to Dr. Iverson's office where she found Alice consoling Mrs. Soames, who had come out of the back room to see what was happening. "There, there, dear," Alice said, "it's just a bit of broken glass. Let us go back and see to your husband, shall we?"

Hannah turned up the lamp on the desk and, with racing heart, lifted out her father's portfolio. Hidden knowledge that is nearby, Hannah thought as she untied the ribbon and lifted the top cover, setting it aside. Something that will heal the sacred land ...

Was it the letter?

Before she left England, she had searched the cottage from top to bottom, finding nothing. She had assumed it would be with the rest of his important medical papers—in the portfolio. But she had examined every scrap of her father's notes and still had found nothing that resembled a letter.

Hidden ....

Hannah shifted her attention to the two loose covers of the portfolio. They were old and tattered and looked as if they had once bound a book. She scanned every inch of the top cover and, finding nothing, set it aside. The back cover was even more ragged, testament to her father's thriftiness. When Hannah saw that the endpaper had been neatly cut, she brought it into the light and saw that something appeared to have been tucked beneath the end sheet.

With rising excitement, she used the ivory-handled letter opener that lay on Sir Marcus's desk, and gently coaxed the item out. It was an envelope. On the back, she read three German words: *Wiener Allgemeine Krankenhaus*—Vienna General Hospital.

Hannah was flung back to the day a curious envelope with a foreign postmark had arrived. It was four years after her mother's death, and her father had been in his laboratory, assembling the new microscope he had recently purchased. Hannah, seventeen at the time, had been taking scones out of the oven when the postman had knocked at the front door. Hannah's father had read the letter in private, to emerge from his laboratory visibly shaken, saying he was going to the cemetery. He had been gone for hours by the time Hannah went searching for him, to find him lying face down on Louisa's grave, sobbing bitterly, the letter from Vienna clutched in his hand.

Hannah never saw the letter after that, and her father would not speak of it, but in the two years that followed, his drive to perfect the formula became obsessive. Whatever was in the letter, it had changed his research from one of inquiry to actively using chemicals on himself, to the ultimate detriment of his own health.

This must be the letter her father had spoken of with his dying breath, the one that revealed the "truth" about her mother's death. But it was in German.

I shall have it translated at once, Hannah thought as she folded the page. As she began to slip it back into the envelope, she found a second sheet of paper inside. Unfolding it beneath the oil lamp, she saw that it appeared to be a second letter, written in English. But when she compared the two, she realized that the second sheet was an English translation of the first.

Holding her breath, trying to keep her hands steady as the sheet of paper trembled in her grasp—and praying that these words contained the solution to the crisis outside—Hannah read her father's anguished words.

"My God," she whispered when she was finished.

Papunya was right! The answer had been here all along!

She ran through the foyer, but when she emerged on the other side of the main door, people in the crowd began immediately shouting questions at her, surging up the steps as if to engulf her in their desperation and fury.

"Can you cure my sister?"

"Can I take my mother home?"

"Wait—" she said, overwhelmed.

Hands reached for her. Someone grabbed at the letter.

"Stop, I can't—"

She was pushed back against the doors as the mob rushed her, shouting questions, pecking at her with their hands like a flock of starving ravens.

And then two strong arms were around her, drawing her sideways, away from the frantic mob, down the steps. Fintan.

"Where is Dr. Iverson?" Hannah gasped. "I must show this to him."

"He is with Neal, protecting the aborigines."

"Help me to get through."

Holding tightly to Hannah, Fintan managed to force his way through the milling throng, whose shouts and cries rose to the stars as if from a single throat. At the center of the angry mass, Hannah saw Neal and Dr. Iverson trying to stave off an assault on the natives.

"Stop!" Hannah cried. "Listen to me! I have found the answers! All of you! Think of your loved ones."

Fintan joined the defense, and so did—to Hannah's surprise—Joe Turner and his brother, until the mob was pushed back, their voices dying down, so that Hannah was able to face them and, holding up the letter, say, "This is what the aborigines came to tell us. Here is the solution to the contagion inside the hospital. You must all calm down and allow us to do what has to be done.

"Dr. Iverson," she said, turning to Marcus while the onlookers shifted nervously and exchanged skeptical looks. "I have found the answer. Please, read this. Tell me if I am right."

The crowd fell still and waited in hushed silence as the sheet of paper in Dr. Iverson's hands fluttered in the night breeze.

His black brows came together as he read, at the top of the translation, John Conroy's preface: "I wrote to learned men in several foreign institutions, explaining that a few days prior to Louisa's death from childbed fever, I had visited a farm wife who had the same childbed fever, and while I was away, Louisa went into labor. I came home in time to deliver our child. When she then came down with childbed fever, I was baffled because our residences are miles apart, we do not share a water supply with that farm, we are not subjected to the same prevailing winds. How was it possible for the two women to come down with the same contagion? Several men to whom I wrote responded that there is a radical new theory that infection can be transmitted from patient to patient by way of a doctor's hands. But the mystery is, where did the original infection come from? If I contracted it from the farmwife, how had *she* gotten it? And so I decided to write to the top authority of the day, the Vienna General Hospital. Here is the response."

While the crowd watched Dr. Iverson, and people at the back demanded to know what was happening, Sir Marcus read the translation of Dr. Semmelweis's response to John Conroy, explaining that he had noticed that the mortality rate from childbed fever on one ward in his own hospital was far higher than that on another ward. Herr Semmelweis said he analyzed the discrepancies and discovered that the ward with the high death rate was attended to by medical students; the other ward, by midwives. What, Herr Semmelweis had asked himself, was the difference? His discovery astounded him.

When he realized, Dr. Semmelweis said, that the only difference was that the medical students attended post mortems before making their rounds, whereas the midwives did not, he could only conclude that the source of the contagion had to be the autopsy room, and that doctors came away from the post mortem with 'cadaver particles' on their hands. He went on to explain to John Conroy that the final proof was when one of the medical staff accidentally cut himself in the post mortem room, and died soon after of childbed fever.

"My God," Sir Marcus murmured as he read a notation added at the bottom. "I am called occasionally," John Conroy had written, "by the coroner in Maidstone to examine the body of someone who has died under suspicious circumstances. And what I learned when I read this letter from Vienna, is that when I went directly from an autopsy in Maidstone to the farm wife to deliver her child, that I had unwittingly infected her, for although I rinsed my hands and they appeared to be clean, they obviously were not. And it was directly after I delivered the farm wife's child that I delivered Louisa's baby."

Iverson lifted his head and looked at Hannah in astonishment and disbelief. "I hardly know what to say, Miss Conroy. When I wondered what was in the hospital that had caused the contagion, I had not thought of the post mortem tent because it is not part of the main building. Even though we isolated the female ward, doctors were going directly from post mortem to the men's ward, infecting three patients there."

Marcus Iverson massaged his stubbled jaw. "This Viennese doctor says that one of his staff died of childbed fever after receiving a cut in the cadaver room. And I recall Dr. Soames telling me that he had cut himself during an autopsy the other day."

"Molly Higgins had an open sore," Hannah said. "As did Mrs. Chappelle. And all three new cases in the men's ward are in the hospital for wounds that won't heal."

Iverson met Hannah's eyes as the crowd watched in anticipation, not comprehending the dialogue but sensing that answers were about to come, as the lady had promised. "That is the answer, Miss Conroy. The streptococcus organism enters through the blood stream. They are all suffering from a form of septicemia. We have our source. We can stop the contagion."

He addressed the onlookers in a loud, authoritative voice, "The threat is gone. We have found the source of the contagion, and we will eradicate it. The sickness will not spread to the city, and by tomorrow this hospital will be safe. Please, all of you go home. I promise you that our doors will soon be re-opened and access will be available to all."

But no one moved. "I ain't leaving until I see my Mary."

"And I ain't going home without my Sam."

"But there is no further cause for alarm," Marcus said. "We have everything under control."

An angry grumble rippled through the mob. This was not the message they had wanted to hear. "Prove it!"

Realizing that things could quickly spin out of control, Hannah raised her arm and called for silence. "Please listen to Dr. Iverson. The contagion will run its course and will soon be gone. There is nothing to fear."

"We ain't leaving and that's that."

Hannah conferred briefly with Sir Marcus, and then she addressed the angry mob: "We understand your concerns. Those of you with loved ones inside will be allowed in for short visits. But we must think of the patients. This will be done in an orderly fashion. There will be no pushing or rowdiness. You will line up and will be given a fair turn inside. If, after visiting your friend or family member, you still wish to take him or her home, then we will make sure he or she is free of the contagion and will assist you in the discharge."

When Hannah saw sudden suspicion in their eyes, saw how men and women shifted uncertainly on their feet, she realized that they had not expected this compromise, and now that they had won their right to enter the hospital, were suddenly thinking of the contagion within. "We will take precautions for your own health and safety," she said, her long skirt stirring in the night breeze, lamplight flickering on her face. "We now know where the contagion originates and how it infects a person. You will all be quite safe visiting your loved ones."

Finally, she saw cautious smiles, people nodding in vague understanding, talking amongst themselves, the tension easing.

As Sir Marcus handed the letter back to Hannah, he said quietly, "Well done, Miss Conroy. I shall ask Blanche to organize the orderly admittance of visitors and will give Dr. Kennedy instructions to seal off the post mortem tent at once."

He addressed Joe Turner, who was looking lost and bereft, laying a fatherly hand on the young man's shoulder and saying, "I am terribly sorry for your loss, son."

With a tight throat, Turner could only repeat what he had been saying all evening: "Please may I see my Nellie now?"

Marcus thought for a moment and then signaled to Fintan. Out of the earshot of the two brothers, Iverson said, "Mr. Rorke, will you please see to it that Nellie Turner's body is brought out of the post mortem tent and into a private area of the women's ward? And will you please ask one of Blanche's ladies to see to it that Nellie is clean and presentable?"

Marcus turned back to Joe and Graham and said, "Please come inside where you can wait in the lobby. I'll see that someone brings you tea."

As she watched Dr. Iverson lead the two brothers up the steps, while Neal helped Dr. Kennedy to move through the crowd and ask them for their patience, that they would soon be allowed inside, Hannah turned to Miriam, who had been silent and watchful through the whole event, and said, "Please tell your grandmother that she was right. I did have hidden knowledge, and I found it. I can indeed heal the sickness in this place."

After her granddaughter translated, the old woman held Hannah for a long moment with her enigmatic gaze and then, through Miriam, declared the sacred land healed. Planting her wooden staff firmly into the ground, Papunya turned away without another word, her companions silently falling into step behind her. Everyone watched as the aborigines walked across the vacant lot that would soon be a formal English garden and disappear into the darkness, like ghosts returning to their supernatural realm.

When Neal joined Hannah, to wearily inform her that the crowd was being cooperative, she said, "With his dying breath my father told me that I needed to know the truth about my mother's death, that it was in a hidden letter. I didn't know that I had had it with me all this time."

She brought the translation into the light and, in the glow streaming from one of the hospital windows, read her father's final note at the bottom: "And so, Dr. Semmelweis has informed me that *I* killed Louisa. Although it was the streptococcus that made her ill and caused her to die, she died by my hand, for the microbiotes were on my hands, they were the weapons I brought into my home. I killed her as surely as if there had been a pistol in my hand, and I fired it. May God have mercy on me."

Now Hannah knew why the letter from Vienna had driven him to the cemetery to spend hours at her mother's graveside. It was to beg Louisa's forgiveness.

In the foyer, as Marcus Iverson saw to it that Joe Turner and his brother were placed in Margaret Lawrence's capable and motherly hands, he went in search of Blanche Sinclair, and he found her in the women's wing, where already she was readying patients for visitors, and informing such visitors as were already there that they must leave and allow others their fair turn. It was so like Blanche, he thought in admiration. She had overheard what was being said outside, and had immediately gotten busy preparing for a parade of hospital visitors.

When he looked at her, wearing a homespun apron over her stylish gown, her red-brown hair caught up in a washer woman's kerchief, Marcus thought of his fleeting attraction to Hannah Conroy, and he realized now that those feelings had been a way of suppressing his desire for Blanche. But that desire had never really gone away, no matter how much in this past year he had tried to convince himself that she had betrayed him. He had heard that Miss Conroy and the American were engaged to be married, and he wished them much happiness.

He kept his eyes on Blanche, who was unaware of being observed by the man she loved. Marcus had seen her work wonders in these past twenty-four hours, organizing her friends and patients' visitors into an efficient team of bedside attendants. Blanche had even asked if any knew how to read and write, and those women were given the job of recording all bedside tasks, such as feeding the patients, emptying bedpans, at what time dressings were changed, or patients turned on their sides, so that no one went hungry or neglected.

Blanche Sinclair was a woman with an amazing mind. He wondered if she would care to listen to his ideas for change and progress in the hospital, and perhaps offer a few suggestions of her own.

He turned away, remembering poor Dr. Soames.

Blanche glanced up in time to see Marcus Iverson turn and walk away from the ward, his back still erect, his shoulders square despite lack of sleep and taking almost no food. She felt love and admiration flood her heart and excitement at the thought of the days to come.

She could not believe how alive she felt, despite having taken only brief naps in the past twenty-four hours, and nibbled on biscuits hastily washed down with tea. She was more than alive, she was filled with *purpose.* For the first time in her life, Blanche Sinclair felt as if she were exactly where she was meant to be. It amazed her to realize how there had been nothing to fear in the hospital after all, and she wondered now if perhaps it was not the hospital itself that had frightened her, but the unknown. In her child's mind, a hospital was a place of chaos, an environment out of control. But Blanche was in control of things now, and the fear was gone.

As she gave instructions to her ladies—"Remove those chairs, otherwise newly arrived visitors will be less inclined to leave and not allow others to take their turn."—she decided that after she had time to reflect on what she had done here, what she had seen and learned, she would sit down and put ideas to paper. And then she would present to Marcus the proposal that had been born and flourished and grown in her mind as she and Alice and Margaret and Martha had bathed patients, dressed their wounds, fed them porridge, changed their sheets—all in a much more efficient manner than when it was left up to family and friends.

A fresh new idea made Blanche nearly giddy at the thought of it. Proper bedside attendants. Not the floor moppers who were illiterate women trained to do little more than keep oil in the lamps, or the infamous "nurses" of London hospitals who came from the lower rungs of society and were notorious for being alcoholics and stealing from vulnerable patients. No, Blanche's staff would be trained and educated ladies of good breeding.

I shall establish the criteria myself, she decided. There are many gentlewomen in Melbourne who would welcome taking up a profession, especially as I will see to it that this will be a respectable one. I will personally screen applicants and make sure they are of high morals and good character.

She marveled that she had once wondered what it felt like to have a calling, to know what one was meant to do in life, because she realized now that she had known it all along, ever since she was a child and had taken charge of the other children in the nursery, supervising the games, making sure everyone played fair, acting as mediator between hurt feelings.

I will inform Marcus that we will want structured hours, I shall want an office of my own, and that I am to be paid. I might be wealthy in my own right, and not in need of money, but it is the wage that makes one a professional. It is how I shall be taken seriously.

Outside on the lawn, Alice found Hannah looking at a small piece of notepaper while Neal asked the visitors to line up, people who now cooperated and looked forward to being reunited with loves ones they had feared dead.

"That was a brave thing you did, Hannah," Alice said, giving her friend's arm a squeeze. "You probably saved us all." Alice gave her friend a quick hug, and then said, "Have you seen Fintan?"

Neal came up and gestured toward the unfinished children's wing. "I saw him go that way. He said something about finding scrap wood to cover the broken window."

As Alice lifted her skirts and hurried away, Neal said, "She looks like a woman in love."

"I know how she feels," Hannah said with a smile. "What now, Neal? Will you go back to the Cave of the Hands?"

"Not right away." He placed his hands on her arms, drew her to him and looked deeply into her eyes. "As I was riding back to Melbourne, I was terrified I might lose you. I am going to stay a while, dearest Hannah. The caves can wait."

As they turned toward the hospital, to go up the steps toward the golden light that streamed from the open doors, Hannah looked at Papunya's staff still standing where the old woman had planted it, the seeds and feathers and teeth gently dancing in the night breeze.

"Neal, do you know where Papunya's people live?"

"Miriam said that their home lies far to the north, many days journey from here. Why?"

"I know there are no tribal aborigines close to the city, and so I wondered how they knew about the fever before even *we* knew—before Nellie Turner even came to the hospital. If as you say they would have journeyed for many days."

"I have no idea."

Hannah pondered this for a moment, then she pointed to the mysterious staff rising from the ground. "Do you suppose Papunya was marking her territory?"

Neal looked at Hannah and said with a smile, "Or marking *yours*."

SIX MONTHS LATER

"I'll take that, Mrs. Scott," the housekeeper said. "You shouldn't be lifting heavy things. Not in your condition."

Hannah smiled and let Mrs. Sparrow take the box, which was not at all heavy, up the steps and into the house. I'm not an invalid, Hannah wanted to say, I'm just going to have a baby. But ever since she had announced her condition, everyone treated her as if she were made of glass.

Hannah paused in unloading the wagon, which contained the last of her possessions from her house in town, to look around their new home. It was no longer Brookdale Farm. Hannah and Neal had restored the original native name—Warrajinga—which was aboriginal for "The place where rainbows are born."

The May weather had brought cool autumn winds and white puffy clouds to the clover farm that also ran some cattle and sheep. Hannah gazed at the house that shone blinding white in the sunlight, with its fresh paint, new windows and doors, and wind vanes on the gabled roof. At the bottom of a sloping green lawn, a pond had been installed, complete with ducks and black swans. It was a replica of the one at Seven Oaks.

They had eventually found Charlie Swanswick up in the Bendigo gold field eager to sell his property. A Melbourne lawyer drew up the contract and deeds, Neal and Hannah paid the full price, and three days later were married beneath the ghost gums of their new home. Fintan Rorke was best man, and his new bride, Alice, was Hannah's matron of honor. Dr. Iverson and Blanche Sinclair, who were now courting, stood as witnesses, while seventy guests, including Dr. Soames who had miraculously recovered from the childbed fever, had sat on lawn chairs and fanned themselves in the summer heat.

That was three months ago, and now they were finally moving in. When she heard the familiar sound of hammering inside the house, Hannah smiled. Neal, creating cabinets for his new darkroom.

Turning her face into the wind, Hannah recalled how she had once wondered if she and Neal could live together, with their different callings. But now she saw it all: Neal going out periodically to explore and photograph the natural wonders of Australia, always to return to Hannah and Warrajinga. And Hannah, going about the countryside in her buggy with her doctor's bag, with occasional excursions into the city, to visit the hospital and confer with Dr. Iverson, but always to return to Neal and Warrajinga. An unconventional life to be sure, she thought, but a life that was going to be rich, rewarding, and no doubt full of surprises.

Although their new home was in the country, they had kept the photography studio in town, and Hannah's office, where she would go periodically to see patients. But the baby would be born at Warrajinga, to start its life on the red soil of this new land. Hannah had turned one of the rooms into a nursery, and the room adjacent to it a writing studio, where she planned to compile her Home Health Manual, which had undergone a change since the childbed fever outbreak six months ago. Hannah's prior emphasis had been on treatment and nursing care ("In The Event Of Fainting: red face, raise the head; white face, raise the feet."), but now she would stress prevention, with the first chapter covering cleanliness. Perhaps the manual's introduction would include the story of Hygeia, daughter of Aesculapius.

Hannah understood at last what her father had meant with his dying breath. He had not meant that iodine was the key to health—rather, *antisepsis* was. There was suddenly so much Hannah wanted to explore. Why were aborigines who lived in the wild so healthy and robust? Why did the natives, with whom Neal had lived, know little illness? It was no longer enough, Hannah knew, to take care of the sick and prevent disease. She wanted to find sources and cures.

She paused on the verandah to look back at trees that had once been foreign and exotic but which were now familiar, the bushy gray emu trotting by on the road, a flock of white cockatoos, the red earth and blue sky. And as she felt the new life stirring in her womb, she thought of the people who had come before her, criss-crossing this vast continent with their timeless tracks down through the centuries—the ancestors of Papunya, Miriam, Jallara and her people, those of Galagandra, too, fighting to protect their sacred ground. She then thought of those who came later to these shores— the Merriwethers with their good intentions, Mr. Paterson who turned himself orange with carrots, and a lad named Queenie MacPhail, baptized in scotch. New people settling in an ancient land. It reminded Hannah of her father's last words to her: *Thee stands at the threshold of a glorious new world.* And she wondered: had it been a prophetic vision of his daughter's future? Hannah liked to think so.

She turned at the sound of a horse and saw a wagon coming up the drive. It was the rural mailman bringing the weekly post. "Good day to you, Mrs. Scott!" he called.

Hannah waved and smiled, and when he pulled up, took the bundle of envelopes and newspapers from him.

As she sorted through it all, she saw that Liza Guinness had written a letter of congratulations to Hannah on her marriage. The Gilhooleys, with whom she had stayed in touch, had written as well, and other friends from Adelaide and the Victoria countryside. Hannah had sent them all an open invitation to visit, including Liza, should she and her husband ever return to Australia. One of the property's outbuildings had been converted into a guest house.

Hannah was suddenly arrested by a pale blue envelope with a curious postmark on it, and she realized it was a much-redirected letter from America.

Jamie O'Brien!

"Dear Hannah," he had written in a familiar cramped hand, "I think of you often and pray you are well. I've done a good job here in California, finding gold. I invested in a stagecoach line and made some money, and now I'm thinking that the new railway will be a good bet. I love this new land, Hannah, it's fresh and bold and a man can spread his wings. But I'll always love Australia first, and my first real lady-love who I once rescued from a dingo in a rose garden."

A photograph was included in with the letter. Hannah's eyes misted as she gazed at a grinning Jamie O'Brien in front of what looked like the mouth of a cave. A sign at the top read, "The Lucky Hannah Gold Mine."

Pressing the sheet of paper to her breast, where she felt beneath the fabric of her bodice the stone talisman with magic powers, Hannah looked back seven years to that fateful night at Falconbridge Manor. She saw herself boarding the *Caprica*, bound for an unknown land. Young and naïve, with some laboratory notes and a handful of medical instruments, Hannah had been alone in the world and uncertain of her path. But now she had come into her own. She had shaped her own destiny in this land of fresh starts and new beginnings, and looked forward with great eagerness to the new life that lay ahead—to the songline that she would follow.

Starting here at Warrajinga—Rainbow Dreaming.

LaVergne, TN USA
15 February 2011
216648LV00003B/1/P